BLOW THE TRUMPET IN ZION

Book I in the Tribulation Chronicles Series

RICK PIETLICKI

WESTBOW
PRESS®
A DIVISION OF THOMAS NELSON
& ZONDERVAN

WestBow Press books may be ordered through booksellers or by contacting:

WestBow Press
A Division of Thomas Nelson & Zondervan
1663 Liberty Drive
Bloomington, IN 47403
www.westbowpress.com
1 (866) 928-1240

ISBN: 978-1-5127-5366-0 (sc)
ISBN: 978-1-5127-5367-7 (hc)
ISBN: 978-1-5127-5365-3 (e)

Library of Congress Control Number: 2016913373

Print information available on the last page.

WestBow Press rev. date: 09/28/2016

PROLOGUE

Ariel, angel and scribe of the most high God have been commissioned by my Lord to write down in a book the final chapters of the history of earth. The events listed herein begin shortly before the fulfillment of the prophecy of the seventieth week of years given to the prophet Daniel by my fellow-messenger Gabriel.

This book of Daniel's prophecy, which was, during his time, commanded to be "shut up and sealed until the time of the end," is now opened for all heaven and earth to see.

CHAPTER 1

A black cloud oozed through the window, and entered her room. A lifeless, yet palpable mass, it blotted out the walls and furniture as it moved towards the bed. Swaddled in her blanket, she stirred uneasily, unaware of the approaching menace. Outside the open window, huge sheets of lightning danced to the music of hammering thunderclaps, spraying the walls with incandescent light, and momentarily repelling the dark presence inside.

In the distance a muffled sound, like an old record skipping, then repeating itself, drew closer. The darkness quickened its pace, filling the room. Another series of hot, white streaks, followed by peals of thunder, scattered the dark anew.

The skipping sound outside trumpeted loudly, as the dark blob loomed over her bed. She awoke with a start, too terrified to scream, while the darkness perched above her, prepared to pounce.

"A trumpet is sounding!" She cried out. "No, the sound of words: N--th, ni--th, ninth, NINTH!"

Mira sat up in her bed with waves of fear washing over her trembling frame.

"Only a dream!" she exhaled, while quickly scanning her room for any sign of trouble, and clutching her pillow tight to her chest for comfort. The familiar surroundings assured her that all was well, just as the first fingers of daylight were chasing away the darkness outside her window.

Miriam Rosen flung herself out of bed, stretched her still tired body, and made her way to the kitchen to start the coffee and her morning routine, hoping that she had not awakened her housemate, Marcia.

"What could've brought that on?" she wondered, while taking a deep sip from her favorite cup, and chased a shiver down her spine. She wished she had something a bit stronger than Columbian coffee to help disgorge the cold fear that had welled up in the pit of her stomach.

"Okay Mira, forget about it girl. Put it out of your mind!" She resolved, and quickly downed her coffee, showered, threw her clothes on, and bounded out the door, determined to do just that.

Stepping out into the muggy Washington, DC morning, she was embraced by the throbbing life that never seems to stop in the city. Her mood brightening, she quickly forgot the events of the past evening. Surrounding sounds reassured her. The hum and bustle of traffic, the quick clip-clop of others, like herself, briskly walking off to work, even the *chirp-chirp* of her car alarm signing off from its guard duty, all comforted her, and made her feel that things were back to normal once again.

Life in the city, a far cry from her gentrified roots in nearby Arlington, Virginia, never seemed to sleep, much less rest. Even through the recent upsurge in crime, and the constant threat of renewed terrorist violence, life went on. Just yesterday, a bomb had exploded in a Hassidic Jewish delicatessen, killing fifteen people and wounding twice that number. Time clocks still had to be punched, offices filled, and merchandise sold. It was a city living on the edge of a precipice; both scary and thrilling at the same time.

She started up her Black BMW 950i, told the voice-activated MP3 player what song to play, and sped off to the mid-town offices of WKBC, Washington's premier cable television station. As Mira snaked her way through the typical stop-and-go traffic that seemed to be getting worse every day, she commanded her in-dash phone to call up her voicemail, and retrieve the morning messages.

The voice of her secretary, and dear friend, came on first. "Mira? Carla. You've got an appointment set up for 11:00 a.m. Some corporate moneybags is dropping in for a meeting or something. Oh, don't forget my onion bagel and coffee. Cream only. I like it light. Thanks, hon."

The next message intrigued her. "Miss Rosen, this is Brant Armisted, Prince George's County prosecutor. Just wanted to thank you for that piece you did on the Luchese case. Great journalism! Really raised the roof over at mob central. You stuck your neck out, and I appreciate it. Let's have dinner and talk."

Mira smiled as she drove through the security checkpoint, and into the parking garage next to the WKBC studios. She would enjoy a night out with Brant, the handsome, thirty-something lawyer, who had quickly made a reputation for himself as a hard-nosed prosecutor. The talk around town was that he was being groomed to be the next Maryland state attorney general. Nailing the notorious Fabio "Big Fats" Luchese on a five-to-ten-years racketeering conviction wouldn't hurt.

Maryland politicos loved to irritate the mob, as long as someone else did the dirty work. Mira's part had been to ferret out a key witness through the many sources she'd developed. Luchese had gone state's witness when he realized that his days as a Mafia capo were numbered. There had been too many nights of drinking combined with too much bragging. It was her timely news coverage of the events, as a feature reporter, that had helped bring about the conviction, and gave a boost to her career. Mira was afterwards promoted to a co-anchor position at WKBC.

By the time Mira had picked up the bagel and coffee at the commissary, and exited the elevator at the tenth-floor suite of offices, she was relaxed and confident, ready to dig into Monday's news traffic.

Carla, busy as ever, smiled briefly, handed her the daily intel sheets, and quickly resumed her mesmerized posture behind the computer. "Meeting's moved up to ten," Carla called out, her eyes never leaving the screen. "Thanks for the B&C."

Mira walked down the hall to her private office that still filled her with a sense of awe. She sat down behind her polished cherrywood desk, and logged into her computer. The word *ninth* echoed in her mind once again.

What does it mean? she wondered. *It's nothing. Absolutely nothing,* she finally determined, and plunged into the events that would occupy her day. After voicing her password to the computer, and pulling up her personal diary, she recited the following entry:

Monday, June 23

Ninth, Ninth, Ninth--what?

Does it mean the ninth inning? Ninth Street? Ninth Avenue?

I don't understand..."

* * *

Pauli Donati loved playing with gadgets. As a boy, he would take apart anything he could get his hands on, including, much to his mother's dismay, clocks, radios, or anything else that had a few nuts and bolts in it. Because of a conscientious high school science teacher at PS #228, in the Flatbush section of Brooklyn, he learned that the joining of certain electrical components, with mechanical or chemical ones, could produce amazing results. During the long, hot, summer days, while his friends opened fire hydrants to stay cool, Pauli would find some shade, and with a battery, some wire, and a pack of fire crackers, or a few cherry bombs, would blow the lids off the garbage cans in the alley behind the tenement apartments.

It was no coincidence that Pauli found himself in a demolition squadron, soon after graduating from Army boot camp. When his four-year Army hitch was up, having become a demo expert in plastic explosives, he was recruited by another army, this one led by Washington crime boss, Vito Bonaserra.

"Hey Paul-i, you takin' an art class or sumthin?" his friend Tony jokingly asked, while taking a short pull from the longneck beer in his right hand.

"Yeah, Tone, this is what you call a real work of art. A real hot property," Pauli laughed at his own joke and stepped back to admire his work. He squashed the butt of his cigarette with his high-top, black boot, and unrolled a pack of cigarettes from the sleeve of his once white T-shirt, now covered with black and green grease stains. Pauli offered a cigarette to Tony, who took one, lit it, and sat down on a wooden crate, the only other piece of furniture in the sparse basement. The modified Semtex charge sitting on a piece of plywood before him, had a newly acquired mercury detonator that, when tripped by a very narrow radio band frequency, would detonate enough explosive to blow up a tank. So small and compact, it inspired a smile from Pauli, and awe and amazement from his friend.

"Someone buys 'dis piece, they can retire real early-like." Pauli remarked. He got up, took a short swig from Tony's beer, and placed the plywood pallet into a small box. "Come on Tone. It's showtime!"

* * *

Mira kicked off her shoes, threw the pile of assorted newspapers, magazines, and mail she had brought home on her dresser, and fell backward, exhausted on her bed. The bloodshot numbers of the alarm clock on her nightstand read 12:30 a.m.

After gently rapping on the door, Marcia, her housemate, walked into the room, clothed in a pink terry-cloth bathrobe, and sat down on the edge of the bed. Her long, auburn hair was knotted in pigtails that fell on both sides of her pert and pretty, middle-aged face, and reminded Mira of her Tri-Delta sorority house mom, during her college days.

"Late night, dear?" Marcia asked in her gentle, southern drawl.

"You have no idea." Mira replied, still lying down, and having covered her eyes with her forearm. "How are things at the White House?"

"Are you looking for a reply on or off the record?" Marcia teased.

"Off the record, but I must warn you that anything you say may be used against you."

Both women laughed.

"Just the usual suspenseful, nail-biting, intrigue." Marcia replied, while stifling a yawn. "I'll fill you in on the details later. Now get some sleep." She fussed, patted Mira on her shoulder, and left the room.

It had been another long, but exciting day for Mira. First, she had met with a potential corporate advertising client and her boss, Larry Kratzert, the executive producer. The meeting lasted through lunch, and resulted in the signing of a six-figure advertising budget. From 1:00 to 3:00 p.m., Mira met at different times with the managing editor and her co-anchor, Jason Ward, to discuss the stories and clips that would be used for the evening news. After that came more meetings and phone conferences with assignment and feature reporters, for another hour, then off to the editing room for a final wrap of the video clips.

At 5:00, she reviewed her notes, checked the wire services for any late breaking news, and met with "Mr. Ward," as he liked to be called, to pencil in any last minute changes. Then it was off to the set to perform before millions of viewers,

WKBC was a super station with hundreds of cable outlets throughout the country. Mira was still awed by her role as co-anchor, almost to the point of stage fright. Yet as soon as the countdown began, she warmed to the camera, and her bubbly enthusiasm became a compelling counterpoint to Jason Ward's, dust-and-cobwebs, dry humor. She once overheard Antwone, the tech on camera three, tell the producer, that the camera "ate her up." Evidently the ratings agreed with Antwone's assessment. Their show was the highest-rated news program in their market.

After the brief half-hour show, Mira ate her hot pastrami on rye and diet coke, ordered from Paisan's Deli down the street, while watching out-takes of the new WKBC news-launch promo. Between 7:30 and 9:00 p.m., there were more meetings, a videoconference call, and a late-breaking, local story to contend with. A final meeting with the producer and Jason Ward, and it was on to the 10:00 p.m. news. The news ran past the normal half-hour by an hour, due to a breaking story of a high-speed chase through lower Washington, which finally ended when a car-jacking suspect was apprehended at a police roadblock, just outside the beltway.

Physically and mentally exhausted, Mira allowed her body and mind to go limp, and the accumulated tension to dissipate. With eyes closed and without looking up, she voice commanded the communications center in her bedroom to locate CNN news. The command was instantly obeyed, and the polished voice of Vanessa Cutler came through the surround-sound, stereo system.

"In other news, Russian Federation President Yevgeny Primakov arrived in Washington today to discuss plans for a joint Euro/Russo/American space venture to build an international colony on the moon. The 1.2 trillion Euro project would be funded by loans and grants from the G-10 group of nations."

"CNN correspondent Grant Tinker has more..."

"Smiling broadly to the enthusiastic welcome he received, Russian President..."

"...this day will be remembered..."

"...White House officials now confirm..."

...Mira stepped out of the forest, and into a beautiful sunlit meadow that rose quickly onto a commanding hill. The wind blew gently through her hair, rustled through the tall grass and the wild spring flowers that were seemingly everywhere. Barefoot and dressed in a long, flowing, cotton gown, she walked slowly up the hill, stopping only to pick up flowers every so often, until she held a rich, fragrant bouquet in her hands. As she crested the ridge, the meadow became an open prairie. Waves of wheat, like a grain-filled sea, were tossed and whipped by violent gusts of wind. Ominous, dark clouds now gathered in threatening heaps, as if a huge furnace had spewed them into the air. The gusting wind was quickly replaced by a howling gale. The noise of the wind, as it raked the tops of the wheat, seemed to form distinct sounds, and then the words--

"ninth...ninth...NINTH!"

* * *

The next morning, Carla Nordquist, a paper-thin, fortyish spinster with dyed, light brown, permed hair, watched as Mira came into the office and stopped at the assignment desk to read the twenty four hour summary; a continuous review of daily news items. Carla favored a retro 1960's look in clothing and accessories, and wore wire-rimmed, granny glasses, that sat easily on her prominent, thin nose, which seemed to be perpetually red from the host of allergies she suffered from.

Never one to hide her opinion from others, Carla came up and stood beside her boss, and whispered in Mira's ear, in her usual blunt way.

"If you don't mind me saying so, and even if you do. You look terrible!"

Indeed, Mira had bags under her eyes, and had come to work in a rumpled, dark blue dress.

"Yeah, well, I haven't been getting much sleep lately. We've been having a lot of late coverage this week, and--"

"Listen," Carla interjected, in her best mother-hen voice. She really cared for Mira, and tried to keep an eye on her, as she would her own child. "You don't have to tell me anything." She looked around to make sure no one was listening, and continued her probe.

"Now, if it's nervousness, or a hangover, or a man!"

"Carla!" Mira cried. She turned to face her, and blushed six shades of red at the last possibility. "It's, it's really none your business, miss busy body." She pouted playfully, and started to walk away, then abruptly turned, and with an impish grin, smiled at her. "Thanks for caring, mom, but I've got to get to work."

Safely ensconced in her office, Mira closed the door, and leaned her back up against it. After rubbing her eyes and downing a cup of coffee, she dove into the mound of work piled on her desk, eager to get past this day and then...what? It would be night again, and those terrible words might come back to haunt her: *ninth, ninth.* She didn't have a clue what they could mean. Yet those simple words were the one constant in the weird dreams she'd been having.

"This is so bizarre. What is happening to me?" she asked out loud.

No one was there to answer back.

"I've got to talk to someone. If I don't I'm going to explode," she said to herself, and began pacing the room.

She walked over to the mirror hanging on her closet door. What she saw shocked her! Her graceful, five-foot seven frame was marred by the wrinkled, navy blue, satin dress she wore, giving her a disheveled appearance. Mira hadn't slept much of the night. After showering and getting dressed at 5:00 a.m., she had lain down on her bed for a moment, and promptly fell asleep. Waking up with a start, she dashed off to work, tired and rumpled.

"Carla was right, I look terrible!" She conceded, while noting the creases on her forehead, and the dark patches under her doe-like, brown eyes.

"Makeup will have a fun time with me tonight. I'll be their challenge for the week," she quipped, while combing out her medium-length mahogany hair with a brush. She quickly shrugged off her concern, and with youthful zeal went back to work, booted up her computer, and opened up her appointment book.

"Oh, my! Lunch with Congressman Prentiss at noon, and look at the way I look!"

She made a hasty call over the voicestream. "Carla, can you get me an iron or something?"

"A what? Oh, I get it, the dress. Yeah, I'll get on it right away."

Mira looked at her watch. Almost 11:00 a.m. Just enough time to go over today's rough outline of probable stories on her computer, dash off to Heather in makeup, while getting her dress pressed, and then off to lunch.

She hurriedly spoke to her diary, and recorded a new entry:

Friday, August 15,

I've had more dreams, and am not getting much sleep. The word "Ninth" keeps recurring, though not every night. I have to talk to someone…

CHAPTER 2

"Comrade Borodin!" The aide to Generalissimus Yuri Ivanovich Borodin said crisply, while snapping to attention. Borodin was the de facto president of all the Russia's, but concealed the fact by maintaining a lesser position as general, and head of the Russian Federation's C-10, Special Intelligence Unit.

"Please, Pavel Illych, don't call me comrade. What would our Western friends think if they heard you? After all, we are now capitalists!" He spit out the last word sarcastically.

"Sorry sir, old ways die hard, even after all this time," the major replied, pouring the general's favorite Turkish coffee, swimming in coffee grounds, with two sugars, and just a touch of cream, which he served in Bavarian bone china services.

He handed the steaming cup to Borodin, whose large barrel-chested frame filled up the red leather chair sitting behind an enormous English oak desk.

"It is…how the Americansky say it? Okay. It is okay, Pavel Illych. He laughed softly under his breath, as he took another sip of coffee and a perfunctory drag from his half-smoked cigarette. The smoke exited slowly through brown-stained teeth, curled around his jowly face, drawing attention to a large, thick nose, and bushy eyebrows, before rising, ghost-like, above his bald pate. The scene conjured up images of the gargoyles atop the Cathedral de Notre Dame in Paris.

"What have you got for me major?"

"Morning dispatches sir, and a report on the progress of Project Scorpion." He handed him the papers and poured the general another cup of coffee.

"Any news from Mercury yet?" Borodin asked without looking up?

"No sir, he's due to report anytime now. I'm sure that he will confirm that the Americansky are far ahead of schedule, and have already completed the final phase of their Salt IV reductions, just as we suspected they would."

"Da, da. President Williams, our country's best friend…and comrade."

They both laughed at the joke and the sweet irony it implied.

President Clayton Jefferson Williams, though elected as a moderate Democrat, promising to keep America's defenses strong in the face of an increasingly hostile and oftentimes violent world, had early on in his administration caved in to congressional doves, and the new Environmental Peace Party. The EPP had made serious gains in recent congressional elections, capturing thirty-percent of the House seats, and a full twenty-five seats in the Senate. Strongly influenced by Secretary of State James Hughes, his political, and some would say, philosophical mentor and EPP chairman, Williams systematically dismantled both nuclear and conventional armaments, downsized military personnel by fifty percent, and drastically reduced the nation's defense capabilities. Declaring to the world that the arms race was officially over, he quickly signed new treaties with the major powers, and began weapons reductions well ahead of other nations, pledging to lead the world into a new paradigm of peace and prosperity.

The minority, and now third party, Republican Party, shocked by the speed with which Williams accomplished his new peace proposals, became paralyzed and unable to marshal the courage necessary to resist the president's strategic initiatives. Its leadership seemed to be constantly embroiled in one scandal after another, and could not muster any meaningful interest in its own agenda.

Armed with controlling majorities in Congress, and a patronizing and oftentimes adoring press corps, the president's popularity soared both at home and abroad. He had already been chosen as one popular magazine's, Man of the Year, and was considered by many as the only viable candidate for the Nobel Peace Prize.

"Let me know the moment his dispatch arrives. That will be all for now." The general said, dismissing his aide."

The major saluted, and quietly closed the massive, ornate, wooden door behind him, leaving the general alone in his spacious office.

General Borodin took another drag from his cigarette, and then vigorously crushed the half-smoked stub in his ashtray.

"*Americansky cigarettes,* he said to himself. *What would we do without you?*"

* * *

Andy Stern reflected on the recent death of Andrei Velikovsky as he sat outside the oval office in the White House, waiting to see the man who held the most powerful office in the world. Velikovsky had defected to the U. S. in 1989, after having been the KGB Middle East bureau chief for twelve years. The following year, he wrote a national bestseller entitled, *Truth Never Dies,* that presaged, among other things, the dismantling of the Berlin Wall, the breakup of the former Soviet empire, and the rise of democracy in Russia. Two years later, he was awarded an honorary master's degree in political science from Georgetown University, and from there began an upward spiraling courtship dance with the media, while earning praise and fat paychecks on the lecture circuit, and through numerous guest appearances on the various talk mills. His celebrity came to a crashing halt just west of the town of Morningside, close to Andrews Air Force base, where he was driving to catch a chartered plane for the West Coast. Though reports were sketchy, and his body was said to have been burned beyond recognition, witnesses stated that the car carrying Velikovsky had been forced off the freeway, hit an abutment, and burst into flame, instantly killing everyone inside.

Stern was chuckling softly to himself when Marcia Thompson, the President's personal secretary, informed him that the President would see him now.

"Good morning, Mr. Prezident," he offered with a discernable accent, as he stood in front of the desk that Queen Victoria of England had sent as a gift to then President Rutherford B. Hayes in 1880. You couldn't walk anywhere in the White House without a piece of history staring you in the face. Indeed, history was a daily occupation there.

On top of the desk in the Oval Office was a voicestream, a multi-line vis-a-phone that, with the flick of a switch, would show live streaming video of the person you were talking to, another ordinary looking secure phone, and the requisite stack of folders and papers. President Williams was frowning at one of these papers when Stern walked in.

"Ah, Andy, so good to see you," Williams remarked as he rose and extended a hand to his Special Assistant to the President on the Russian Federation. He clasped his hand in his usual campaign stop, vise grip way, and motioned him to one of the more comfortable chairs located in the middle of the room, These sat on gold, short pile carpeting, embedded with the blue, black, and gold image of The Great Seal of the United States.

A steward silently deposited a silver tray of fresh croissants and coffee on the table between them, and without looking up, went back to the kitchen adjacent to the Oval Office.

Another door opened; there were three coming into this room, and Jack Quinn, the president's National Security Advisor, walked in with his usual brisk step. He poured a black coffee, and sat down, looking directly at the President, without so much as acknowledging Andy Stern.

"How's traffic this morning Jack?" the President asked, looking over his half-lens eyeglasses, wryly noting that his ever-punctual friend and advisor was five minutes late.

"Typical D.C. boondoggle Mr. President," he said with a heavy sigh, venting his own frustration, and looked past his own glasses to the sheaf of papers he had pulled out of his briefcase. He unbuttoned his tailored suit jacket, which perfectly fit his just under six-foot frame, and took a deep breath. "The downpour outside just made it that much worse, of course."

Inwardly Jack was quite ruffled by his tardiness. Punctuality was more than a virtue to him; it was a badge of honor he displayed with pride. He had even taught a session or two about the subject when he had been an adjunct business law professor in his ethics class at Georgetown University. Jack was too well disciplined to let it affect him for more than a moment though. After sorting through some more papers, he confidently launched into his briefing, and gave a brief synopsis on several trouble spots, including the continuing standoff in Kashmir, between Indian and Pakistani forces, and a reported Middle East flare-up at the hotbed town of Hebron in Israel, finally finishing with a report on the European Union. "Our so-called allies in Europe seem to be towing the line, vis-à-vis, our nuclear weapons scale down initiative," he began, and looked up to see a knowing smile spread across the president's face. Both knew that Europe was anything but unified, and the thirty-three countries that comprised the Union, rarely if ever agreed with each other or with the United States. They tended to look on the U. S. as spoiled children might eye their doting parents, always wanting something more, but never giving anything up.

"The Netherlands have already abandoned all their weapons, the Brits are down to a quarter of theirs, as we are, and Prime Minister Jaques DuLong insists publicly, that what France does with its weapons is her own affair, but privately, he insists that France has already cut its resources in half, and pledged another quarter by the end of the month."

He looked up from his notes, paraphrased from NSA and CIA documents, and closed with a personal observation. "With no major hurdle to overcome sir, except for verification of Russian Federation compliance, your goal to eliminate all nuclear weapons by the end of the year, I think, has moved much closer to reality."

The President smiled contentedly. "Don't let those hawks on the Hill hear you say that. They're still trying to sell rat traps, even though the rats have all left Hamlin-town!" He replied with a chuckle. Williams loved using the allusion to the medieval Pied Piper story, ever since an editor for The Washington Post pinned a label on him with an article entitled, "The Pied Piper of Washing-town." That editorial piece, as well as other plaudits from around the world, had caused his popularity to soar. His current approval rating was hovering at a whopping seventy-three percent.

"Andy, what about our Russian friends?" the president continued. "Are they doing their part?"

"Yez, Mr. Prezident," Andy replied. De Russian Federation has exceeded target projections, and has now scaled back nuclear inventories forty-two percent from Cold War asset levels. I think it is safe to assume--"

"What about verification, ah, Mr. Stern?" Jack interrupted, barely disguising his anger, which caused his freckled cheeks to flush crimson, almost matching the color of his hair. "Have on-site investigators verified your figures? Where are you getting your numbers from?" He shot out these questions in rapid fire, hoping to entrap and put to flight the man he considered an adversary.

Stern was unruffled by the attack. "Mr. Prezident, on-site inspections have been going on for years, and continue to this day through competent United Nations inspectors--"

"Competent?" Jack shot back. "You call a team made up of a mixture of former Soviet satellites, and Third World nations, who may not even know what they're looking for, competent?" Jack's normally quiet and reserved demeanor was gone now, and he felt his face flush again as he pressed his attack. "Let me ask you this. Why are American inspections only being handled by trained Russian engineers?"

"I do not dictate policy regarding inspector billeting," Stern replied. "I would suggest that you take the matter up with your ambassador to the U.N.?" Stern was beginning to get nervous over this intense scrutiny, but was outwardly calm and self-assured. "As I was saying Mr. Prezident, I feel confident that Primakov iz keeping up his end of the treaty."

"Tell me then, what does *Borodin* say about it?" Jack pressed with a knowing half-smile. The three men knew that General Borodin was the real power behind the scenes in the Russian Republic. "I'm not ready to sign off on that statement until I see reliable figures from reputable sources, and--"

"Gentlemen!" The president interrupted. "Let's not quibble over who's doing what, and how much. We're all in the same camp, and I think we can all agree, that mutual reductions are occurring ahead of schedule."

Jack tried to pursue the point he was making. "That's true from our side sir, but without verification--"

"Jack, the days of taking sides have come to a close. The Russian's are our allies, and I trust Primakov, or should I say Borodin, is telling the truth, when he says he's decreased his stockpile by...how much did you say, Andy?"

"Forty-two percent, sir."

"That's right, which means that he's in compliance, and ahead of schedule."

"But sir?"

"That's all I want to say about the matter, Jack." The president, once again, looked over the rim of his glasses, giving him his most adamant fatherly glare. "Now if there is nothing else this morning gentlemen, I have to meet with the Defense Secretary in a few minutes."

He stood up and walked to his desk, signaling that the meeting was over.

"Oh, Jack, could I see you for a minute?"

Stern left the room, and went straight to his second floor office in the northwest corner of the West Wing of the White House.

The President sat down, hands entwined on top of his desk, much like a judge preparing to render a verdict. At seventy-three, and standing six feet-two, with medium length blue-gray hair, swept back at the sides, President Clayton Jefferson Williams presented a formidable figure.

"You know that I hold both you and Andy in the highest esteem. You're both hard working, intelligent, and very capable counselors, and I truly respect the job you're both doing."

Jack had heard this tone before and knew what was coming.

"Nevertheless, it troubles me to see this infighting, this sophomoric bickering between two very bright individuals."

"Sir, if I might--" he said, trying to head him off.

"No Jack, please listen." The President got up and looked out of the bullet-resistant window that, because of its thickness, gave a distorted picture of the western lawn. "I know that you have a problem with Andy because, well, you believe once a Russian always a Russian. You also believe him to be some low-level former intelligence operator, who somehow found his way into this country, and wormed his way into a very sensitive security position. Isn't that about the gist of it?"

"I don't trust him sir!" Jack replied bluntly.

The president walked over to the portrait of John F. Kennedy that hung in a special niche he had built for it when he took office.

"Do you recall a Soviet defector by the name of Andrei Velikovsky?" He turned and looked at him, arms crossed over his chest.

Jack pulled out the folder marked, "Velikovsky, Andrei Ivanovich," from the vast file cabinet, that was his photographic memory, and began reciting the facts.

"Born November 1942, during the siege of Stalingrad, joined the Comsomol, Communist Youth Party, at age twelve, graduated form the University--"

"All right, all right," the president chuckled while looking down at the floor. "I should've known better than to tap into that fertile mind of yours. Then you also know that he defected to the U. S. in 1989, wrote a best seller, received an honorary doctorate from Georgetown University, and was killed in a fatal car crash on the Capitol Loop."

"Yes, that's right. The bodies were never recovered, as I recall."

"What you don't know, because even though you have the highest level security clearance, you haven't had the need to know until now, was that Andrei Velikovsky is our own Andy Stern." The President leaned against the wall, and waited to see what impact the bomb he just released, would make on his National Security Advisor.

He wasn't disappointed.

Jack Quinn, felt as though someone had just kicked him in the gut. Andrei Velikovsky had been a true Cold War hero; some say he was a pivotal figure in the dismantling of the Soviet empire. He had even read Velikovsky's book, and still referred to it from time to time for its political savvy. He put his face in his hands and shook his head. "Boy, do I feel stupid, I thought--"

"That his intentions were less than honorable? That's why I had to let you in on our little secret. Andy Stern is one of the bravest men I know. He's lost his name, his homeland, even agreed to alter his appearance, and go through that crash scenario, all for the cause of freedom. I'd trust him with my life, Jack. I think he's proven himself, don't you?"

The president patted his now humbled advisor on the back, and resumed his position behind the large wooded desk, watching, as Jack left and closed the door behind him.

* * *

The tall man in dark clothes left the White House around eleven, pulled his sleek, black Chrysler New Yorker out of the parking garage, and drove north on Sixteenth. He took a sharp right into a one-way alley, went south for a block, turned right again into another alley, and right again onto Sixteenth. A few blocks north, he pulled over to the right, and parked in a metered parking spot. He put in his government supplied smart card, and walked briskly north until he got into the drivers' side of a late model Buick Supreme. He drove north again on Sixteenth, and, a few minutes later, turned left on Monroe. Driving on, he suddenly pulled up in front of a small cigar store. After a few minutes he drove off again, made a complete circle, turned around, and parked on the other side of the street across from the store.

Entering the dilapidated cigar store through a large glass door with wrought iron security bars and a simple bell, now ringing on the inside, he went up to a short, heavy-set man with a receding hairline, and bulging black and gray beard tending the counter. "Do you have any Cuban's senor?"

The clerk looked at him intensely, stroked his beard, and answered, "No, but I do have a fine Jamaican Macanudo."

At a nod from his customer, the storekeeper produced one from a humidor kept in an antiquated and dusty glass display case, beneath the equally worn counter, and handed it to him.

His customer brought it to his nose, sniffed the cigar, and then slipped it stealthily to his waist. In a practiced, swift motion, he deftly pulled off the paper band around the cigar, and replaced it with another.

"Maybe some other time," he said handing back the cigar and quickly exited the store.

CHAPTER 3

Brant Armisted arrived at Mira's brownstone condominium, located in a fashionable section of Mount Vernon, exactly an hour and a half late. She had only just arrived herself, after having been called in at the last minute to edit a sketchy news item that was being broadcast that evening by the weekend news team, and was not ready. She invited Brant into the bare bones living room, while she finished with her makeup.

"I'll only be a minute," she announced while putting on an earring and running down the hall to the bathroom in her nylon stocking feet. "Make yourself at home!"

Brant shook his head at the modern painting on the wall, a jumble of colors and geometric shapes that he couldn't make any sense of. Though the dimly lit living room was sparsely furnished with retro 1960's style furniture, Brant noted with pleasure that everything was in its place, and you could have eaten off the highly polished oak flooring. He smiled at the wall plaque in the shape of a red metallic heart that read: "a heart is what you give to others during the course of your day."

"You know we can do this some other time if you'd rather," he teased, shouted down the hall.

"You're not getting off that easy," Mira replied from the bathroom. I'll make you pay for being late."

"Excuse me? If I'm late and I'm still standing here waiting, then what does that make you?" He answered, enjoying the game, while folding his arms together over his chest, as if he had just given a successful summation to a jury.

"It makes me hungrier than ever," Mira replied, slipping in, looking marvelous in a form-fitting, satin evening dress. She gently placed her arm in his, as he led her to his new bubble-gray Lexan IV convertible.

"Oh, wait! Mira cried, while jumping out of the car, leaving Brant smiling and shaking his head.

She soon reappeared, and bustled into her seat. "I had to leave a note for my roommate, Marcia. I'm under strict orders to let her know where I'm going," she explained with a grin.

It was a short drive to Tino's just off of the Beltway, one of Brant's favorite Italian restaurants. A light mist was falling, which, coupled with the blinking neon sign on the awning attached to the façade of the old brick building, reminded Mira of a scene right out of the classic movie, *Casablanca*. An impish smile curled up from her lips as she imagined "Bogey" leading the beautiful Ingrid Bergman out of the restaurant, and on toward their destiny. She loved the old movies, and to her Bogart and Bergman were the best.

Brant parked in the customer parking lot adjacent to the restaurant, and after a brief walk on the damp sidewalk, guided Mira down the short flight of stairs, and through an ancient looking oak paneled door that opened into a darkened, old-world Italian setting.

The cavernous room was dotted with round tables, filled with lively, chattering guests. On the center of each table was a floating candle, encased in a larger crystal bowl filled with water, sprinkled with several miniature pink roses. The candlelight cascading onto the white linen tablecloths seemed to dance to the Straus waltz being played by a trio of violinists, somewhere in another part of the restaurant.

Mira drank in the scene all at once; her senses bombarded by the cozy, romantic atmosphere. At the same time she wondered what kind of statement Brant might be making. Was this a well-conceived plan leading to an eventual conquest, and its attendant fringe benefits? Her analytical mind and reporter instinct had not taken the night off. Or was this just the product of a boyish *joie de vivre*, his love of life? The notebook in her mind opened now, she decided to find the answers during the course of their meal.

The waiter, a thin, middle-aged man, dressed in a tuxedo-type black vest with a shirt and tie, seated the pair in a comfortable corner table, and produced two large menus written in Italian. By prior arrangement Brant took charge of the ordering, while Mira delighted in the sweet strains of a Vivaldi piece echoing from the now-closer musicians.

Brant broke through her reverie. "In case you're hungry…" he began, pausing until she was listening. "I've ordered a bottle of their best Chianti, not too dry, a little antipasto, followed by a splendid *Vitello Valentino* and the best *Taleggio alla Marinara con Acciughe* in the world. That's the house veal for you, and fried cheese with tomato sauce for me." His following smile, both warm and generous, caused Mira to avert her eyes towards the waltzing candlelight.

"Impressive summation counselor. The court rules in favor of your choices," she joked, while hitting the table with an imaginary gavel.

They both laughed as Brant accepted the newly proffered wine from the waiter.

"Here's to the end of the Luchese case," Mira offered, raising her glass. They clinked crystal glasses and took a brief sip.

"And here's to you Mira, someone who's as courageous as she is beautiful."

They tapped each other's glasses once more, while Mira felt herself turning numerous shades of red. *Be careful Miriam*, she told herself, and quickly tried to deflect attention away from herself.

"So, do you think the Luchese case is really over, or are we going to hear from those thugs again?

"Ah, always the reporter," he laughed.

"I'm sorry. It's just that…" she replied, blushing more deeply than before.

"I know, Mira." He gently patted her hand. "Let's forget about everything else, but the night before us. I promise to be a good boy if you'll drop the interview, deal?" He reached out to shake her hand.

Mira laughed, while vigorously shaking hands, and remembered a line from the last scene of Casablanca. "Brant, this looks like the start of a beautiful friendship."

* * *

The couple spilled out into the foggy night, breathing in the damp, moisture-laden air. Mira laughed at a silly joke Brant shared; the wine mixing with her youth allowed for a certain giddiness that made everything seem funny. The night had been a dreamlike collection of romantic ambiance, fine Italian food—the best she had ever tasted—and, once she had allowed herself to put down her reporters note pad, lots of fun. Brant, she found, was as personable as he was intelligent, yet without the arrogance she had seen in other high-octane professionals. Whether it was his charm, or a little too much wine, or a combination of both, Mira really enjoyed being with him, and was already hoping that this date would not be their last.

Several yards from the car, Brant abruptly scooted ahead of Mira, and with feet together and the right index finger pointing toward the overcast sky, produced a long, exaggerated bow. "Your coach awaits you m' lady."

A stab of fear raced through Mira for an instant and then disappeared. She wondered at it for a moment, but then quickly shook it off, and joined the play being acted out before her. "I am thy most humble servant sire," she replied, curtsying with her head bowed.

"Stand behind me and watch this Mira. This is the latest feature in automotive excellence. What we have here is voice recognition technology, or, if you like, VRT, the latest from the fertile minds of the automotive industry. We're about thirty feet away and I'm now going to command the doors to open and the engine to start. This actually should work from fifty feet, but let's try it from here just to be sure." Brant faced the 2-door Lexan and spoke to the vehicle. "Doors op--"

A huge fireball lit up the night sky as the car exploded. What had been a state-of-the-art vehicle was quickly reduced to a pile of smoldering, blackened, rubble.

* * *

The phone ringing beside her bed woke Carla up with a start. "Hello," she said a bit irritably at the noisy speakerphone that had invaded her sleep.

"Carla it's Jan at the evening news desk, turn on--"

"Jan, do you realize what time it is?" she grumped. Her eyes were still closed; her right arm draped over them to keep away any potential light, while her left hand was trying to shut off the phone. (She was accustomed to the old ways, and forgot that she could end the call with a simple voice command).

"Carla, please listen to me!"

"Time." Carla commanded, after being wakeful enough to remember.

"The time is 1:48 a.m.," exclaimed the computerized voice.

"It's about Mira!" Jan yelled.

Carla sat bolt upright, moved her feet off to the side of the bed, and stared wide-eyed at the voicestream. "What's happened to my baby?"

"We're all watching it Carla, just turn on the news." With that, Jan hung up, while Carla found her glasses, and raced into the living room of her small, one bedroom apartment. She groped for the on-switch of the button-less video center that was actually part of her wall. "O for heaven's sake! Television on! Thirty-two!" she finally commanded.

"...firefighters are still trying to determine if anyone else might have been in the wreckage at the time of the explosion, Jason..."

"Oh my! No, it can't be. Not Mira! Please God, not my Mira."

"To recap what we know at this point." Jason Ward remarked in his most somber and sympathetic voice, looked straight into the camera, and began the sad litany. "A car explosion, possibly a car bomb, but I caution you, it's much too early to tell, exploded just outside Tino's Italian Restaurant at approximately 12:45 a.m., this morning. Emergency crews quickly responded, and took as many as three and possibly four victims to Riverside Medical Center, about a ten minute drive from the accident scene. The explosion knocked out many of the windows in the area, as you can see from our SkyCam3 video relay, and police are busy assessing the damage and questioning any--"

"Get to the point Jason, you long winded--windbag! GET TO THE POINT! WAS MIRA HURT? THAT'S ALL I WANT TO KNOW!" Carla screamed at the videostream.

As if on cue, Jason Ward continued: "There are reports and, we must again caution you that these are yet to be confirmed, that one of the victims was possibly WKBC's own Mira Rosen."

"Oh no! It can't be!" Carla covered her mouth with her hand in disbelief, a trickle of tears forming at the corner of her eyes.

"Witnesses close to the scene have indicated that Mira Rosen was last seen going into Tino's with, uh, please standby! We do have a confirmation? Let's switch live again to Pat Savidge. Pat, what can you tell us at this time?"

"Jason, I've just talked with lead detective Tom Delaney of the Washington D. C. police department. Lieutenant Delaney believes that Mira Rosen, along with an as yet unidentified white male, left Tino's Restaurant sometime around 12:30 a.m., local time. They were both involved in the explosion along with maybe one or two others, and were then taken to the Advanced Trauma Center at the Riverside Medical Center. There is no independent confirmation at this time, and we'll obviously be following these events very closely. Back to you, Jason."

"Thank you Pat. WKBC's live team coverage of 'An Explosion Rocks Washington' will continue after a short break."

"Video Off! And good riddance! Typical that they would interrupt a major news story with some soap suds commercial." Carla scolded, while rummaging for her car keys.

During the commotion, her three cats, ever alert for any signs of activity, kept watch over the unfolding drama with her, but were now clamoring for their share of attention by alternately rubbing their sides up against her legs.

"Not now sweet-ums." She gave each a pat on the head and a small treat. "I've got to get over there." She bit her lower lip as tears filled her eyes. "Mira...my baby, she needs me.

Good. Found the keys. Got my purse. Let's go!" She stepped into the elevator and gasped at what she saw in the mirror-walled compartment.

She had left her apartment with her pajamas on.

* * *

Carla had to park in the overflow parking area, some distance away from the Emergency Room entrance, and was quite out of breath and soaked from the steady, early morning rain that had descended on the city. She walked briskly through the first set of automatic doors that spoke to her in a mechanical, computerized, voice: "Welcome to Riverside Medical Center, please proceed to the blue information desk for immediate processing. Approximate waiting time is now fifteen minutes."

"Humph!" she groused. "Some immediate processing; look at this crowd."

The second set of doors opened into the middle of a large, rectangular room, about the size of a high school gym, divided off into four colored sections: yellow, green, red, and blue. Carla, dripping wet, her permed hair matted down on her head, made her way to the nearest counter, the green one, and stood behind one of the three lines that had already formed there. Behind the green counter sat three young men, passively looking and talking into the computer screen. The only other movement they made was to order the incoming patients, many moaning in pain, others in crude bandages, the lesser emergency cases, to place their right hand, palm down, on the micro-feed scanner on the counter. Carla noted, as a cold shiver ran up her spine, that if a patient did not have a microchip implant in their hand, one was quickly inserted by a technician standing nearby, who was armed with a device that resembled an old flu-shot gun. (Riverside was one of several social welfare hospitals where the new microchip technology was being used).

Politely standing by the counter, but receiving no attention whatsoever, Carla abruptly called out to one of the attendants. "S'cuse me. Hey you! Bright eyes. Listen, I've got a friend in here and..."

The caseworker ignored her for a moment, and then turned his mannequin face in her direction, "You'll have to proceed to the blue counter for processing." He replied sharply, and then turned back to his screen, and the next patient in line.

"Hey! Listen bub!" Carla was wet and annoyed, and not about to be put off. "My Mira's in here somewhere and I *will* see her." When no response was forthcoming, she stomped off in a huff to the three lines of the blue counter, which by now had grown to at least a half an hour long.

"This is ridiculous." She exclaimed, standing with her back to the counter, and surveyed the mass of groaning, complaining, humanity inhabiting the room. She noted that after processing the patient would then go through some doors behind the blue counter, which would open automatically, and remain open for about five seconds after the patient walked through.

"Don't see any guards or anything," she said to herself, while scanning the room. Slowly, stealthily, she positioned herself between the green and blue counters, and, when the next patient walked through the doors, followed her into the emergency area.

Once inside she faced a beehive of activity. The doors opened into a small rectangular room that led to two corridors, each containing several examination rooms where doctors and nurses huddled with their patients. Occasionally a gurney would wheel into a room, destined for an x-ray or operating room. Carla knew she had only a few minutes before she would be discovered and, acting as if she belonged there, walked down the far right corridor.

About half way down she noticed an equipment room, ducked inside, and found some blue scrubs and foot protectors, along with a stethoscope, and decided to put these on.

She bounded out of the room, and mingled easily with the throng of workers and patients jostling in the narrow hall.

"But where would Mira be?" She wondered. "Obviously she wouldn't be in the examining rooms." Her best guess was that she would be either in the operating room, or in ICU. She decided to make her way for the operating theater.

Carla followed the signs, but found that there were several operating rooms. She decided to wait in a small waiting room, which was furnished with several fabric-bound chairs, and a small table containing several magazines, when an orderly walked in.

She jumped up out of her seat, and almost ran into the arms of the surprised orderly. "S'cuse me. I'm trying to find a patient who would have been admitted sometime in the night. Her name's Mira Rosen. Car explosion."

The orderly backed off and examined his attacker. "And you are?"

"Doctor, uh, Car--that is, Doctor Frannie Davis. She poked out her bony hand, which the orderly shook, while trying to place the name.

"She's an acquaintance of mine. I'm off duty now, and I just wanted to check up on her." Carla folded her arms across her chest and tried to relax.

"Well, I don't recall anyone by that name. Have you checked the status computer?" He asked and started walking, while Carla fell in beside him.

"No, I was about to check that when you came out, so I thought I would ask." She replied, hoping her nervousness didn't show.

They walked through several doors, and finally entered a large office area with a long bank of computer screens on the wall. The orderly sat down in front of one of these, while Carla took the chair beside him. He spoke to the blackened screen, "Emergency Room, status report." The monitor came to life and immediately a long list of several columns appeared.

"Key traffic status, Mira Rosen."

The screen blinked, and a personal information sheet on Mira Rosen appeared. At the bottom of the page a red rectangular box blinked off and on. Written in the box was the word, "Deceased."

The orderly turned to Carla. "Sorry about that. Was she close?"

Carla was transfixed by the screen and felt hot tears welling up.

"She was my baby."

* * *

The incessant ringing of her cell phone finally woke Marcia Thompson from a deep sleep. As President Williams' appointments and personal secretary she could be called into work at any time, night or day. This night found her coming home to her shared apartment at 2 a.m., only to find that her roommate, Miriam Rosen, was not home yet. She had smiled at the note Mira had left her, and was happy to find that Mira had found time in her busy schedule to actually go out on a date.

"Heh-hello? Marcia answered grogilly, when she finally found her phone.

"Miz Thompson?"

"Yes, this is Marcia Thompson."

"This is the duty nurse at the Advance Trauma Center in Riverside Medical Center."

"Yes." Marcia replied with rising alarm.

"You know a person by the name of Mira Rosen?"

The hair on the back of Marcia's neck rose. "Yes, we share an apartment together. Is everything alright?"

"Unfortunately, Miz Rosen was involved in an accident; a car bombing."

Marcia put her left hand over her mouth and sat down on the bed. "A bomb?"

"I'm sorry to have to inform you that Miz Miriam Rosen has passed away."

CHAPTER 4

"Ladies and gentlemen, mes dames e messieurs, please take your seats."
Dinner and dessert now finished, the tall, lanky Anglican-turned-Roman
Catholic cleric with meticulously groomed gray, wavy hair, and fine,
chiseled face, brought the crowded room to attention.

"The annual meeting of The Bilderbergers—no, the Club of Rome—
no, the Illuminati, will now begin."

Spontaneous laughter, followed by hand clapping, attended the
obvious joke. The group had been called many things in the past, but the
names, like shadows in the dark, missed their true nature and purpose.

"First, I would like to thank those news correspondents amongst us
from Time, Le Monde, Das Bilde, and the like, who have agreed that these
proceedings, because of their implications for the future of the planet,
should be kept, shall we say, private."

More laughter, followed by shouts of One World! One World! filled
the ornate, multi-frescoed ballroom that had once hosted popes, princes,
and pastel-gowned dowagers, the toast of medieval Europe.

"We have among us tonight an august presence. Beside you, before
and behind, are kings and princes, prime ministers and presidents, leaders
in academia, the sciences, arts, letters, the world's foremost religions, and
the very *crème de la crème* of world consciousness."

Loud claps and cheers followed, while all stood up and began a chant:
One World Now! One World Now! ONE WORLD NOW!

Benjamin Stuart smiled as he surveyed the crowd before him. He was Captain Ahab at the helm of the Pequot, both hands gripping the sides of the podium, and shouted out to the throng, "We are the One Hundred and Sixty-Nine! The few, but chosen ones! We worship the Fell Star! ALL BOW DOWN TO THE FELL STAR!"

Stuart abruptly fell to the floor as if dead, while the crowd fixed its attention to a point just above the dais, where a huge, brightly illuminated five-point star, tipped upside down, descended to a point just above the speaker. Suddenly, the lights went out, and in the midst of the star a holographic image appeared. It had the head of a goat, looking down at first as if asleep, and then it slowly raised its head, and began speaking in a flat, unearthly voice.

President Williams, who had been enjoying the proceedings to this point, was visibly alarmed at the apparition before him. He looked to either side of him to see if anyone else seemed to be upset, and was shocked to find that all appeared to be in some kind of a ghoulish trance, absently staring at the image on the stage. Even his good friend seated beside him, the Prime Minister of Great Britain, Sir Thomas Hood, was apparently caught up with the rest.

"This is preposterous!" he shouted as he turned to Sir Thomas, and shook him by the shoulders. "Tom, snap out of it man!"

There was no response. Hood's eyes, along with the others, were fixed on the goat's head. A low murmur, almost like a silent prayer, "one world now," filled the hall.

As if in response, the unearthly form of part-goat and part-man, framed by the red glimmering star, began to speak. "That which we have toiled for in patience is soon to come to pass. The critical mass needed to usher in the Aquarian Age, foretold by our seers and psychics, is at hand. Our mortal enemy, and that of all mankind, of all who love peace, the Judeo-Christian conspiracy, retreats on all fronts. Their malevolence, and the bane of all true god-fearing peoples, will be a thorn in our side no more! Soon, every nation on the planet will have a ban in place against these pious beasts. They will each be registered, and a dossier will be on file detailing their peculiar practices and rituals. Then, unless they join us in the new world order, they will be hunted down and eliminated."

To President Williams' horror, the whole auditorium, in a frightening display of unity, jumped from their seats, thrust their right hands towards the podium, thumb and pinky extended outward in the goat salute, and chanted in a steadily rising voice: one world now! ONE WORLD NOW! ONE WORLD NOW!

Men and women, dressed in tuxedo's and gowns, jumped wildly from their seats, some vigorously clapping, others writhing in an almost epileptic frenzy, their eyes rolled back into their heads. Many began falling over one another, some headlong into the aisle, twitching and contorting as if electrocuted.

The President of the United States had had enough. "Tom! Tom!" He shook the prime minister once more, but to no avail. Sir Thomas, possessed of a spell of some sort, stood shaking beside him, his face and both arms reaching for the stage.

As he was making his way to the aisle to leave, the voice on the stage stopped him in his tracks. "President Williams will now come forth to receive his initiation."

The lights now came on to half power as a spotlight focused on the crimson faced, gray-haired man, caught now between two large ushers, who quickly escorted him to the podium.

The crowd roared its approval as the President of the United States stood beside the now revived Benjamin Stuart, and reluctantly shook his hand, while Stuart whispered in his ear. "You have the full support of your people, your Congress, and the world, as you become one of the 'new elite' tonight. Wave to your adoring admirers."

Stuart put his right arm around Williams, faced the crowd, and waved with his other arm.

The president was too stunned to respond immediately.

"I, I can't do this. You can't--" He started to say, then looked at Stuart and noticed for the first time the vacant, yet hypnotic eyes, full of hidden malevolence and resident evil.

"You can and will, mister President," Stuart hissed through a feigned smile. "If you don't your country and presidency will lie in ruin within twenty-four hours. You did not choose to come here my frightened rabbit. We have chosen you!"

Williams turned once more to the mob, which roared back their clapping approval, and realized that he was teetering on the edge of a deep chasm. One step in the wrong direction could be fatal. *Where are Jack and James when I need them?* he wondered. They, for some reason or other, couldn't come with him to this meeting. Had this been prearranged? Was the power of this group that great? If so, how could he resist?

He had never been a forceful man and had always ridden the crest of an expediency wave. Bravery under fire had never been a political prerequisite. He left the tough decisions and any dirty work to his political handlers. They had always known what was best. Had they known that this would happen? Where were they now? He was utterly alone and only had one choice.

This is, after all, just politics. Sort of like a nominating convention, isn't it? he thought to himself. *I must survive at all costs, and if that means that I have to shake hands with the devil? Well, so be it. I'll win him over as well. Who knows, I might be in for a choice position. There were possibilities here."*

The argument was settled. He placed his arm around Stuart's waist and waved to the crowd.

"Look how they love you, mister President," Stuart gushed as they both acknowledged the applause of the crowd.

"You win Mr. Stuart," Williams whispered, as he smiled and waved.

"We always intended to." Stuart replied without hesitation.

CHAPTER 5

Binyamin Cohen looked east over the windswept dunes that marked the perimeter of Tel Nof airbase in the central Negev desert of Israel. The hot, *khamsin* wind, bone-dry, laced with fine dust, and gusting through his short-cropped brown hair, threatened, once again, to scrub the mission for another day. Benni looked on apprehensively to see if the telltale clouds of dust, indicating a *shamal,* or quick gathering dust storm, had appeared on the darkening horizon. His force of eight planes had lost two days to the fickle dust storms, which blew in from the eastern desert with ever more frequent regularity, and seemed bent on frustrating their flight plans. A Moslem poet had once written that the desert was Allah's anvil, and the *khamsin* was his hammer.

He now found that the hammer had surrendered. There would be no storm tonight. Elohim had overruled Allah once again. Green combat flags were hoisted as air crewman and pilots scrambled for their planes, poised on the black tarmac, like angry killer bees, ready to take wing.

Benni shed his leather aviator's jacket, and gently placed it in his locker. He smiled as he stroked the soft brown sleeve and tenderly touched "The Bold Tigers" patch, the insignia of the United States Air Force 391st fighter squadron, sewn on the left shoulder of his jacket. Jamie "Nimrod" Davis, an American pilot he had trained with at Nellis Air Force Base in Nevada, had given it to him just last year. "I finally found someone crazier n' me," he had said, as he toasted Benni and other members of the Israeli contingent at a farewell dinner party. "He gives me the shivers when he drives that Eagle, so I can just imagine how cold he really must be up there." Laughter and clapping accompanied Benni as he took a hug and the jacket from Jamie.

"Maybe you should change your logo from 'The Bold Tigers' to 'The Cold Tigers,'" Benni had quipped, holding aloft the coveted team jacket, while the pilots laughed and gave him a standing ovation.

He now quickly donned the one-piece pressurized flight suit, over his six-foot tall and lean frame, laced up his combat boots, and with his blue and white helmet in hand, dashed off for his Eagle.

"Shalom *layish*, lion," came the exited, high-pitched voice of Dov Horowitz, his new Weapon's System Officer, affectionately known as the "wizzo," as he boarded the plane. Benni shook his head and smiled as he climbed into the pilot seat of the modified two-seater, Israeli F-15EV Strike Eagle, and fastened his seatbelt. "I'm surprised the engines aren't warming yet Dov?" he joked, while continuing the preflight checks that had become second nature to him.

"I would have, but I couldn't find the key," Dov retorted with a smile that lit up his freckled face.

Benni liked Dov, who had graduated first in his class and was, like so many of his generation, filled with patriotic zeal and *"chutzpah,"* raw nerve. He was maybe a bit green, this being only his tenth flight with Benni, and first real combat mission, but he had already displayed an exceptional grasp of advanced avionics and weapons skills as well as a cool head under pressure.

Benni completed the checks, and started the twin Pratt & Whitney turbofan engines, which also brought to life the HUD (Heads-Up Display) on his helmet visor. While down on his right and left he noted the monochrome and full-color Multi-Function Displays (MFD's), that act like computer monitors, and can be seen by the pilot even in broad daylight. In the rear seat Dov was also busy programming his weapons systems to "ready" status, and followed closely Benni's preflight.

At "all systems green," the slowly accelerating whine of the engines was soon replaced by a roar, as Benni jockeyed the Eagle to the rear of the eight planes of Layish flight. While waiting for clearance from the tower, impatient and fidgety, he lifted his helmet visor, and caught his reflection in the canopy. He noticed for the first time that a few lines were appearing on his bronze, chiseled face, and telltale "crow's feet" were developing on the outside corners of his eyes, underneath his black eyebrows. *"Oy. Monika was right,"* he said to himself. *"Next comes the premature gray and then…"*

He smiled at the thought of his beautiful Monika, who playfully teased him last night about his age, in the vain hope that one day soon her *sabra* would at last have his wings clipped, and would settle down behind a desk somewhere. Only then would they be able to lead a more normal life, if such a thing could be had in the Israeli Defense Force.

At thirty-two, Benni was considered the "old man" of the flight. As commander of an air wing he could have easily let someone else lead this mission, but its importance to the future of Israel had compelled him to take an active role.

"Not bad for an old lion," he allowed, while tousselling his hair and then stroking the sandpaper rasp of his unshaved face. *"It will come soon enough Moni, too soon for me, but very soon, motek."*

Benni pulled out the small photo of his wife he had secretly hidden in his undershirt pocket, and admired it for a moment. One of the flight rules for all aircraft personnel flying into enemy territory was that personal effects of any kind, rings, cigarettes, lighters, or letters, were forbidden to be carried onboard. In the event of capture, any personal items confiscated might be ruthlessly employed to extract information from captives. Benni allowed himself this one indulgence. He lovingly placed it to the left of the HUD console, and gently stroked Monika's face with his gloved finger.

"Tower, this is *Layish* flight. Danni, what's the holdup this time?

"Layish, standby. By my life we're on hold from Central Command," was the exasperated reply.

"Roger tower!" Benni replied gruffly, but couldn't hide the irritation in his voice. *"It could only mean one thing. Our 'political' leaders haven't finished arguing amongst themselves,"* he said to himself. "Some countries have baseball as their national pastime, others soccer, or chess, to the Jew it's the love of argument!" He could just imagine the smoke filled room of Central Command, where the Prime Minister and his cabinet ministers, with shirtsleeves rolled up and arms flailing, standing toe-to-toe in a fog of tobacco smoke, were arguing over some minute detail of the mission. "Just let Yossi do his job!" he would say if he could. Yossi Peleg, the head of the Israeli Air Force, was one of the brightest stars in the *Zahal*, the Israel Defense Force, and could be trusted to bring this mission to its successful conclusion.

"Those nuclear plants cannot go online if Israel is to survive," he said out loud, with a fierce resolve that he wished would, by itself, settle the issue once and for all. "After all, there was, *en brerra*, no choice!"

"*Layish*, this is the tower. Wonder of wonders the *balagan* finally broke up! You'd better sortie before they change their minds."

Benni knew the other crews were probably laughing while he blew out a deep sigh of relief.

"Roger that! If you call us back, I'm afraid we won't be able to hear you," he joked as he eased his throttle forward, and taxied into last position on runway two.

"*Mazeltov, Layish*. Good hunting, and may the Eternal One guide you back safely."

With foot brakes on, Benni ran the engines up to maximum dry power. The Strike Eagle shook slightly in response. He next levered through the throttle gate into afterburner, and felt a shuddering against the brakes. After a final thumbs-up salute, he released the brakes, pushed the throttle contol to the stops, and heard the violent scream of thundering engines. The sudden thrust of power quickly lifted his plane, and sent a lightning bolt of adrenaline racing through his body, as it always did at takeoff.

After the flight leveled off at an altitude of 30,000 feet, Benni quickly assumed lead position of the six fighters and two fighter-bombers, lined up in their prearranged arrowhead formation. Benni's F-15EV Strike Eagle formed the head of the arrow, followed closely by two other F-15 fighters. Next came the two modified F-15E fighter-bombers, each carrying a payload of two, two-thousand pound, laser guided bombs, capable of decimating a small city. In the frigid calculus of the military it was known as a "clean bomb." The remaining three fighters completed the small but deadly force. Several other flights were also taking off from other bases for various targets of interest. These would be other reactor sites, missile bases, and factories being used to advance Iran's nuclear ambitions.

Heading due east, the thickening cobalt darkness quickly swallowed the flight as they crossed into Jordan, and in a few minutes reached their first waypoint, Wadi-as-Sirhan, on the Jordan-Saudi Arabian border.

Soon after entering Saudi Arabia, two Israeli KC-10 tankers met them at their pre-arranged rendezvous. Each tanker could nurse four of the fuel guzzling Eagles, as one by one they lined up in station behind the tankers, waiting, while the boom operator, gazing at them through his window in the rear of the tanker only a few feet away, slowly lowered his boom arm into position to lock onto their fuel receivers.

Stripped down, the Strike Eagles carried 23,000 pounds of fuel, giving them a range of 2,878 nautical miles. Layish flight had the advantage of having additional FAST packs. These packs, despite their name, would not increase air speed (FAST stands for "fuel and sensor tactical"), but are really long-range spare fuel tanks. The extra 5000 pounds in each FAST pack boost, now increased their range to 3,450 miles.

The refueling now complete, Benni, as he had done so many times before, replayed the flight plan in his mind, going over each part of the mission in detail, until it became automatic.

"Hey Benni are we there yet?" Dov joked. He had checked and double-checked his weapons systems, and now began the boring task of monitoring his threat indicators for any enemy activity. The problem was that, while flying over miles and miles of trackless desert waste, they were about as likely to make enemy contact as they were to see an igloo.

Benni laughed. "No, but the stewardess will be by in a moment with hot coffee and sandwiches. I hear that the in-flight movie tonight is *Ali Baba and His Forty Thieves*."

Even without his mike on, Benni could hear Dov's cries of laughter. "Did you have to mention food Benni? I'm starving!"

"I'll buy you breakfast when we get back," he shot back, but felt a sudden chill course through him. *"When we get back, Dov...when we get back..."*

* * *

37

He scowled in frustration at his antagonist and good friend Rabbi Chaim Podhoretz, as he often did when confronting some difficult passage from the Torah, or a particularly tough question from one of his *talmidim,* his students. He took off his ancient wire rim glasses, wiped them with a pocket handkerchief, put the glasses back in place on his large nose, and stroked his medium length white beard. Shlomo Berkowitz got up from the small kitchen table with the half-finished tea services on it, and, with hands folded behind his back, went to the large rectangular window that looked out over the now darkened courtyard of *Ha'Kotel,* the Western Wall of the Temple Mount, in the Old City of Jerusalem.

"Its heresy pure and simple, Shlomo," shouted Podhoretz, who would have pounded the table with his fist if could have found room to do so. The red-faced, portly Rabbi, opted instead for composure and, after another sip of tea, folded his meaty arms across his chest, awaiting a reply he knew would soon come. They had had this argument several times in the past with neither of them yielding his position.

"Chaim, my dear Chaim," Reb Berkowitz began with a sigh, "put away your commentaries, and the *Midrashim,* the writings of the sages, you're so fond of. Take only the *Tanakh,* the holy scriptures." He replied, while holding his old, black, leather-bound bible in both hands for emphasis. "Let the Eternal One, may His name be blessed forever, take the scales from your eyes so that you may find *Yeshua Ha'Mashiach,* Jesus the Messiah."

"Impossible!" Podhoretz shouted, his patience shattered. The Rabbi grabbed the edge of the table with both hands, as if to pull it, and the argument, out from under his friend. "You would have me believe in the gentile 'god,' the god of the Catholic Crusades, the god of the Spanish Inquisition, the god of the Nazi HOLOCAUST!" He bellowed out the last word, which turned his normally pink face into a perspiring beet red.

"Have you forgotten already the *Shema,* Shlomo?" he asked in anger. He walked quickly to the window, using the Western Wall as a backdrop, turned, and with his right hand covering the black *kipa,* or cap, on his head, bobbed forward and back, as he recited the central tenet of the Jewish faith: "Hear, O Israel, the Lord our God is ONE Lord! Not two or three or however many you would have us believe Shlomo. No, I cannot accept this concept, this god of yours. It is impossible Shlomo. Impossible."

Exhausting his zeal he walked back over to the table, put a sweaty hand on the shoulder of his friend, sat down, took another sip of the now cold tea, and abruptly changed the subject. "So how are Benni and that Monika he married then?" He pulled out his pocket watch from the side of his black vest, making it obvious that he was not interested in carrying the argument any further.

"Benni and Monika are fine. They're both down in the Negev and--"

"*Oy vey*, Shlomo," he interrupted. "Time flees indeed like the sands of the Negev and my hourglass is now empty." He got up abruptly from the table, and made quickly for the door that opened into the hallway of offices and other small, two-room apartments.

"Shalom, Shlomo," Chaim said giving his friend a quick hug.

Berkowitz held him by the arms and looked deep into his friend's eyes. "Chaim. Would you read something for me without your commentaries or ancient sources, would you please prayerfully read Isaiah fifty-three? Would you do this for me?"

Podhoretz slowly removed his arms, and was visibly taken aback by his friend's urgent request. "I don't even have Isaiah fifty-three in my bible, Shlomo. It's forbidden you know."

"Why is that so, Chaim? Tell me. Why would they take that chapter out of the prophets, when it's there for the entire world to see in the Dome of the Book Museum, eh? Don't you remember seeing the huge round showcase that contains all sixty-six chapters of the book of Isaiah?"

Podhoretz nodded his head absently, trying desperately not to make the mental connection.

"Think Chaim, please think!"

Rabbi Podhoretz nodded his head in assent, without looking into his friend's eyes, then backed out the door and walked briskly away, putting the whole matter in the back of his mind, and sought out the sweet comforts of his own flat just down the hall.

Reb Berkowitz reluctantly closed the door, walked into the bedroom, knelt beside his bed in the only other room in his apartment, and prayed for the truth and the light to find its way into his dear friend's heart, and into the hearts of his people.

* * *

Layish flight had spent the few hours since takeoff; flying over hundreds of miles of endless desert sand, the only combat they experienced being the fight to stay awake in the moonless, inkwell of darkness. Now the Saudi Arabian coast on the Persian Gulf loomed before them; a faint, sinuous thread, dotted with occasional shimmering gemstones of light. Looking to his left, Benni could see the large diamond cluster that marked their next waypoint, Ras al Khafji. It was here that Iraqi forces made their only thrust into Saudi territory during the Gulf War of 1991, only to be beaten back by coalition forces two days later.

In the back seat Dov was wide-awake and glued to his sensor display, ever alert for a possible threat alarm. From this point forward he would have to be extremely vigilant, always on the lookout for enemy patrol boats and missile batteries. The Persian Gulf was teeming with ships of all kinds, and they would be crossing numerous offshore oil rigs, some of which were known to possess high-tech surveillance equipment.

As they passed Zuluf, and their final waypoint at the Marjan oil rig, the flight was now less than 185 nautical miles from their target. At this point they descended to an altitude of 500 feet in order to avoid radar detection, dropped their spent and now unnecessary FAST packs, and made final preparations for the attack on the Iranian Nuclear Weapons Complex at Rishahr.

With the approach of the Iranian coast and the battle to follow, the usual, noticeable dryness occurred in the back of Benni's mouth. He ran through the details of the mission, and locked the data in his mind for the last time.

"*Remember! The complex is about 16 kilometers south of Bushehr in the villiage of Rishahr. Aproach from south, winds will be out of the southwest. Commence bomb run, split nail formation, leading units driving right and left to deflect enemy counterattack. Probable Hawk, SAM 5 and 6 sites at Bandargah to the east, and there will be a rocky outcrop to the northwest.*"

Sites are manned by Russian techs, so they will be good! Deliver the package. We must, at all cost, deliver the package. The life of Israel depends on this!"

* * *

The oncoming duty officer at the Iranian Air Force base in Heleyeh, began his watch arguing with his counterpart at the Nuclear Weapons College guard post in Rishahr. "Hamoud, listen to me. What are you doing? You must tell them. Tell the Russian dogs that the fire control system must be online at all times. May Allah turn you into a jackal, Hamoud if you do not tell them that we cannot have this system down unless we have a backup, and we do not have a backup at Heleyleh at this time! We wait for parts, and do not have a backup. Do you understand me? It is important that you understand me now, Hamoud."

"You can argue with me all night if you wish Farik, and the missiles will not come online tonight. The Russian infidels have had too much vodka, and they are all asleep. I am sorry, but it is impossible you see? These Hawks have American designs, and we have no treaty with the Great Satan, and we cannot get the parts now you see. Yes, I know Farik, we are in jeopardy. Allah help us, but it is altogether impossible."

With that he hung up, leaving Farik al-Karzemi in a black mood on the other end. He slammed the phone down and cursed his fate, and the fate of his people. With the toppling of Shah Reza Pahlevi, and the ascension of the Ayatollah Khomeini and his Republican Guards, the Iranian military became more and more dependent on foreign nations to fulfill their military needs. Iran simply did not have the will or means to begin manufacturing weapons, and assembling the accompanying infrastructure necessary to make it a proper industrial-military complex.

"Iran is chosen by Allah to be a light to its people, and through the sword of jihad, a blinding light to the four corners of the world," he mused, quoting from Khomeini.

"Allah willing, we will use the tools of the infidel to bury him," he shouted out loud, and smiled, while he stroked the short-cropped black beard on his thin, dark skinned face.

He noticed a large cockroach skittering along the makeshift kitchen counter, and with one swat, dispatched the unsuspecting insect.

"Jihad, my poor friend," he said as he wiped off the crushed remains of the insect from his hand. "Life is meaningless without Jihad."

* * *

Benni toggled his ULF radio switch, and opened up a secure comm line to the rest of the flight. Although the messages sent out would be secure, the ensuing scrambled wave of static could provide a positional fix, if a sharp radar operator was listening. That is why radio silence had been maintained from the moment the flight had exited Israeli airspace.

"Layish flight commence target run at 0445." Benni quickly turned off his radio, and activated the Heads-up Display (HUD) on his visor. His helmet now became an advanced virtual reality computer, extremely technical, but similar to the kind he used to play with as a boy. With this new weapons system, he was now "hands free," and could direct the movement of the Strike Eagle, and its weapons and countermeasures, by simple voice command.

By prearranged design Benni now took the lead of the right hand group, while his wingman, Marvin Chertok, led the group on the left, and less dangerous position.

Both groups maintained a distance of a quarter mile, the split nail, while the two bombers positioned themselves in the midst of the gap, and a quarter mile behind.

* * *

The phone ringing twice in sequence sounded like an alarm going off to Al-Karzemi, who had just nodded off to sleep in his chair. He angrily lifted the receiver, his heart pounding from the sudden adrenaline rush, and exploded into the mouthpiece. "What! What is it?"

"Commander, this is the tower radar operator. We picked up a contact bearing 215, for about five seconds and then lost it. The bearing was constant."

Al-Karzemi rubbed his eyes awake, and tried to digest this unwelcome intrusion into his rest. "Did you get a distance? You say it was a constant bearing?"

"It was about 150 nautical miles, and a steady 215 relative sir," said the operator, a bit more relaxed, as he scanned the radar screen for any updated blip that would help identify a threat.

Al-Karzemi walked over to the dish-strewn sink, hoping to find a clean glass for a little water to help wake him up. Not finding one, he picked a dirty one from the pile in the sink, filled the glass, and poured it down the back of his neck.

"Are you sure it is not a false echo? Did you check your instruments?" Karzemi asked.

"No, sir, it's not a false echo. I performed a routine maintenance sweep just before making contact."

"Very well then, continue the search, concentrate on that bearing, and report back on anything you find."

Al-Karzemi quickly hung up the phone, and rang up Hamoud at Rishahr, his hands visibly shaking from a fear welling up in the pit of his stomach. He was comforted by the fact that Hamoud had picked up the phone after two rings.

"Hamoud, listen to me, there is no time to argue. Scan your radar in the direction of 210, and tell me if you're picking up anything there."

"Sir, a thousand pardons, but, but..."

"Hamoud, you are mumbling like a school child, what is it?"

"The radar sir. The radar is also down. The Russian technicians, they--"

"Yes, yes, I forgot."

Al-Karzemi slammed the phone down in frustration.

"Infidels! May Allah strike them blind for their incompetance," he mumbled to himself, while pouring a stale cup of black coffee that quickly heightened the acid burning of his stomach.

Farik quickly downed the coffee as the phone rang. "Yes! What? Are you certain?

"Yes sir, the reactor complex at Rishahr is under attack. I repeat Rishahr is under attack!"

* * *

About 225 nautical miles south of Rishahr, an American AWACS surveillance plane, patrolling over the Gulf, had been watching the drama unfold.

"Sir, I've got multiple hostile contacts converging on that nuclear weapons facility at Rishahr," Staff Seargent Earl Monroe declared, as he swiveled away from his radar console to face his senior watch officer, Major Frank Collins.

The AWACS had been following the Israeli flight across the Saudi desert, and although it was never acknowledged, Collins knew for a fact that they were going to take out the nuke weapons plant "as sure as a Georgia bullfrog was gonna' catch a fly." It was his duty to report all theater activity, even though he knew that this case was different. He had been pre-briefed that the United States and Saudi Arabia were giving this mission, and the others, when and if they occurred, tacit, but not overt approval. Should Iranian nuclear facilities ever come online the whole region would be threatened, and that was in no way acceptable to American interests.

"Ain't nothin' like that gonna' happen on the Collins watch," the major thought to himself. He looked up from his logbook; a slight smile barely creeping past his lips. "Sergeant, as far as I'm concerned y'all found a flock of pheasants flying in from the Gulf."

"Oh, come on Major," the sergeant replied laughing. "A flock of pelicans maybe, but I can't see there would ever be pheasants flying over Iran. Ain't no pheasant around here, and anyway they don't fly worth a darn!" They both laughed.

Just then the threat alarm sounded on Monroe's console. "Iranian fighters scrambling out of Heleyeh, sir." Monroe was all business again, as he "painted" the mass of blips heading for the Israeli's. "I count eighteen fighters. Holy smokes, they're Russian Fulcrums sir, and they are hot to trot."

Collins jumped out of his swivel chair, and positioned himself behind Monroe to better assess the situation.

"Well son, Layish flight has taken the kickoff, and they are runnin' up the field. Now we'll see what the de-fence can do."

CHAPTER 6

He paced nervously on the granite steps in front of St. Ignatius Loyola church in the Washington, D.C., suburb of College Park. It was a broodingly gray, cold, and windy, late November, Sunday morning, and looked as if it might snow again. Jack pulled up the collar of his camel hair tan coat, and was glad that he had remembered to bring his scarf and black leather gloves. He took a drag from his newly lit cigarette, and promptly tossed the butt to the ground.

"I'd given up smoking ten years ago, just after Evalyn died. Why am I starting up again?" He said out loud, scolding himself.

Jack nodded absently to a young couple, locked arm in arm, and leaning into each other to ward off the cold, while hurriedly making their way into the church for the 11:00 a.m., high mass about to start. He wished he could join them now, listen to the sermon, and maybe take communion.

"No, it had been too long. When was the last time I went to confession?" He couldn't remember.

Jack looked across the street at George Washington Carver Park, its ten wooded acres honeycombed with walkways and bike paths, where the majestic elms and maples of summer, now seemed to be desperately scraping the clouded sky for any warmth they could glean.

He thought back to the sunny days of his youth when he was in awe of God, and, as an altar boy at this very church, was often swept into the heavens by the angelic singing of Sister Mary Anastasia. He once believed that one day he would join the priesthood like his uncle, Father Francis Marion Quinn, a jovial Irishman with a small, feisty stature, whose short cropped, reddish-blond hair, Jack clearly inherited. Uncle Frank always seemed to have a good joke to share, especially after a few shots of his father's Irish whiskey, or, as Father Francis liked to put it, "a wee bit of the necessities."

Jack shook off a shiver from the cold, just as a black Lincoln Town Car pulled up in front of the church. The front passenger side window rolled down revealing the face of his friend, and White House correspondent for American Public Service News, Harry Stanton.

"You're eleven point five minutes late Harry, and I've been frozen for fifteen," he joked as he buckled himself into the seat, took off his gloves and scarf, and unbuttoned his coat, thankful for the blowing warmth of the car heater.

"You'll live I guess. Besides, I don't have to tell you about the Beltway traffic, even on a Sunday, do I?" Harry replied in a Brooklyn accent as he drove off down the street.

Harry had been a tough beat cop in the notorious Bedford Stuyvesant section of Brooklyn before turning in his badge for a laptop and a desk job at APSN. After his daughter graduated from City University of New York, and moved with her husband to Washington, it seemed natural for Harry, who had lost his wife to cancer many years before, to move to Washington as well. When the White House correspondent position opened up, Harry seized the opportunity and the job.

"Tell me about it." Jack said sarcastically as he sat back in the plush leather seat and stared out the window.

"So, what's up Jack? I don't hear from you in a month, and then, all of a sudden, I get a call, and it's like, Harry, I've got to talk to you." He glanced over at his friend with a concerned look on his face.

"I don't know Harry, I really don't." Jack responded, continuing to look out the side window at the quickly passing landscape. "It can wait until lunch."

Harry pulled into the parking lot of Russo's Steakhouse, found a spot quickly, and both men walked into the upscale restaurant where they were quickly seated.

Both ordered steak; Harry preferring a rare filet mignon, while Jack opted for a medium New York strip, while both men added a baked potato and salad. Neither man drank much alcohol so they ordered coffee with their meals.

The waitress served the coffee, freshly ground and piping hot, which appealed to both men on this frosty day. Harry stirred in his usual two teaspoons of sugar, and waited for his friend to speak first.

Jack was restless and didn't know where or how to begin. He knew that he had to open up to someone, and Harry, despite the fact that he was a network news reporter, was one person he could trust. He looked down into the black coffee inside his mug, as black as the mood he was in, and finally opened up to his friend. "Harry we've known each other a long time," he began and looked up into his friend's questioning face, then back down to the coffee. "You know a lot of people and you hear a lot of things." He paused and groped for the right words, then fixed his eyes on his friend, and finally asked the question that had been haunting him for weeks. "Was there some problem with me at the White House?" He shook his head from side to side as he said this, a look of grave concern on his face.

Harry looked down at his coffee and continued stirring, and Jack felt that there was something there. Harry knew something.

"Tell me what you know Jack?" Harry asked in a stiff tone.

Jack relaxed a bit and thought back to the last few weeks at the White House. "There's not much to tell, really. At first the routine was the same; daily briefings with the President, meetings with various staff people, group discussions; a very hectic, but rewarding and productive schedule. Then the President goes off to Europe and--"

"What happened in Europe, Jack?"

"What do you mean, Harry? He had the Bilderberger meetings, briefings, and a ceremonial dinner. Just the usual state visit stuff." He replied, and looked at his friend for an explanation.

Harry's eyes bored into him. *"Was Jack part of the conspiracy, and just play-acting, or did he really not know?"*

"Do you recall the reception the president went to in Florence, Jack?"

"Only that it was put on by something called the G-169 summit group. I was supposed to be there with the president, but was called away on urgent business for him at the last moment. Funny, but when I got to New York, to courier some paperwork to the U. N. Secretary General, I was told by the one of Stanas' aides, that the matter had been dropped, and the papers were no longer necessary."

"You know anything about the G-169?" Harry asked

"No, not really, just a consortium of some notable politicos, with a sprinkling of academia, I guess." Jack shrugged and took another sip of coffee. He really wanted a cigarette, but fought the impulse.

"So the president gets back from his trip, and then what?" Harry asked, and lit a cigarette, making Jack want one even more.

Jack put both arms on the table and leaned in for emphasis. "That's when it all changed Harry. I'd go in for my normal briefings, but the president seemed distant, distracted. He was indecisive, and once, when I asked if anything was the matter, he snapped at me, and told me to mind my own business.

The briefings started to fall off then. First it was every other day, and then once a week. One day I'm in the oval office, and there's a new secretary sitting in Marcia Thompson's desk. When I politely asked where Marcia was, I got an icy stare on top of a cold reply from a thin, butch haircut, fifty-something-or-other, and was informed that Marcia had been terminated. I was shocked. Marcia and the president go way back to the old barnstorming days when the president first started his political career. Well, I waited that morning until noon for a 10:00 a.m. appointment, when the president comes out, and looks genuinely surprised to see me. Another man came out with him, whom he introduced as his new UN liaison, Zoltan Bielczek. The president, later that day, claps me on the back, thanks me for all the hard work I've done on his and the country's behalf, hands me my resignation letter, and asks that I have it back to him by the end of the day!"

"So, he cut you out of the loop." Harry reponded, sighing in relief. "You're not part of the inner circle anymore buddy." He smiled, reached over and patted Jack on the shoulder.

"You make it sound like that's a good thing Harry. If I didn't know you any better I'd be offended right now. I've given my life's blood to this country, its president, and--"

"Now you're on the outside looking in." Harry finished the sentence.

"Yes. And I don't know what I've done or not done. That's why I wanted to talk to you. I was hoping you could shed some light on it."

"Well, you're right Jack, I could, but I won't." Harry motioned for the waiter and handed him his credit card over his friend's objection.

"Not here Jack, too many ears in the place." He explained, while quickly scanning the room. "In every place these days."

They went through the door, and were greeted by a wintry blast of arctic air, that scattered some brown, withered leaves, and sent a chill down Jack's spine.

In the car, Harry handed Jack his business card with an address written on the back. "There's a meeting I'd like you to come to this Wednesday at 7:00 p.m. Perhaps a lot of your questions will be answered for you."

"Sounds kind of spooky, even for a snoop like you Harry." Jack kidded.

"Point taken." Harry chuckled. "I've learned that sometimes the truth is stranger than fiction."

Jack took the card, and put it in his wallet, even more perplexed now than before. Outside, the wind chased snowflakes to the frozen ground.

As the black Lincoln pulled out onto the road heading back to College Park, a figure dressed in a black coat emerged from the restaurant, and mentally jotted down Harry's license plate. Entering and starting his car, he then accessed his slide-away computer under the dashboard, and keyed in the numbers.

* * *

Jack, holding an umbrella in one hand against a driving, windy, rain looked down at the address on the back of the business card his friend Harry had given him, checked his watch, and saw that he was five minutes early, as punctual as ever. He then glanced at the building numbers of the similar looking houses in the fashionable Georgetown section of Washington. Finding number 1455, he went to the call button, and pressed the vis-a-phone. On the inside, Jack's picture was broadcast to the assembled group, which included his friend Harry Stanton.

"Yeah, that's Jack Quinn. I'll vouch for him." Harry acknowledged.

He heard a snap and a buzz, and opened the door into a large, closed foyer that had an interior door leading to the main part of the house. He hung up his jacket and folded his umbrella, as Harry came into the foyer.

"Jack! Glad you could make it," Harry said, patting him on the back, and leading the way into the large living room. Jack scanned the room and noticed that there were stairs going up to the second floor on the left, and a sunken floor with a comfortably lit fireplace on the right. On both sides of the sunken floor were two large couches, a pair of lounge chairs close to the stairs, and a large, round, wrought iron, glass-topped coffee table. The table was filled with trays of cookies, pastries, and a large assortment of finger foods.

As Harry led the way to the fireplace, Jack was interested to note that the room contained about thirty men and a sprinkling of women, and several faces he knew or had seen before at various government functions.

"Jack, let me introduce you to our host, Major General Thomas Hood." Harry offered.

General Hood was dressed in his dark blue Air Force uniform, and had just finished talking to one of his aides.

"Pleased to meet you Jack, Harry's told us a lot about you," he replied, while clamping his right, sixty-two year old hand on Jack's in a vigorous handshake. He was six feet tall, about the same height as Harry, in top physical shape, and seemed to dominate the room. His imposing short-cropped gray hair, square jaw, and straight shoulders, were balanced by a warm and generous smile.

"Likewise here, General. How are things at the Pentagon these days?" Jack asked, recalling that the general was the head of the Phalanx missile defense project for the Air Force.

Hood wondered how he knew that he worked in the Pentagon. "About the same as going duck hunting without shells I'm afraid," he quipped. "Getting Congress to vote in enough money to protect our country is harder than getting blood out of a rock these days."

"General we're gonna step over to the bar for some adult refreshment, care to join us?" Harry asked, while pulling Jack by the arm to follow.

"Thanks no, I need to find Rose, and make sure she's got everything under control. I'll see you fella's later." He replied and briskly set out for the kitchen.

Finding a newspaper colleague of his, Harry excused himself, after serving himself a quick beer from the tap.

Meanwhile, Jack poured himself a cup of black coffee, and, as he turned to find a seat, nearly ran over Marcia Thompson, President Williams' former secretary.

"Why Jack. How wonderful to see you again," she cooed in her dainty southern drawl that always reminded Jack of peach blossoms in springtime for some reason. She looked marvelous, dressed casually in a white open-collar, silk shirt and black slacks. Her straight, shoulder length, auburn hair was pulled over to one side, and provided a perfect backdrop for her diamond studded earings. She wore very little makeup, which gave her face a porcelain quality, enhancing her natural beauty, and brought several shades or red to Jack's cheeks.

"Marcia! Forgive me for almost running you over." He shook her hand, hoping that his palms were not sweaty. "After I found out that you were no longer working for the president, I was afraid I'd never see you again."

She dropped her eyes, obviously pained by the memory, but recovered quickly. "Thank you Jack, it's so good of you to say so. I wondered why you weren't coming around as often as you had been, but then so much about the president has changed."

She smiled brightly. "But now I see that you've joined our little conspiracy." She replied, while putting her hands behind her back, and cocking her head to one side.

Jack was taken aback once more. "Well, er, I haven't joined anything, at least not yet." The thought of joining any group without complete information and documentation was totally foreign to his thinking.

Marcia gently touched his left arm, which sent a chill up Jack's spine.

He had always been quite taken with Marcia, her winsome manner, and statuesque beauty, but because of the non-fraternization employee policy at the White House, had never shown anything other that a cordial demeanor to any of the staff.

"You will Jack. Once you come to understand what's happening to our government, and the rest of the world, you'll join us."

She looked over to the fireplace and saw that the meeting was about to begin. "Jack, won't you sit with me through the meeting?" She asked, batting her eyes ever so slightly.

"I'd be honored," he answered with a smile, and offered her his arm.

General Hood stood to one side of the large open hearth fireplace, that had several three-foot long seasoned oak logs burning brilliantly behind a large folding screen, while everyone took their seat, or stood along the perimeter, eager to hear what tonight's speaker had to say.

"For those of you, who are new to our 'gatherings,'" a ripple of laughter went around the room, "you'll note that the very nature of our relationships to one another, and especially our meetings, are necessarily clandestine. I believe, if Von Clauswitz, that brilliant military strategist, were to write about our times, he would refer to them as the days of conspiracy. For whether you choose to accept it or not, we are all of us, involved in a conspiracy. This, of course, is nothing new. Our country was founded on a premise that refused to accept oppression, and above all tyranny. We face the same situation in our country today, and it is the reason why you are all here tonight. This being said, I yield the floor, once again, to our distinguished speaker for this series, professor emeritus, and head of the political science department at George Washington University, Dr. Horace Clark."

A warm applause greeted the professor, while a portable podium was set into place in the middle of the room. The professor was a thin specter of a man, about sixty-eight years of age, standing a bit stooped, with long legs and arms. He was haphazardly dressed in brown corduroy pants, Birkenstock sandals and brown socks, and a long-sleeved turtleneck shirt, which lead up to a thin neck and face. His long, coarse brown hair, mingled with gray streaks, was tied back in a ponytail, and formed an outcrop over a pair of thick eyeglasses, and a scruffy, short beard. As he settled his papers on the podium, Jack chuckled at the thought that he reminded him of a daddy longlegs spider.

"Thank you General Hood. Ah, It is good to be with you all again, and in such times as these, eh? Last we were together; we followed a conspiratorial thread that quickly wove its way through the cloth and patterns of history to our modern times. Indeed, conspiracy has been a sort of handmaiden, or henchman, if you prefer, to history, and, as the general has mentioned, even aided a one-time fledgling democracy that we all hold dear to our hearts.

He looked up, squinting through his glasses, and scanned the room. "So, what's all that got to do with us, you may well ask? Everything, I'm afraid. Because the conspiracy afoot today in our land, is one that will tie us inexorably to the stream of events that are leading the world to the edge of a precipice, and quite possibly, the end of the world as we know it." He paused for effect, and then began again. "How can I make such a brash statement? Let's weigh the facts." He shuffled more papers around the podium, looked directly at Jack, and then shuffled again.

"For the sake of the few that may not have been here before; I note that the distinguished Mr. Jack Quinn, former counsel to the president is here with us," Jack squirmed in his seat and was beginning to wish he were somewhere else, "we'll do a brief recap, so that we'll all be on the same page."

"My particular journey on the very narrow road of conspiracy began back in the late 90's, when I read, for the second time, a book by Carroll Quigley, professor of history at the Foreign Service School, and a former colleague of mine at Georgetown University. The book title is *Tragedy and Hope: A History of the World in our Time.* I would suggest you read this book, if copies are still available, maybe Amazon still carries them, because it deals precisely with the nature and practice of the globalist agenda being played out in our time. H. L. Mencken once said that the whole aim of politics is to keep the populace on edge, clamoring to be led to safety, by threatening it with an endless series of ghosts and ghouls, all of them imaginary. Sounds rather creepy doesn't it? Yet we know that a careful study of history reveals the truth of these words. Why, the Roman Empire lost its republic, and embraced emperorism from just such a scenario."

He paced back and forth with his left hand in his pocket, while the right gestured for emphasis. "Give the people chaos, disrupt their normal every day routine, and they will clamor for change, and follow anyone who will give it to them, even at the loss of lands or liberty. Ever heard of the French Revolution?" He grasped the podium with both hands and leaned over it looking out and scanning the crowd. "Did you know that the monarchy was, just before the revolution, conducting some of the most serious reforms ever undertaken by France? Just one example of this was that food destined for starving peasants in Paris, just before the outbreak of hostilities, was waylaid, and held captive by those who sought to destroy the status quo. Before the French Revolution there were forces at work that wanted to destabilize the existing government, with the aim of bringing about a new order in Europe, and eventually the world. The Illuminati, a secret society founded by Adam Weishaupt in 1776, infiltrated various Masonic orders in Germany, France, and England, themselves secretive groups, with the purpose of fomenting chaos, and bringing about change. This clandestine plan eventually included a fledgling democracy in North America. You'll note that many of our founding fathers, including Washington, Franklin, and Jefferson had significant ties to Freemasonry, especially the more powerful Scottish Rite sect. Indeed, the more one delves into some of the more esoteric history of our country, the more you will find that much of what is our own city of Washington was built around Masonic plans and specifications! There has also been some scholarship surrounding the fact that our own one-dollar bill has some distinctive Masonic symbols incorporated into it."

"*Hocus pocus,*" was all Jack could think of at the mention of Clark's, so-called, new world order. "*It's so childish. The boogey-man under the bed! This is just another escape from reality,*" he thought to himself, and looked around to see if he might be able to escape. He glanced over at Marcia, who was looking at him with those big and beautiful, "I told you so" eyes--how did she do that? It made him stone cold angry, and melted him at the same time. He decided to stay; for the time being.

Dr. Clark walked, spider-like, back to his web behind the podium, and shuffled his papers once again. "Now this is all quite interesting, though admittedly speculative—not much fact to back some of this, eh? After all, secret societies are by their very nature, well, secretive." Several laughs and hushed comments rose from the group. He stroked his beard thoughtfully. "Let's get back to Quigley, and hear what he has to say. Please bear with me; we'll bring this up-to-date shortly.

"Quigley says in his book that this form of governing is 'subterranean,' and may even be occult. Subterranean? As in underground, behind the scenes, secretive, shadow? Yes! And always with the plan in view of bringing about a new society, one that is founded and controlled by an intellectual and financial elite!

Quigley further states that there has existed for a generation, an international Anglophile cabal, which acts in a way that most people believe the communists act. In fact these groups, known loosely as the 'Round Table Groups,' frequently do cooperate with communist groups. He knows about this because, in the 60's, he was allowed to examine certain secret papers and documents from their meetings. He goes on to say that he believes in most of the goals of these groups, and only objects to the fact that they chose to be so secretive. I can find no clearer example of an international conspiracy, designed by a powerful elite, with the goal to eventually bring about a *Novus Ordo Seclorum*--A New World Order!"

The professor stepped to the right side of the podium, took off his glasses, dangling them in his right hand and leaned on the podium. "Is this really such a foreign concept? Do you remember your bible about the Tower of Babel?"

That brought about a hushed discussion around the room. Jack had to think hard, back to his catechism classes in parochial school, and still couldn't quite get there.

"I know, it has been a long time for me as well." Clarke acknowledged, "I had to dust off my old King James version, and look it up in a concordance, before I could find the reference. In the book of Genesis," he began, and went back to his notes on the podium, "chapter eleven, verse one, it says that,

...*the whole earth was one language, and of one speech.*
Then in verse four the people said:

...let us build us a city and a tower, whose top may reach unto heaven; and let us make us a name, lest we be scattered abroad...

Then in verse six it reads:

...the Lord said, Behold, the people is one, and they have all one language; and this they begin to do: and now nothing will be restrained from them, which they have imagined to do.

You see, the reason God judged the earth in the Noah story can be summed up in chapter six and verse five:

And God saw that the wickedness of man was great in the earth, and that every imagination of the thoughts of his heart was only evil continually.

Now God saw the same thing beginning to happen after the flood, and He decided to do something about it. In chapter eleven, verse seven, God says:

...let us go down, and there confound their language, that they may not understand one another's speech.

So the Lord scattered them abroad from thence upon the face of the earth:

...and they left off to build the city.

Now I don't know about you, but I've done an about face with my relationship to God and the bible." Professor Clark looked down as he said this, and seemed to struggle with the words. "I used to think all this talk about a personal God was all mythology and man-made trash. I've come to realize that there's more than meets the eye to this book," he explained. as he raised his old leather-bound bible, "and I would advise each of you to thoughtfully and, dare I say it, prayerfully, look into its contents, precisely because of the days we are in." He wiped a tear from his eye, cleared his throat, and shuffled his papers once again.

"We'll let all this simmer for awhile, and take a break for some refreshment."

Immediately, several in the group came up to the professor, and peppered him with questions, which he calmly answered with much gesticulating of his hands and arms.

Jack squirmed in his seat. He hadn't seen, much less picked up, a bible since high school, and suddenly felt the need for some tobacco.

"Marcia can I get you something to drink?" he asked, as he stood.

She looked up at him with those eyes. "Why Jack, how sweet of you? An iced tea with some lemon would be nice."

"And a good scotch whiskey for me," He thought to himself, as he proceeded to the service bar.

After downing a quick shot, and chasing it with some soda water, he was about to head back with two iced teas, when Harry tapped him on the shoulder. "Hey Jack, so what do you think so far?"

Jack put on a thoughtful face. "He's certainly raised some interesting and provocative issues. You know me Harry, I've got to digest things before I can respond conclusively."

"Same old Jack," he chuckled. "I was skeptical at first too, you know. After a lot of research, the cop and reporter in me, I can tell you that what he's saying is true." He took a long pull from his beer. "Wait till we get to what's happening now. There'll be some answers in it for you and your situation. I'll catch you later." He walked off as Jack, and everyone else, headed back to their seats, signaling the beginning of the next segment.

CHAPTER 7

Benni had expected to hear his threat alarms sounding by now, like so many angry bees, sounding out from Iranian radar. Only minutes now from target, they had expected to see enemy SAM 5's or 6's, or at least radar guided triple-A fire, which could be even deadlier than a launched missile.

The six Strike Eagle fighters, defending the two bombers, were more than able to handle any opposition that might come their way. Each plane carried AIM-7, and AIM-9 air-to-air missiles, better known as the Sparrow, and the Sidewinder, to thwart any airborne assault. Should enemy radars become active, Layish flight also carried HARM, air-to-ground missiles, which would home in on an active radar set, and take it out before the SAM's could be launched.

The trouble was, there was absolutely no defensive activity. The enemy could be waiting until the last moment to surprise them, but that scenario just didn't fit into either the Iranian, or Russian, defense doctrine.

"We're feet dry, skipper! I still hold no contacts." Dov's excited voice, coming over the intercom, brought Benni out of his reverie, and to the job at hand. They were now over dry land, and only two minutes from their target and closing: too late for nervousness. Benni said a quiet prayer: *"God of my fathers, I'm not altogether sure I believe in you, but others do, and I guess I'll side with them for now. Help us to destroy this malignant creation of our enemy. Deliver us again. Omain."*

"Layish flight, this is Layish leader. Commence bomb run," Benni ordered.

Immediately, the six covering Eagles gained altitude, and peeled off to the right and left to hold the perimeter against any inbound hostile forces, while the two bombers dove straight through the opened gap, without hearing so much as a whisper from the Iranian deactivated radar sets, which were laying in various pieces around the Iranian Nuclear Weapons Complex at Rishahr.

* * *

He sat at the end of a long wooden table that was centered in a cramped classroom located just above Wilson's Arch, which overlooked the broad plaza, and massive stone blocks of *Ha'Kotel*, the Western or Wailing Wall; Judaism's holiest spot. Shlomo looked out wistfully at the wall, which sat in an early morning shroud of shade, and thought of Christ's words in Matthew 23:37:

O Jerusalem, Jerusalem, thou that killest the prophets, and stonest them which are sent unto thee, how often would I have gathered thy children together, even as a hen gathereth her chickens under her wings, and ye would not!

Tears formed in the corners of his eyes as he thought of his people, and the scales that still covered their eyes from the truth about their *Mashiach*.

"*How He longs to know you, and love you my people, but you will not.*" He said to himself. "*Another will come, a deceiver, and him you will embrace.*" He took out a handkerchief, wiped the tears away, and blew his nose.

He was gently shaken by one of his *talmidim*, a student, who had been standing and pondering an argument proposed by the rabbi. "Reb Berkowitz," he asked softly, "are you well? May I get you some water?" His pale face, with adolescent stubble forming on his chin, framed by long curly forelocks, and capped by the black "kippa" of the orthodox, showed genuine concern for his teacher. The other three students looked up from their commentaries, and wondered what great passage of scripture, or theological principle had produced such emotion.

"Thank you Barak, thank you." He replied, while polishing off his wire-rim glasses and clearing his throat to speak. "Sometimes the very air of the eternal word leaves me gasping for breath. My *talmidim*, how precious are His words; they are more than life. Omain?"

"Omain." They all replied.

"Nu, young rabbi." He said, and lovingly patted Barak on the head, while leaving his hand there for a second, and saying a quick prayer for the young scholars' salvation. "We are discussing the book of Psalms, yes? Psalm 110 and verse 1:

The Lord said unto my Lord, Sit you at my right hand, until I make your enemies your footstool.

What does David mean by this? How could David call his son, Lord?"

One of his students stood up and replied, "This is a very hard saying. Contemporary commentaries say--"

"Put away the commentaries for now." Reb Berkowitz interrupted. "Put them aside, please. I want you to search your hearts and minds."

"But rabbi?" another began. "We cannot understand this by ourselves. Scholars have struggled with this verse for centuries. How can we discern the meaning?"

"Sit, sit." Shlomo gestured with his hands, sat down at the head of the table, and looked at each perplexed face with a smile and a twinkle in his eye. "Do you believe that the Lord desires for you to know his will?"

"Yes, but--"

"Your goats are butting again, Ehud." He joked, which produced a chuckle from the boys.

"Listen closely. The Eternal Lord of the universe desires that each of you know His will. True?"

They all nodded in agreement.

"To know His will, you must also know His mind. This is also true? Of course true. Does this include difficult passages? Hmm?" They all nodded. "Then tell me what is meant by this."

The four students were genuinely perplexed, and hung their heads in defeat.

"Nu, it is difficult, is it not, to understand some things right away. Choice treasure takes much digging. If you want to find the costly pearl you must sacrifice much time and energy to find it. This will also take time. You must spend time with the Lord. Not in your books and notes, but take time to learn from Him."

He stood up, and paced back and forth. "A question? If David calls him Lord, how is he his son? Answer? There are several possible answers to this question. David wrote Psalm 100 by divine inspiration, yes? By the Spirit of the Eternal One, if you will, and he wrote about *Mashiach* to come. David could only call his son superior to himself because He, *Mashiach*, is superior, that is divine. The only way this could be possible would be through a virgin birth, where the line of David would be preserved, and at the same time, be superceded by the divine nature of that birth."

He looked at faces and was pleased to see the beginnings of comprehension.

"Therefore, we can paraphrase the text and say:

The Lord God said to Lord Mashiach, sit You at my right hand, until I make Your enemies Your footstool. Omain."

Waiting patiently at the door, but unseen until now, was the rabbi's friend, and fellow rabbi, Chaim Podhoretz.

"Shalom Chaim, you're just in time for an interesting discussion."

Podhoretz was obviously troubled by something. "Shlomo, a word please?"

Berkowitz walked out of the class and into the hall. "Dear friend, what is it?" He asked with concern.

"Shlomo, this is hard for me. I did what I could do. The council..." He paused, and looked down at the floor. "You're to appear before the council. They want you should be questioned about certain statements you have made concerning your belief in Yeshua!"

* * *

The first Strike Eagle bomber began its bombing run, while his backup held station thousands of feet above. Skimming just above the wave tops, he punched in the new coordinates that would take him over the nuclear weapons complex in a matter of seconds. At the same time he went to LANTIRN, a military acronym for the illuminated, infrared pods located under his wing, which allowed him to clearly see the landscape before him.

Streams of information were now flowing down the side of his helmet visor, giving him course, height, speed, and time to launch. As the Eagle went "feet dry," or, over land, he climbed up at a sharp angle, and, at a prearranged point, released his bomb. With the additional weight now gone, his Eagle clawed for more altitude, while the bomb ascended at first, then felt the tug of gravity, and began to fall.

In the bomb's nose, infrared seekers sniffed for the guiding beam from the Eagle, acquired it, and locked onto the nuclear weapons facility. With a huge *whummp*, the bomb dug into the building, buried itself deep into the ground, and then let out a thunderous explosion, leveling the complex, and most of the surrounding facilities. When the second bomber commenced his run, there was little left to destroy. The coordinates were pre-set for a concrete hardened storage bunker, which was now little more than a pile of rubble. The pilot made a slight adjustment that would allow the second bomb to explode above ground in a surface blast, and would impact a large area outside the now-decimated nuclear complex.

As the second Strike Eagle approached the target, it was greeted by triple-A fire from postings outside of the complex perimeter. Several missiles were launched as well, but without radar guidance, both missiles and cannon fire completely missed their mark. The second bomb exploded with a terrifying blast, and silenced the feeble opposition.

Their job complete, both bombers rejoined their support fighters, who were already winging their way back to the coast.

"Commander! Numerous contacts are lifting off from Heleyeh. Not everyone was sleeping in tonight, I guess," Dov joked, but there was a strain in his voice. He realized that there would be a battle after all, and while he was prepared for it, indeed had worked hard to be cool under fire, the strain of combat was new to him.

"Layish flight! Bandits on your o'clock!" Benni announced calmly, and, along with three other fighters, banked his Eagle in the direction of the incoming attack, according to their prearranged plan of defense. This gave the two bombers and their two support fighters, the ability to go to afterburner and make their escape.

Benni had already toggled off one of his Sparrow missiles as soon as he got a long distance lock from his combat radar. The missile split the formation of eighteen hostiles, and homed in on the last fighter, now desperately trying to make an evasive maneuver. The unfortunate pilot tried to evade the missile by reaching for the deck, and launching countermeasures, but it was too little, too late, and he disintegrated into a fireball.

The rest of the chase group split into two sections. The first eight put on afterburners, and tore after the fleeing Israeli bomber group. The rest formed a column of three groups of three planes, and attacked from three different angles.

"Benni, Fulcrums! They've got Fulcrums after us!" Dove yelled into his mike. The Fulcrum was the most advanced fighter in the Iranian arsenal. A Russian design, it had advanced avionics and weaponry and could match the Israeli Strike Eagles stride for stride.

"That explains their quickness, Dov.

Layish three and four peel off and intercept that chase group. We'll mix it up with these *goyim*.

Marvin, take the left and I'll take the right two."

"Side 1and 2, fire!" Benni barked the command that sent two Sidewinder missiles hurtling after the enemy.

"Seventy down, bank hard right. Counter right and left," he ordered. The Strike Eagle instantly obeyed the commands to dive and veer right, and simultaneously launched countermeasures against the incoming missiles.

"Benni, alarm threats all over the clock!" Dov cried out. His voice was now boyish and shrill in the midst of the massive Iranian missile barrage.

"I've got it Dov. Stay with me now." The inside of Benni's visor showed multiple moving circles, some trying to lock onto his aircraft, others following Chertok's Eagle, and still others doubling back on the Iranian flight.

As they passed under the enemy column, and crossed over to one side, they saw three of the enemy go down in flames from the Israeli

Sidewinders, and another two shot down by enemy missiles gone astray. The first attack had lasted thirty seconds, and had decimated the enemy by more than half.

"Layish, Layish, Benni I'm hit!"

Benni could see smoke trailing from the port turbofan engine of Chertok's Strke Eagle

"Marvin, it doesn't look bad. Head for home."

"I can still fight! This lion hasn't lost its claws yet. I need to cover you Benni."

"That's an order Marvin! Return to base!" He barely got the words out when new threats lit up his visor once again. He pushed the yoke down, causing his Eagle to scream for the deck. Benni leveled off just above the wave tops, and with two enemy missiles in hot pursuit, made for an oilrig just off the Saudi Arabian shoreline. He launched a round of countermeasures, and swung around the square platform in a tight, clockwise turn.

The missiles, momentarily confused by the chaff, reacquired the metal signature it was programmed for, and exploded on impact. It hit the metal oilrig derrick, and sent it toppling into the sea, causing no little commotion on the platform itself.

Having escaped again, Benni sent his Eagle soaring into the sky, and came up behind the pursuing Mig 27's. He quickly toggled off two more Sparrows, and voice-guided them to the two pursuers, and saw them go up in flames. He also noted that another Fulcrum at his five o'clock also went up in smoke.

"Dov, did you catch that splash to starboard?" he quickly asked. *"Were there other friendlies aiding us in the fight?"* He wondered.

"Mazeltov, Benni! Got that one for you. I couldn't leave without a parting gift." Marvin Chertok's voice came merrily through the headset.

Benni smiled and shook his head. "You should be court-martialed; but thanks for the help."

"En brerra, no choice. I will be happy going to prison knowing--" Suddenly, the communication went dead, and to his left Benni saw a fireball erupt where once Marvin Chertok's Strike Eagle had been.

Benni bowed his head and prayed, a hot tear forming in the corner of his eye. *L'Chaim, dear friend. You gave your life so that others may live. May the Eternal One give you rest. We'll say kaddish for you when we get back to base,"*

"Layish--BEHIND!" Dov yelled. The last remaining Fulcrum had crept up below and behind their Eagle and peppered it with fifty-millimeter cannon fire. The bullets danced diagonally across the right side of the plane and through the rear half of the cockpit.

Benni instinctively commanded his plane to bank hard right and down, bringing seven g's of gravity against his chest, and almost causing him to pass out. The maneuver didn't fool the Mig. It kept up with him through the turn, and his many counter-moves.

Benni noticed a thin trail of smoke coming from his own plane. The gauge symbols on his visor showed the hydraulics icon blinking, indicating that a leak had sprung in his steering system. He would eventually lose control of the plane if he didn't get out of there.

"This Iranian--couldn't be an Iranian, he flies too well. These are the moves of a veteran, like the veteran pilots we used to practice with back in the States."

"Gotta be a Russian!" He shouted.

Just then another volley from the Fulcrum peppered Benni's tail section, damaging his rudder, and causing his yoke to stiffen.

"Going manual." He told the computer and seized the stick so that he could gain better control while rolling his plane back and forth to avoid any more damage from the trailing Mig.

"Dov, I'll need your help to shake this guy."

"Dov!"

"Dov, do you copy?"

Nothing came back over the two-way. Benni craned his head back as far as he could, and saw the bullet-hole tracks along the canopy.

Dov would never answer again.

Another volley from his pursuer missed, but Benni was now having difficulty controlling the Eagle.

"Time for one last shot." He said, and raced his engines to full throttle. He was heading west, his back to the rising sun, and noticed an intermittent hum in one of his engines.

"Must be why it's smoking."

He punched the throttle through the stops and into afterburner, felt a slight hesitation then an abrupt leap forward.

The Fulcrum was not about to lose his "kill," and the pilot punched his aircraft into afterburner as well.

"Come on. Come on. That's it, a little more…"

The Strike Eagle vibrated wildly, while the Russian closed in for the finish.

"NOW!"

Benni pulled the throttle back, hit the airbrakes and looked up to see the Fulcrum zip past him. He immediately toggled off his last Sparrow, and voice guided it onto the target. The billowing, ball of flame marked the end of the pursuer and the chase.

Even as Benni eased the Eagle down to a safe cruising speed, and now exhausted from the adrenaline producing tension suddenly released, the Eagle began vibrating wildly, until a loud metallic grinding noise, culminating in a loud boom, told him that one of his engines was gone.

The stick, which had been fighting him to begin with, now became stiff and inflexible. At the same time a flashing red light, accompanied by a relentless "beep, beep, beep" indicated that his plane was losing power and beginning to stall.

As the altimeter began its counterclockwise descent, Benni struggled to maintain control, and throttled up to the stops, desperately trying to regain the vital airspeed necessary to reverse his downward death spiral.

The Strike Eagle was still falling, a critically wounded fighter seeking the sanctuary of the desert sands below. At approximately 2000 feet Benni put the F=15EV into a shallow dive to increase speed. Then his controls seized up, and he lost complete steerage. With the ground coming up fast, Benni had only seconds to eject. He pulled at the emergency handle, located down between his legs, with both hands. Small charges in the cockpit exploded, lifting the canopy safely away. Moments later the thruster rocket beneath the seat lifted the seat up and away from the stricken craft.

The sudden launch, and tremendous force of the ejection, caused Benni to black out. Had he been able to see behind him, he would have noted that the casing of his primary parachute had been ripped apart by the fifty caliber bullets from the Mig-27 Fulcrum.

* * *

Monika Cohen slept fitfully the previous night. She was getting better at this. She hardly slept at all on any of her husband's previous missions. The early morning sun streaming through their bedroom window tried to reassure her that all was well. She turned her petit frame to the emptyness beside her, half-hoping that her handsome sabra would still be occupying it.

She took Benni's pillow and buried her face in it and smelled the spicy fragrance of his cologne: her cologne actually, for he wore it for her. She brushed her long, black hair aside, and kissed the spot, which would have couched his face, and then laid it back gently in its place.

"*Where is my Zahal flyboy?*" She wondered. "He must be...," she glanced over at the alarm clock sitting on the non-descript night stand beside their bed: It was eight fifteen. "He's on his way home!" She cried.

She bounded out of bed, and jumped into the shower, ready to put the long night behind her, and enjoy the delicious expectancy of her love's soon return.

Donning Benni's terrycloth robe, and using a towel to dry her hair, Monika made her way to the kitchen, and began her breakfast of black coffee and a single slice of toasted bread topped with a wedge of goat cheese.

She was almost too excited to eat. As an intelligence staff officer on the base, she knew that the raid on the nuclear site took place in the dawn hours of that very day. Given the operational parameters and time-at-site assessment, which she helped draft; Layish flight should be several hours over Saudi Arabia by now. Their estimated time of arrival was projected to be about 10:00 a.m., Israeli time.

Smiling over her cup of coffee, tears of joy filled the corners of her hazel eyes. *"I can't wait to tell Benni the surprise!"* She thought to herself, and gently rubbed her stomach feeling for any telltale signs.

It was still too soon. She had just found out yesterday when her pregnancy test came back positive.

"Perhaps this will finally ground you motek." She shouted, and smiled at the thought of her husband safely behind a desk, and coming home to his family each day.

"Another sabra, Benni. A *different* eagle for you."

CHAPTER 8

"The council will come to order please." The head of the seven-man Rabbinic Council, seated in the middle of a long classroom table, dressed in the black garb of the Orthodox, looked out over the top of his black glasses, and began the meeting. It was held in Reb Berkowitz's own class, which was a small ten-by-twenty foot room that was now packed to the walls with black clad Hassidim, the rabbis and scholars, who made up the bulk of the Sephardic branch of Jerusalem's Jewish population.

The mood in the room was tense. Everyone present sensed that something very important was about to take place. In the background, arguments, as well as whispered conversation, could be heard. Speculation about the old rabbi's fate ran rampant through the crowd.

Reb Berkowitz, dressed in a long black coat and worn black shoes, that sharply contrasted with his white shirt and equally white beard, sat down in the single chair placed before the table occupied by the Council.

"Nu, It is a good thing for the tired feet of an old rabbi to sit down. True?" The Rabbi looked around from face to face.

A nervous laughter and response broke out.

"True, true."

"Of Course, true."

"Well spoken, eh?"

The crowd quieted to a few whispers as the Chief Rabbi, Shmuel Neumann, his two curly forelocks bobbing as he coughed to clear his throat, started to speak.

"Rabbi Shlomo Berkowitz, we are here in an official capacity to explore certain allegations brought to us concerning your teaching philosophy." He paused and looked over his glasses to see what reaction, if any, his opening statement might have produced.

Reb Berkowitz sat motionless; hands folded one over the other on his legs, with a calm, even expression on his face.

"In particular your teaching about…" Neumann paused again, closed his eyes, and raised his two hands, palms upward, a few inches above the table. "Yeshua, the so-called Christ of the Christians."

With that, the whole room began to buzz in rapid conversation.

"You mean Yeshua Ha'Mashiach," Reb Berkowitz countered.

The crowd was shocked again to silence, and then exploded into heated denunciations.

"Traitor! Idolator!"

"Not my Mashiach!"

Neumann leaned forward, now visibly red in the face, and pointed a finger at the accused. "Then you admit to the charges?"

The crowd in the schoolroom was hushed in anticipation of the rabbi's response. Having prayed, Reb Berkowitz chose a text from the book of Acts.

"Men and brothers, many centuries ago, other disciples of this same Yeshua were brought before a council much like this one." He paused and looked around at the stunned and hushed, black clad men, some now scowling with angry faces. "I must respond to you as they did in their generation." With that he stood up and faced Rabbi Neumann. "Whether it is right in the sight of God to hearken unto you more than unto God, judge for yourselves. I cannot but speak the things that I have seen and heard."

With that he turned around, and walked out of the room.

* * *

Monika was putting on her sandals, while attaching a loop earring to her ear, when she heard a knock at the door. She opened to find a female

Zahal major, an administrative officer from Benni's wing, standing hat in hand with head bowed.

"Mrs. Cohen may I step in for a moment," is what she said, but what Monika heard that made her blood run cold was, "*Mrs. Cohen your husband has given his life for Israel.*"

Monika's normally dark-skinned face turned pale, and she almost fainted.

The major reached to catch her from falling. "Are you alright Mrs. Cohen?"

She had seen it before. Next door to their flat the messenger of death had come. A young pilot Benni liked was killed in a skirmish somewhere in the north. A shoulder fired SAM had extinguished his life, and crumpled his family. It had happened too often to so many in Israel.

"Not my Benni." She cried, and wept into her hands.

"Mrs. Cohen, please..." The major pleaded, while taking a chair across from her. She offered her a handkerchief, that Monika gladly accepted.

The officer looked down again, and spoke softly. "I've come to tell you that Benni is missing in action." She paused, and looked up, hoping that there would be some encouragement in this. "We believe that his plane was shot down near the Saudi-Iraqi border. We have received a radio beacon from one of the ejected seats and..."

Monika sat up straight at the news, and somehow knew in her heart that Benni was alive.

She turned and smiled at the worried officer. "Thank you major. I'll be alright now.

"But, we're not sure if it is him, Mrs. Cohen. We only have one--"

She gave her a fierce, knowing look that stopped her in mid-sentence.

"Benni is alive!"

* * *

He drifted in and out of a restless dream. Monika was running through a spring meadow, clothed and bejeweled with myriads of brightly colored flowers; the train of her flowing dress trying to keep pace with her bare feet. She looked back at him, and laughed at the chase. He ran after her with his arms outstretched.

"The ground motek; the ground is coming," she cautioned, still running away. "The ground Benni!"

He awoke a few hundred feet above the desert floor, just in time to turn his parachute into the wind, and touch down roughly, but safely, on the sand. He lay there for a minute, gathering his wits about him, while shielding his face from the fierce sunshine, which, even at mid-morning, was unforgiving, and brought on a sweat that would soak through his clothes in no time.

"*What happened?*" He wondered. "I remember the dogfight, the ejection, and then...nothing more." He looked at his discarded parachute, and noted immediately that it was the emergency backup chute, not his primary one. He stumbled through the hot sand to his pack, and saw instantly why the main chute had failed to open. A trail of bullets from the attacking Fulcrum had penetrated his backpack, and cut the lines to the parachute. Somehow, he had deployed the emergency parachute.

"*But how?*"

He tried to rub out the throbbing headache in his forehead, couldn't, and attempted to recall the events of the ejection. Nothing came to mind. Somehow the emergency had been pulled open. He looked at his pack again. The emergency pull ring was still in place! It wasn't pulled!

His bewilderment, compounded by the headache, and the apparent haziness of his mind, were disrupted by the sound of machine noises echoing across the dunes, coming from an easterly direction. The adrenaline rush, produced by the excitement of this newfound discovery, instantly brought his senses into sharp focus. He scrambled to the top of the dune he was lying on, eager to find the composer of those sounds. Carefully peering over the edge of the dune, he saw, about a mile away, a large oil rig shimmering through the mirage-like waves of heat emanating from the sands. Benni pulled out a small pair of collapsible binoculars from one of the many pockets on his flight suit, and found it to be a relatively new site, noting that the drilling derrick was still in place. He scanned the area for any workers, saw no one, and, apart from a trail of black smoke that he knew was from his own downed fighter, found that there was no discernable landmark anywhere else to be found.

That brought Benni to his immediate predicament. *"Where am I?"* He wondered, pulled out an area map from another pocket, and tried to calculate his position. He had flown approximately twenty minutes west of the coast at roughly six hundred knots. That would mean he was some two hundred miles inland. How far north or south of his ILF (intended line of flight) would only be a vague guess.

"I could be close to Qulban Layyah in Iraq, or Al Waqqbah, or Ath Thumamah, in Northern Saudi Arabia, if I calculated correctly that the oil rig I wheeled around was indeed Safaniya #2." He pulled out his pocket GPS tracker and found that he had landed some twenty miles south-southeast of the Iraqi village of Qulban Layyah.

"That would put me within radar range of both Kuwait City and Basra in Iraq." The thought of being greeted by Iraqi troops sent a chill down his spine. Even though Iraq and Iran were bitter enemies, and had fought several long years of war, they had recently formed a cooperative alliance, and the capture of an Israeli pilot would be a noteworthy prize for either country."I would just as soon deprive them of a trophy."

Yet another pocket yielded his pre-programmed sat phone that would enable him to call for help. His head swam for a moment, and he became dizzy as he lifted the cover and looked at the screen.

"Must've been shaken up a bit."

He tried to focus his eyes on the dial pad and found that he couldn't. The sand dunes began swirling now, and he felt nauseous. He doubled over from a sharp pain in his head and stomach, lost his balance, and rolled down the side of the dune.

Then he passed out.

* * *

The phone rang just as Shlomo Berkowitz was sitting down with his morning tea. He grumped at the clanging modern contraption, once calling it a disturber of the peace.

"Let it ring itself to death!" he shouted, and then thought better of it.

"Nu, and what if it should be important?

And what am I that I should be so important?

There is none important save Elohim.

So what am I, pickled herring?"

The argument over, he picked up the phone, and heard an excited and emotional Monika on the other end.

"*Zeide*, grandfather, I'm so glad you answered, I know how much you hate to talk on the phone."

"Nu, I'm talking already. What could be so urgent that my tea should get so cold for?"

He was joking with her for he truly loved Monika and relished the few times they had been able to talk, even if it had to be on the phone. Life for Benni and Monika, on a frontline airbase, had not been conducive to much verbal exchange with him. They would rarely leave the base, and Reb Berkowitz was semi-cloistered in the religious world of Jerusalem. Besides, Benni had grown more distant with the discovery of his grandfather's newfound Christian conversion. It grieved him to see that the boy he loved, and had raised from six years of age, was now so closed to him.

"*You said Lord, that You had come to bring a sword:*

For I am come to set a man at variance against his father…and a man's foes shall be they of his own household,

I now see what you mean, Lord."

"*Zeide*, we're pregnant. I mean…I'm going to have a baby, but also--"

"May the Eternal One be blessed, and may he bless the fruit of your womb."

"*Zeide*, please!" Monica interrupted, and started to cry.

Shlomo continued without heeding her. "How truly does the psalmist say:

As arrows are in the hand of a mighty man; so are children of the youth. Happy is the man that hath his quiver full of them.

"Monika, I'm so proud of both of you. My joy is full."

Monika regained her composure. "It's also about Benni…" She lost what little strength she had, and sobbed over the phone.

Reb Berkowitz was alarmed now. Something was seriously wrong.

"Monika, tell me, What's wrong?"

"B-Benni's been shot down!" She finally managed. "I don't know if he's alive or dead."

Shlomo felt as if someone had thrust a hot poker in his stomach. He sat down heavily, and propped his head up with his left hand. *"Father, by the life of your Son Yeshua, help us now,"* he prayed quickly to himself.

Monika cried until the cloudburst of tears was spent. "I believe Benni's alive. Somehow I know in my heart that he's still alive."

The moment she said that, faith rose up to meet her words and Shlomo had a witness in his heart that Benni was indeed alive. "Yes, Monika. I too believe that he lives."

"Zeide, can you come to the base. I'm having pains and I'm worried. Would it be too much to ask you to come...soon?"

"Monika, get to a doctor now!" Please go now. I will come as soon as arrangements can be made." He was already calculating the arrangements he whould need to make as he spoke.

"I will. Come soon, and thank you."

The minute she hung up the phone, the burden to pray had set Reb Berkowitz on his knees once again. He would not rise again until the burden had been replaced by God's peace that passes understanding, given to those who know Him as Lord.

* * *

Benni chased Monika into gentle surf of the Mediterranean Sea. He watched as she slipped beneath the waves with the grace of a dolphin. He dove in after her and swam until he found her and pulled himself up to her waiting arms, and sweet embrace.

He awoke from his dream by a splash of water on his face, slowly regained consciousness, and then felt pressure applied to his chest making it hard for him to breathe. Benni opened his eyes only to have them stabbed shut by the fierce rays of the mid-day desert sun. Using his hand as a shield, he focused on several dark shapes standing around him. One of them had his foot on Benni's chest.

"You are Yahud? Yahud?" The tormentor asked in Arabic. When his questions produced no immediate response, he shoved his sandaled foot onto Benni's neck producing a painful groan.

Benni passed out again.

"Pick him up! We take him with us," ordered the leader.

With that command the two closest figures hoisted him between them, placing one arm over each shoulder, and dragged him over to the waiting camels. They draped him over the saddle of one of the baggage camels, and tied his arms to his legs underneath the camel's belly, to keep him from sliding off.

The small band straddled their camels, adjusted their *kaffiyeh*, or head wraps, over their eyes, and with a brief "hut, hut" command, rode off in a northwesterly direction. If Benni could have seen it, he would have noticed that one of the pack camels carried pieces of his own plane; a desert camouflaged wing piece, that bore the insignia of the Star of David.

The setting sun painted the endless canvas of dun-colored dunes with a rose hue, as the band neared its destination. The vast desert sea finally gave way to a slim green island of a thriving oasis. Grouped together on one end, an expansive tent encampment of the Bedouin tribe now appeared. The children, accompanied by the camp dogs, outran their elders to meet the returning troop, while the women lined the route into camp, and ululated the tongue-clucking trill of greeting, to their brothers, husbands, and sons.'

The Bedouin raiders rode proudly on their mounts, as if they had just returned from a famous battle, carrying with them the spoils of war. Yosip bin Saladen, son of Sheik Wallid Haj Saladen, sat tall in the saddle of his white steed, and, with his vintage AK-47 submachine gun in hand, fired several rounds into the evening sky.

As he approached the largest tent, Yosip deftly slipped off his horse and bowed low to his father, who was standing in the door.

"*Salaam Alaikum*, Abu."

Haj Saladen bowed in return, gave him the appropriate Muslim salute, and then kissed his son on both cheeks.

"Alaikum Salaam. Al-lah has blessed me with your return, my son. May his wisdom guide you all the days of your life." He put his arm around Yosip and ushered him to the main tent.

Yosip abruptly stopped short of it. "Abu wait! Look what Allah has given us!" He took his father's hand, and led him to the rear of the column of camels that were already being refreshed at a nearby watering pool. "He has gifted us with a falcon fallen from the sky." He grabbed a handful of Benni's hair, and pulled his head back for his father to see.

"Yahud, Abu!! He was one of fifty enemy beasts shot out of the sky by our victorious brothers. They litter the desert floor like carrion, and their wives and mothers wail for them tonight. This one gave us a vicious fight, but I subdued him and brought him to you." He put his hands on his hips, thrust out his chest and smiled wickedly, as if he had truly accomplished his boast.

"Insh' Allah!" as Allah wills." Haj Saladen replied, patted his oldest son on the shoulder, and thought only of the handsome reward that he was sure would be paid for a prize such as this. "Truly it is said that the biter has been bitten."

He turned to his son. "Go to your mother and tell her of your exploits. Tomorrow we will hold council with the muktars, to decide how we shall dispose of this falcon with the clipped wings. But tonight we must have a feast!" Haj Saladen shouted to the gathered crowd of people, who began celebrating once again.

"Jabril!" Haj Saladen called to another of his five sons, this one in charge of preparations.

"I live to serve you, Abu." Jabril acknowledged, and bowed low as he came up to his father.

"Muster the women and make ready the feast."

"As you command," his son replied.

The Sheik already knew what the outcome of the council would be. His will would dominate the council's decision as he always had. Since the death of Mohammed, the Wahhabi sayyids claimed direct descent from the prophet. The Bedouin had always considered themselves to be the elite of the Arab: the true Arabs. They had been the original driving force behind Islam, and spearheaded the Moslem conquests by the

Caliphs. The Bedouin payed no landlord, owed no taxes, and held to no borders. The Middle East desert was their home, an area that had proved to be too remote and desolate for the ambitious Egyptians and Romans. Theirs was a cruel culture, developed from the harsh extremes of the desert, one that honored and encouraged the plundering of the weak. The Wahhabi Bedouin had always wielded and been governed by the sword. The ceremonial, jewel encrusted scimitar was passed down to the one who possessed the most cunning and ruthless skill. Haj Saladen himself had secretly slit the throats of two usurping muktars, when he was only sixteen. His ferocity and bravery, quickly quieted any other dissent, and surrendered the ruling sword into his capable keeping. During his rule, he had increased his tribe's holdings from a single village and one hundred dunams of land, to hundreds of villages and several hundred miles of territory. His enemies feared him, and both the Baghdad elite and the Sunni rulers in Riyadh had courted him. He had spit on their overtures of peace and offers of wealth, and remained to the present day fiercely independent.

"Like the Shiite Fatimids of old." he said to himself. *"I owe allegiance and pay tribute to no one but Allah! I am one with the desert wind and the wind blows wherever Allah wills."*

Now he held a prize that would gain him further prestige throughout the Arab world. He walked out of camp to the darkening dunes, looked in the direction of Mecca, and fell into deep thought. *"It is the will of Allah that all his Moslem children unite for a Grand Jihad against the infidel. The Shiite Imams have proclaimed that the twelfth Mahdi, a prophet in the spirit of the Prophet Mohammed, is already here! As Allah wills, the Mahdi will be revealed in his time, and Islam will unite behind him. Then the Zionist entity in Palestine will finally be driven into the sea. The infidel nations will tremble, and quake with fear, when the hammer of Islam is unleashed once again! Only when the blood of the infidel flows freely down the streets of every city and village will true peace be possible. Then, and only then, will peace reign under the flag of the Crescent Moon!"*

Haj Saladen walked back, and smiled as he touched the sign with a picture of the Ka'aba above his tent door, and quickly turned to the voice of the muezzin as he sang out the call to evening prayers.

He gathered up his prayer rug, and placed it in the sand in front of his tent, facing southwest. He then knelt on one end, bowed down at the other, and called upon Allah to make it so.

Haj Saladen uttered the same prayers he learned as a child. A blind, old Imam from the Iranian holy city of Qom, had once prayed over him, and told him that Allah would one day give him a sign when the time for Islam's glory was at hand. *"You will catch the infidel by the neck, like a fowler snares a bird in his trap,"* he had said. *"Then you will gather the children for jihad, and Allah will prosper your hand.*

"As my son so wisely said, I now have a falcon with clipped wings."

* * *

After the long dusty ride in the slow moving armor-plated bus, and a thorough search at the airbase gate, (even Rabbi's had to endure the painstaking search that had become second nature to Israeli citizens), Reb Berkowitz went to Benni and Monika's flat. Finding it empty, he hastened to the base hospital to see if Monika had been admitted there. A stern, olive-skinned nurse took him through the intensive care section doors, to a small room across from the duty nurses station.

"She's lost a lot of blood. Stay only a few minutes, and do not upset her!" The commands were followed by a blistering stare from her heavily creased face that eased only when the concerned Rabbi nodded his head in assent.

As she began walking back through the doors they had come through, Reb Berkowitz plucked up the courage to ask the question that weighed heavily on his heart.

"Please nurse; a lot of blood. What of her child?

"Mrs. Cohen had a miscarriage," she stated flatly, without a trace of emotion. "She's in critical but stable condition. Remember only a few minutes," she commanded, turned crisply from the door, and was gone.

The weary Rabbi sat down in the chair next to Monika's room, buried his face in his hands, and wept. With tears hot on his face, he prayed that Monica would regain her health both physically and emotionally, and would find peace and rest in Yeshua.

"Blessed are you, King of the universe, who gives life so that we may live. *L"chaim*, Elohim. To life!" He prayed with eyes closed, and lifted up his hands in praise.

"May Monika and Benni, Lord Yeshua, find life in You!"

* * *

His head swimming in a whirlpool of confusion, Benni finally found the strength to focus on his surroundings. He noticed a sharp pain coming from his wrists, and saw that his hands had been tied to a tent pole.

"I'm a prisoner!" He thought to himself.

His head had been resting on a large goatskin blanket draped across some of the baggage, and placed in the far corner of a large rectangular tent. The rest of the tent was quiet and dark, except for a few oil lamps hanging from the tent roof. These revealed several bunched shapes of men huddled closely together; the still night punctuated, now and then, with their loud snores.

Had he been conscious, Benni would have witnessed a celebration right out of the tales of *The Seven Voyages of Sinbad the Sailor*. After the ritualistic handwashings, the food prepared and served by the women came in waves and torrents. Salads, stacks of flat and round bread There were steamed grape leaves topped with currants, hummus, tahini, and falafel; plates of olives, pickles, peppers, lamb livers and eggplant dishes. Other dishes included cheeses, yogurt and pomegranates. There were also pies of lamb and poultry, squash dishes, and several different types of mixed and mashed beans.

Then there was the main course.

Huge and heavy platters of chicken covered with couscous, lamb and rice, goat and cabbage came next, smelling of dill, garlic, and saffron.

At one point in the meal the wing section from Benni's aircraft, bearing the Star of David, that Yosip bin Saladen had brought back, was produced and passed around the room amid shouts and yells of *"Allahu Akbar!* Allah is great."

Then there was dessert, consisting of baklavas, other cakes, figs, grapes, and other fruits.

Cardamon-laced, double-boiled coffee capped the meal, and after fingers were licked clean, a barrage of belching ensued, while the women cleared the plates.

Finally, the *narghiles* or water pipes were produced, while the men recounted tales, mostly fictitious, of their personal valor in battles real and imagined.

After a short time the glut of food settled in and one by one the men prostrated themselves on the oriental rugs or were propped up on blanketed camel seats and fell asleep to a chorus of snoring.

"Where am I? How long have I been here?" Benni wondered. He began to fight against his bonds, only to find that his feet had also been tied, and that further attempts to free himself would be useless.

Out the shadow of still more bags to his left, a dark figure suddenly emerged, pulled out a small angled knife, and held it close to Benni's throat. "Any sound other than your breathing will be your last," hissed a male voice in Arabic. "You must come with me."

He deftly cut the cords from Benni's hands and legs, quickly tied his hands behind his back again, and led him quietly into the black night, where two saddled black horses awaited.

The phantom helped Benni onto his saddle, and, after mounting his own steed, silently rode out of the Bedouin camp with Benni's horse in tow.

As he rode awkwardly into the night, Benni wondered what awaited him at the end of the ride. *"Was there a firing squad in my future: a ransom perhaps?"* From what he had been briefed on before his ill-fated flight, he knew that he was obviously a worthy prize. Had his captor spirited him away from the camp so that he wouldn't have to share a reward? Thievery was commonplace among the Bedouin.

Looking into the moonless sky, an ebony carpet strewn with diamond-studded stars, he felt utterly and hopelessly alone. "I might be riding off to torture and death, and no one would know." The thought produced an involuntary shiver, as fear, an emotion he had rarely felt, welled up in the pit of his stomach. His heart began to race, and his breathing quickened, as fear produced fright, and fright looked for an opportunity for flight.

He was still too weak to resist. His elevated pulse rate produced hammer-like pains, causing his head to swim from time to time, as he fought to stay conscious.

Miserable and weak he cried out to God. *"Eternal One of my fathers, if you are there, please help me! God of Abraham, Isaac and Jacob, have mercy on me!"*

As he finished his prayer, great rogue waves of sobs crashed against his chest, and released a flood of tears. As his cries grew to a crescendo, he lost his balance, fell off his horse, and plunged head first onto the cold desert sand.

The black rider with one quick movement sprang from his horse, and lifted Benni to a sitting position.

"What are you doing? We cannot stop here."

Benni looked into a masked face above, showing only dark eyebrows and eyes and angrily demanded an answer. "Who are you and where are you taking me?"

"Up! Now!" the black rider commanded.

"No! I won't go on like this. Untie my hands!" He replied

The black rider stood motionless for a moment, seemingly unsure of what to do. Then, in one quick movement, he produced the glittering knife again, placed the blade deftly under Benni's chin as a silent warning, and then cut the cords that bound his wrists.

They rode on for some time into the cold night, riding through hill country, and finally, just before dawn, trotted down a small cart path that led into an equally small village. As the horses walked softly through the slumbering town, Benni looked up into the sky to see a shooting star streak through the newly risen crescent moon, forming, for a brief moment, the shape of a cross.

CHAPTER 9

General Borodin steered his bulky body into the only empty chair at the end of the long mahogany boardroom table that could comfortably seat thirty people. It was centered in an ornate conference room looking out through four, large, bullet proof widows onto Red Square, brooding it seemed, with the rest of Moscow, over the oppressive and gloomy gray skies. The wind-whipped, light snow outside, heralded a major snow storm yet to come. Seated at the table, immersed in agitated discussion, were President Primakov, several cabinet ministers, and a few selected members of the Politburo. All eyes were on General Borodin, who had called this meeting, and who alone might be able to make sense out of the debacle that had occurred in Iran.

Borodin poured himself a glass of water, and lit a cigarette from a gold case given to him by Vladimir Putin, then head of the KGB, for his service to the now defunct spy agency.

"Da, da. So we've had an incident in the Middle East," he began, downplaying the Israeli surgical strike that had once again wreaked havoc upon the sensibilities of the world. He calculated the impact of his offhand remark on each face.

Primakov cracked the slightest of smiles, while Defense Minister Boris Ivanoff launched into a tirade, as if a starting gun at a race had been fired.

"Incident? With all due respect, this was a complete fiasco! Several major Iranian nuclear centers have been bombed and destroyed; their nuclear potential and capabilities eliminated in one swoop!" Ivanoff swished his right hand across the table, as if clearing a space for emphasis.

Next it was the Energy minister's turn. "We have already established from our men on the scene that ninety to ninety-eight percent of Iranian nuclear capability has been destroyed, effectively wiping out the Iranian nuclear program for years to come." He sat down as murmuring discussion filled the room.

Ivanoff, a young thirty-five year old newcomer to the game of party politics, who sported a short cropped, black beard, as a counterpoint to his prematurely balding, swept back hair, raised his thin frame from his chair, and took up the distressing litany once again. "Only an *incident* you say." He spat the words out and looked directly at General Borodin. "What of the hundred Russian advisors and soldiers who lost their lives, the millions of rubles in destroyed equipment, the time and effort wasted?" He paused for effect, but failed to see the slightest response from the general, who stubbed out his cigarette, and immediately opened his gold case for another. "What of the loss of face to our allies, to the world?" he continued and looked around the table for support, but found none.

Borodin took a full drag from his cigarette, and actually looked bored.

Failing to get a rise from the general, Ivanoff turned his wrath on Air Force General, Sergei Chertov. "What of our vaunted air defenses, General Chertov? He quickly scanned his notes. "Missile defense systems down for repair, 27 planes grounded for maintenance, flight crews missing key equipment, or away on leave?"

Chertov, sporting a uniform encrusted with several medals, and now wearing a crimson- tinted, moon face, immediately stood to attention. "I must remind the minister that Russian forces are in Iran as guests. As such we must try to fit our military doctrine and equipment into a society and form of governance that is one step removed from the Stone Age!" Murmurs and nods of approval surrounded the table. "The Iranian government has been reluctant to allow us to install our latest equipment, with the exception of our vaunted Fulcrum fighters, or to establish an orderly command and control system of any kind. Instead they place their poorly trained, and under equipped personnel as operators and technicians of equipment left over from the Cold War. The result is what will happen when the Iranians come up against any disciplined encounter, and mind you, the Israeli defense forces, behind ours, are probably the most disciplined in the world!" With that he abruptly sat down.

Ivanoff, still standing, was not done yet. He looked down at his notes again, and then up again at Chertov. "Tell me general. Were our Fulcrums manned by our own pilots?"

Chertov glared at the Defense Minister, and knew where the question was heading. "Our brave pilots manned all but a few of our Fulcrums, yes."

"I have a report here," Ivanov continued, "from the attack on the Rishahr facility. The attack began just before dawn, and yet there was little or no ground-to-air response. Then a scrambling of eighteen Fulcrums out of Haleyeh airport, several minutes after the attack was completed? May I ask why?"

"Am I on trial here?" the General shouted in anger.

Ivanoff had crossed a line that experience would have told him never to cross. It's never wise to make a general officer look bad in front of his peers, and his questions were doing just that.

"I'm sorry General. You're certainly not on trial and I'm not trying to be rude." He backed off and sat down again trying to diffuse the tense situation.

Chertov was unforgiving, gave the defense minister a withering look, and replied still standing. "As I said before, and any *fool* can find out with even a cursory inquiry, the conduct and deployment of our brave men and women, given all the mitigating circumstances previously mentioned, fought with courage and conviction under near impossible conditions. Add to that the superior numbers of the Israeli forces arrayed against them..."

At this General Borodin raised an eyebrow, and stifled a laugh with a congested cough. He knew that Israel had launched four strike forces of eight planes each, hardly a superior force. He also knew that the full force of eighteen Fulcrum jets that had set out from Heleyeh had all been destroyed, with only two Israeli fighter escorts lost.

"...and you can see that this action was lost before it even began." Chertov sat down quickly, just as Ivanoff rose to continue his inquiry, amid nods of acclamation for the general's response.

"May I then ask the general--?"

President Primakov, who had been bemusedly quiet all this time, finally put an end to the debate. "I think we have heard enough for now, Defense Minister. We will now hear from General Borodin, and the purpose for calling this meeting."

Borodin crushed his cigarette in an ashtray, while looking out at the darkening gloom outside the window, stood up, and looked over at the Defense Minister. "I still say this was but an incident!" he shouted, and pounded his fist on the table, "one that, sooner or later, had to take place. Our Moslem allies will now be forced to unite with us in our common purpose of destroying the renegade entity known as Israel!"

"What about us, my friends," he pleaded, as a defense lawyer might for the sake of a client. "What has the *Rodina*, Mother Russia, whom we all love and serve, gained from all of this turmoil, and the billions of rubles spent on years of fruitless effort? Where is the warm-water port we so desperately need for the security and safety of our people? What of our lifeline of oil from the Middle East? Can we say today that it is truly safe from the tampering of outside forces? As we speak, Ilya Stanas, that sly fox of the United Nations, has safely ensconced himself and his forces in Jerusalem! Their troops safely deploy in Haifa harbor every day.

We've also received reports from our agents that there is now talk in the General Assembly, of moving the United Nations to Rome of all places!" He leaned heavily at the end of the table again for emphasis. "Can we passively stand by, and in good conscience continue to allow Israel to run roughshod over our Arab clients?"

To a man, all but President Primakov, stood up and shouted, "Nyet! Nyet!"

Borodin nodded at the president, who was now standing and clapping, while the rest began to chant, "Ro-di-na! Ro-di-na!" The same chant that had carried Mother Russia through to victory in the Napoleonic War and in World War II.

The general raised his arms to gain attention once again, knowing that he held his comrades by the scruff of the neck. He would not let them go until definite plans were drawn for the conquest of Israel!

* * *

She awoke, and was startled by the fact that she didn't know where she was. There was a thick cloud of darkness all around her, except for a small blue light on the wall above the foot of her bed. She sat up, and put her feet delicately over the right side of the bed, almost afraid that there might not be a floor to stand on. Dizziness took hold of her at first, but was soon replaced by a general grogginess.

"*If I didn't know any better I would say that I have a hangover,*" she said to herself.

"Hangover? Have I been drinking?" Her voice echoed in the dark room.

The darkness scared her, much like a child's fearfulness after having a nightmare, and she groped for anything familiar. A quick search produced metal bars framing her bed. Then, in a frenzy, she knocked something to the floor from a small table close to her pillow. The constant darkness haunted her, nurturing her fear, and seemed to be getting thicker, and yet strangely familiar. Finally, the physical exertion caused her head to swim, and she settled back on her pillow and closed her eyes.

"Where am I?" She asked in a loud whimper, choking back a sob that was starting in her throat. "What's happened to me?" Her voice trailed off, and she was embraced by sleep once more.

* * *

The dawn broke over the horizon with a dazzling display of dancing colors. It grew from plum to orchid, magenta to pink, and then from tangerine to fluorescent yellow as the sun began its daily pilgrimage across a crisp, blue, cloudless sky. The teal-colored blanket of the sea was calm as glass, with gentle rolling swells that ended in foaming laughter as they tumbled towards the shore.

She walked down the sandy, palm-treed beach, a gentle breeze wafting through her shoulder length hair, and thought that there could not be a more wondrous place in all the world.

Suddenly, as she looked to the north of the island, huge roiling black clouds boiled up, laced now and again with hot streaks of lightning, and came cascading toward her with frightening speed. She ran away in terror, trying to gain traction in the loose sand, stumbled, and saw a small piece of wooden wreckage that had washed up on the beach. She picked it up, and saw that some writing had been chiseled on the board. As soon as she read it, she threw the board down, and it was immediately taken out to sea again.

She opened her eyes, and focused on what was clearly a brightly lit hospital room.

It had been a dream! Another one of *those* dreams! She quickly put it out of her head, and considered her surroundings.

She was in the same bed with the metal rails that had confused her in the dark.

"Was that last night?

She pulled herself up to a sitting position, relieved to find that there was no dizziness this time, and looked around the room. There was another bed, close by the entrance door that was neatly made and empty. Everything in the room was a sterile white, except for a six-inch ribbon of powder blue that ran around the perimeter of the walls, acting as a painted chair rail.

"I'm in a hospital room but…where?" She wondered in confusion. *"How and when did I get here? Who am I?"*

* * *

Dr. Clark assumed his position behind the podium, and called the gathering to attention. "Well now, we are all refreshed and ready to begin our next session, which I will call, bringing the conspiracy up-to-date.

Several decades ago, a powerful financial elite centered in London, with offshoots in New York, and Paris, formed what became known as the Roundtable Groups. Their goal was to take the old disorganized system of handling money, through localized holdings of capital and credit, and organize them into an integrated, *international* system, which has worked quite well for many decades now. I emphasize the word international, so that you can bear in mind what the bigger picture is. These elite, because of their purchasing power, swallowed up whole industries, such as mining and transportation, first locally, and then internationally.

Since government could present severe obstacles to their overall plans, it too had to be controlled, and because schools would produce the next generation of the elite, it also had to be manipulated.

None other than Albert Einstein once stated that the ruling class has the schools and press under its thumb. This enables it to sway the emotions of the masses. The function of the roundtable groups was to enable the power elite to have secret discussions, review where they had been, and make plans for where they were going. The foremost roundtable group is known as The Bilderbergers. It was formed in 1954, and was named for the Bilderberger hotel in Oosterbeck, Holland, and the site of its first meeting. The group also meets yearly around the world at various sites."

Hearing this, Jack straightened up and paid close attention. He'd known about the Bilderbergers for some time, and it was after one of their meetings this year that President Williams had changed so much, leading to Jack's being pushed away from the inner circle.

"Because of its secretive nature, we only know a few bits and pieces about what goes on in these meetings; with the exception of the last one in Florence, Italy, which we will get to presently. It suffices to say that The Bilderbergers have been one of the leading roundtable architects of the globalist agenda."

The room was abuzz with conversation, and even Jack, who had been puzzled by many things he had seen and heard at the White House, began to see the pieces falling in place.

"Now, if this is the case, what will it take to see the plan through? You've heard the expression: follow the money trail? This plan is being accomplished through the implementation of a global banking system, and the interlocking of the boardrooms of major world corporations, all run by a small, powerful elite, bent on achieving the dream of a one-world society; a new, Tower of Babel, if you will."

"Next, you'd have to get government out of the way. This has yet to be fully accomplished, but the process is inexorable. Way back in the 1970's, another roundtable group called the Club of Rome was founded to assess the world's problems, and prescribe viable solutions to pressing global needs. They realized early on that they needed to shock the world out of its stupor, and force it to realize, what it termed, 'the predicament of mankind.' You'll note a similar, and by and large successful attempt to shock the world was done several years back by former Senator Al Gore and his global warming crowd. The Club of Rome authored a book that spells out the need to divide up the world into ten regions, or, if you will, kingdoms. These are to be: Western Europe, Japan, Australia and South Africa, Eastern Europe, including the Russian Federation, Latin America, North Africa and the Middle East, Tropical Africa, South and Southeast Asia, China, and NORTH AMERICA!"

Clark lifted his head and looked out at the stunned crowd. "Yes, you heard correctly, I'm afraid, not the United States, but North America, or more accurately, The North American Union. May I say to you, that after exhaustive research, I have found these ten 'kingdoms', though in various stages of incorporation, to be virtually complete!"

"You'll note that our own country's movement towards this so-called North American Union, starts with Nixon's regionalization plan in the early 1970's, goes on to the North American Free Trade Association (NAFTA), then the building of a major 12-lane superhighway from the Texas/Mexican border to Canada. It also includes, Mexican consular offices in each of our country's regions and eventually each state of our country, the free-falling dollar and subsequent rise of the Canadian dollar and Mexican peso, and now the creation of a 'euro-like,' North American currency, called the 'Amero.' I could go on and on. Our country has been handed over to an elitist conspiracy, whose worldview is an eventual one-world empire!"

Again, the room came alive with a rumble of hushed and shocked discussion.

"Jack, how can this be?" Marcia asked, while looking up at him with what he saw was fear in her eyes. "Is this why you can't find any mention of the United States in bible prophecy?"

Marcia had been raised in a typical Southern Baptist family in Charleston, South Carolina, and was home schooled by a doting mother, who fiercely taught her to know her bible, while living a life-style far removed from its teachings. This disparity caused Marcia to drift away from her biblical roots, while attending the University of North Carolina, where the full weight of her liberal education bore down on her, and all but erased her early upbringing. Then as a staffer for Senator Biron Nowles of South Carolina, and later, as an appointments secretary for President Williams, she led a life of growing despair, and became disillusioned by the parasitic pretentiousness of the Washington elite. Her despair heightened when she had learned that her roommate, Mira Rosen, had died tragically in a car bombing several weeks ago.

During their brief meetings at the White House, Marcia had always thought of Jack as a solid, down-to-earth kind of guy. He seemed to shy away from the public scene. She only saw him once or twice at government functions, and then always in the background. Now he was here beside her, and maybe...

Jack was taken aback by the question. Marcia had assumed that he was up on his biblical eschatology, when in fact he would have a hard time finding the book of Matthew in the bible. He was well adapted to the situation though, and put on his scholarly, contemplative face. "That's surely a possibility. I'd have to look into it more to be sure."

* * *

She awoke to find an elderly, short-cropped, gray-haired man, wearing silver, wire rim glasses, and a short gray goatee, sitting close to her bed. His slumped shoulders, coupled with a rather dishelved look, was sharply contrasted by his neat, charcoal turtleneck under a gray tweed jacket. He put his hands on hers, which sent a creepy chill up her spine.

"I'm glad to see that you are getting well, my dear."

She slowly withdrew her hand away. "Um, are you a doctor? She asked innocently.

A look of stunned surprise washed over his face. "Don't you know who I am?"

She looked hard, and wrinkled her brow in thought for a minute. "No, I don't think so."

Sitting back in the chair, he crossed his legs and stroked his beard in contemplation.

Just then the duty nurse, followed by a short, stocky, middle-aged doctor, walked briskly into the room, clipboard in hand. The visitor quickly pushed his chair, and himself, out of the way, lest he become trampled under her tall and burly frame.

"How you doin' baby? She asked, while munching on some bubble gum, and, seemingly timed to its beat, took her temperature, noted the values on her monitors, and punched in the data on her hand-held computer notepad, all in one dizzying display of efficiency.

"You lookin' good darlin'," she gushed, not looking up from her notepad, and handed the printed readout to the doctor. "I'll be by later, baby. You take care, hear?" She said smiling, and then whisked her way out of the room as quickly as she had come in.

"My, yes!" The doctor exclaimed, while slowly approaching the bed. "Very nice. Good progression. Everything now in the normal range, I see." He folded his hands over the clipboard, and sat down on the edge of the bed. "That's the first part of the evaluation; the second is for you to say."

"Me? I feel great. My head's not swimming now, and my appetite is back." She replied brightly, and hoped that maybe the next step would be for her to go home.

Home? Where was home? She couldn't remember. She'd been told that she had been in a car accident, where she had suffered severe head trauma. Nothing from the past revealed itself to her.

The doctor looked over at the man in the chair. "Do you know who this man is?"

She looked at him once again. "Another doctor? A psychiatrist maybe?"

He chuckled. "Well he is a psychiatrist, but that's not why he's here." He studied her face for any glimmer of recognition.

"No. I've never seen him before. Should I know him?" She asked innocently.

With that the man walked over to her, and stood beside the bed, as the doctor rose to stand beside him. He looked at the doctor, and then at her, and with pleading eyes answered her. "Dear...I'm your father."

* * *

Professor Clark leaned both arms against the podium, took off his glasses with his left hand, rubbed the topmost ridge of his nose, and began again. "Now let's bring this all up to date, shall we? Most of you know that earlier this summer President Williams went to a summit conference in Florence, Italy. What you may not know is that while he was there he also attended a special meeting of the Bilderbergers. I know this because a friend of mine, a newspaper reporter, had secretly covered the event. The story he related to me would make your hair stand on end, but it's not germane to our discussion at present, except for the part that President Williams played in it. The president was an invited guest, but evidently did not realize, at first, that this meeting was actually meant for him. He was to be initiated into what is known as, 'The Plan of the 169,' or as it casually called, 'The Plan.' This clandestine group of one-worlder's is bent on destroying democracy, and seeks to gain control of the planet by the creation of a totalitarian world order. President Williams is now a member of this group, and has in tow a man by the name of Zoltan Bielchyk. Technically, he is a United Nations liaison, but he's been secretly placed in a position at the White House to keep the president, and other key members of the G-169 in his cabinet, under control."

Jack looked over at Harry, who was leaning against the wall with a grim expression on his face. As their eyes met, he nodded, and Jack knew the reason Harry had wanted him to come to this meeting. All the questions he had, like several streams merging into a river, were being answered for him. He now understood President Williams' sudden change, and why Jack lost his job at the White House. This conspiracy had produced a silent coup-d'etat, which now meant that the United States was no longer the nation he once knew, but a gross appendage onto a monstrous beast! Without realizing when it had happened, in the course of the evening, Jack knew that he had joined this little group, and made a vow to fight this one-world beast!

He looked over at Marcia, who was lost in her own thoughts, gently took her hand in his, and when she acknowledged him with a surprised, but welcoming look on her face, gently whispered in her ear: "I'm in."

CHAPTER 10

He sat beside Monika's bed in the small room of the airbase hospital and beheld her ashen face.

So peaceful.

So serene.

Shlomo gently and lovingly stroked her sweat encrusted hair, hoping that the mere touch or his hands might wake her from the coma she had dropped into. She had lost the baby to a miscarriage, and also lost a great deal of blood, which resulted in this deep sleep.

"How long have I been here?" He asked himself, while stroking his beard. *"The scowling nurse, (may the Eternal One give to her a new and more pleasant face!),* had come and gone with her threats of eviction, twice. *"It must be about two hours now. May you also bless her for her patience, Lord."*

He had prayed for both Monika and Benni and, although he felt a calm peace regarding Benni, believed that he must continue to pray for Monika. There was a battle raging for her life. Physical? Spiritual? Maybe both? He could only keep praying.

"So, you're still here then?" The scowling nurse was upon him again. "Do you think by your bother she should get better?" she scolded, while taking readings from the monitor beside the bed. Her face softened as she walked over to the bed, and gently stroked Monika's face with her hand, and adjusted the blanket. She did this with such loving care that it brought a tear to Reb Berkowitz's eyes.

"Praise be to you, O Lord. Monica is in good hands." Shlomo prayed silently.

The scowl returned again, though, when the nurse positioned herself at the end of the bed, her arms crossed over the clipboard hugging her chest. She didn't have to say a word.

"Nu, already I'm going. I'm going!" The rabbi announced in mock anger. Shlomo lifted his tired body slowly from the chair, and stood to face the resolute woman.

She helped him with his black great coat, and walked him to the door.

He abruptly turned, and gave her a great hug, that was also returned.

"A warm heart you have. I have asked the Eternal One to grant that it should reach your face one day!"

They both laughed, and went their separate ways.

* * *

He walked on, while the heat of the desert mid-day sun bore down upon him. His flight suit, torn and saturated with sweat, weighed heavily on him, as he plodded through the sea of dunes ranging for miles in every direction. In the distance, a black speck appeared in the cloudless sky. As it drew near, a large flying creature appeared, swooped down and picked him up. After many miles, it let him down on grassy field. In the midst of the field was a large, gnarled, olive tree, where thousands of bees were busily attending the hive they had built, in the bosom of the tree. Off to the north, a black cloud appeared. As it drew near, he could make out the shapes of huge locusts flying towards him. As they drew closer, he could see their faces, as it were, the faces of men. He realized that they were coming to destroy the olive tree, and he frantically looked around for something or someone to help.

Benni woke up to find that the sun was up, and the wind was rattling the canvas tent he was in. He sat up quickly, only to find that his headache had come back with renewed force.

"It was a dream." He said to himself, wondering what it could mean, and shook himself awake to collect his thoughts. How long had they been traveling? It seemed like months since he had bailed out over the

Saudi desert, but it was only a few days. They had been riding by night, according to Benni's star field navigation training, on a general, westerly heading, stopping, but not staying, at various oases along the way. How he craved his area map and GPS right now.

Breakfast and dinner, now in reverse order because of their night flight, consisted of small pieces of dried goat meat, goat cheese, and a few dates. When they had stopped, their morning camp was made in the shelter of an outcrop, or cleft of overhanging rock, and consisted of a single, low-slung, rectangular tent that could sleep two. Unless the wind was severe, Benni slept in the tent, while M&M, (Benni's acronym for his unnamed captor, "man of mystery"), slept no more than a foot outside his tent door. While they seemed to be making good progress along their journey, there was always urgency in their movements. He oftentimes had the sense of enemy eyes searching for them in the darkness. The Bedouin were master trackers, but their pursuers were at least a day behind. That, coupled with the recent windy conditions which covered their tracks, was aiding their escape. Still, they could only travel by night, while their pursuers could pursue them day and night, if necessary.

Benni's captor was all business. During their infrequent conversations, he never discussed the purpose or plan of his capture, much less their destination. He did, however, learn how they had escaped from the Bedouin encampment. Evidently there had been an accomplice inside Haj Saladen's stronghold, the night that Benni had been brought into the camp. During the Bedouin feast, certain tasteless sleeping potions were added to the drinks, insuring that the entire household would be fast asleep throughout the next day. The getaway was then swiftly accomplished, and he was whisked away into the fastness of the Arabian desert night.

Benni suddenly stiffened, when he heard voices talking in hurried conversation outside his tent. The flap of the tent suddenly burst open, and his captor spoke to him in hushed, but urgent Arabic. "We must leave at once! The Bedou patrols are upon us! We must make for the caves!"

Within minutes the camp was broken up, and the six riders, (they had been joined by four others sometime in the night), fled northwest to a low line of barren hills. At a signal from M&M, one pair of riders broke off to the right and north of their line, while a few miles later the two other riders broke off to the left and south.

"They're trying to throw off the pursuit behind us," Benni thought. Judging by the sun just overhead, he knew that it was sometime near midday. Soon a line of hills appeared, and a few tall mountains loomed into view. An hour later, they came to a dusty wadi, and turned a sharp right to follow it on its northward course. They climbed up a narrow pass between two bald hills, and followed what appeared to be a narrow goat trail that hugged the side of a hill. After several minutes, and many turns and dips, they came to a valley with a long wall on the north side, that contained numerous caves. Following the valley floor, the riders turned left at the end of the wall, and climbed a steep bank onto a flattened hill. From there, on a height that gave them a good view of their escape route, they stopped for a moment, while M&M turned his horse around, checking for any pursuit. In the distance, some twenty miles away he spotted two low clouds of dust rising above the desert. One group headed north, evidently following the two riders who had banked away some time ago. The other and larger group was following their escape route. By the amount of dust they were kicking up, it became painfully obvious that the pursuers were also on horseback.

M&M wheeled his horse, Benni following, and raced across the rocky plateau and still higher hills. Above and several miles away loomed the tall mountain he had seen from the desert floor. It was pyramid shaped, had a blackened feature, like a black ribbon, snaking over its peak and down both its flanks. The ribbon had a glazed appearance in the waning afternoon sunlight, and Benni knew from his pilot training that here was Jebel al Lawz, the mountain of almonds. He remembered from countless arguments with his *zaide,* that this mountain was one of the sites, indeed the only site according to him, that many claimed was Mount Horeb of biblical fame, where Moses received the Ten Commandments from God. Interesting as that might be, Benni now realized that he was ever so close to his homeland, and his precious Monika. If he could find a way to shake his persistent captor, he knew he could find his way home. His survival instincts now aroused, and the fresh scent of his homeland in the air, Benni began formulating a plan of escape.

* * *

When Shlomo entered the makeshift bedroom, which had been converted from a base supply office, and contained a military cot, a small desk, and a tiny table and chair, he felt that it was enough. "Nu, Rabbi Paul once said, that we must in all things learn to be content. So it is good for me, this room," he said, as he unpacked the few necessities he brought, from his black leather bag. Gathering up his worn bible, he held it close to his chest, and knelt beside his bed. He spread it open to one of his favorite passages, Psalm 91, and prayed. "Oh, Lord, you are my strength, and have become my salvation. For this I praise and worship you, now and forever, omain." He took his white handkerchief from his pocket, wiped the tears that had formed from his eyes, and continued his prayer. "My Lord, I pray this, your Psalm, for my dear Monika. Gather her to your bosom. Hide her under the protection of your wings. Give your holy angels charge over her. Lord, I call upon your holy and wonderful name! May you ever be praised. Lord, through the death, burial, and resurrection of your dear Son, Yeshua Ha'Mashiach, show her your salvation!

* * *

Sheik Wallid haj Saladen walked to his pavilion, and paused to see the smoke rising from the ancient city of Tobuk, the primcipal and provincial city of northwestern Saudi Arabia. It had been at one time the home of the Royal Saudi Arabia Northern Military Command, and the Royal Saudi Air Force.

"*It was the will of Allah, blessed be his name, that we overcome the infidel Saudi king in Riyadh, and pluck for ourselves one his choice figs.*" He thought to himself as he entered the main room of his pavilion and seated himself on the gilded, high-backed chair, that served as a mobile throne, while several of his concubines fussed over him with offerings of food and drink.

The battle for Tobuk had lasted an hour. His horde of thousands had descended from the high hills, and quickly overran the token resistance offered by the Saudi defenses. He had put most of the city to the torch, ordered the captured leaders beheaded, and caused those that remained to swear an oath of allegiance, and pay a generous ransom. This money, he told his newfound subjects, would be used in the struggle to take back the holy sites of Mecca and Medina from the Saudi usurpers.

He thought of his son, Yosip, now riding with the best and swiftest trackers he had, in hot pursuit of his stolen prize. *"Somehow, the Israeli falcon had taken flight again, but not by himself. The treachery that produced his escape shall be rewarded with a slow and painful death to the conspirators,"* he vowed to himself.

The call to evening prayer by the muezzin quickly disolved the dark spell of his mood. He took the large ornate prayer rug offered by one his servants, gently placed it on the sand facing south, and kneeling in an attitude of prayer, urged his son on. *"Insh' Allah.* As Allah wills. Speed to the prey my son. Bring back the falcon and the vipers!"

* * *

"Pigs! And sons of pigs!" shouted Yosip bin Saladen. He was frustrated by his band's inability to catch up to their quarry.

His second in command groveled, kneeling at his feet, not knowing whether his fate because of this failure would produce a quick sword blow to his neck.

"Get up Mahmoud! You disgust me!" Yosip commanded, He paced back and forth to disgorge his anger. He suddenly mounted his white Arabian stallion, with its distinctive gold rimmed, leather saddle and tasseled bridle, sprinted northward, gained the summit of a small hill, and waited for his troop of fifty Bedouin to catch up with him.

Yosip abruptly halted, got off his horse, and looked off to the northwest, as if he were trying to see his quarry. "These are not falcons, majestic and doughty raptors, but rabbits and weasels," he shouted. "They are not worthy of our pursuit. May it please Allah, blessings on his name, to find them in a sinkhole buried in a pit of their own stench!"

"Mahmoud the map!" He demanded, while dismounting. One of his men produced a folding table, where a map scroll of the region was quickly unfolded.

"We are here." He pointed with his black and gold riding crop to a spot on the map nearest their site. "Where will they go?" He wondered and stepped away, while another attendant produced a goatskin of water and a towel. He took off his white keffiyeh headress, looked for a moment at the black and gold braided *agal* headband, which signified him as a prince of his people and, after taking a long drink, poured water over his short-cropped, black hair and mustached, dark-skinned face, and walked back to the map table.

"My prince, the infidels will track up the Wadi Ifal," Mahmood offered. He traced the wadi with his black-gloved finger. "If they continue on this northwest track, and this they must do within the wadi, then they will either follow the road here," he again traced the line of the road, "from Al Bi'r to Haql, or proceed northward into Jordan."

"The Hashemite kingdom of Jordan must be their goal." The prince replied, taking his riding crop and striking it into his left hand. "Their sniveling king has ever resisted the will of Allah in our attempts to forge a Caliphate, and unite all Islam for holy jihad."

He turned sharply, pointed his crop at Mahmoud, and then at the map. "You will take ten men and proceed at full speed around the Al Hijaz, then north by northwest across the desert here, driving west along the Jordanian border. You will stop at Aba al Hinshan, ask our brothers there for any rumor of the infidel's flight, leave five men there to patrol the area and bar any passage, and then take the rest on to Haql. There you will alert our people in the city and wait. If they are not found quickly, you will take your remaining men, and drive south along the coast to Al Humaydah. We will move north along the wadi, take up the road from Al Bi'r, and drive them towards you, *Insh' Allah*, as Allah wills it, into your waiting arms." He looked up and saw a smile creep over Mahmoud's face.

"Salaam Alaikum, my prince." Mahmoud acknowledged, bowed low, and kissed his hand. "We live to obey."

"One last word, Mahmoud. The *Yahud* is to be unharmed. He will be taken back to my father the king; for his pleasure." He drew out his curved, gem encrusted jambiya knife, and pointed it at his second in command. "The rest of the vermin you'll keep for me and *my* pleasure."

He explained, and with a wicked smile, sped off in a swirl of dust to join the rest of his men.

* * *

"Shlomo... Shlomo Berkowitz, rise up!" came a voice to the heavily sleeping rabbi.

"Nu, a dream this is, I'm having." He closed his eyes again, and drifted off to sleep once again.

"Shlomo, you must get up!"

"Already I'm up. I'm up." He replied wearily, and sat up on the edge of his cot.

After rubbing his eyes, Reb Berkowitz realized that this wasn't a dream at all, but the voice of the Lord calling him to get up. Awake now, he knelt by the side of his bed and began to pray. "Lord, forgive my lack of responsiveness."

He stayed in an attitude of prayer for some time, praying for his grandson Benni, who he knew to be alive, though still unaccounted for. He then began to pray for Monika. In the midst of his prayer, he heard the Lord, not audibly but in his spirit, say to him, *"go now to Monika and pray over her."* He had learned not to question the Lord in these matters. There was a vital reason for him to go to Monika, and he would simply obey.

He got dressed, picked up his bible, looked at his watch, and saw that it was nearly 3:00 a.m. He prayed that the "iron nurse" of his past acquaintance would not be on guard duty this night, and laughed to himself, as he exited his room.

He made his way across the base compound of barracks and offices, which, even at this early hour, were busy with activity.

Shlomo entered the base hospital; a long, rectangular, single story, tan colored building (all the buildings on the airbase were the same tan color, to better camouflage them), and was surprised to find that the usually locked door to the intensive care unit was open.

"Nu, of course opened, this door is. Of a truth does the psalmist say: *Your word is a lamp unto my feet and a light unto my path.*

He walked past the nurse's station, which was also empty, and quietly opened the door to Monika's room. She was lying on her back, her face ashen colored, under a dim fluorescent light, keeping vigil over her head.

He took a seat on the far side of the bed, regained his strength, then knelt beside her and began to pray. He found himself in deep intercessionary prayer for her, and soon realized that he was locked in a battle for her soul. The words from Ephesians 6: 11-18 dropped like welcomed rain on his spirit, and quenched the burning fire of spiritual battle he was engaged in:

Put on the whole armor of God that ye may be able to stand against the wiles of the devil. For we wrestle not against flesh and blood, but against principalities, against powers, against the rulers of the darkness, of this world, against spiritual wickedness in high places.

He prayed in the Spirit for some time, perspiration building on his forehead, until a calm peace came over him, and he knew that God had answered his prayer, and that Monika would be saved.

* * *

Benni had been walking in the heat of the morning desert sun for some time when his strength ran out, and he fell, face first, into the burning sand. He looked off into the distance, and could barely make out the figure of someone walking ahead of him, beckoning for him to follow. Somehow he managed to get to his feet again, determined to find out if this person was just a mirage. With sudden strength, he ran over the sandy tracts, and drew close to someone he soon found to be a woman. She looked back with a playful smile, and motioned for him to chase her. Suddenly, she disappeared into the clouds above an oasis, which seemed to hover over the desert sands. Upon reaching the oasis, he found a basin of water with a washcloth and a large pitcher of water. He happily washed himself, and then drank in the ice-cold water until it was gone. Refreshed, he walked in the cool shade of the palm trees, until he came upon a huge red Persian rug, overflowing with every kind of food. He began to eat, and wondered at the woman who was now nowhere to be seen. *"She looked so much like Monika, Monika…Monika."*

Benni awoke from the dream when his horse stumbled over stony ground. They had been following the road northwest, and he found that they had left the main road, and were following a goat trail into the hills. They followed the winding path, gaining the summit of a hill, until they stopped for a moment to take in the view.

There to the left, some five miles to the west, was the Saudi Arabian city of Al-Humaydah, and just about five miles north of Al-Humaydah, was the city of Haql, hugging the Gulf of Aqaba, but now shrouded in fog. Benni knew that both cities were tourist sites for wealthy Arabs, and even some Westerners. He also knew that he was only twenty miles or so from Eilat and his beloved Israel. The thought of that, and his recent dream involving Monika, brought tears to his eyes, and he bowed his head and prayed a silent prayer, that it would not be long before he regained both of his loves.

He looked up to see that M&M had been watching him intensely and probably guessed what he had been feeling. Was this why he brought him this way, to tease him with the sight of home and freedom, and then take him away to some dank cell of a prison?

"*Not if I can help it.*" He thought to himself, and vowed again to do everything he could to escape from this nightmare.

They traveled downward for some time, and came to a long, flat defile that would eventually rise again into another hill. What appeared to be a wall of rock on their right was actually a cleverly disguised gray and tan tarpaulin, made to look like the adjacent rock. The canvas covered a ten by ten-foot cave mouth that opened into a huge cavern.

They led their horses to the back of the well-lit cave where a much appreciated water trough awaited them. M&M then led Benni past several small stacks of crates and boxes, to a long makeshift table with a few folding chairs, and a prepared platter of goat cheese and flat bread. M&M picked up a piece of the bread, and walked over to the cave mouth where he was soon joined by a tall man dressed in tan kaffiyeh and cloak. They conversed briefly, and the man left the cave.

Benni marveled at all the provision and preparation that had been made for his kidnap. "*All of this couldn't be just for me? There were long lasting designs and purpose at work here,"* he wondered, as he took another bite of cheese, and washed it down with a bottle of wonderfully cold water.

The cave seemed to be a staging area for this group led by M&M. Everything had been meticulously planned and executed with precision. *"This is so unusual."* He mused; now full, after just a few bites of cheese and bread. *"It looks for all the world like a special forces operation. But how could that be? There are no Arab countries I know of that could pull off something like this, except maybe the Iranians."*

He thought long and hard. *"If it were them, I would have probably been shot by now, and we're definitely going in the wrong direction."*

* * *

Monika, stirring, woke Reb Berkowitz with a start. The early morning sun streamed through the window as he quickly got up from his chair and sat on the bed beside her. She tossed her head from side to side, softly moaning, then opened her eyes, and fastened them on him. *"Zeide, you came."* She smiled softly, and closed her eyes once more. "Why hasn't Benni come with you?"

"Yes my dear, I am here now." He took her hand and gently patted it. "Benni will be along soon enough, as the Almighty One wills it." He smiled warmly, and saw that her face was troubled.

"He will return won't he?" She asked, her voice trembling at the realization that he was still lost somewhere in the Arabian Desert. "He must come soon. I have news…" She suddenly burst into great sobs, and reached out for her grandfather, who held her in his arms, until the wave of emotion subsided.

She looked up at him again. "The baby. What of the baby?"

"Elohim, praised be His name, has taken the child to be with Him." He answered, holding her head to his chest, as tears formed in his eyes. "It is His will, no? One day you will see your child again safe in the arms of Yeshua Ha'Mashiach." He smiled, and lovingly held her head to his chest once again.

Monika held his hand, and gently sobbed at the loss of a life so dear to her and the promise it held, now gone to a place where she could not follow.

"You've always been there for us, even though we've rejected you time and time again. Yet, I have seen by the love you've displayed for Yeshua, for Benni and me, that Yeshua must be real."

She sat up abruptly, her long, black hair framing her now animated face. "Do you know that I had a dream about him? I was wandering alone in a desert place, starving for food, when I heard a voice behind me, gently calling to me. I turned around and saw a figure dressed in white, standing on the bank of a river. He said: 'I am the bread of life.' Then a carpet appeared on the ground filled with every kind of food. I ate until I was full, and looked up to thank Him, but found that he had gone. It was Yeshua, wasn't it *zeide*?"

"Yes, my child. It was the Lord of Glory." He wiped a tear from his eyes, and opened the bible he had laid on the bed beside him. "Do you know that earlier this morning the Lord woke me from my sleep, and urged me to come here to be with you? I came and knelt by your bed and prayed for your healing, but also for you to receive Yeshua Ha'Mashiach as your Lord and Savior. My hands tremble to read the words of your dream shown in God's word. This is in the gospel of John in the new covenant, chapter 6 and verse 35:

I am the bread of life: he that comes to me will not hunger; and he that believes in me will never thirst.

He looked up at her and saw the wonder on her face.

"Then it was real. It was Him!" She exclaimed lying back down, awed by the implications of her dream. After a moment she turned her face away. "I've been so wrong about so much, and have sinned against Him. How could He ever forgive me" She asked, as tears formed in her eyes once again.

"Nu, my dear, it is for this cause that Our Lord died on the cross, so that our sins He would forgive. Let me read to you what one of our great prophets wrote about Him. It says in the book of Isaiah 53, verse 5:

But he was wounded for our transgressions; he was bruised for our iniquities: the chastisement of our peace was upon him; and with his stripes we are healed.

He paused and saw her turn to face him once more.

"I've never seen it like that before. We had always been taught that this referred to Mashiach who is to come. It must have been for us."

"True. Yes my dear. It was for us and the descendents of Abraham, and, as the Eternal One promised in Genesis 12:1-3, for the sins of the whole world!" He paused to let all he had said sink in.

"Then when did the execution take place?" She asked, taking his hand once again.

"Exactly four days after his triumphal entry into Jerusalem, my dear. The same crowd that praised him would shout: 'Crucify him!' in a few short days." He bowed his head and praised God for His mercy and goodness.

Monika lay down on her pillow and closed her eyes deep in thought. After a few moments she looked at him once more. "Then *our* Mashiach has already come," she replied with a smile.

"Yes, my child." He looked deep into her eyes and saw salvation, like a seed under the pressure of heat and moisture, burst forth into newness of life.

She raised herself up, held his right hand in both of hers, and closed her eyes in prayer. "I do believe. I believe in Yeshua Ha'Mashiach, and I ask you my Lord and Savior, to forgive me of my sins, and come into my life to live."

"Omain." Was all he could say as he hugged Monika, and cried tears of joy.

Suddenly, Monika's body went limp in his arms. Alarmed, Reb Berkowitz gently laid her back down on the bed, and put his left ear close to her mouth. He let out a sigh of relief when he found that she was still breathing, and offered a quick thanks to the Lord. He gently covered her with a blanket, and kneeled down beside the bed to pray. After some time he stood up and gently caressed her dark hair.

"*She's too pale*," he thought, and realized that she had now lapsed into a coma once again.

* * *

Benni could not rest. He tossed and turned in the sleeping bag provided for him, serenaded by the loud, nasal snores of his captor, who had drifted off into a deep sleep. Whether M&M intended to sleep, knowing that they were securely guarded in this hideout, or that he was simply exhausted, Benni didn't know.

It didn't matter. It was now or never!

He offered a quick prayer, and felt a keen stab of excitement mingled with fear, much like the feeling he had just before the bombing of Rishahr.

He had to make his escape--NOW!

He slowly slipped out of his sleeping bag, M&M lying only a few inches from him, grabbed his sandals, a sand colored keffiyeh and cloak, and a few morsels of cheese and bread, and stuffed them into an old Bedouin hang bag that had been lying on a pile of old clothes by the rock wall. He needed some kind of weapon. M&M's pistol was holstered at his side, so that was out. He quietly rummaged through another pile of old clothing, every so often looking over to his heavily snoring captor, and found the prize he had hoped to find; a short bladed scimitar in a worn scabbard and belt. He quickly fastened it to his waist, adjusted his travel bag and water skin and quietly made for the cave opening.

"I can't take a horse," he said to himself, *"it would make too much noise and they're spent from the long travel."*

He thought of Monika and how close he was to holding her in his arms once again. He quietly slipped through the folds of the canvas covering the cave mouth without making a sound.

"This could be the shortest escape attempt in history if the guards are watching the cave entrance." He whispered.

With a bold burst of energy, he sprinted to the other side of the defile, and looked up quickly into the hills to the right and to the left.

"No one there," he whispered again.

Walking north through a narrow passage at the end of the defile, Benni reached the top of a small hill that gave him a panoramic view of the area. He crouched beside a large overhanging boulder that provided him with shade and a covert against possible discovery. There to his left, about five miles distant, lay the Gulf of Aqaba shimmering in the sunlight. Lost in the haze to the north was Israel, home, and Monika. Truly it had become Benni's "promised land". He yearned for it now as Moses must have, when leading the children of Israel through this area several thousand years ago.

"Which way should I go?" he wondered, then prayed silently for guidance, and took his first step to what he hoped would be his eventual freedom.

CHAPTER 11

The dreams she'd been having fell into two categories; both were distinctly black and white, which made them even more alarming, since her "normal" dreams were in color. They were, she now realized, in fact nightmares, and yet, where she was personally involved in the first dream, she was strangely detached from the second.

In the first dream she was a child of three or four, and was running through a field of tall grass, away from something or somebody. A boy, several years older than her, was running at a faster pace ahead of her, occasionally motioning for her to hurry. There were sounds of gunfire all around them. She tried to catch up to him, but her little feet couldn't keep up.

"Help her! help her!" she cried out in her dream.

Suddenly, the child tripped and fell. A man in uniform, with a kind face and a gun slung over his shoulder, picked her up and took her away. She looked for the boy she had been following, but he had disappeared.

In the second dream, she was walking alone in the desert under the scorching rays of the sun, dressed in a chador, a long black hooded robe worn by Muslim women. She stood at the top of a broad plateau, which somehow she knew to be the Golan Heights, the land in the northeast corner of Israel that was taken from Syria after the Six Days War in 1967. In front of her, looking east toward Damascus was a wide plain flanked by two, long, chains of hills. The hills seemed to beckon to her. "If I could only get up into those hills, I know I would be safe."

She turned to the right, and thought she'd found a path that led up to the top of one of the hills, but as she began to climb, the path dead-ended into a steep slope of loose rock. Desperate to gain the height, she stepped onto the pile of stones, which caused a rock slide that carried her back to the foot of the hills once again.

She tried this several times, with the same result, and finally gave up the attempt. As she sat defeated in the desert sand, battered and bruised, she looked again to the heights, and saw thousands of people standing on the hills, all dressed in white. "How were they able to get there?" She cried, and buried her face in her hands until she looked up again and found that they had vanished!

Suddenly, the earth began to shake violently, causing the hills to tumble to the ground. As she looked off to the east, she was blinded by a sudden burst of light. Moments later, she looked again, and saw with shock and horror, a huge mushroom cloud of an atomic blast rising into the sky!

"What could this mean?" she wondered to herself.

Too stunned to move, she heard a sound drawing nearer. The sound became a voice. She could almost make out what it was saying...

Then she awoke!

* * *

Jack Quinn held his arm around Marcia Thompson, snuggling close, to ward off the cold, as they descended the long run of stairs from St. Ignatius Loyola Church, after the morning mass, on a crisp, blue, Sunday morning. He hummed a Straus tune, and waltzed her from side to side, until they reached the walkway below, where he bowed low with a flourish of his arm. "You dance magnificently, m'lady."

Marcia, looking radiant, her mid-length auburn hair draped over a red, full-length coat, bowed slightly. "T'is more than could be said for *you*, my bonny rogue prince," she replied and threw herself into his waiting arms. They kissed deeply, impervious to the others coming down the stairs around them, and walked down the sidewalk towards his car.

Jack marveled at how quickly they had fallen in love. He never dreamed that he would find someone to replace Evalyn, who had died several years before. In fact, he'd stopped looking long ago, and had buried himself in his work at the university, and then at the White House, in part, to repress her memory. He now realized that the long winter of his isolation was quickly melting away.

After meeting again at General Hood's home, they came to embrace both the conspiracy and, after many subsequent dates, each other. They were now inseparable, and oftentimes counted the minutes between their meetings.

As they walked arm in arm down the walkway, Jack looked down and kissed the top of her head. She responded by drawing closer to him, and he in turn wrapped his right arm around her.

It had been somewhat easier for Marcia. She had gone through college, then straight into public service, and had never been comfortable with anyone in the "power elite" of Washington. She dated from time to time, but her cherished homespun morals and values seemed to collide with the "anything goes" philosophy of those she came in contact with in the nation's capitol.

She had heard whispers of "prude," and "namby-pamby," behind her back, but considered the disparaging remarks to be a badge of honor. She believed that there was only one man for her, and that he would be "the right man".

Marcia looked up at Jack with love, as they walked. She had truly found the one she had been looking for in Jack Quinn. The first time she had met him at the staff introduction party several weeks before the president's first inauguration, she found him to be stiff and formal. When he shook hands with her, he was all business. His eyes, though, betrayed a hidden warmth and depth of character, which she came to appreciate more and more. She sensed that he was warming up to her, but there seemed to be a wall between them, one that Jack would not, or could not, surmount. It was after the fateful night of their coming together at the Minuteman meeting, and several dates later, that the wall between them came crashing down, and was replaced by a deep and abiding love. She responded in kind and, as she pulled him close to her now, was thankful that she had found the answer to her heart's desire.

They were stopped in their tracks when a black limousine pulled up quickly to the curb nearest them. Jack walked up to the car when the passenger side window opened.

He turned back to Marcia and held both of her hands. "I've got to go with him," he said softly, handing her his car keys, and kissed her on the cheek. She looked at him with alarm, and wouldn't let go. He hugged her and whispered softly, "It'll be alright; just something I've got to do. He looked at her again, kissed her gently on the lips, and walked over to the waiting car.

*　*　*

She looked around the room; a familiar room painted a light orchid color, with a flower border tracing the ceiling. The dresser at the opposite end was hers, as was the desk by the window, and the pictures she took while in college still hanging on the wall in several places. She looked out at the morning sun streaming in through the window, and felt that cozy warmth of waking up in happy surroundings, with the whole bright day ahead of her. She was home!

Looking over at her desk, she noticed a clipboard sitting there. Curious, she got up, reluctant to leave the warmth and security of her white down comforter, and sat down on the desk chair to read. It was in the handwriting of her father, who had apparently been taking notes of some kind.

Saturday,

-12:15 AM: Exhibited normal sleep patterns with active dream state.

-6:00 PM: At dinner, brought out a mixed group of pictures from childhood to young adult, probing for cognitive/sequence recognition. None found.

She leafed back through the pages to an entry made while she was in the hospital.

-Wednesday,12:00 noon: Accident trauma has produced aggravated memory loss--She doesn't know who I am--Some of hospital staff said to be praying for her. Ugh! They ought to lock them up!

She winced at that last statement. She couldn't remember ever being a religionist, but something in her heart was repelled by his accusation. Besides, the thought of others caring enough to pray for her, brought a certain peace to her. *"I hope I can find out who those people are so that I can thank them,"* she said to herself, and continued reading the notes on the clipboard.

-1:00 PM: Met with Dr. Abrahamson. ML could last a day or a year or...I don't want to think about any other possibility. The nagging question has come back to haunt me. If only Anna were here, she would know what to do. Should I have told her about her earliest childhood? Should I do so now in hopes of recovering her memory? Much to ponder.

She sat bolt upright in her chair, now alarmed, and threw the clipboard back on the desk. *"Earliest childhood? What happened there?"* she wondered, rubbed her forehead; a headache was coming on, and tried to think back to her earliest memories.

It was too much. The strain brought the headache into full bloom. She walked over to her bed, and sought the refuge of her comforter.

"Must ask dad...must ask dad," she thought to herself. *"Where have I said that before?"* Another thought from sometime in the past fought to push itself into her consciousness. She snuggled up to the cool softness of her pillow, knew it would have to wait, and then dropped off into sleep once more.

* * *

"Iz good to see you again," Andy Stern said from the dark confines of the luxurious Mercedes, stretch limousine. Jack sat down next to him on a dark gray, leather bench seat, while Andy quickly produced a small bottle of brandy and two shot glasses from the beverage console on the sideboard beside him. He filled the glasses half-full, and handed one to Jack, who felt a bit uncomfortable, having just come from church, and was not used to drinking very much.

"Salut!" he said, clinking Jack's glass, and downed his drink in one gulp.

It was obvious to Jack, as it would be to anyone who didn't drink much, that Andy had already had a few drinks before meeting with him.

"*Na zdrovye!*" Jack returned in perfect Russian, and took only a sip, which burned as it went down his throat, and placed the glass on the tray beside him.

Andy leaned back and laughed, while producing a silver cigar case. "You are truly a *tovarich,* a comrade, my dear Jack Quinn, but you drink like a Cossack."

He laughed again, poured another drink, downing that one as well, and pulled a cigar from his case. He removed the paper cigar ring, Jack observed, and rather than throw it out, deftly placed it in the breast pocket of his tailored black suit coat.

"*Why did he do that?*" Jack wondered.

Andy then cut off the end of the cigar with a specially designed clipper, lit the other end, and, after several forceful puffs, produced a large cloud of smoke that filled the back of the car.

"Where to sir?" the driver asked over the voicecom.

"Take de Beltway and drive north. Thank you Max." Andy replied and turned his attention to Jack. "*Da, tovarich,* you haven't summoned me only to share a few drinks. What iz I can do for you?" he asked, and leaned back puffing on his cigar.

"I'd like to thank you, first of all, for seeing me," Jack replied, while turning to face Andy. "I know that I'm *persona non grata* at the White House, and that you and I haven't always been the closest of friends."

"Iz nothing!" Andy replied, waving his cigar with his right hand. Jack noted that Andy's speech was beginning to slur. "We are comrades, yes?"

"Well I'm glad that you consider me your friend--"

"Not friends, my dear Mr. Quinn!" he shouted, and sat bolt upright, pointing the cigar at Jack. "Maybe later." He relaxed again and took another long drag on his cigar. "But still we are comrades, no? Fighting the good fight, as you Americansky say." He closed his eyes and rolled the cigar around in his mouth.

Jack was taken aback by Stern's outburst, and thought it best to change the subject. "So, tell me Andy, what happened to you when the shakeup at the White House occurred? How is it that you survived Bielchek's housecleaning?"

Jack knew from his friend Harry, that there was an ongoing tension between the president's new chief of staff, Zoltan Bielchek, and Andy. When all the dust had cleared, Andy had become nothing more than a figurehead at the White House.

"That Bulgar peasant!" he fumed, while vigorously crushing his cigar in the ashtray. He poured himself another drink, vodka this time. "When that swine settled into the White House, nothing iz same." He gulped down his drink in one quick motion. "Iz that Ilya Stanas behind this. He and heez United Nations ilk now in de White House! Before, when you were there, I have complete access to de prezident, and all de major foreign relations talks, yes? Now--nothing! I am, how you say it, a lapdog. The prezident brings me out on leash at banquets and dinners, and after keeps me confined to de kennel!" He poured himself another vodka, offered one to Jack, who declined, and sat back heavily in his seat. "Cossacks and peazants Jack. That is all iz left. Cossacks and peazants." He closed his eyes as if trying to forget a bad dream.

Jack knew that Ilya Stanas' meteoric rise to power as Secretary General of the United Nations, was the talk of world. He was also a member of the G-169 summit group. Zoltan Bielchek was Stanas' special envoy to the White House, who then became the president's chief of staff. Since then, he learned from his clandestine meetings at General Hood's home that the United Nations and G-169 people planned to eventually replace the entire White House cabinet. The result was that the country was now in a severe depression. The US dollar fell from its perch as the world's pre-eminent currency in favor of a "market basket" of various world currencies. Unemployment had now reached a staggering twenty-percent, and hyperinflation; in boa constrictor-like fashion, was slowly strangling the country's goods and services.

Several states were distancing themselves from an impotent federal government, joining with other states to forge a commonwealth. New "local" currencies were now being created in the vain hope of staving off the effects of what economists were saying will be an inevitable national bankruptcy.

With prospects for any kind of recovery grim, the call was going out from several quarters for the United States to become partners in a new government with Canada and Mexico, and for the trio to form a new identity, one modeled on the European Union: a North American Union.

"Max drive to cigar store, I am almost out of cigars," he shouted into the voicecom.

"Yes sir."

"I vill get out and Max vill drive you wherever you want to go," Andy said. "Now, *tovarich*, what iz I can do for you? He asked in a slurred, but businesslike manner.

"I would like to have a private meeting with the president. Can you arrange it?"

Andy thought for a second. "I think iz Impossible! Even I can't see him alone." He poured a half glass of vodka and downed it like the others. "The Cossacks have him under heavy guard, *tovarich*." He sat back again in deep thought as the limousine pulled up beside the cigar shop.

Andy opened the door to leave, stepped out, and turned again to face Jack. "Still, there may be a way. Leave Max your bizness card, and I may be in touch with you."

"*Dobryj dyen!* Good day, *tovarich*." He offered smiling, and reached into the car to shake Jack's hand.

"*Spasiba*, thank you, Andy," Jack replied, as the door closed.

Jack gave Max his address over the voicecom, and sat back wondering exactly what Andy had in mind. He glanced over to where Andy had been sitting, and noticed the cigar ring Andy had tried to put into the breast pocket of his coat laying on the seat. He looked it over, found nothing unusual about it, but decided to keep it just in case.

CHAPTER 12

M & M woke up with a start from his death-like sleep, only to find that Benni had escaped! He looked at his field watch, it was near seven in the evening, and realized that he had slept through the day.

"A complete *balagan*!" he shouted. The rock walls of the cave echoed back as if to mock him. "*To come so far…I should have tied him up, or cuffed him to me. Then again, he should have been as exhausted as I was, and slept through the day as well.*"

He searched through his travel bag, and pulled out his satphone, to communicate with his two watchmen stationed on the heights above their compound.

"Levi, we've got an escape in progress. Get down here right away.

"We'll be right there. Out"

"Never underestimate the powerful lure of freedom! That is the lesson here." He pulled out a map of the area, and spread it out on the table.

* * *

Benni hid in a shaded, rocky covert, as the sun disappeared over the darkening mountains. He opened his canteen, allowed himself two full swallows of the precious liquid, and paused to review his progress.

He had been on a steady northwesterly march for three hours, and was now somewhere between Al-Humaydah, which he could see dimly to his left, and Haql, a mile or so up the coast to the north. The main dirt road that would take him to Haql, lay a hundred yards away from him, but he wondered if he could take that road, and also avoid capture.

"*Well, which way should I go?*" He asked himself. "*Al-Humaydah, with its Western tourist appeal, would be a good place to find possible help, or perhaps an escape vessel of some sort. Still, it's not quite the best time for tourists of any sort, and even if I found a boat, the Saudi border patrol squadron could still track me down.*

Haql it is then." He said in a whisper.

He got up, as dusk crept slowly over the landscape, and struck a path through the rock-strewn heights above the roadway. It was slow going, but he had to avoid any contact with the local population, and stay out of sight as much as possible. The night would help keep him anonymous, and he welcomed its onset.

After an hour or so, Benni climbed a ridge, and saw to his left the city lights of Haql; the Gulf of Aqaba forming an ebony backdrop in the distance. He now realized that he was a mere eighteen nautical miles from Eilat, and only fourteen miles from the Israeli border. So tantalizingly close, he felt like he could almost reach out and touch the hand of his beloved Monika, yet the most dangerous aspect of his improbable journey was still to come. He knew that the Saudi's had a military contingent, as well as a naval base, in Haql. "*How will I ever break through?*" He wondered.

Fear, such as he had never experienced before, suddenly gripped him, and he dropped to his knees and began to pray. "*God of my fathers, Eternal One of Israel, I ask you for help. Show me how to proceed. Keep my path straight, and allow me to win through to my beloved wife and country. Cover me in the shadow of your wings and help me fly to safety.*" Refreshed in spirit, he started walking toward the city, but abruptly halted when he felt a tug at his heart. "*I believe you're telling me that I'm not to go this way. Then I will make my way north to the Jordanian frontier.*" With that he started out once more as the night closed around him.

* * *

M&M, also known as Major Moise Azerah of the Israeli Mossad, the secret service branch of Israeli intelligence, stood before his two abashed watchmen, hands on his hips, with an incredulous look on his face.

This special operations group consisting of five men, code named FO-9, had been tasked with shadowing Benni's flight group in the event of a downed Israeli plane. They had responded quickly when Benni's plane came down, homing in on the Strike Eagle's distress signal, and arrived on the scene only minutes after his capture. They followed the raiding party back to Haj Saladen's encampment, and were able to engineer Benni's successful escape.

Because his was a clandestine operation, and secrecy was an absolute requirement, Major Azerah was not at liberty to reveal himself, his men, or their mission to Benni, and was forced to treat him as a virtual hostage, until he could get him safely into Israel.

"So Levi, my eagle-eyed boykin, what do you have to say for yourself? How could he have gotten by you?" Major Azerah asked.

"Sir!" he replied, and snapped to attention, "I beg to report that I was standing my watch as closely as possible from noon until just now, with only two nature breaks during that time."

Major Azerah wore a frown, but smiled to himself. "At ease Levi, we're not going to be formal out here. I'm sure you stood a vigilant watch."

"And you Natan, what's your story?" He asked, while looking at the outstretched map once again.

"Major, I stood the initial watch from six to noon while both of you slept, and apart from a single nature break, saw nothing out of the ordinary.

Thank you. You both did your job as professionals, and I appreciate your efforts. If there's any blame here it's mine. I believed the commander to be physically exhausted, as I was, and let him sleep without restraint, never thinking he would attempt an escape on foot. Still," he looked up at each man, "the yearning for our beloved homeland runs deep in the soul. Let this be a lesson to us all, that we should never underestimate the sacrifice one is willing to make for freedom."

"Now, let's get down to business and see if we can track down our Strike Eagle."

The three men huddled around the map. "There are three lanes of pursuit, and each of us will take a different route. Levi you'll drive north as quickly as possible, pick up our other two brothers near Aba al Hinshan, then ride to the Jordanian border closest to Haql and patrol the area. I believe he will try to make his way to Jordan rather than risk being found in one of the coastal cities. Natan, you and I will proceed to the crossroads between Al Humaydeh and Haql. You'll go into Al Humaydeh and inquire of our contact there, and see if he had heard anything about the pilot. I'll move on to Haql and do the same. We'll all rendezvous at the Wadi al De'ir encampment, just across the Jordanian border, at eighteen hundred hours tomorrow." They all nodded in agreement. Each man quickly obtained the necessary provisions, saddled their refreshed horses, and silently, but grimly, strode out in the humid night air.

* * *

Yosip bin Saladen looked to the north as the thickening gloom of night approached. He had sent his trackers into the hills to scout for any sign of his quarry, and expected them back at any time, but chafed at the wait, and began to pace. Patience had never been a virtue to Yosip. He sensed that they were close to their elusive prey, and silently prayed that Allah would graciously bring their chase to a successful end.

"*Insh'Allah*," he concluded, and walked to the top of the highest point of the coastal hill they were on. To his left he saw the lights of Haql, and its prominent well-lit jetty that sheltered the Royal Saudi patrol boats. He spit contemptuously in that direction. "Go hide in your detestable wormholes, House of Saud! Your days of malignant rule are coming to an end. The caliphate of my father, Haj Saladen, approaches, and he will show you no mercy!"

He sat down on a nearby hillock, refreshed by a cool desert breeze wafting in from the coast, and thought for a moment. *The Yahud will not go to Haql. He will fear the Saudi boats. There is no help for him at Al-Humaydah as well.*

He looked north, and could just make out the lights, glittering like a handful of gemstones, of the Israeli port city of Eilat. Beyond that, he knew, loomed Jerusalem, the noble city. *"All Islam craves her as one craves a dearest love."* He said to himself with a sigh. *"Within its walls is Al Quds, the Dome of the Rock, on the Noble Sanctuary where Mohammed was said to have ascended to Allah's glories. May Allah grant that one day I may walk along the courtyards of the Harem Serif!*

"My prince! The riders have returned!" shouted one of his bodyguards.

He ran to the horsemen, who had quickly dismounted, and awaited him at the campsite. They kneeled and bowed low at his approach.

"Rise and speak! What have you found of the jackals?" Yosip commanded, and began to pace again, hitting his side with his riding crop.

The foremost tracker now spoke. "We scoured the hills and found not a trace of man or beast. Then, as the sun cast its last shadows and we were about to return, a worn path brought us to a long canyon that emptied on the north to a bald height. There we found fresh horse marks leading off into three different directions: one due north, another to Al-Humaydah, and still a third heading to Haql. After a short time the light failed us, and we rode back to camp." He bowed low, hoping that his report would be well received, and that he would not have to receive any lashes from bin Saladen.

"Break camp and gather the horses! Yosip commanded. "I have communed with Allah, and he has shown me, blessed is his name, that we are to ride for the Hashemite kingdom of Jordan. There we will bring a snare to our prey!

As quickly as it was made, the camp was broken up, and the horsemen rode briskly into the night.

* * *

Benni tripped and fell down hard to the ground. He had been pushing himself beyond his exhausted state, but realized that he could not go any further that night. Even though he had found a broad wadi north of Haql heading in a northerly direction, the fear of discovery and leaving any telltale tracks in the sand, kept him on the slow and ponderous trek through the rock-strewn heights above the wadi.

He sat down heavily on a flat-topped boulder, rubbing a now bruised knee, and considered his situation. It was now somewhere past midnight, and that would put him over the Saudi border, and into Jordan. Benni smiled, while rubbing his tired eyes, at the thought that he would now receive fair treatment, and eventual freedom, should the Jordanians capture him. Jordan, while politically neutral in its relations with Israel, had been for years now, a covert ally of his homeland. Both countries had even conspired on a few clandestine Special Forces operations, when it was in the interests of both countries.

He woke up startled, and found that he had drifted off to sleep. *"I've got to find shelter,"* he mumbled to himself. After his weary eyes adjusted to the dim light, he scanned the hills to his right, hoping to find a place of refuge for his weary body. There, about two hundred meters away, was a concentrated mass of large boulders that he hoped would provide a covert for him, and the respite he so desperately needed. He forced himself to move, and trudged up the rocky hillside, tripping every so often, until he gained the boulders. After a brief survey he found a flat rock slab covered by two huge rock monoliths leaning one against the other. It wasn't a cave, which he would have preferred, but it would give him coverage against discovery, and protect him from the heat of the sun. He collapsed onto the slab, stretched out his arm towards Israel and Monica, and drifted off into a deep, dreamless sleep.

* * *

The crash of a boulder shattered the deep sleep Benni had been having, and instantly put him on alert. He crawled from his rock slab bed to a large boulder, and carefully peered over the top of it. The setting sun winked at him over the now darkened western hills, and temporarily limited his vision of the terrain.

"I've slept for the entire day," he noted. Moving to the left side of the boulder, Benni looked down the rocky expanse that led to the wadi. What he saw there took his breath away. There in the midst of the boulder field, some fifty yards away, was a black-clad Bedouin armed with a rifle, searching for tracks that would bring him to his hideout. Further down

the hill, in the wadi, were the black shapes of two other mounted riders and another horse.

Benni collected himself, and, with his years of training kicking in, evaluated his situation. *"I cannot go further up the hill, or to one side or the other, without being seen."* He said to himself with alarm.

Darkness was his ally and would allow his escape, but it was still a half an hour or so away. At the rate the Bedouin was climbing, he would be on him in a few minutes.

"There's no way out!" he whispered.

Benni fought against the rising panic, and whispered an urgent prayer:

"God of my fathers; the Eternal One, help me now I pray. Save me from the snare of the fowler!

"The snare of the fowler?" He thought, and suddenly recalled one of his favorite Psalms as a boy:

He that dwelleth in the secret place of the most High, shall abide under the shadow of the Almighty. I will say of the Lord, He is my refuge and my fortress: my God; in him will I trust. Surely he shall deliver thee from the snare of the fowler...

The dark specter now stood on the same rock Benni was crouched beneath.

...Thou shalt not be afraid for the terror by night; nor for the arrow that flieth by day; nor for the pestilence that walketh in darkness; nor for the destruction that wasteth at noonday...

Benni stayed in silent prayer, while his pursuer stood perched on the rock.

He then heard the sound of the Bedouin's rifle being loaded.

"This is it. I've been discovered!"

...A thousand shall fall at thy side, and ten thousand at thy right hand; but it shall not come nigh thee...

Suddenly, a shot rang out! The man on the rock took a step, and then collapsed in a heap in front of the rock.

...Only with thine eyes shalt thou behold, and see the reward of the wicked. Because thou hast made the Lord, which is my refuge, even the most High, thy habitation...

Stunned by the change of events, Benni slid to one side, and peered over the rock at the scene in the wadi below. There he saw two machine gun toting, jeep-type, military vehicles confronting the two waiting Bedouin, who were now being handcuffed, and roughly thrown into the back of one of the vehicles. Two others, apparently Jordanian soldiers, were making their way up the hill towards Benni.

The dusk had now deepened enough for him to make his escape. Slowly he slid off to the north, moving stealthily from boulder to boulder, until he gained the top of the ridge. Hiding behind a large rock, he saw in the dim light that the two soldiers had retrieved the body of the dead Bedouin, and were slowly making their way down the hill.

Benni sat down, took a deep breath, and thanked God for his deliverance. As he decompressed from the tension, the thought occurred to him that he now had the opportunity to surrender himself to the Jordanians. They would treat him fairly, and in a few months probably release him to Israeli authorities. As he considered the idea, the option disappeared with the last jeep leaving the area.

"As you will, Adoni," he said, and began walking north along the ridge. He stopped for a moment to look at the brightening stars, and then heard a voice behind him.

"So, we meet again."

CHAPTER 13

Jack had been right all along, Andy Stern was an agent of the Russian Republic. A few days after Stern's driver had dropped him off at his house, Jack had taken the cigar ring band he had found in the limousine, and inspected it carefully. He found that there was an oval black spot about five millimeters wide on the backside of the band. Though he didn't know very much about cigars, he knew that the black spot was an anomaly; there shouldn't be anything on the inside of a cigar ring.

He rummaged around his attic until he found an old microscope set he had, and, placed the black dot under 300x magnification. Although still unreadable, definite lines of print appeared. What he found was evidently a cipher of some kind. The next day he took the band to a friend at Georgetown University, and under far greater magnification, saw distinct Cyrillic characters, all in a coded sequence of some sort.

"This was spy craft pure and simple!" He realized, and returned home, now in a quandary about what to do about this new discovery.

That night, with Marcia curled up beside him on the couch, and warmed by a well-constructed fire dancing in the fireplace, he considered his options.

"Should I turn this over to the FBI? The DEA? Should I confront Andy and ask him what this was all about?

He patted his pockets for a cigarette, forgetting for a moment that he had stopped smoking some time ago, abruptly stood up, and walked over to the fireplace. On the mantle, he found a pipe and tobacco, and placed them on the rough-hewn cedar coffee table. He filled the pipe, lit it until the flame caught, and soon produced a bouquet of Cavendish tobacco aroma that soon filled the room.

"I didn't know you smoked a pipe?" Marcia remarked, while curling up beside him once again.

"Haven't smoked this in years, and only when I tried to quit smoking before," Jack replied absentmindedly, trying to focus on the problem confronting him. He then realized that he was drifting away from Marcia in his thoughts, and hugged her close.

"Do you like it?"

"It reminds me of my grand-dad." She replied. "He had a different pipe for every occasion. His office would always have a different fragrance every time I visited him.'

Jack took several solid puffs from his pipe, and wandered off to his thoughts again.

"What are you going to do, Jack?" She asked softly, not expecting a quick reply. Instinctively she knew that he would, in his analytical way, mull it over, until the best solution was found.

After several moments and not a few drags from his pipe, he finally answered her. "I'm not sure, dear. I just don't know."

His cell phone on the coffee table chirped, and he picked it up.

"Hello. Andy? Oh, Andy Stern.

"I do not dizturbing you now, tovarich?"

"No, not at all, um, how have you been?" Jack replied, trying not to show the nervousness he felt.

"We do not have de time for pleazantries. Another time perhaps. Can you meet with me at the Global Peace Forum, at the Watergate, tomorrow night at nine?"

"I, er, that is…" Jack's mind raced for a quick out.

"Tovarich. You wish to meet with Prezident Williams, yes?"

"Oh, sorry. I'd nearly forgotten. Yes of course.

"I leave de card for you at the regiztration desk, and de room number we will be meeting in."

"We'll be meeting? Andy, I had hoped to have a private meeting with the president."

"Iz best I could do. You can meet him with me, or not all. I am sorry tovarich, it must be thiz way."

"I'll be there Andy," he replied, hoping his voice didn't sound too strident.

"Oh, iz another matter, er, Jack. Did you happen to find a small, um, slip of paper in back of de limousine?

Jack could feel the hairs stand up on the back of his neck. He remembered the same feeling he had as a boy when he was caught in a lie. "A piece of paper you say? No, I don't recall seeing anything like that Andy."

"Iz no problem really. I collect cigar ring bands, and am missing one iz all. Andy paused, as if he were trying to detect some misstep from Jack. "I will see you tomorrow, tovarich."

Jack hung up the phone, a myriad of thoughts now competing for his attention.

* * *

The scene before her stretched on for miles and was filled, wave upon wave, with golden stalks of wheat. She walked through the field, gently caressing the plump, ripe grain, marveling at the abundant crop. She crested a hill, and found herself on a high ridge overlooking a deep valley. Above that was an old city built on top of a hill. Shielding her eyes from the intense sunlight, she recognized the walls and ramparts of the city.

"I know this city. This is Jerusalem." She said to herself.

She walked down to the valley, took the Jericho road going north, entered into the city through the Lion's gate, and walked onto the Temple Mount. An eerie stillness greeted her. There was no one to be found, and the only sound she heard was the freshening wind whistling over the ancient stones. As she walked past the Dome of the Rock, she noticed that the sun had darkened, and, looking back to the north, found that thick clouds were looming up over the distant heights. She watched as the clouds turned black, became illuminated by flashes of lightning, and echoed huge peals of thunder; so loud that the ground shook violently beneath her feat. The wind grew to a gale, and pushed her to the pinnacle of the Western Wall, where she saw with horror, that the plaza below was filled with throngs of people.

"You can't stay there!" she shouted, trying to be heard above the noise of the now hurricane force wind. "Please, please, there's a storm coming!"

A strong gust of wind almost sent her falling from the height, and sounded out the words: "It's the Ninth...the NINTH...THE NINTH!

* * *

Jack walked into the main lobby of the Watergate Hotel complex, the same Watergate Hotel made infamous by the bungled burglary during the Nixon administration. He found the reception desk for The Global Peace Forum, and saw that, true to his word, Andy Stern had left him a card with the meeting room number inscribed. Jack checked his watch, and found that he was fifteen minutes early. With a few minutes to spare, he walked over to the bar and ordered a scotch and soda. Though he rarely drank anymore, he felt like he needed one tonight. He took a large swallow, put the glass down and proceeded to the meeting.

The entrance to the Gateway Plaza suite of meeting rooms was cordoned off and manned by a squad of Secret Service Agents, some of whom Jack knew from his days at the White House.

"Jack, good to see you again," Tom Armey, head of the president's detail said. His muscular build was barely contained by his white shirt, tie, and black suit coat.

"Great to see you, Tom. It's been too long."

"I know you're not packing, but I've got to do the search you know." Tom replied apologetically.

"Same old drill, no problem." Jack walked through the body scan doorway, and was cleared to enter the plaza.

"Is the old man in?" Jack asked as he walked down the hall.

"Yeah, you've got the room number. Just knock before you go in."

Jack walked briskly to the door and checked his watch. *"Eight fifty-nine. Right on time."*

He took a deep breath, adjusted his tie, and knocked on the door.

* * *

"Mira…Mira…Miriam! Dr. Rosen cried with alarm, sitting on the edge of her bed, trying to wake her up.

Mira sat up with a start, held her pillow to her chest, and realized that she had had another one of thoses dreams.

"I'm alright dad. It was just a dream, or more like a nightmare; a little of both I guess.

A look of bewilderment crossed her father's face. "You called me dad! You know who I am?"

Mira looked at her father, and realized that she did know him. Tears welled up in their eyes, and both hugged each other for some time.

"Where's Carla?" She asked, now holding her father at arms length.

"Oh, yes of course, Carla's still in New York, dear. She's called every day to see how you're doing.

"And Marcia? Has anyone contacted her?

"Oh, that would be your roommate. I've tried your phone at the apartment, but it's been disconnected. I also tried the White House, and found that she's not working there anymore." He explained.

"Not working there? That's strange." She replied, and considered that for a moment. Then what about..?" she hesitated, and tried to focus on images that seemed to be scattered about in her memory, like so many shards of broken glass. She lay back down on her pillow, and covered her eyes with the back of her right hand.

"What is it dear?" He asked with concern. "Maybe a little more rest is in order. After all it's only five o'clock in the…"

"Brant!" She shouted, while sitting up. "What happened to Brant?"

Dr. Rosen hung his head, took off his glasses, cleaned the lenses with her bed sheet, and thought about how he should answer. Mira's memory was apparently back to normal. She was now probing the depths of what had happened to her on the fateful night of the car bombing. He could defer the truth, or tell her the facts. He wasn't a strong man, and often found truth to be blurred or confused, but he now felt that it might be best to get everything out on the table.

"Miriam." He spoke softly, while placing her right hand between both of his. "What do you remember about Brant?"

"I remember our date. It was a dark, misty night that reminded me of that old movie, *Casablanca* with Humphrey Bogart and Ingrid Bergman." She sat up again, pulled her knees up, and wrapped her arms around them. "The restaurant was marvelous, red checkered table cloths, violins playing in the background; real old-world stuff. He was so charming and so handsome..." She looked off in the distance as tears formed in her eyes. "We walked outside, he wanted to show off his new car, how he could open the doors and start it with a simple voice command, and..." She couldn't finish the sentence, and slumped back onto her pillow and began sobbing.

"I know dear." He replied, and gently placed his right hand on her shoulder.

"There was a terrible explosion, and because he stood in front of you, you were shieldedfrom the worst part of it. Brant saved your life Miriam. That's why you're still here."

"Then..." She couldn't bring herself to say it, and buried her face in the pillow.

"Yes dear, he protected you, and paid with his life."

Mira didn't respond. She turned herself away from her father, and cried.

He wanted to be there for her, but was unaccustomed to showing much emotion, and didn't know what to do. He sat on the bed for a few minutes, while Mira grieved over her loss, and finally thought it best to leave her alone for the time being.

* * *

The door opened to the president's room, where two other Secret Service agents Jack didn't know, immediately searched him once more. Jack saw that he was in a large apartment suite that was separated into several compartments. He was led from the small foyer into a large room that contained a modern cherrywood executive table and twelve chairs that looked out of place when seen against the ornate French provincial furnishings in the rest of the room. It reminded Jack of a funeral parlor.

When he approached the second room, a towering figure loomed before him in the doorway. He had seen Zoltan Bielchek before, when he was dressed in a three-piece business suit, but now he wore a long black cloak, like a priestly cassock, down to his shoes. His mid-length, black beard pointed to a large gold medallion hung from his neck, while his head was capped with an equally black turban. The cap added to his already tall six-foot five-inch frame, and that, coupled with his brooding dark eyes, and a malevolent look on his face, had a daunting effect on Jack. He imagined that an incarnation of Merlin or Rasputin might be standing before him.

"Zoltan! It's all right. You can let Jack pass." The president's voice boomed from inside the room, and sounded as if he were calling off a guard dog. "You and the others can wait in the lobby while Andy, Jack, and I have a little chat."

"As you wish master," Bielchek responded. His fixed stare into Jack's eyes had a mesmerizing, almost hypnotic effect, and he was relieved when the dark figure left the room.

"Jack! It's been too long my old friend," the president said, with his best campaign smile. He rose from the couch, and shook his hand, and was alarmed to see that the president had lost quite a bit of weight. His once athletic build was now reduced to a frail, gaunt shell. "You know Andy, of course."

Andy Stern rose from one of the two gilt-edged, French provincial chairs, opposite a matching couch, and reached over the coffee table to shake his hand. Jack noticed that Andy looked down, and would not make eye contact.

"He doesn't believe me! He knows that I have the cigar wrapper." He thought to himself as he poured a cup of coffee from the service tray.

"So Jack," began the president, while staring down at the coffee table, "Andy here tells me that you, ah, have something you'd like to share with me. Out of respect for Andy, and our, er, past association, one which I truly regret, ah, we were not able to continue, um, and so forth..." The president paused as if he were listening to someone. "...To continue, ah, that is, as before, when our mutual acquaintance would have precluded the need for this, um, somewhat special, and I must say with all candor, highly irregular visit."

Jack was stunned. This person sitting on the couch was not the same man he once knew. The creature before him, who would not even look him in the eyes when he spoke, now replaced the strong, powerful man of the past. Sudden anger rose up in him, and he had the urge to shake the President of the United States, and awaken him out of his stupor. He quickly glanced over at Andy, and saw only a bemused smile on his face.

"Thank you for your time sir," Jack began, not really knowing what particular tack to take, but decided to approach him from once familiar territory. "There have been a number of recent international and domestic--"

"Well Jack," the president interrupted, "my policy has always been to, ah, paint these matters with as broad a brush as possible, so to speak." He paused again for several awkward moments, almost as if he had fallen asleep, and then began once again. "Yes, that is, ah, like painting with a brush, see? By the way Jack, do you paint at all?" Before Jack could answer he began again. "I've taken up the hobby and I must say that, ah, putting paint to canvas...well, there's just not anything quite like it you know."

"Sir, if I may, there are troubling developments here and abroad--"

"Oh, to be sure, yes, trouble on every front, to be sure, yes," the president cut in, and then paused again. "As Shakespeare said in *Hamlet*, or, er, was that *McBeth*? 'Bubble, bubble, toil and trouble, cauldrons, and, ah, oh yes, thank you, cauldrons deep and, ah...and so forth."

The conversation was going nowhere, and Jack was losing patience. It was almost as if someone or something was deliberately blocking any attempt at his having a meaningful discussion with the president. He now tried an indirect approach. "How is Mrs. Williams, sir?" He asked. Jack knew that the president's wife had recently left him, and was living in one of their homes in Boca Raton, Florida.

The president sat speechless for some time, and acted as if he hadn't heard the question. "Eh? Mrs. Williams? Yes, of course, you mean Margaret, that is Margie, don't you? Well, I'm sorry to say--ouch! I, I didn't mean that! Um, she's, ah, spending some time in Florida, I think. Oh yes, Florida, that's it."

Just then the tall, dark statue that was Zoltan Bielchek entered the room. "Mr. President it's time for your next meeting." He droned in his monotone voice.

Suddenly, the president seemingly came back to life. He took a long drink of the coffee that had turned cold, stood up briskly, as did Jack and Andy, adjusted his coat and tie, and proceeded toward the door, led by Bielchek. He paused at the door, and shook Andy's hand. He then took Jack's hand, placed it in a vice-like grip, and glared at him through coal-black eyes, which was framed by a menacing look on his face. "I won't be seeing you again, Jack," he said in a threatening, unearthly voice.

"Ever again!"

* * *

Jack got home about 10:30, thoroughly flummoxed by the quasi-interview he had had with the president. When he got to the front door, he found that it was partially opened. His heart began to race, and he paused for a few seconds to get his emotions under control. He then stepped over the threshold, and turned on the light. The scene before him caused him to gasp. The whole house was turned upside-down! Books were scattered on the floor. The couch and chairs were overturned, and drawers were rifled through.

Walking into his office, he saw that the room was in similar chaos. Papers lay strewn over the desk and on the floor, more books littered the floor. His file cabinet drawers were opened and disemboweled.

He pulled out his wallet, and removed the cigar wrapper from an inner secret compartment. "All this for a little piece of paper." He said holding the wrapper out and examining it. He put it away again for safety and decided to leave quickly. He knew that he was probably being watched.

He locked up the house, got into his car, and looked down the street from his cul-de-sac. There was a car parked at the end of the street.

Jack pondered his next move, and decided to call Marcia.

"Marcia, would it be possible to stay at your place tonight?"

"Of course, dear." She replied, noting the tension in his voice. "Is everything alright?"

"I'll explain later sweetheart. I've got to see someone first, and then I'll be over. The key in the same place?"

"Yes, but I'll be up now for sure, so just come to the door."

"Okay. See you soon."

Jack now realized that he was a marked man as long as he held on to the mysterious cigar wrapper. His next call was to a friend he had in the FBI. He scrolled down his contact list until he found the home number for Bill Young.

"Bill? Hi, Jack Quinn. Look, I know it's late, but I've got something important I need to talk to you about."

"Jack, it's been awhile. Sure, let's talk. How about my office at 8:00 a.m. tomorrow."

"Bill, could we meet tonight? This is rather urgent."

"Um, okay. Let me shake the cobwebs out for a moment. Anywhere in particular?"

"There's that little all-night coffee shop close to your place."

"Ernie's?"

"Yeah that's the one. Just give me about a half and hour. I've got to shake off a possible tail and it might take me some time."

Bill tensed. "Sounds like you're in some kind of trouble, Jack. You sure you don't want me and maybe a few others to come by your place?"

"Thanks, but it's not safe for me to stay here any longer. My house has been ransacked and I think I'm being watched. I'll explain everything at Ernie's. See you there."

"Okay buddy. You take care. I'll have a couple of guys meet with us just in case."

"Great. Thanks Bill. I owe you one."

He hung up the phone and started his car. As he came to the end of the street he saw that there was a dark figure in the car, parked on the right side. Jack turned right and after a few moments noticed the same car following him.

He felt a shiver of excitement run down his spine. "So this is what a chase feels like." He took a deep breath, and pondered what it would take to shake this guy.

* * *

Miriam had cried herself to sleep, and slept through the day. She looked over at the alarm clock, and saw that it was now past midnight, and her growling stomach prompted her to go downstairs for a quick bite. She turned the teakettle on, and found the herbal tea and honey that she liked in the cupboard. The fridge produced some turkey, cheese, and mustard and, oh yes, kosher dill pickles. Mira assembled the ingredients on the counter, added two slices of deli rye bread, and after the sandwich and tea were prepared, moved to the kitchen table.

She could not stop thinking about Brant, and after a few bites of her sandwich, lost her appetite. She looked out at the darkness outside the kitchen window, through eyes blurred with tears.

"Mind if I join you?" Her father asked.

"Hi dad. Sure, I could use the company." She replied, still looking out the window.

"I see you've made yourself some tea. I think I'll join you." He warmed up the teakettle once again, and when it came to a boil, prepared a cup of hot chocolate, and sat down beside his daughter. He looked down at his cup while stirring, not knowing what to say, and decided to stay quiet.

"Anna would have known what to say." He thought to himself. *"I'm the quiet, analytical one, while she was always so warm and outgoing. Oh, how I miss her."*

"Dad there's something I've got to ask you." Mira suddenly announced, while turning to face him. "The other day, I read something on the clipboard you left in my room. You wrote that it might be helpful if you told me about my earliest childhood." She paused, and saw that her father was affected by what she had just said. She gently touched his hand. "It's okay dad. I just want to know."

The dreaded moment had finally come. He had insisted on putting it off all her life, thinking that it might somehow hurt their relationship, or put some distance between them. Anna had tried to convince him that it would be all right; that love would bridge the gap. But he had been stubborn, and, dare he say it, afraid to act. Now there was no way out. The story had to be told. He leaned back in his chair, took off his silver, wire-rim glasses, closed his eyes, and rubbed the bridge of his nose.

Taking her right hand in both of his, he began the tale.

"Let me start at the beginning."

* * *

His car, a late model electric car, was not up to the challenge. A half-hour from College Park, Jack realized that he couldn't shake his pursuer. He decided to head for Ernie's, and hope that Bill and friends were waiting for him. As if reading Jack's thoughts, the pursuing car suddenly became more aggressive, came up close, and bumped him. That angered Jack, but he pressed on, dodging right, then left, and down side streets, while trying to keep his attacker at bay.

"It'll take about ten minutes to get to Ernie's." He thought to himself, just as another jarring bump came from behind. "I've got to stay close to the city." He turned the wheel hard to the left, and went down an alley, behind a shopping center. His pursuer overshot the turn, and lost him for a moment, but then picked him up again at the end of the alley, bumping him once again.

The chase continued through Bladenburg, and down Landover Road. A split second decision found Jack going up the ramp to the I-295 freeway heading south. Again, the attack car overshot the turn, allowing Jack some precious time to get ahead, in the thick, late night traffic. "How I wish I had my old Corvette right about now," he mused. He pushed the pedal to the floor, but saw that the speedometer showed only 70 miles an hour. A quick glance in his rearview found that his nemesis was gaining on him once again.

He got off the freeway at the East Capitol Street exit, heading west, crossed the Anacosta River, drove past RFK stadium, and down Constitution Avenue into the heart of central Washington. The black car behind him had closed the gap, and continued bumping him with renewed vigor, at one point causing Jack's car to swerve sharply to the right. He continued to drive well over the speed limit, and went through several red lights, hoping to attract the attention of the Capitol police.

Just then, a bullet crashed through the rear window, and became lodged in the passenger side dashboard. This new development only angered Jack more, and steeled his resolve. He cut in front of a car on the inbound lane of the four-lane boulevard, causing it to come to a screeching stop, then turned sharply left, and drove off in the opposite direction. His attacker, desperate now, followed suit, as gunshots rang out once again. Jack came to another light, and noticed a police cruiser waiting for the light to turn. He slowed down, enduring several more bumps, and went through the red light once again.That was enough to alert the police car, and he immediately closed behind his pursuer, with lights flashing and siren on.

Jack pulled over to the side, and saw his tormentor zoom past him, followed closely by the police car. The chase continued for several blocks, aided by several other patrol cars, until he lost sight of them.

* * *

"Miriam," he began, looking down at his cup. "This sort of thing has always been hard for me. I'm not a strong person, and usually shy away from confrontation. I always relied on your mother to handle difficult situations. Then, when I almost lost you…" he paused, reached out for her hand once again, and looked her in the eyes. "I deeply regretted not having told you, ah, certain things about your past. At one point, when your memory was in a hiatus, I thought that telling you about these things might just shock you back to clarity. Hence the note you found on the clipboard."

"I know dad." She said, covering his hand with both of hers. "I'm alright now. I'm a big girl, and I need you to tell me all there is to know about my past."

He patted her hand and took a sip from his cup. "Yes, yes of course. I can see that there is no other way." He leaned back, took his glasses off, closed his eyes, and summoned his courage.

"Miriam, you are not our natural child." He looked at her with a pained look on his face. "You were adopted."

She looked down in shocked silence. "Go on." She replied after a few moments.

"You were born in Israel, and we adopted you when you were a little over three years old. You were found wandering in a wheat field, after a terrorist attack on your kibbutz had killed your natural parents." He paused to see her reaction.

She looked out the window, tears welling up in her eyes, and then remembered her dream:

She was running through a field…the sound of gunshots in the distance filled the air…she couldn't keep up with him! Help her! Help her!

"I, I had what I thought was a dream about this." She replied. "I see now that it wasn't a dream at all, but a flashback to something that really happened." She then recounted the story to her father.

"I had no idea, Miriam. Your mother and I were afraid to bring up the subject. We wanted to give you a new life, and hoped that an effective home environment would displace the trauma of your early childhood." He looked down at his cup once again, and realized that he had been wrong. He should have told her the truth long ago. He would have to tell her the whole story now.

"Just recently I found out, after some research on the web," he began again without looking up at her, "that you have an older brother, who also survived the massacre. I don't know much about him, except that he's taken the family name of Cohen. Binyamin Cohen, to be precise, and that he is a fighter pilot with the Israeli Defense Forces." He paused once again, fearing to heap too much information on his now distraught daughter.

Mira continued to look out the window. "A brother! I have a brother?" It was almost too much. Her whole life had just been turned upside down.

* * *

Andy Stern, a.k.a., Andrei Velikovsky, furiously packed his personal items into a large black suitcase that he had brought to his White House office.

He had no time to lose. The plot to retrieve his lost cigar band had failed, and he knew that he had to leave the country at once.

"That Americansky, that Jack Quinn! He was nothing but trouble from the beginning." Andy said to himself. *"If I hadn't been drunk in the car..."* He stuffed the last few items in the bag, and quickly zippered it shut.

"Nyet! Was time for me to go." He acknowledged, and looked around for anything he might have missed. "The president is lapdog to that peazant Bielchek...they closed me out of the loop...they..."

Andy picked up, and gently caressed, one of his framed collections of butterflies. Whenever he went on speaking engagements, or government business, he would take time to scour the local countryside for the elusive insects. In a way, they nurtured his alter ego; the gentle bucolic farm boy of his youth. The hobby kept him sane through the months of espionage insanity. He laid it down gently on top of the others, on the chair beside his desk. There were five of them, but they would have to stay.

His driver hurried the bags into the trunk of the limousine, and drove out of the White House main gate heading for Dulles International Airport. Andrei had already sent his last cable to Moscow, alerting his superiors that his cover had been blown, and that he was "coming in". An Aeroflot Tristar passenger jet was already waiting for him on the tarmac at the airport.

The George Washington Memorial Highway was busy with bumper-to-bumper traffic at five in the morning, but there was no need to rush now. The plane would not leave without him. *"Was a good posting."* He thought. *"The faked accident, new identity, and all confidence of the prezident."* He chuckled, and lit a cigar—he actually did smoke cigars. After a few large puffs, and a shot of vodka, he relaxed and felt the tension drain away.

The log jam of cars broke free, and they continued on past McLean, Virginia, and exited onto the Dulles International Airport road. After several minutes, the limousine pulled up to the airport terminal. Briefcase in hand, he entered through the pneumatic doors, not even acknowledging his driver, who dutifully unloaded and signed for his baggage.

At the security checkpoint, Andrei pulled out his diplomatic credentials, walked quickly past the military guards, and down the pedestrian walkway that would take him to Concourse B and his awaiting flight. Along the way he paused to get a copy of the latest Washington Times and Izvestia newspapers, found his departure gate, and, after a brief exchange at the counter, boarded his plane. Upon entering, he found, without surprise, that he was the only person on the eighty-seat jet.

He settled in to his comfortable, first class seat, and pulled out his copy of Izvestia, while the Tristar began taxiing toward the runway that would soon whisk him away to his beloved *Rodina*; mother Russia.

Suddenly, the plane came to an abrupt stop, and after a few moments, proceeded slowly to the left, and away from the runway. Andrei looked outside the left window with concern, as the plane stopped on the tarmac, a short distance from the gate he had just left.

A ramp vehicle was brought up beside his plane, and after a few tense moments, several men in dark suits came up the ramp, and when the front hatch was opened, into the cabin. Two men with short-cropped dark hair and muscular builds, pulled the seats around, and faced Andrei, while two others, clone look-alikes of the first two, manned the seats behind him.

"Andy Stern, or should I say, And-ray Velikovsky, erstwhile spy for the Russian Federation, I'm special counterintelligence agent, Bill Moore of the Federal Bureau of Investigation, and these are my associates." He declared in a monotone, matter-of-fact voice, while producing his wallet badge.

Andrei was too stunned by the sudden change of events to quickly respond, but soon recovered his composure. "I am not sure what you mean by spy, but I have diplomatic passport, and am on official Russian Federation bizness. You are trespassing on government property, and a complaint to that effect will be lodged with your State Department."

"No need for that And-ray." Moore replied with a wry smile, sat back, crossed his legs, and unbuttoned his suit coat. "Y'all are still on American soil," he replied, "and because you're implicated in espionage activities against our country, we have the right to detain you, without a warrant, for up to thirty-six hours. Now get this. If we conduct a search of your office or baggage, and find any incriminating materials, such as, say, a cigar band with an imbedded microchip?" He leaned close, pulled out his vis-a-phone, and showed him a picture of the cigar band Andrei had lost. "Why shucks, we could hold you indefinitely, and let our two governments haggle over you."

Andrei sat motionless, distraught over what he had just seen and heard. His only out was his diplomatic immunity, and he hoped that it would be enough. "I must state again that I am official of the Russian Federation government under diplomatic cover--"

"Relax And-ray; we're not going to take you in." Moore replied, leaning forward, with his arms on his knees. "Naw, that would be way too much trouble. This is just a friendly visit to let you know that we've been on to you from the beginning: even before you became involved with the president. You see, when you had that little car accident on the beltway? While you were knocked out for awhile? We went ahead and implanted a little chip into your right hand. Right there between your middle and ring finger." He pointed to his hand, causing Andrei to once again feel the need to involuntarily itch the spot. "That's right. You probably felt the urge to itch, but didn't know why? Well, now you know." He explained with a grin, and leaned back once again. "From that point on we fed you with all the information you could swallow; like an Arkansas razorback feeding at a trough." This produced a chuckle from the other men. "So, And-ray," he continued, as all four men stood up to leave. "We just thought y'all would like to share in our little secret."

Moore buttoned his jacket, and put on his black sunglasses. The three others filed out of the plane while he turned to face Andrei once more. "Oh, by the way. You know that butterfly collection you were so fond of? The framed ones you left in your office? Yeah, you'll be pleased to know that we're going to put them on display for you." He teased, and could read the despair in Andrei's face. "In the FBI museum." He said grinning, and walked out into the bright early morning sunlight.

CHAPTER 14

Benni sat down heavily on the first rock he could find and buried his face in his hands. The gathering gloom of darkness matched his depressed mood. "*To be so close!*" he chided himself. Amazingly, it seemed as if a huge weight had been lifted off his shoulders. He felt an inner peace, and somehow knew that everything would be all right.

"So, how did you find me?" He asked while looking up into the darkened face of M&M.

Major Azerah sat down on the opposite rock, and leaned forward. "You're quite easy to track you know. I reckoned that you wouldn't make for the city, and would probably head for Jordan. Two of my compatriots checked the cities just in case. I picked up some solid tracks of yours, as well as those of the Bin Saladen band you ran into here, just inside the Jordanian border. I followed them, and waited for the right opportunity, found you asleep in that covert, and decided to let you sleep. Had the Jordanians not taken out that tracker, I would have had to shoot him, but fortunately they intervened just in time."

Benni marveled at the news, and the fact that this was the longest conversation he had ever had with M&M. He would attempt to keep the conversation going. "Where do we go from here?"

Major Azerah was at a crossroads. He could keep up the ruse of being the mysterious captor, or break his silence and reveal his true identity. Mossad intelligence protocol demanded the former; he decided on the latter.

"First I must properly introduce myself." He said in Hebrew, standing up to his full, almost six foot height. My name is Major Moise Azerah of Mossad intelligence in charge of special operations. I was tasked with retrieving you from hostile territory after you went down in Saudi Arabia. We followed your captors to their encampment, and forced your extraction when conditions warranted. You know the rest of the story, except for the fact that, for your protection and ours, we had to treat you as a hostage, until such time as we could deliver you safely to freedom. Of course you gave us the slip, because of your *hutzpah,* and so now, here we are."

Benni rose up and tried to come to grips with this new revelation. He didn't know whether to laugh, cry, be joyful, or angry. After a few moments, he reached over to Major Azerah and hugged him, tears filling his eyes. "I'm so glad to know you Major. I feel like I can finally breathe again."

"*B'seder,* I understand." The major replied, and awkwardly hugged Benni back. 'We have to move fast. The Jordanians are now on the hunt. They will launch a full air, sea, and land search until we're found. We also have to deal with the determined pursuit of bin Saladen and his men. The Jordanians, who are not fond of trespassers on their soil, might neutralize them, or they might join together. Either way we must go."

"What is your plan then?" Benni asked, his spirits lifted, knowing that he was now part of a team.

Major Azerah dropped to a knee beside Benni, pulled out a terrain map of the area, and a palm-sized flashlight. "We're approximately here, about five kilometers south of Ra's an Naqb. Soon the major border crossings will all be heavily guarded with both air and land patrols, searching along the Arabah between the Negev Desert and the Jordanian frontier." He moved his finger along the winding border between Israel and Jordan. We will reconnoiter with my men at a small oasis, just north of Bi'r Abu here." He pointed to a spot on the map. From there, we'll hear their report, and decide on the best course of action." He stood up, stowed the map and flashlight in his backpack, and prepared to move out.

Benni stood as well, stretched his legs and arms, and looked west to his homeland and freedom. They were so close. He felt like he could almost jump across the border and into Monika's arms.

Moise looked over at Benni, and sensed what he was feeling. "It is that close we are to home." He allowed, walking along the ridge. "By the Eternal One, we'll be there soon."

Benni followed him into the inkwell of night, glad to be in the company of a fellow countryman.

* * *

Yosip rose wearily from his prayer mat as the early morning sun rose above the eastern hills, and filtered through the palm trees of the oasis. He walked slowly back to his pavilion, while his men began to move about in preparation for the new day. They had all, individually or in small groups, spread their prayer mats, as he himself had done, faced Mecca, and recited the *shahada,* the Muslim creed, and then entered into *salat,* or prayer, for a short period. This was one of the five times they would do this in the course of the day. Thus, they will have fulfilled two of the "five pillars" of the Muslim religion. These five are: reciting the creed-*shahada,* prayer-*salat,* almsgiving-*zakat,* fasting-*saum,* and the pilgrimage to Mecca-the *hajj.*

Yosip had already accomplished four of the five pillars, but had yet to go on a pilgrimage to Mecca. The thought of taking the pilgrim's road, walking counter-clockwise with thousands of others around the Ka'aba, drinking from the Zamzan well, and performing the *Stoning of The Devil* on the plains of Mt. Arafat, brought a sigh and a smile to his face, along with an intense desire to fulfill his final pillar of faith.

He entered the opened door flap to his pavilion, sat down heavily on his ornate throne-like chair, took off his gold-banded keffiyeh, and rubbed his scalp. *"I'm tired of chasing this desert monkey."* He said to himself. *"I've lost a man and others have been captured..."*

His thoughts went out to his father who was undoubtedly preparing for an assault on another Saudi city. He longed to be in the vanguard, at the head of charging horses, routing the enemy at every turn. "One day soon, all Islam will be united under one caliphate, and that caliph will be my father, and I will be his proud son." He vowed.

Without warning, the encampment erupted into random shouts and yells, men running about with guns at the ready. Bin Saladen rose up, put on his kaffiyeh and agal, and walked to the tent opening, just as one of the men came up to report to him the nature of the disturbance.

"My lord, I beg to report", he said, bowing low to the ground, and rising only when bin Saladen raised his hand.

"A Jordanian army jeep and troop carrier has just passed one of our lookouts, and are heading this way." He stayed bowed and walked backward away from his master.

Yosip walked back into the tent, sat down on his throne, and ordered his servants to quickly arrange for some refreshment.

The Jordanian column pulled up to the encampment, and were quickly surrounded by bin Saladen's men.

A short, dark skinned man dressed in green camouflage army fatigues with black jumping boots, and wearing a green beret and sunglasses, stepped out of the lead vehicle. His two stars on both shoulder boards indicated that he was a Jordanian general.

Mahmoud, bin Saladen's second in command, stepped forward to meet him.

"I will speak to your commander," the general demanded in fluent Arabic, his black moustache twitching slightly.

"As Allah wills." Mahmoud replied with a bow, and led him into the tent. The general and his aide-de-camp walked into the tent and stood before bin Saladen.

"I'm General Fawad Haroun, commander of the Jordanian 5th Airborne division." He announced slowly and deliberately, while taking off his black leather gloves, and placing them under his left shoulder board. "Major elements of my division are bivouacked only a few kilometers from here.".

"My apologies general. Fatigue and weariness have cost me my manners. Mahmoud, guide our guests to the couches, and lay on refreshments. See that his men are comfortable and well cared for." He commanded. Yosip saw that his position was precarious. His small band had come into Jordan without permission and could be arrested.

Mahmoud led the men to a large carpet covering the oasis sand, where cushions were placed around a large tray of dates, nuts, cakes, and a tea service.

The general and his aide sat upright with legs crossed, and did not take any of the offerings, which told Yosip that they were going to be all business. His servant poured some tea, while Yosip took a bite of a fig cake. "Come general, enjoy my humble offerings." He insisted, and took a sip of tea.

"Let me come directly to the point, Yosip bin Saladen." He looked up to see the surprise on Yosip's face. You are the son of Sheik Walid Haj Saladen. Oh yes, we have dossiers on both you and your father. "He paused, enjoying the cat and mouse game being played out: the cat now toying with his trapped mouse. We know of his recent raid on Tobuk, and that you are here, trespassing I must say, and hunting for an escaped Israeli pilot." He paused again,and nodded to his aide, who took a small ceramic cup, poured in some tea, and handed it to the general.

The mouse wanted to squeal, but tried very hard not to appear surprised. He took another bite of his fig cake, washed it down with a sip of tea, and sat upright. "You are well informed general, but it only seems that you have the upper hand." He replied with a dark grin. "As you can see, we have you and your men hostage. A handsome ransom, wouldn't you say?" He lay back down again and sampled another cake.

The general did not flinch. "I have given orders that if my detachment is not back in," he looked at his gold Rolex watch, "thirty-five minutes from now, then my battle group is to follow with a massive strike, one that will eliminate your little band of cutthroats, and deprive your esteemed father of his gifted son."

The cat had tossed the mouse in the air. Bin Saladen was trapped. His bluff had not worked, and he was now at the mercy of this Jordanian.

"Insh' Allah. I am your humble servant, and also the servant of your king." He replied meekly, rose to his knees, and bowed low to the ground in a gesture of submission.

"Thank you. If you had done that in the beginning, it would have saved us both a lot of time. Accompany me to my Jeep."

The general stood, and waited for Mahmoud to lead the way out of the tent. Yosip's men had made an armed circle around the oasis, but he now ordered them to back off, stack their weapons, and wait in the center of the oasis.

At a word from the general, the aide produced a folding table with a field chart on it, and placed it beside the Jeep. "It is the will of my king that we join forces in the pursuit of the Israeli pilot." The general said factually. You are now under my command, and will gather your men to meet me at the village of Ma'an, here," he pointed at a spot on the map, "at 1200 hours. From there we will brief you, and give you additional orders. Understood?" He ordered, and fixed a dark, sun-glassed stare at Yosip.

"From my mouth to Allah's ear, I will be there with my men." He promised, amazed at the turn of events that had seen him first become a prisoner and now an ally.

The general's detachment sped off in a cloud of dust in the same direction they had come, and arrived at their camp five minutes before the scheduled deadline to attack.

Yosip walked briskly back to his pavilion, picked up his riding crop, and angrily paced back and forth on the carpeted floor, flogging his right side as he walked. "Pigs and sons of pigs!" he shouted. "Do these Hashemite swine think that Yosip bin Saladen, son of Sheik Wallid Haj Saladen, soon to be caliph of all the Arab people, can be so easily intimidated?" He walked to the door of the pavilion.

"Mahmoud!" He shouted.

Mahmoud understood the anger in his master's voice, having felt the fire of angry lashes in the past. He ran, knelt, and bowed down in the sand at his master's feet. "Your servant, my lord."

"Break camp quickly, and be ready to move out." He declared, and wheeled back into the tent.

"We are to join our Jordanian brothers?" Mahmood asked hopefully.

Yosip turned sharply on his heel, raised his crop to strike, but held back. "No!" He yelled. "We will not share our prize with the Hashemites. It is Allah's will that we find and capture our desert viper, dead or alive."

* * *

Standing up with difficulty from his kneeling position Reb Berkowitz stood beside his bed in the cramped quarters of his two-room flat overlooking *Ha'Kotel* in Jerusalem. He had been intensely praying for Monika, who had once again lapsed into a coma following his visit. He would have stayed with her for several more days, but an urgent message from his dear friend, Chaim Podhoretz found him, and he decided to leave at once.

He put on his worn but comfortable slippers, and strode into the tiny kitchen to make some tea. While the kettle warmed on the two-burner gas stove, he walked over to the window, and gazed out at *Ha'Kotel,* now shaded from the early morning sunshine. Even now there were several men praying beside the massive stone blocks that formed the foundation of the Temple built by Herod the Great. He looked down at the plaza, now some thirty feet above the original first-century groundwork, where, in 70 AD, greedy Roman soldiers, lusting for gold they believed had melted and filled the cracks between the platform slabs, pried the stones apart and threw them over the wall. This act fulfilled Yeshua's prophecy that:

"…there shall not be left here one stone upon another, that shall not be thrown down."

"Nu, truly are you, blessed Lord, "the way, the truth, and the life".

The teakettle whistled for his attention, and Shlomo walked over to the stove, and fixed his favorite orange-pekoe tea, flavored with a teaspoon of honey. As he was stirring in the honey, a loud rap sounded at the door.

"Yes, yes, come in, come in," he shouted, and opened the door to find an agitated and sweating Chaim Podhoretz standing there. Without a word of greeting, he walked briskly through the door, and took a seat in front of the window. Podhoretz immediately took out a handkerchief from the sleave of his full-length black topcoat and patted his brow. "It is only seven in the morning, and it's that hot already, Shlomo."

"Is it tea then for you, Chaim? I just made a fresh pot."

"Yes, thank you. Some chala bread if you have it. I'm also hungry, but Shlomo, I had to see you before they--have you heard from anyone since you've been back?

"Chala I have, though it's a bit dry. Some currant spread will help, nu?" He placed the tea and plate before his friend.

"Thank you. But has anyone been to see you?"

"First to pray, and then to talk, yes?"

Both men bowed their heads as Reb Berkowitz lead in prayer. "Blessed art thou, Lord of the earth and all its fullness. Bless now this food for our needs, and this time together, we pray, in the name of Yeshua Ha'Meshiach. Omain.

"Shlomo! You know I can't acknowledge that name! Couldn't you have settled for the G-d of your fathers?"

"But I did. Yeshua has ever been in the bosom of His Father. Does not the Torah say from the beginning, *"let us make man in our image"*. He took a piece of bread and lathered it with the black currant spread. "Who is this "us" and "our" then, but the Almighty One, blessed forever be His Name, found in three persons, one of whom is His Son." He looked at his friend for confirmation, but Podhoretz was shaking his head.

"We've been all around with this, Shlomo. I must admit though, dear friend," he allowed, taking a generous bite of chala, "you do raise some interesting questions."

"Yes, and another point I should raise for you my dear Chaim. What hope have you that Ha'Mashiach could come anymore from the line of David, eh? All previous records have been destroyed, without any hope of tracing anyone back to our father David?"

Rabbi Podhoretz reacted as if he'd been punched in the stomach, pulled out his handkerchief again, and mopped his perspiring brow. He hated being put on the spot with such questions, and there were so many of these in their discussions that he had no answer for. "True, true, Shlomo. Nevertheless, will not the Almighty, He is holy, provide those documents when the time is right?"

"Manufacture them out of thin air then I suppose, eh?" Shlomo asked sarcastically, folding his arms across his chest. "No my dear friend. *Ha Shem*, the Name, has already provided Him, yet you and all others who reject Him will surely find another, who will promise you peace and safety, and then will come sudden destruction. As Yeshua has said in the book of Yochanan:

"...I am come in my Father's name, and you receive me not: if another shall come in his own name, him you will receive."

Chaim looked down and took another sip of tea. He had no answer for this as well, and was quiet for some time.

Suddenly a loud rap at the door broke the silence in the room.

Rabbi Berkowitz opened the door to a tall, much-too thin young man, dressed all in black, with short black hair, and forelocks bursting beneath a black kipa. He recognized him as being a former pupil of his, and an officer of the Sanhedrin.

"Yitzak my boy, how are you?" He asked, and shook the boy's hesitant hand.

"Reb Berkowitz, I'm fine and...that is..."

"Yes, yes, it's alright my son, I understand. Nu, you have something for me?" He asked, and patted the young man's arm reassuringly.

"I regret...well, this is a summons from the Sanhedrin." He replied and produced a formal document, gave it to the Rabbi, and ran away down the dark hallway.

Shlomo closed the door while reading the single page summons, and then turned to face his friend.

"I'm sorry, Shlomo. That is why I came to see you. They intend to sack you."

Reb Berkowitz sat down heavily on his chair, and looked out towards *Ha'Kotel*, silently praying for strength. "My dear Chaim. As Reb Sha'ul, also known as Paul, said in his book to the Romans:

all things will work together for good according to His purpose..."

CHAPTER 15

She awoke to the sound of loud conversation coming from somewhere downstairs. Mira looked at her alarm clock and saw that it was almost noon. She stretched, and then buried herself in her down comforter to try to block out the noise, but soon heard loud footsteps coming up the stairs.

"Mira!" called out an excited voice, after bursting through her bedroom door.

She threw off the covers, sat up, and knew immediately who it was. "Carla? How did you--" was all she managed before being smothered in a huge bear hug. Both women rocked back and forth, with tears of joy streaming down both faces at the glad reunion.

"I knew it wasn't true," Carla said, while taking off her wire-rimmed glasses, and wiping her swollen eyes with a handkerchief. "They told me you were dead, but I knew it wasn't true," she continued, and began to weep.

Mira wiped her own eyes with her comforter, and gently touched Carla's shoulder. "Who told you that I was dead?"

Carla collected herself, and recounted the story. She then looked up, a huge smile spreading over her face, hugged Mira once more, and drew back at arms length to look at her. "You are fine now aren't you? I mean the memory and all."

Mira laughed, and lay back down on her pillow. "Who did you say you were?" she teased. "Seems like I know you from somewhere?" She laughed again, and covered herself with her pillow.

"Stop that. That's mean." Carla chided and pushed down playfully on the pillow. She took Mira's right hand in both of hers. "I'm just glad you're okay.

"Carla, how did you get off? Where are your cats? What's going on at the station? She asked, in rapid-fire succession.

Carla leaned back and laughed. "Whoa, gal! We've got all day." She looked at her watch. "Well, what's left of it, sleepyhead." She reached over and mussed Mira's hair. "My kittums are fine, and staying with my aunt. The cheapskates at the studio gave me time off—whoopee! two whole days so that I could see you, and pass along some news to you. They're planning a big shindig for you when you return with all the corporate bigwigs coming by. Hey—they've even got the mayor coming!" She looked at Mira expecting to see her excited, but instead found her face clouded, with downcast eyes.

She reached over and touched her arm. "Everything alright dear? If this is too much, too soon?

"No, it's okay. It's just that things have changed. I mean, I've learned some things that are going to take awhile to sort out."

"You're not pregnant are you? She asked, craning her neck forward

"Carla!" Mira shouted with a laugh, turning brightly red. "No, of course not, silly." She hesitated for a moment, questioning whether she should share her secret with her friend. Carla had always been like a combination best friend and mom to her, and she knew from experience that anything she might tell her would never go anywhere else.

"My father told me the other day that I'm adopted." She explained without emotion. She looked to see Carla's response, and found compassion in her eyes. "Not only that, but I also learned that I have a brother living in Israel; an Israeli Air Force pilot. His name is Binyamin Cohen." She looked down at her hands, and found a certain relief at being able to share this with her.

"Wow! That's amazing." Carla replied, not knowing how to respond.

"It gets even more interesting. I tried to get in contact with my brother, and finally, after a lengthy military run-around, found out that he's on some sort of 'secret mission'. That's all I know about him."

"So that's why you're not that excited about all the hoop-la for your return." She replied, looking into Mira's eyes. "What are you going to do?"

"I'm not sure. It's taking me awhile to get adjusted to this. I don't know what to do." She replied and lay back down on her pillow.

"Well dear, whatever you decide, I'll be right there with you." Carla replied. "Come on and get dressed. I'm taking you out to lunch, on the company credit card no less!"

Mira got up and hugged her friend. "Thanks for coming Carla, and thanks for not giving up on me."

"Of course I wouldn't give up on you. You're not only my friend Mira, you're my baby."

* * *

Both women bustled through the front door laughing, with several packages in tow.

"Hi Dad." Mira chirped, happy to be out of the cold night, and in the warmth of her home. "You should never have given me your identification card. I'm afraid I've used up a bunch or your credits.

"Your daughter," added Carla laughing, "was like a babe in a candy store."

Mira walked over to the fireplace and warmed her hands. "It seems like ages since I've been shopping." She said wistfully. "I would've done a lot more damage to that card if it wasn't for miss mother-hen over there." She pointed playfully at Carla.

"Ha! Like I could stop a runaway train!" she replied, joining Mira at the fireplace; both women laughing at their playful jibes.

Mira noticed that her father had put down his notes, and had a far away look on his face. "Something bothering you dad?" She asked, and sat down beside him on the long brown leather couch.

"He took off his horn-rimmed glasses and closed his eyes. "The continuing anti-Semitic riots in New York and Chicago have spread to other cities. It appears that the Jews are being blamed for the financial downturn in our country. Now with several states separating themselves from the union..." He let the statement hang in the air, and put on his glasses once again. "I'm concerned for our people, Mira," he said, turning to her. "For us, and for where our country is heading.

So, girls, you've managed to clean out my bank account, eh?" he said, trying to sound more upbeat. "You must be hungry after all that shopping." He looked from face to face and found no objection. "Good. I've got some hot borscht soup to take the chill off, and I'll make us some toasted Reuben sandwiches to go along with that. How does that sound?"

"That's great dad! I'll set the table." Mira replied.

"Count me in, especially the soup." Carla added, still sniffling from her ordeal with the cold night air.

The meal was quickly served and all three cleaned their plates in quick succession; Carla opting for another bowl of borscht garnished with sour cream.

"I love this soup Dr. Rosen. It reminds me of my mother's. We would have it at almost every Shabbat meal." Carla said between spoonfuls. "You make it with that tender short rib beef and you didn't forget to add the beet greens, which gives it that tangy flavor." She cleaned out her bowl and sat back refreshed.

"Carla, I didn't know you were Jewish?" Mira asked, while clearing off the table.

"It's true, but only on my mother's side. My father was from Finland, of all places, that's where they met, and both immigrated to the states before I was born. I get my thin frame from him, but my mother, and my heart, are Jewish." She smiled and helped Mira with the clean up. "Now you can see how I can put up with you all the time." She joked.

"Here's some more for you to put up with." Mira took some soap foam in her hand and blew it on her.

"You're a brat!" Carla scolded playfully while wiping her glasses off with a paper towel.

"Girls, how's some tea by the fireplace sound?" Dr. Rosen asked

"Hot chocolate for me, if you have some, please." Carla replied. "I'm in the mood for something sweet."

"Tea's fine for me dad, thanks. I'll just go upstairs and change into something more comfortable."

The drinks were prepared, and placed on the thick glass coffee table in the living room. Dr. Rosen sat down in his favorite leather recliner, while Carla stood with her back to the fireplace.

"Carla, while we have a moment. Have you been able to talk to Mira about what plans she might have?" He asked in a whisper.

"Well, we talked about her coming back to her job at the studio, and about finding her brother. I'd say those are her main concerns right now. Is she closer to making a decision on going back to Washington? I'd have to say no."

"What concerns me, with regards to her job, is that the threat of violence may still remain." He took a sip of tea. "It's my understanding that they've never captured those responsible for the car bombing."

"No, the perps are still at large, though it's common knowledge that the Mafia, and that Luchese fatcat, were behind it." She said with some anger. "They covered their tracks pretty well, that's for sure." She sat down on the couch and took a sip of hot chocolate.

"So is it safe then? Won't they find out she's back in the city, and try to finish the job?"

"That's a risk, and I don't like it any more than you do." She allowed.

Both were lost in thought when Mira joined them, sat down beside Carla on the couch, and poured a cup of tea from the tea caddy, adding some sugar and cream. "Let me guess? You're both discussing my plans for the future, right?" she asked cheerfully.

"You're psychic!" Carla exclaimed.

"Not really, I just overheard some of your conversation on the way down the stairs." Mira replied, while tucking her feet under her powder blue, terrycloth bathrobe.

"Really dear, we're just concerned for you." Her father explained.

She reached over and gently touched her father's shoulder. "I know dad. It's all right. I'm a big girl now, and I can handle this as well."

"So you've decided to go back then?" Dr. Rosen asked.

"Not yet. But I'm leaning that way."

* * *

Jack and Marcia walked briskly through the chill night air until they found Jack's car, and quickly entered and closed the door. He turned on the ignition, both cuddling close, until the heat broke up the cold, and quietly reflected on the meeting they had just come from.

They had arrived at the Hood's home for their weekly meeting at 8:00 p.m. sharp, and were ushered in as usual into the large living room, where they were greeted by the warmth of their friends, and the oak logs vigorously burning in the fireplace. As the men made their way to the open bar, Rose Hood came up to Marcia, took her by the arm, and led her to the Dining Room, where several of the wives had gathered.

"Jack, I believe you know everyone here?" Tom asked, while Jack acknowledged the men around him.

"What you don't know is that we're not going to have our usual meeting tonight. Dr. Clark was arrested today by the FBI." Several heads nodded, while others, including Jack's, expressed shock at the revelation.

"What's he being charged with?" Jack asked.

"There have been no formal charges at this point, but we may find out more shortly, if that's who I think it is." Tom replied as the doorbell rang. He walked through the foyer, and opened the door to a medium build, bespectacled, balding figure, dressed in a black wool coat, gray silk scarf, and black Stetson hat. Jack recognized him right away as Secretary of State, James Hughes. Tom walked him to the living room where he was introduced to the men in the room.

"Jack, it's great to see you again." James said, while shaking hands. "You're expert advice has been missed at the White House, especially at times like these."

"Thank you, sir. The pleasure is mine." Jack replied, as all took their seats by the fire.

"Jim has been in sympathy with our group for some time now, and has just recently decided to join our cause." Tom explained. A murmur of approval circled the room.

"I'm sorry to say that I've been witnessing the dismantling of our country for some time now, and I, like you, am deeply concerned. I've heard the recordings of the meetings you've been having with Dr.

Clark, and I must say that, apart from the religious vein in the talks, I wholeheartedly agree with what he's been teaching."

"That brings us to some news we've learned today, Jim. I understand that the FBI has arrested Dr. Clark. Do you have any information on that?" Asked Tom.

"I heard about his apprehension only a few hours ago. I called the director of the FBI, but he was out. I then talked to one of his deputies, who told me, off the record, that Dr. Clark was going to be charged with sedition."

"Jim, if that's what he's charged with, what will State's position be on this,?" Jack asked.

"Today's State Department is different from the one you knew, Jack," he began, while sitting down on the couch across from Tom. "Thanks to an overindulgent Congress, the new presidential appointments, and especially Zoltan Bielchek's constant meddling, State has become nothing more than a rubber stamp for the president. Now with the seceding of several states, and martial law being declared in others, all members of the Cabinet are being told to accede to the president's wishes, or get out! The last cabinet meeting we had was terrifying, and made me realize that time is short, and we must resist at all costs. "Of course I'll do all I can to see that Dr. Clark gets a fair trial, but I'm afraid there's not much that can be done for him one way or the other. I must tell you that if he's found guilty, and that's almost a foregone conclusion in the political climate we are in, because of the declared marshal law, he will be executed." Jim's frank summation produced a stunned silence.

"This turn of events has profound implications for every man in this room as well." Jim added, scanning each man's face. "I don't know if any of you noticed the black car with its motor running, parked across the street? That car has government plates, and is tasked to follow someone in this room. Whether you know it or not Tom, the government is on to you, and probably knows about every man in this room. Right now they're just watching, but they will eventually make moves against you and these meetings.

Looks like we're in the crosshairs men." Tom allowed. He turned to the Secretary of State. "Jim what do you think? It pleases me to note that each of you men is solidly behind what we've begun here. Our stance is in the finest traditions of our country. During the Revolutionary War each representative from the thirteen colonies had the threat of execution hanging over his head as well, and I see that the same now applies to us. I'm honored to be standing together with you here."

"I heartily agree, Tom. This is the type of group I was hoping for. Without a spoken pledge, we've yielded our lives to the cause of true freedom, and away from the tyranny that is now gripping our nation. As Thomas Paine once said during a similar time, 'these are the times that try men's souls.'"

* * *

Dr. Rosen sat at the kitchen table hunched over his newly made cup of tea, a look of sadness etching worry lines on his face. "So, you've decided to go back then?" he asked looking across the table to his daughter.

"I'm all packed." Mira replied, trying to sound upbeat. They had just finished a quiet supper with hardly a word exchanged between them, each lost in their own thoughts.

"Mira, I'm just concerned that…"

"I know, dad." She said, reaching across the table to hold her father's hand. "It's alright. I'll be fine. If nothing else, I just need some closure before I can…" She let the thought hang in the air, not wanting to reveal to her father the other plans she was considering.

"Before you can rest?" He interjected.

"You've been great, dad. You helped me through a really trying time." She walked around the table and hugged her father from behind.

"All right. I give in." He said chuckling, and raised both hands in mock surrender.

"Thanks, dad. I knew you'd understand." Mira walked over to the stove to warm up the teakettle. "Another cup of tea?" she asked.

"No thanks dear. But let's go over to the living room and bask in some of that fireplace glow. Sound good?"

"I'll be right there."

Dr. Rosen took his customary spot on his plush recliner, while Mira curled up under her mother's favorite afghan pullover.

"Dad can I talk to you as Dr. Rosen for a few minutes." She asked.

"Hmm. Sounds serious, but sure, go ahead."

Mira hesitated. She didn't know how to broach the subject, but decided to start at the beginning. "I've been having some strange dreams, and I'm not sure what to make of them." She began and took a sip of her raspberry tea.

"Should I be taking notes?" He teased.

"Dad! Enough with the notes! She playfully scolded. Both laughed.

"Last summer, although it seems like ages ago, I began having dreams that were terrifying, and yet strangely interesting, and even fulfilling."

"That is a strange combination, go on."

"Each of them would start innocently enough, but then erupt into a threatening, sometimes violent scene. The first had this huge black shadow in the middle of a violent thunderstorm ready to pounce on me just as I woke up. Another found me walking through a lovely field of wheat, when a huge dark storm came out of nowhere, threatening to overwhelm me. Then there was the nuclear explosion to the east of the Golan Heights in Israel."

"Nuclear blast! How strange." He replied, now alarmed, and began pulling on his gottee.

"Yet the most bizarre thing of all, dad, is that almost all of these dreams were followed by the haunting words, 'Ninth, Ninth, Ninth.'" She explained, looking off into the fireplace, while wrapping herself tighter in the afghan. "That's the short version. I can fill in some details if you like."

Dr. Rosen stayed silent for a few minutes, and mentally evaluated his daughter's story, while Mira sat quietly, sipped her tea and gazed into the crackling fire.

"I must say, first of all, that what you've relayed to me is not unusual. I've done some work with Early Childhood Trauma Syndrome, and it's possible that you may be suffering from this as well. Recurrent dreams are one of the symptoms of ECTS, but they usually begin and end as nightmares, and seldom start out serenely and then end violently. Then there's the matter of those last words you heard, 'Ninth, Ninth.'" He paused and stroked his beard once again. "That's a tough one. I've never heard of that before."

"So what do you think is wrong with me dad?" She asked with concern.

"Wrong with you? No, there's nothing to worry about dear." He shrugged his shoulders, trying hard not to show his concern. "Your childhood trauma has just now caught up with you is all." He turned to look her in the eye. "It may even be that these dreams will all go away, now that you know something more about your past."

She turned once again to watch the dancing fire, and wanted to believe him, yet, except for the one dream about her running away from someone or something as a child, (could the fact that this dream appeared to be true, validate the others as well?), all the other dreams seemed to portend some imminent danger or disaster. Then there was the cryptic, 'Ninth, Ninth.' *Was it a place, a time? What did it mean?* She wondered once again.

* * *

With the decision to meet each week at different times and places, the meeting at the Snow home broke up; some leaving immediately, while others remained behind, engaging in animated discussions. Jack was just about to collect Marsha and leave, when he heard Jim Hughes calling him.

"Jack, have you got a few minutes? There's something important I'd like to talk to you about." He asked.

"Sure Jim. Marsha's still holding her own with the women in the kitchen, so I guess I'm free."

"Great," he replied, and walked over to the colonel and whispered in his ear. "Tom, can Jack and I use your office for a bit?

"You bet. It's all yours."

Both men walked down the short hall toward the kitchen, and turned left into Tom's office.

"Ahh, this is nice, isn't it?" Jim said, sitting back in the burgundy leather reclining chair. "Quiet, peaceful." He sighed and closed his eyes for a moment. "I'm afraid there will be little of this from now on." He abruptly sat up, and leaned over the desk. "Jack, the country we love and serve is in dire straights tonight. We are being torn apart from within and without. I know I'm preaching to the choir here, but I want to impress upon you the truly perilous condition we face."

"Sir, I appreciate the situation we are in. In fact, when you told us about your last cabinet meeting, and the way the President acted there, it reminded me of the meeting I had with him a few days ago."

"Really, how so?" Jim asked and leaned back again in the chair.

"I assume that you know about the Andy Stern affair?"

"The Russian Republic spy. Yes, I was briefed on that."

"I arranged a meeting with the president, by way of Andy, ironically enough, to forewarn him about some covert activity I had chanced upon.

"The 'cigar band caper' we called it." Jim recalled. Both men laughed.

"When I finally got to meet with him, it was like I was talking to a different man, or maybe, two different men."

"I know exactly what you mean Jack. I had the same feeling at the cabinet meeting. It was like he was fighting himself. He finally gave up and let Bielchek run the rest of the meeting.

"Exactly. I never got a word in edgewise, and when we all left the room, the president turned to me, and in an other-worldly voice, full of malice and hatred, warned me never to try to see him again."

"He's not the president we once knew, Jack, and now we are on opposite sides of the battle for the heart and soul of the republic." He leaned over the desk once again. "Our immediate concern is the looming takeover of our country by the United Nations. I don't know what the timetable for that is, but if I know Stanas, he'll move quickly. The only thing that might slow him down is his plan to move the UN from New York to Rome."

"Move the UN to Rome?" Jack exclaimed in surprise.

"Oh, sorry Jack, I forget that you've been out of the loop for a while. Hush-hush negotiations are under way as we speak. The fear is that with martial law in place, and the threat of violence in the air, the time is right to make the move. Besides, the building itself in New York is in need of a serious overhaul, It will cost billions of dollars, and with the dollar in a tailspin, that amount goes up almost daily. Yeah, I think it's a done deal, Jack; which brings me to the point of our meeting tonight." He said knitting his fingers together on the desk, while fixing his eyes on Jack. "I have a proposition for you." He paused for a moment, lighting the fuse to the bombshell he was about to drop on Jack's unsuspecting lap. "I want you to become the new assistant to our ambassador at the United Nations."

Jack was too stunned to speak, and tried hard to process what he had just heard.

"I know this is sudden, but believe me when I say that it is absolutely essential that we have a man on the inside of the UN who can monitor its movements. Someone who can keep tabs on that wily fox, Stanas." He turned and faced Jack once more. "That man is you."

The room grew silent as Jack weighed the possibilities of what was being offered. On the one hand, the thought of going into government service, and especially clandestine service, (would he be a spy?), produced a thrill that raced up and down his spine. Then there was his logical side. He had his teaching post at Georgetown University. He would have to move to New York City and potentially, *Rome*? What about Marcia? How would she respond?

As if reading his thoughts, Jim began to answer some of his questions. "I know you're probably concerned about your present job, and having to make a move. Let me assure you that you will be able to keep your tenured teaching position at Georgetown, much the same way as when you worked at the White House. As for moving, you'll be able to live in Washington, and maintain a government paid residence in New York. As for the potential move to Rome, ah, we'll have to cross that bridge when we come to it." Jim sat down again and leaned back in his chair.

"How will you be able to get me into the post? Isn't there some kind of confirmation process that has to take place?" He asked.

Jim smiled, and knew that Jack would come onboard. "The ambassadorship goes through confirmation, but assistants are billeted by the State Department, and hence the Secretary of State."

Jack let out a sigh, smiled, and leaned back in his chair. "When do we start?"

CHAPTER 16

"Just as I suspected. The Jordanians are in force at Wadi Musa." Major Azerah observed as he handed the binoculars to Benni. Both men were on a high hill overlooking the town of about two thousand people that took its name from *Ein Musa*, or spring of Moses, on the northeastern edge of town. Tradition held that God created this water source for Moses and the host of Israel, during their wilderness march, prior to entering the Promised Land.

"It's almost dark, and by now I know that you probably have a plan for this situation." Said Benni, smiling.

Major Azerah laughed softly. "So, commander, you've come around to trusting me, eh? A wise move." He joked, took the binoculars from Benni and scanned the town once more. "Let it grow a little darker, there will be no moon tonight, and I'll make my way to the rendezvous with my men.

"You mean, we'll make our way to your men, don't you?"

"No. You'll stay here with my pack. It's too dangerous for both of us to go down." He pulled a long, one-piece, Bedouin *galabia* cloak from his backpack, put it on, tied it in the middle with a sash, and doffed a matching turban or *ihram*. With this outfit and his dark complexion, he could easily pass for a traveling Bedouin.

"*Mazeltov*, Benni, he said and quickly disappeared over the edge of the rocky outcrop.

* * *

He would miss his small apartment, his students, but especially the quiet times of prayer and the reading of the God's Word. The Sanhedrin had passed their judgment…

"…Rabbi Shlomo Berkowitz you have been warned in the past not preach, teach, or make mention of the name "Yeshua," the so-called Mashiach, in all our precincts and jurisdiction. You have steadfastly and stubbornly opposed our ruling, and the laws of our fathers, and continue to practice and teach in this name.

By the majority vote of this council, and the power vested in me, the High Priest of the Sanhedrin, I hereby banish you from the council, and remove herewith all rights and privileges associated with your position as a teacher of Israel. May the Eternal One, *Baruch Ha'Shem*, have mercy on your soul…"

The remembrance of his last official meeting as a Rabbi brought him to prayer. "Oh my Jerusalem," he whispered softly with deep emotion in his voice, "if only you had known the day of your visitation, when your true Mashiach came to you with open arms. Now you are desolate and alone, until another will come as a ravening wolf in sheep's clothing, and will devour you and your children." He sat down heavily in one of the kitchen chairs, and bowed his head. "Father above; you are the Eternal One. Praise and glory be to you now and forever. Let your kingdom come, Lord Yeshua. Save your people Israel. Gather them into your loving arms, and carry them into your kingdom. Omain." He continued for several minutes in reverent prayer, until he heard a knock at the door.

"Nu, come in already." He shouted, and walked to the door, just as Chaim Podhoretz burst through.

"Shlomo, my friend, it's good to see that you are well, and at such a time." He made his way to the kitchen table, and sat in the chair by the window. "A wonder this view, no?" he said looking out at the wall, "and now…no more."

"Nu, the view will still be there, Chaim. Only the one who sees it will be different." Shlomo replied as he walked over to the stove. "Some tea for you my friend? I still have a bit of chala bread if you like?"

"Just the tea would be fine, thank you. So then what will you do now? Where will you go? You're abandoned and alone. Who will care for you?" He asked in a mournful voice.

Reb Berkowitz walked over to the table with the two steaming cups of tea in hand. "So then, who should take care of me, but the one who has always done so, eh? Is it not written in the Psalms, ninety-one I believe,

Because you have made the Lord, who is my refuge, the most High, your habitation; there will no evil befall you.

"True, true, Shlomo." Reb Podhoretz replied, taking a quick sip of his tea. "But will the Eternal One, blessed be the Name, come to your aid when you've been dispossessed by your people? Not that I'm one of those. You know that I am your friend, Shlomo." He stirred another teaspoon of sugar into his cup.

Reb Berkowitz was looking out the window, away in his own thoughts, and didn't respond. "The same Psalm also says, my dear Chaim, that,

he will call on me, and I will answer him: I will be with him in trouble; I will deliver him, and honor him.

"Honor him? Where is the honor in being banished from your people?" He asked with irritation in his voice.

Shlomo acted as if he hadn't heard him. "Did you know that Yeshua was tempted by the evil one by this very Psalm, Chaim?" He continued without waiting for a response. "Just as Eve was tempted by the lust of the eyes, the lust of the flesh and the boastful pride of life, even so, was Yeshua tempted after he had fasted for forty days." He paused to let the thought sink in. "I find that fascinating, don't you?"

"Well, um, I suppose that if one believed in, ah, that sort of thing," he answered uncomfortably. "But really, Shlomo, what are you going to do? Do you even have a place to stay?"

"My friend, in the New Testament book of Rabbi Shaul's letter to the Philippians it says that,

My God shall supply all your needs according to His riches in glory by Christ Jesus.

A beautiful promise, true? Indeed true. He has provided for me because of His love and grace." He got up to warm the kettle on the stove once again. "In fact, my dear Chaim, I hear His supply for my needs coming for me down the hall."

A few moments later a series of small raps were heard at the door.

"Come in, come in, children," Reb Berkowitz replied, happily taking his seat once again.

Two young boys popped through the door, both dressed in long coats and gloves, followed by several men. "Shalom, Rabbi Berkowitz," they both chimed in at once. "We've come to take you to our home, right abba? Said the taller of the two, adressing his father, who followed them through the door, along with several other bearded men?

"Yes, my son." Avram Shmuel, a burly, black-bearded man with a deep baritone voice replied. "With your permission, Rabbi, we've come to move your things for you." He offered, bowing his head. "Rabbi Podhoretz it's good to see you once again."

"Er, yes, Avram, it's been a long time. So, your family is well?" He asked awkwardly.

"As you can see," he replied, putting his large hands on both boys' shoulders. The Lord Yeshua has blessed us with two strong olive saplings. May they grow into strong trees in the service of our Mashiach."

"Oh we will abba," the shorter one said with a smile.

The men laughed at the spontaneous response.

"So, if you'll excuse us, we've got work to do. This way men." Avram led the group into the bedroom where boxes were already prepared to go. Each man grabbed one, the boys each took a smaller one, and all walked out the door.

As he came to the kitchen, Avram paused for a second. "Rabbi Berkowitz, Marta is cooking a special treat tonight in honor of you, so you should bring your appetite with you." He said smiling. "Rabbi Podhoretz, you're welcome to come as well."

"Thank you dear boy," The rabbi replied uncomfortably. "Perhaps another time then."

With that Avram picked up his box, and joined the other men on the street below.

"Nu, Chaim, do you still have any concerns about what will happen to me?"

"Where did you find them?" the Rabbi asked.

"I didn't find them; they found *me*." Shlomo explained and took another sip of tea. "They are part of a messianic group called Congregation Beth Israel. They were in a prayer meeting recently, when one of the members had a burden to pray for a certain rabbi, a believer in Yeshua, who was being banished by the council. They all prayed for me, and then sought me out. Then they immediately took me under their wing, so to speak, and found me a place to stay, and offered me a teaching position in their church."

Chaim was stunned to silence.

"So does Isaiah truly say," Shlomo continued,

They that wait upon the Lord shall renew their strength; they shall mount up with wings as eagles; they shall run, and not be weary; and they shall walk, and not faint.

Rabbi Podhoretz took out his white handkerchief, and mopped his perspiring brow. All he could manage to say was, "Omain."

* * *

Benni awoke as the first rays of sunshine crept over the ridge on his right. He collected himself quickly, scanned the area below him with the major's binoculars, and shook off the early morning cold he felt. Finding that all was clear, he lay back down again, and thought about the dream he had had. They were in two parts. In the first, he was wading in chest-deep water at night, frantically trying to get away from pursuers, who appeared to be closing in on him from behind. Coming to a shore, he ran across a beach and then a field, leading to a dome of light in the distance. Racing forward with incredible speed he gained the edge of the light, and soon found that, in the middle, someone was lying down on a bed of roses. He walked up to the sleeping figure, who was apparently a woman dressed in a long white gown, and saw that it was Monika! He reached down to kiss her, and then the second part of the dream immediately took over.

He was running away from a pursuit again, but this time through a wheat field. He was only a boy, maybe six or seven, but knew that he had to get away or die. He heard gunshots off in the distance, and as he looked back, caught glimpses of a grown woman following after him. He noticed that he was also now a grown man, and that the fields behind him were on fire. "Run! Run fast! He called to the woman behind. When he stopped to allow her to catch up, she had disappeared!

"Nu, commander. All is well?" asked Major Azerah, who had crept in stealthily from the overhanging rock behind Benni.

"Major Houdini, I presume." Benni joked, a bit startled. "How were you able to get behind me without my notice?"

"I had planned on being here just before daybreak, but had to wait until a squad of Jordanian soldiers moved away from their bivouac. After they left, I found a goat trail just outside the city that led in this direction. I followed it and found that it came past our little redoubt here and gave me the protection I needed against discovery. And...I brought presents!" he declared, and pulled out two large flat breads, some dates, goat cheese, and two water bottles from a goatskin bag he was carrying.

"Breakfast Bedouin style! I'm that hungry I could eat a camel." Benni exclaimed.

"These will have to do. We're in short supply of camels these days." The major quipped.

Both men ate vigorously, until all but the water bottles were consumed. "So, Major, what news from the front?"

"The situation is more desperate than I first thought. The small force of Jordanians in Wadi Musa is soon to be reinforced by no less than a combined arms battalion of around five thousand soldiers. From what my men have told me, the pincer movement the Jordanians are applying, is closing in on this area. We have little time to spare." He pulled out some Bedouin clothing from his bag. "Here, put this on. We'll leave what we don't need in the hideout."

Benni quickly changed into his new outfit, which he found to be quite comfortable. "How do I look?" He asked, while crouching under the rocky overhang.

"Like the Israeli sabra that you are, commander." Azerah said smiling. "These disguises will work for us if we happen to get stopped."

"Then, where to from here?"

"My men have already left our safe-house, and are on their way to Petra."

"Petra? *The* Petra?" Benni asked with surprise.

"Yes, we're to meet my men, just before dusk, at the home of a Bedouin friend, not far from the Petra Visitor's Center. One of the men has already gone down into Petra to arrange for a safe place to camp. We'll leave shortly after dawn tomorrow, or the next day, and make our way down to the Theater ruins and meet him there.

"And after that? Benni asked.

"Let's get down to the campsite first, commander, and then we can discuss our next move." He replied, placing the bag over his shoulder.

After scanning the slope leading to the town, and finding it clear, each man slipped around the back of their hideout, and found the goat path leading them to the outskirts of Wadi Musa.

* * *

The band of Yosip bin Saladen's men had quickly broken camp, and turned southwest moving steadily away from the Jordanian troops stationed in Ma'an. After several kilometers, they found the rocky slope where one of the trackers had died, and where they had last found traces of their quarry. Scrambling up the hill like spiders, two other trackers reached the top of the hill, and explored the area. After a few minutes, one of them raced down the slope to bring word to his master. "I beg to report," he said kneeling and bowing to the ground. "We have found the infidel tracks, and also another set of tracks with him."

"So, our desert rat has found a helper." Bin Saladen observed, while flogging his right thigh with his riding crop. How old are the tracks, and in which direction do they lead?" He demanded.

"They are but two days old, and are heading north, my lord." The tracker replied, as bin Saladen dismounted from his horse.

"Mahmoud the map!" Yosip shouted.

Mahmoud came up, and handed the map to his master, who spread it over the back of the still-bowing tracker.

"Where might they be heading?" He asked himself. "The Hashemites are here in the northeast at Ma'an. By now the Jordanian northern army is encamped at Ash Shawbak, here, while the southern group has probably reached Ra's an Naqb." He drew an invisible circle around the three points and found only one place that could provide shelter for the Yahud.

"Wadi Musa!" He declared, and rolled up the map. "Get up Khaleed, and join your brother. You will track the vermin, and report to me at Wadi Musa. We will go on ahead, and find lodgings there close by the mosque. Make haste! There's no time to spare!" He commanded and mounted his horse.

"Your desire is my will, excellency." He said, still bowing, and backed away. In no time, the pair of trackers had scrambled up the hillside, and were hot on the trail.

"*Yallah*! My brothers! We ride to Wadi Musa!" Bin Saladen shouted to his men. He reared his horse, and galloped off to the north, his men following him, leaving a cloud of dust in their wake.

* * *

The Jordanian major saluted the guard, who allowed him to pass, walked into the general's pavilion opening and stood at attention.

"At ease major. You're report?" General Abdullah Husseini, head of the Jordanian Joint Chiefs of Staff asked, without looking up from the large map of Western Jordan spread out before him.

"It has been more than twenty-four hours, and bin Saladen and his band have not reported in, sir." He stood in a relaxed position with his hands clasped behind his back. "I sent a squad to reconnoiter their encampment, and found it empty, with horse tracks running in a southwesterly direction."

"So he has taken the bait then, eh?" General Husseini replied with a wry smile. "I knew that sly fox wouldn't come into our camp in Ma'an." He strode over to the tent opening, the Major following him, and leaned against a support post. "By now he's backtracked to the last place tracks were found for the Israeli, and has sent his trackers off in pursuit." He chuckled and took a long drag from his cigarette. "What he doesn't know is that we are shadowing him and his trackers, until they lead us, like falcons, to our prey. Then, after they have done all the work, we will go in for the kill."

* * *

The two men were slowly walking through the outskirts of Wadi Musa when a Jordanian Land Rover military vehicle, open to the air on all sides, and manned with a fifty-caliber machine gun in the back, skidded to a stop in front of them. A young lieutenant dressed in khaki pants and shirt, and wearing a red and white-checkered kaffiyeh, jumped out of the front passenger side and confronted them.

"Salaam Alaikum." Major Azerah offered, bowing low in his best Bedouin Arabic.

"Alaikum Salaam." Replied the officer gruffly. "Papers?".

"Sir, we are but humble farmers from Wadi al Q'tub, who have come here to buy a few goats for our families. We have had no need as yet for papers of any kind."

"The city is under military control now. You must come with me to our field office where papers will be issued for you." He declard.

"Sir, if you please, we are weary of our journey, and the heat of the day is upon us. May we first find lodgings, refresh ourselves, and then report to you at any time of your choosing?" Benni asked in equally proficient Bedouin Arabic, surprising Major Azerah with his fluency.

The Jordanian major considered their request. He looked them over with a critical eye for a few moments, and then decided. "You have twenty-four hours to report to our office on the north of town. If you fail to keep your appointment, a military warrant will be issued for your arrest." He turned sharply on his heals and took his seat once again in the Land Rover. Both men kept their heads bowed until the vehicle was well out of sight.

"That was close." Benni sighed with relief.

"You gave a good account of yourself, commander. You're Arabic dialect was excellent!" Azerah acknowledged, as both men continued to walk.

"That was one language course that truly paid off." Benni replied. "Now where's that safe house? I wasn't joking when I told the Jordanian that we were weary from the day. I could use something tall and cold right about now."

"It's just down this lane." The major said pointing. "We'll be alone until one of my men comes for us in a day or so, and there will be refreshments and rest for us until then.

"I'll take a large serving of both of those please." Benni joked, and they both laughed.

CHAPTER 17

Mira, with Carla beside her, walked through the double glass doors, and into the tenth floor suite of offices belonging to WKBC, only to find it empty! She gave Carla a questioning look, and saw that she was surprised as well.

"Must be a meeting going on or something." Carla said. They walked past the reception desk on the left, into the large maze of cubicles and desks, and found that these were empty as well.

"Maybe we should come back--"

"Surprise!" Came shouts from every direction. Suddenly the room was alive with administrative staff, reporters and news people, They converged on Mira, who blushed several shades of red, and welcomed her back with hugs and handshakes. After a few moments, Larry Kratzert, Mira's boss, walked over to her, to say a few words.

"Mira, darling, I can say darling because I'm that much older than you," he joked, and hugged her close. "It's obvious that you are well loved, and that you've been missed by all of us. Welcome back! We look forward to great things from you in the future." He reached over and kissed her on the cheek, while applause filled the room. "We've arranged a little reception for you. There's a catered buffet in the back, and quite expensive I might add, so everyone enjoy already!"

A round of cheers and applause erupted as the crowd filed over to the buffet.

"Mira, please meet me in my office when you're done here, okay?" Larry whispered in her ear.

"You're the boss," she said enthusiastically. "Oh, and thank you for all of this. It was totally unexpected." She replied, eyeing Carla, who shrugged her shoulders, and wore sheepish grin.

* * *

After enjoying the buffet and the heartfelt welcome she had received, Mira walked into Larry Kratzert's office, on the 24th floor suite of executive offices. It was much the same as she remembered it. His large, rectangular cherry desk, piled high with newspapers, magazines, and ratings books, was offset by a panoramic view of Central Park, displayed in a floor-to-ceiling row of windows behind him.

"Mira, darling, nice of you to come." He said in his usual nervous way, while clearing some space on his desk.

"It's been awhile Mr. Kratzert." She replied.

"Please, it's Larry." He offered, and shuffled through some of the papers on his desk until he found what he was looking for. He was in a difficult position and didn't like it. Mira had been his "star" when she had been on the news team. After Mira's accident, he had scrambled to find a replacement for her, and fortunately found someone who had since grown to be a celebrity in her own right. There was no room for two celebrities.

"Thank you Larry. I was about to say that it's good to be back, but I'm not sure how long I'll be staying."

"Yes, well…hey, look at our ratings sheet for this month." He replied, handed her a copy of the sheet, and had not comprehended what she had just said. "We're first in our market once again." He noted with pride. "Jason's done a fine job and Sophia Lynd--have you two met by the way? No? Well, she has been a super co-anchor since you were, ah, gone." He paused to think for a moment. "Now what did you say? I thought I heard you say something like you're not sure you'll be staying?"

"Yes that's true. You see, there have been some changes in my life since the, ah, accident." Mira looked down at the floor. It was still difficult for her to deal with what had happened. In fact, although she had finally contacted Marcia and was welcome to come back to their shared apartment, she couldn't go back just yet, and had been staying with Carla since her return. "I just found out that I have a brother living in Israel. Well, he's not there right now; he's a fighter pilot missing in action--"

"Wait, wait!" He put his cigar in a large ashtray. "You've got a brother and you just found out about it?"

"That's right. You see I was born in Israel, and my brother and I were separated during a terrorist attack on our kibbutz when I was about three. Both our parents were killed in the attack, and I was placed for adoption soon after. That's how I came to be in the states."

"So then, you are a Jewish girl after all; a daughter of Israel." He sat back in his chair and smiled. "This is marvelous, marvelous, Mira."

"Thank you, Larry. I'm still adjusting to it all, but it is fascinating. Because of this, my priorities have changed, and I feel like I need to dig into my Jewish roots, and find my brother. So, I won't be coming back to work for you." She said softly but firmly.

Larry Kratzert looked shocked by this news, but was inwardly sighing in relief. A huge weight had been taken off his chest and he could now relax. "I'm very sorry to hear that Mira, very sorry." He replied. "Don't get me wrong, I understand. Family--it's everything. My wife and children, Mira, I would do anything for them. So then, how can I help? Surely there is something I can do for you. Just name it, and I'll do it."

"You're more than generous, Larry. I truly appreciate your willingness to help. Actually I was hoping that you would ask. Last year, at one of our end of the year corporate parties, I met an executive from the Reuters News Agency. He told me that if I ever wanted to work as a foreign correspondent I should look him up. I didn't think much about it at the time, but now the possibility intrigues me, especially if there might be a posting around Israel."

Kratzert leaned forward and consided what he had just heard. "I've got it darling. Let me make a few phone calls, okay?" I know some people, and maybe we can put something together." He stood up and walked over to her.

Mira stood up and hugged him. "Thank you Larry. You've been great to work for. I somehow knew you'd understand." She reached up and kissed him on the cheek.

"A daughter of Israel, wanting to make an ascent, an *aliya*, to the homeland?" He patted her on the back. "I'm there for you, kid.

* * *

He walked through the pneumatic glass doors of the Secretariat Building in the United Nations complex, and took an elevator to the twenty-fifth floor. As the doors of the elevator opened, he was greeted by two athletic looking Marine Corps guards, who checked the identification badge pinned to Jack's left blue blazer pocket, against an authorized personnel list found on a hand held computer. When Jack's name appeared, the authorizing guard saluted, while the other escorted him to the reception area.

Jack sat down in one of the leather office chairs and looked at his watch. It was 9:00 a.m., and he was on time. *"But on time for what?"* he wondered. *"I don't even know what I'm going to be doing here, except, of course, keeping an eye on Stanas' business."* It was the "not knowing" that bothered him. He would have liked to know all the details about his position beforehand, so that he could be properly prepared. *"Well I suppose the ambassador with fill me in."* he thought.

"Jack Quinn." said a tired looking, gray-haired, bespectacled man, in his early seventies. As soon as he got Jack's attention he reversed direction, and headed back into the suite of offices, expecting Jack to follow him.

"I guess that must be me," Jack quipped, following close behind. The two men zigzagged through a maze of cubicles, until they reached the northeastern corner of the building where the office of the United States Ambassador was located. Jack sat down in one of two chairs sitting in front of a large oak desk, and noticed that behind the man sitting in the brown leather swivel chair, (is this the ambassador?), was a view of the East River and the borough of the Queens beyond.

"I don't know what Jim was thinking about when he sent you to me." The ambassador huffed without looking up. He found a file he was looking for on his cluttered desk, opened it, and began reading. "Says here that you were a counsel to the president, before he gave you the boot. Tenured professor at Georgetown, graduated Magna Cum Laude from

Brown University, impressive, Mr. Quinn." The ambassador paused and put down the file. "What it doesn't show me is whether or not you have any diplomatic experience to speak of." He leaned back in his chair and folded his arms behind his neck. "So what are you doing here, Mr. Quinn?

Jack was taken aback by the ambassador's less than cordial manner. "Could we start at the beginning? Hi, I'm Jack Quinn and you are, sir?" He reached across the desk to shake hands.

"Thomas Stanton, US ambassador to the UN." He replied dryly. He shook Jack's hand, and then quickly withdrew it.

"Thank you, Mr. Ambassador. To answer your question, Jim Hughes thought you could use a hand here, especially with all that's happening in our country. I agreed to come on board, and here I am." He sat back and crossed his legs.

"Well that's just like him, isn't it? Never bothered to discuss it with me though. He pops in here, and takes over the show when he pleases, and now sends me a greenhorn to train up. As if I didn't have enough on my plate." He groused, never looking at Jack, who sat quietly, uncomfortable with the ambassador's unprofessional diatribe against a man Jack respected and admired. "Not much I can do about it, I guess." The ambassador sighed. "I've got an office for you close by me here," he pointed to his left, "get yourself settled in and--"

"--Ambassador Stanton, the Secretary General and aide are in the reception area, and he would like a word with you sir." the Marine guard stated over the intercom.

"I'll be right there," the ambassador replied, surprised by the news.

"Jack, you'd better come with me. It's a good time to introduce you to Ilya Stanas, the secretary general." He said nervously.

Both men weaved their way through the office, and into the reception area, where Stanas and an aide were waiting. "Your excellency, what an unexpected pleasure." Ambassador Stanton gushed, while reaching out to shake hands.

Jack stood beside the ambassador, and sized-up the man who had quickly become one of the most powerful men in the world. Stanas stood about six-foot two, somewhat on the thin side, with angular, intense, facial features, that easily formed into a broad smile, and had a prominent, yet distinguished nose. His wavy black hair was meticulously well groomed, and was complemented by the charcoal gray, tailored suit he wore.

"The pleasure is all mine, my friend." Stanas replied. "I trust this in not an intrusion?"

"Not at all excellency. It gives me the opportunity to introduce a new addition to my staff. May I present Mr. Jack Quinn, a senior analyst, and deputy ambassador to our mission here."

"Sir, it is a privilege to meet you." Jack said, while firmly shaking his hand. The sense of raw power eminating from Stanas almost took his breath away.

The Secretary General looked long and hard into Jack's eyes, as if he were examining his very soul, unnerving him by doing so, while holding Jack's right hand in both of his own. "You are the Jack Quinn who was at one time senior counsel to President Williams, yes? Stanas asked in a barely discernable accent, finally yielding Jack's hand, but still looking into his eyes.

"Yes sir, that's correct." Jack allowed, barely keeping his composure. "I had the distinct priviledge of serving the president, and our country, in that capacity."

"Splendid! We have a true patriot here." He gushed, and then turned his attention back to the ambassador. "You must be excited to have such a valuable asset at your disposal, Mr. Stanton."

He turned back to Jack once more, and spoke in a gently threatening voice. "We'll be watching you with great interest, Mr. Quinn. I'm sure that you will be a credit to all of us, and to the mission of the United Nations."

He turned to leave, followed closely by his aide.

"Ah, excuse me, your Excellency? The ambassador called out. "Was there something you came here to talk to me about?"

Stanas turned sharply on his heel and smiled. "I came to meet your new protégé, ambassador; and so I have." He replied, eyed both men with a bemused look on his face, and walked into the elevator.

Jack walked back to his new office, sat behind his desk, and was visibly shaken. He had never met anyone like Ilya Stanas, and it totally unnerved him. On the one hand, he felt an intoxicating exhilaration at being in Stanas' presence, on the other hand, an incomprehensible fear and dread.

"I will have to be very careful in my future dealings with this very dangerous man."

* * *

Great, black clouds loomed over the heights of the mountains. As she focused on them, she realized that they weren't clouds at all, but thick plumes of smoke billowing from somewhere in the distance. Lightning and thunder lit up the sky roundabout her--or so it seemed, but they were actually the bright flashes and sounds of explosions in the distance. Then she saw large burning embers, like you might see raining down after fireworks show; only these were huge, and seemed to come from everywhere.

"This is the sound of warfare," she realized, bracing herself from the cold that blew in from the direction of the battle.

In the now gale force wind she heard a sound like a voice…*"Ninth of… ninth of…NINTH OF AV!"*

Mira awoke to the sound of her vis-a-phone ringing. She jumped out of bed, and noticed that the alarm clock by her bed stand read six-thirty in the morning. She answered with a weary, "Hello."

"Mira darling, Larry Kratzert here. Did I wake you? Of course I woke you, but this is urgent, okay? I've set up an appointment for you this morning at 10:00 a.m. I found out at a dinner party last night--oh, by the way the shrimp bisque was superb-- that a foreign correspondent billet is opening up at a new communications company called Global Satellite Network. I'm not sure about the position, or if it will include Israel, but the Mid-East is definitely in the mix. I told Harold Klein, the CEO, he's getting his seed money from some overblown Euro consortium, that I have someone for him that will knock his socks off. So, go sell yourself, darling, and let me know how it turned out, okay? Great talking with you, kiddo."

"Larry--wait! What's the address?" she asked, still trying to digest all that he had just said.

"Oh, of course, I'm that *meshuggah*, crackbrained, this morning. I haven't had my first cup of coffee yet; it's that early for me as well. I'm sending it to your phone right now.

"Great. Thank you so much, this means a lot to me."

"No problem Mira darling. Talk to you later. Ciao."

Mira sat back in the chair, and began to mentally prepare for her upcoming meeting. Suddenly she remembered her dream. *"Ninth of Av, or is it Ave? Ninth Ave? It doesn't make any sense...*No time to think about it now, though. I've got work to do," she chirped,

* * *

Mira burst through the doors of the tenth floor WKBC offices, and found Carla glued to her computer screen.

"Carla, we've got to talk!" She said excitedly.

"Oh, Mira, um...sure," she responded in a distracted voice. "Hold on--did you get the job?"

"Can you take a break? I'll explain it all to you. Mira replied, barely able to conceal her excitement.

Carla thought for a moment, and then logged off of her computer. "Mary, can you cover for me for a few?" She asked one of her co-workers.

"No problem. Go for it."

Both women walked hurriedly down the corridor, and took the elevator to the first floor commissary. Mira bought herself a herbal tea and a coffee for Carla, and both walked briskly over to a sun drenched table by a window.

"So what happened?" asked Carla nervously. She knew that Mira had interviewed for a foreign news bureau position, and the thought of it made her cringe. She loved Mira like a daughter, and could not bear to think of her thousands of miles away. "By the look on your face, I'd say it was something good."

Mira leaned forward excitedly. "Carla, I got the job!" she almost shouted. "Can you believe it? Not only that, but GSN is going to open an office in...guess where?"

"New York City, I hope." She answered sadly, while looking down at her cup.

"No silly. The land of my dreams. Tel Aviv, Israel! Carla, Israel! Isn't that the best?" She gushed, but noticed that Carla, rather than being happy for her, was saddened by the news. She leaned forward again, her right hand reaching out to gently touch Carla's arm, and saw that tears were welling up in her eyes. "Carla dear, what's wrong?"

"Oh, it's nothing," she lied, and reached into her handbag for a handkerchief to wipe away her tears, and blow her now reddened nose. "I thought I'd lost you once, but I don't know if I can go through it again." She said, sobbing.

"Dear Carla," Mira consoled, while lovingly stroking her arm. "I didn't tell you the best part. I'll be in need of an administrative assistant, and I thought that maybe you would, ah, recommend someone who might be interested in the position."

"Hah! I'm the only one that could put up with the likes of you." She shot back, while wiping her fogged wire-rim glasses with her napkin. "But my job, my apartment—Yikes! My cats!"

"It's okay. It will take a little time to set up the news bureau in Israel so there's no rush. Just tell me that you will go with me." She pleaded, as tears welled up in her eyes. "You see, I also lost you once, and I don't want to go through that again either."

Carla, a new round of tears filling her eyes, reached across the table and hugged her. "I'll always be there for you, Mira.

CHAPTER 18

The men awoke to a knock at the door: three short raps, two long, and two more short ones. Major Azerah slowly opened the door, and saw Levi, dressed as a Bedouin, standing at the door, and quickly let him in, while checking to the right and left to make sure he hadn't been followed.

"Shalom. All is in readiness at Petra. We can leave whenever you're ready."

"We should leave immediately," Azerah answered. "I learned yesterday that the main body of Jordanian troops will be in place by tomorrow. An advance battalion is already here, preparing for the arrival of the main body."

Levi packed the three goatskins with food and water for the trip, and the three men slipped out of their hideout into the predawn darkness. They followed the road for a kilometer or so until they came to the Petra Visitor's Center. There, the road narrowed into a wide lane, enough for two people to walk side by side. The trail, lightened by the early morning sunshine, eventually weaved its way through dark, towering walls of multi-layered red and pink sandstone, called the Siq. It soon became a narrow path that ended at the foot of El-Khazneh, the awe inspiring Treasury Building, carved out by Nabatean and Egyptian stone masons, some twenty-five hundred years ago.

"This is incredible." Benni exclaimed in wonder. "I've seen pictures of this building, but they don't do it justice. Look at the detailed stonework."

"Legend has it that the Treasury was so-named, because the Nabateans, who inhabited this area, buried large amounts of treasure somewhere inside the building, prior to the Roman occupation in 106 A.D." Major Azerah explained. "The myth has slowly died with the passing of time, but some of the locals still believe that one day the treasure will be found."

"Perhaps the treasure will be of another sort." Benni interjected cryptically.

"What do you mean commander?" Asked the major.

"I don't know. It's silly really, but the thought just gripped me that another kind of treasure may one day be found here."

Levi and the major looked at each other. "Nu, Levi, we have a prophet in our midst." The three men laughed.

The small cart path they had followed through the Siq, now gradually widened into a large flat plain. On the left, built into the tall cliffs, was the "Street of Facades." The facades, or false fronts, are four setback rows of large, flat-faced, unadorned, rock-hewn buildings, built one on top of another, and separated by a narrow road leading up to each section.

"There's the theater," Levi said, pointing to the eroded, semi-circular rows of seats built into the hillside, on their left. "We're to meet Natan in one of the caves above and to the left," he explained. He lead the men through the plaza, and up through the rows of seats. On the top row of the theater, they paused for a few moments, making sure they weren't seen, and then followed a small pathway past several tomb niches built into the rock walls, until they came to a large cave opening.

"Shalom!" came a cheerful greeting from deep inside the cave. A moment later a bright light from a lantern appeared, illuminating the face of Natan Hertzel, who had been standing watch.

"The others are posted?" the major asked.

"Yes sir." Natan replied, coming to attention. "Yochanan is just above us here, and Caleb is watching over the site we'll be going to next."

"Has the communication link to command been established?"

"We are in active communication with the FO-9 command in Detanya, sir."

"Very well. Let's move on to our bivouac site. Natan, lead the way."

The four men carefully slipped out of the cave, down the rows of seats, and onto the plaza. They stayed to the left hand side of the broad plain, turned sharply around a towering outcrop, and proceded down a narrow ravine, that contained a series of tombs known as the Garden Temple Complex. Here, after climbing up a winding path along the rock face, they found the large cave that Levi and Natan had previously discovered.

"This will do well, men." The major allowed, while putting on a communication headset.

"Caleb, Yochanan. Comm-check, over."

"Site Alef, Caleb, five by five, over."

"Site Bet, Yochanan, five by five, over."

"Very well, men. Be vigilant. We don't know what to expect. Over, and out."

* * *

"The infidels have been here my prince," one of the trackers proposed. "We have discovered a cave nearby, and have found their clothing." He bowed low, and produced Major Azerah's backpack.

"How long ago?" asked bin Saladen impatiently, while sitting on his horse and rifling through the backpack.

"The tracks leading from the cave tell us that they were here a few days ago, and continue to Wadi Musa."

"Sons of dogs!" He spit, and threw the backpack to the ground. "Too much time! Get me the map!"

Mahmoud ran up to him, bowed down on one knee beside the prostrate tracker, and held the map out at arms length.

Bin Saladen seized the map and then struck Mahmoud in the back with his riding crop. "It is your fault!" He shouted, and pointed the crop at his men. "There is no more room for failure. Allah will not hear of it, do you understand? We will find these desert monkeys, and my father will have his pleasure with them! *Insh' Allah!*"

"*Insh' Allah!*" the men shouted back.

"Get up Mahmoud, and hold the map for me," he commanded. Yosip's servant quickly complied.

"Where do you go, my frightened monkeys?" He hissed, looking intently at the map. "*The Jordanians now hold Wadi Musa. Then, there is only Petra. But why go there?*" He asked himself, and began pacing back and forth while his men waited. "*Perhaps they are hiding, and will wait until the troops withdraw? Yes, that is it then. They are holed up like desert rats, waiting for the heat of the day to cease.*"

He took the map out of Mahmoud's hands, rolled it up, gave it back to him, and mounted his horse. "*We will wait for you to come out of your hole and then swoop down like a falcon to it its prey,*" bin Saladen thought to himself, a fiendish smile crossing his face. "*This is the will of Allah!*"

* * *

"General Hussieni, I wish to report." Declared the khaki-clad intelligence officer, standing at attention. He wore the red and white, checkered kaffiyeh, with the black agal of the Jordanian officer corps.

"At ease major," replied the general, who was sitting behind his desk at the El-Arish Hotel conference room in Wadi Musa. His force of five thousand men had now combined with several other mechanized units from the south and west, and had formed a cordon around Petra. His pursuit of the Israeli group was now in its final stages. "Proceed with your report."

"Yosip bin Saladen and his band are in Wadi Musa, staying with a local contact of theirs. It is unclear at this time what their intentions are, but our best estimate is that they will move into Petra."

"Very well, then. Relax the guard at the visitor's center and the Siq, so that they may have undisturbed passage, but have your men posted along the way to keep track of their movements. We will catch them and the Israeli's in one large net." He stood and pointed to Petra on his map. "It's time we ended this fox and hounds chase."

* * *

He sat on his bed and smiled, as he looked around the small ten-foot by eight-foot room provided for him by Avram Shmuel. By loving design, it was very much like the bedroom he had in his flat overlooking the

Western Wall. Only a single window looked out at the now darkened, flagstone-paved plaza of the Jewish Quarter of Old Jerusalem.

"Thank you, Almighty Father, for your care and provision." Reb Berkowitz prayed, falling to his knees beside the bed. "And bless the house of Avram Shmuel, and his wonderful family for their love and concern for me." He paused for a moment, and felt a burden to pray for Benni, his nephew. "Nu, there is trouble for Benni, dear Lord. He is in a tight place, true? Yet there is no place too tight for you, *Jehovah Jireh*, God our provider. I am reminded of your promise in the book of Isaiah:

They that wait on the Lord, shall renew their strength; they shall mount up with wings of eagles...

"'*With wings of eagles...*'" he reflected for a moment, and then continued his prayer. "Lord comfort, Lord strengthen, Lord return him and those with him, back into the bosom of your people Israel. Omain."

He would continue in prayer for the next two hours.

* * *

The men saddled their horses sometime after midnight, under the gaze of a full moon. Their plan was to overwhelm the Jordanian guard at the beginning of Al-Siq, ride into Petra, and find a suitable hideout among the ruins before dawn.

Yosip looked up, pointed at the crescent moon, and made an announcement to his men. "Allah looks down on us in favor of our pursuit. Let us complete the task, and return victorious to our wives and children. *Yallah* brothers!"

They galloped to the visitor's center, only to find that it was unguarded. Yosip and his men reigned in their horses, and scouted the area for a possible trap.

Two of his trackers rode up hastily to report to him. "There are no soldiers here, my prince."

"Strange...no guard?" thought Yosip to himself. "*I will consider this later. For now we must make haste.*" With that he spurred his horse down the trail, while his men followed. They rode, single file, past the ghostly Djin Blocks on the right, the Obelisk tomb on the left, and then through the Siq, to El-Khazneh, the Treasury building. Even by moonlight the building was impressive; a sight none of the men, including bin Saladen, had ever seen before.

As they rode slowly on through the wide plain before them, Yosip marveled at the multitude of darkened caves, cut into the sides of the hills on either side of them. *"They could be anywhere!"* He said to himself in anger, but would not let his men see his concern.

Taking the right hand side of the plain, they turned around the corner and came to the Silk Tomb, remarkable for the swirls of multi-colored rock that made up its ornate façade. Yosip decided, after sending two of his reluctant men to search it out, to make it his camp.

"Mahmood, send out two of the trackers, and set a watch. The others can find rest within the caves." He commanded.

"I live to serve you, my prince." He replied, bowing low.

"In the morning we'll flush them out!" boasted bin Saladen. Inwardly, though, he was daunted by the task, realizing that even if he had a thousand men, it would take weeks to track them down in this place.

* * *

Benni woke up with a start, and heard Major Azerah talking with Levi nearby. "I'm positive major. They arrived sometime in the night and their scouts are searching us out as we speak."

"Who are 'they'?" Benni asked moving over to where Major Azerah and Levi sat.

"Good morning, or should I say good afternoon, commander. I see that Petra agrees with you." The major smiled.

"Is it really afternoon?" asked Benni, rubbing his bearded face.

"Yes, almost one in the afternoon. You slept like one of these ancient rocks."

"Must be the inspiration from all of these tombs." Benni quipped, while yawning. So we're in trouble again, eh?"

"Levi spotted some men on the other side of the plain scouting out the various buildings. I believe that they are from the same group that has been chasing us all over the countryside. They tracked us here, and are now actively searching for us. Fortunately they are camped opposite us, so it will take some time for them to make their way here."

The major handed Benni a small burlap bag that contained a breakfast of flatbread, a slab of goat cheese, and a piece of goat meat.

"Thanks, but I'm not hungry."

"Nevertheless, you should eat while you can. We may have to move out at a moments notice, and a full stomach would be most appreciated in that case."

"I see your point." Benni acknowledged, while reaching into the bag for some cheese. "What do we do now?"

"We sit tight, keep an eye on them, and make arrangements with central command for an extraction. Things are starting to get a little crowded here, wouldn't you agree?"

"By your life major, that's the best news I've heard in some time. The sooner we leave here the better." Benni agreed, and saluted him with a bottle of water.

*　*　*

Late in the afternoon, and bored by the inactivity, Major Azerah seemed to have everything well in control, Benni decided to explore the depths of the Garden Temple building. The large area just inside the columned opening, called a *triclinium,* or banquet hall, was where the men had camped out for the night. There were several other passages branching off from the hall, and he decided it might be fun, and potentially helpful, if he explored a few of these. Flashlight in hand, he took the first of these tunnels, and found that it housed several burial niches, and soon ended in a dead end. The next one was much longer, winding first left and then right, and contained many of the same type of niches, all of them rifled through, presumably in the pursuit of treasure.

"What's this?" he wondered out loud, his voice echoing down the tunnel. He looked down a straight section of the pathway and saw a large number of boxes stacked neatly in a row, one on top of another. The sight of them was such an anomaly, that it stopped him dead in his tracks for a few moments. He finally walked over to the first stack of three boxes, and opened the top one, to see what might be inside.

"Books? What are books doing in a cave, and in Petra of all places?" He lifted one of them, peeled off the brown paper wrapper, and found that it was a bible! Not only a bible, but a Christian bible! (He had examined one of these in a bookstore many years ago). He looked at the first page, and found that someone had written a note in English, in an old style of handwriting:

To the Children of Israel
May this bible bring you comfort and
Understanding in your time of need!

Benni was dumbfounded. "What does it mean, time of need? Why was this written to the children of Israel, and why here?" He didn't have an answer. It was a mystery, wrapped, like these bibles, inside an enigma. He quickly rewrapped the bible into its package, placed it back in the box, and walked quickly back down the tunnel. He went a few paces, turned back, walked to the opened box, and took the bible he had just put down. *"I'll keep this to myself for now. Perhaps when I've had time to think…"*

CHAPTER 19

Jack checked his watch again as he mounted the steps of St. Stevens Church in College Park, Maryland. *"It wouldn't do to be late for this appointment."* He said to himself as he entered through one of the two large oak doors, then into the vestibule, where he knelt quickly, dipped his right hand in bowl of holy water, and made the sign of the cross. After catching his breath, and adjusting his tie and coat, he nervously opened the door to the sanctuary, and walked down the aisle to the steps leading up to the altar. He stepped onto the platform and shook hands with Jim Hughes, who was also nattily dressed in a black tuxedo and tie. "Glad you could make it." Jim joked.

"I'm not so sure I am." Jack replied with a grin, while turning around to face the small gathering in the front section of pews.

"You'll be fine. The butterflies will go away after the first year or so." Jim quipped, patting him on the back. "Quickly Jack, any news from Stanas' crowd on the United Nations' takeover of the U.S.?"

"Um..." He reached into his inside pocket, his hands visibly shaking, and handed Jim an envelope. "That's my report. You'll find that the UN is well along the road to setting up an interim government with a view to an eventual North American Union."

"Great work Jack. We'll meet again when you get back from your honeymoon. I just wish you'd take more than just three days."

Just then the organist struck the first note, and through the double doors came the procession of cute little flower bearers and three bridesmaids dressed in different hues of pastel, full-length gowns, walking slowly to the tune of *Here Comes the Bride*. Jack noted with a smile that Mira Rosen was the lead bridesmaid. Although he didn't know Mira, he knew that she was a special person to Marcia, and was happy that she was able to attend the wedding even as she was soon to depart for her new job in Israel.

He lost focus and his breath when he saw Marcia, beautifully hidden in a cloud of white, step through the doors. From that moment on he was entranced by her, and the rest of the ceremony became a blur. He recalled saying "I do" at some point, placing the ring on her finger, and hearing the words, "I now pronounce you man and wife". Then the majestic "kiss," and a hailstorm of rice and confetti tossed at them as they ran to their waiting limousine.

Alone in the backseat, Jack took Marcia in his arms and lovingly embraced her. "Hello, Mrs. Quinn," he said holding her in his arms, and gently brushing her hair from her face.

"Hello, Mr. Quinn," she answered with a contented smile. "I guess you're stuck with me now."

"One lifetime will hardly be enough." He replied, as he reached down and kissed her again.

........*

"So, Miz important foreign correspondent, are you all packed then?" Dr. Rosen asked brightly, trying to dispel the somber mood.

"Yes, I believe I've got everything. I might write you to send some other things if I think of anything; like yourself maybe?" She smiled and hugged her father close.

He held her and affectionately patted her head. "I know dear. I've always wanted to visit Israel. Perhaps one day you'll find me at your doorstep."

He kissed her on the top of her head. "So then it's off to the airport for us. The traffic and all the extra security these days, make for long delays.

Mira looked around the house, making a mental image of each room, the sights and the smells, and somehow knew that she would never see them again.

The drive to the airport was a quiet one; both Mira and her father were lost in their own thoughts. The causeway leading to Reagan National Airport came too soon, and before she knew it, her father was giving her bags to a handler, and she was saying goodbye.

"I love you, dad. Will you email me from time to time? I know how much you hate the computer."

"I'll make an exception in your case." He offered with sadness.

They both hugged for some time, tears forming in their eyes, and then Mira was off to face the security check ordeal, and then the boarding of her plane, Delta Airlines, flight 6550, to New York's JFK airport.

Arriving in New York, she deplaned into the always busy airport concourse, where she found an information kiosk, entered her El Al Airlines flight number into the computer, and was given a printout showing step by step directions on how to proceed to the proper gate. She followed the map, went through another round of even tighter security, featuring a sit-down chat with an Israeli security official, and then proceeded to her gate, and finally boarded the El Al jumbo jet.

"Now I begin a new life in Israel." She said to herself excitedly, and then turned serious. "God, if you are there, take care of my brother, and bring him back safely to me."

CHAPTER 20

This is our position as it stands," Major Azerah stated, while drawing a large oblong circle on the sand floor of the triclinium. Five of the six men were in attendance, while Yochanan stood watch on the heights above them. "As you can see, Petra is like a large bowl, or more like the shape of a kidney. We are here," he pointed with the stick, "in the middle right of the plain. Our enemy, fortunately, has taken shelter to the north of us, here. Between us, splitting the kidney in half is the Collonaded Street." He drew a line, from left to right, across the middle of the drawing. "To the west, at the end of the street, are a series of rock hewn gravesites known as the Unfinished Tombs. My plan is to maintain our present position, keeping our sniper post in the rocks above us, and establish another posting, that would be you Caleb, in the Tombs." All the men nodded their agreement. "That gives us a triangulating crossfire solution for anyone crossing the Collonaded Street. We'll put the plan into effect straightaway. Our advantage is that we've stocked enough food and water for a prolonged siege, if necessary. Our enemy may not be as fortunate. They have horses. The horses will need water, and there is no water to be had in Petra. They will eventually have to go back to Wadi Musa, and perhaps be captured by the Jordanians.

"Sir, how long do you expect us to have to hold our position before help arrives?" asked Natan.

"Central Command has informed me that they will evacuate us in force at 2200 hours tomorrow."

A buzz of excitement went around the men.

"Sir, should the enemy cross the Collonaded Street, are we authorized to use deadly force?" Caleb asked.

"We will warn them off with a shot at their feet. If they persist, it will be shoot to kill."

"How many men are on the other side, Major?" Benni wondered.

Major Azerah looked at Natan for the answer. "We've counted twenty-one horses commander, one of them being the white horse of a prince."

"Any other questions?" The major asked, looking from face to face. "Then you're dismissed." He erased the map with his sandals.

"What would you have me to do major? I'd like to help." Benni offered.

He pulled out a 9 mm pistol from one of the supply bags and two extra magazines, and handed them to Benni. "For now, you are to lay low, but you may need to use this before we're done."

* * *

"My prince," whispered one of Yosip bin Saladen's trackers, while kneeling down in the sand, and bowing low to the ground.

"Speak Yusef, and be quick about it." He replied impatiently, whipping the side of his ornate chair with his riding crop.

"We have combed the entire area north of the street of columns, and have found no sign of the infidel, my master."

Bin Saladen stood up, and walked to the large opening of the Silk Tomb. The sun had already set in the west, leaving in its wake a brilliant display of orange and red colors in the sky. Yosip sighed. *"My father, may Allah bless and keep him, watches the same sky. How I long kneel beside him during the time of the evening prayer, and fight with him again in holy jihad."*

"Get up Yusef, station guards at key points, and gather the rest of the men together for evening prayer. We will strike out again at dawn, and see if we may trap these jackals in their lair."

"Your wish is my desire, my prince." He bowed low, and walked backward through the tomb entrance.

The men filed out of the cave, spread their prayer rugs on the sandy ground facing toward Mecca, and bowed down in prayer.

Several hundred yards away, using high-powered binoculars, Caleb watched the scene from the Unfinished Tombs.

* * *

The night was all but spent, as dawn approached. Benni had not slept, and though his eyes were heavy, he urged the day to come quickly and deliverance with it. He was not alone in his vigil. Major Azerah had also forfeited his sleep, kept two of the watches, and was in hourly communication with his watchstanders.

"Nu, Benni, how would you like to go on a little field trip with me?" He offered, smiling.

"What do you have in mind, major? A little sightseeing before we go, maybe?"

"Hah! In a way, yes." He replied, half-joking. "Caleb has just reported that all but three of the enemy has gone off toward the Siq, evidently to continue the search for us." He let that sink in to see if Benni would pick up on the implications of what he had just said.

"So, you're in the mood for some hunting then, I take it"?

"You're too quick for me commander." the major replied laughing. "Let's just say that it's time for the fox to turn on the hounds."

Major Azerah and Benni painted their faces black with charcoal, donned their remote headset mikes and black knitted caps, and stepped out into the cold night. The sky was overcast, so their movements would be difficult to detect. Caleb, watching the enemy with high-power night vision binoculars, had alerted the major that one of the three remaining men was standing watch outside the Silk tomb, while the other two were presumably sleeping inside.

They kept close to the spiny ridge on their right until they came to the point where the slope ran off to the right towards the theater and further on to the Siq.

"Site Alef, Bet, we're at the point of the ridge about three hundred yards across from the tomb, over.

"Site Alef reports all clear, over."

"Site Bet reports the outside guard is sitting down, and may be asleep by the time you get there." Levi reported, stifling a laugh. "No other contacts to report, over."

The two men crouched low and moved warily across the plain listening intently for any sound coming from their right. In a few minutes they came under the sheltering arms of the far ridgeline, and ducked behind the ruins of the Corinthian Tomb, just north of the Silk Tomb. Peering around the edge of some crumbling sandstone, Major Azerah saw that the guard, only fifty feet away, had indeed fallen asleep and was loudly snoring. He took his first step around the wall, when another guard came out of the cave, kicked the sleeping watchman, cursing him with an Arabic oath, and took his place, and sent the other one back into the cave.

Both men hustlled back to the cover of the wall and sat down. "We'll have to wait until the new guard has settled in." Major Azerah whispered.

Benni nodded. "Understood." He leaned back against the wall, and wondered what the next hour would bring.

* * *

It was five in the morning in Jerusalem when Reb Berkowitz abruptly woke up.

"Nu, I'm up my Father. What is your will?" He prayed with half-closed eyes.

"Benni? B'Seder, Adonai." He settled on his knees beside his bed, stayed in prayer until released by the Lord, and fell asleep once again.

* * *

The first light of dawn turned the overcast darkness into a murky gray, matching the mood of Major Azerah. He moved closer to the wall of the Corinthian Tomb and contacted his men. "Alef, Bet, report." He whispered.

"Site Alef, holding no contacts, over."

"Site Bet, guard at the Silk Tomb still alert. No other contacts to report. It's like the search party was swallowed up, over."

"Site Bet, we'll have to move out soon. Let me know when an opening against the guard opens up. We'll be standing by, over."

"Will do, out."

Azerah walked over to Benni who was keeping watch beside the sandstone wall. "We'll have take action soon commander, before the light defeats us." He whispered, gesturing with his hands for effect. "When we move out, follow behind me. I'll make for the guard, while you run left into the cave mouth with your gun drawn. There should be just two of them, and they will probably be sleeping. I'll join you after I've disabled the guard, understood?"

Benni nodded. Up to this point he hadn't really known what they were going to do. He thought that they might be collecting intelligence. He now realized that their mission was more serious than that. They were going after hostages.

The major took up his position at the end of the wall, and watched. Several minutes passed, while the light increased to where he could clearly make out the guard.

Suddenly, site Bet reported in: "Major--go!"

The two men burst into the open, Major Azerah running at top speed toward the guard, who had his back to him, and was relieving himself against the far wall of stone.

Benni, his heart racing, sprinted for the dark opening of the Silk Tomb, and, using his flashlight, quickly found the two sleeping men, who were covered in blankets and spread out on carpets. He held his position with his pistol at the ready, until the major came in with the guard.

"Commander, tie his hands behind him." Azerah directed, his voice shaking a bit from the adrenaline rush of action, while handing him a few large plastic zip ties. He then picked up a rifle lying next to the sleeping guard, and Bin Saladen's *jambia,* his curved knife, and then kicked him enough to wake him up.

Bin Saladen awoke with a start; a look of defiance etched on his face, and immediately realized that he had been captured.

"By my life we meet again, Yosip bin Saladen." Benni remarked, as he crouched down beside him. "The last time we met you had your foot on my neck, I believe. Now you are caught in the snare of the Yahud."

They led Yosip and his two men across the plain, and up the steps of the Garden Tomb, where Chaim was standing guard. Once inside, Major Azerah led his captives to the far end of the triclinium, and sat them down in the sand against the wall.

"Yahud pigs! Kill us quickly, our paradise awaits us!" Bin Saladen spat out in anger.

"We're not going to kill you." Azerah replied in perfect Arabic, while crouching in front of his adversary. "Let's just say that you're under our protection for the time being."

"Because you speak well the language of the Prophet, blessed is he, do not think that we will show mercy when we overcome you. My men will soon return, and turn over every stone until we are delivered into their hands. It would be better if you surrendered to us now." He replied defiantly.

"It's odd then, isn't it, that my lookouts can't seem to find your men anywhere. What do you suppose happened to them?" Azerah asked with a look of mock concern. "Maybe they're lost, or maybe...the Jordanians have found them, eh?"

"You lie! A thousand curses be upon you and the Yahud! Here me well, infidel! My men will find me, and you will not live to see another day with your head in its place! Yosip struggled to stand up, but was restrained by the plastic ties Natan had wrapped around his hands and ankles.

The three Israelis walked a short distance away, so as not to be overheard. "Natan," the major began, "give them water and food, if they will take it, and then try to find out what happened to the rest if his men. We have to know what we're up against before we give the final go-ahead for our evac."

* * *

"Site Bet, Yochanan sir, still no movement from the direction of the Treasury, or the Siq. It's like they've disappeared."

"Very well. Let me know if anything changes." Azerah answered wearily, having just woken up from a very short nap. He stood up, stretched, and looked at his watch, noting that it was now a little before noon. *"Where are bin Saladen's men?"* He wondered, while walking out of the cave, and into the gray-colored day. *"On the one hand, it works to our advantage not to have to fight them. On the other, hand…"* He poured some water on his face, trying to chase away the sleepy cobwebs from his brain. *"They either rode out of Petra of their own accord, or else they were captured by the Jordanians. The Jordanians! That must be the case. They have been captured!"*

He walked over to his satellite phone. "Cental Command, Layish here, over."

"Go ahead Layish, you're five by five."

"Request immediate evacuation. I say again, immediate evac, over."

"*Ruth*, roger, Layish. Understood. Standby."

Azerah paced back and forth and waited.

"Major, this is General Haver. What to all the devils is happening there? We have you scheduled for 2200 hours and now you would we should pack you out of there immediately? Over."

"General we have captured Yosip bin Saladen, the leader of our main pursuit group, two of his men, and…"

"You've what? This is a complete balagan! Your mission was secret, and now you have hostages?"

"Let me explain sir." He replied, scratching his head, and trying to be patient. "Yesterday, a force of twenty men on horseback settled in here not more than a half a mile from where I stand. They immediately started searching for us, and continued again early this morning, when all but three rode off in the direction of the Siq. I saw the opportunity to capture the three remaining men, one of which is their leader, Yosip bin Saladen. Under cover of darkness, we surprised them, and they are now our prisoners." He paused and let that sink in. "I make no apologies for my actions; you can court martial me later if you wish, but we now own a very important bargaining chip in the event of a confrontation.

"Hmmm. Such *chutzpah*, Azerah. By my life, I see your point, but go on." The general was now enjoying this story. It reminded him of his exploits as a tank commander charged with Israel's defense during Israel's Yom Kippur War.

"Since the other raiders left before dawn, we've kept four eyes open for their return, and to this minute they are still nowhere to be found."

"Gone? Gone where?

"There are only two choices, sir."

"Yes, I see. The only true choice is that the Jordanians have them, and they are waiting for dark to strike." General Haver replied.

"Major, you hold tight, and I'll ram this through channels."

"Thank you sir. Shalom."

"Shalom Layish, out!"

CHAPTER 21

Mira walked out of the customs checkpoint, after a half-hour interrogation, (no wonder the Israelis were so effective at keeping terrorism at bay), down a cordoned off-ramp, lined on both sides with friends and family, and into the lobby area. There she saw a handsom young Israeli, not more than twenty years old, dressed in slacks and a tan short-sleeved shirt, holding a sign with her name on it.

"Shalom!" He gushed, with a big-toothed smile. "You are Mira Rosen, yes?

"That's right." Mira acknowledged.

"I am Ari. You come away this, the car, okay?" He explained in broken English, bowed low, and pointed the way with his right hand.

"My bags. What about the luggage? She pulled out her claim tickets.

"I take care, yes? You can to me give, okay?

She reluctantly handed him the tickets, and followed him to an awaiting black late model sedan parked outside the lobby entrance. Smiling all the way, and bowing several times, he opened the rear door for her, and ran off to collect her baggage.

"*So this is to be my new home.*" Mira sighed, looking past the arrival area to the hustle and bustle of traffic near by. After several minutes her bags were loaded into the boot of the car, and Ari leapt into the front seat and sped off in the direction of Tel Aviv. They drove down the causeway, linked up with National Highway 1, north, the United States equivalent of an interstate freeway, and drove through flat, sparsely populated land. Ari, with radio blasting contemporary rock music, passed and swerved through the very congested traffic, shouting out strange Hebrew expressions whenever he cut things a little too close.

Before long they exited the highway at the La Guardia interchange, and traveled due west into the heart of the old city. *"It's not really an old city though."* Mira thought to herself. She opened the travel brochure she had picked up at the airport that gave a brief description of the city:

"Tel Aviv, which means 'Spring Hill,' was founded in 1909 and located close to the ancient city of Jaffa or Joppa. It is the financial capital of Israel and one of the world's formost tourist sites."

That's great! I think I'm going to like this place." She said, while studying the pictures in the brochure.

"Mira Rosen, iz the boss place there." Ari shouted above the loud music, and pointed to his right.

She looked over and saw nothing, but a line of shops and businesses whose architecture reflected the city's famous Bauhaus style. A few minutes later they drove into the Neve Tsedek area, a cluster of trendy homes and apartments, and the oldest housing development in Tel Aviv.

Ari pulled up to a two-story apartment building, frontloaded with pink and purple hydrangeas, blooming wisteria, and a row of fragrant lavenders on both sides of the walkway. She entered the left side door, then up a flight of stairs that rose to a landing, with a quaint straw mat in front of the door, and several small potted plants she had never seen before, lining both walls. She opened the door, and walked into a brightly lit apartment, furnished with the modernistic theme she favored, and thankfully saw that everything was as neat and clean as could be.

"I'll have to remember to thank Mrs. Myerson," she noted, while putting her leather purse on the glass kitchen table.

Ari lugged the last suitcase into the apartment, and then stood awkwardly by the door awaiting instructions; finally catching Mira's attention. We go to boss, ah, no?" He asked with his big toothy grin.

"We go to the office, Ari. Wait in the car, and I'll be down in a minute."

"Yes, I see. I wait, okay?" He replied and walked back to the car.

Mira unpacked a two-piece navy suit and blouse, changed out of her rumpled travel clothes, freshened up in the bathroom, the water had a bit of saltiness to it, and bounded out the door ready to meet her new boss, Raymond Bernstein.

She walked through the modern glass doors, and into the second floor offices of the Israeli branch of the Global Satellited Network. "Mira Rosen to see Mr. Bernstein," she announced cheerfully to the receptionist.

"Mr. Bernstein, Mira Rosen is here." She spoke into the intercom in heavily accented, but good English. "Please take a seat Ms. Rosen, he will be with you shortly."

Moments later a short, rather paunchy man, dressed in a black suit with a white shirt unbuttoned at the collar, bounced through a side glass door and, with right hand extended, came over to greet Mira.

"Ms. Rosen, Raymond Bernstein. I'm so glad to finally meet you." He said with emotion, while vigorously pumping her hand.

Mira was quite taken aback by his exuberance, and gently pulled her hand away. "The pleasure is mine. I'm looking forward to working with you and your staff."

"Great! Let's get started then. I'll show you to your office." He guided her through the glass door, and into the main office which consisted of three enclosed, glass-windowed rooms on the right, and three cubicled desks on the left. Behind the cubicles was a long row of windows which looked down on a sea of residential rooftops.

"This will be your office, Mira. You don't mind me calling you Mira do you?"

"No, of course not." She replied, and placed her briefcase on the desk beside her computer, while eyeing the walls and mentally organizing her new room.

"*B'seder.* That's Hebrew for "of course," or "okay." You'll be learning that in the classes you'll be taking. You can call me Raymond. I don't like Ray, and Mr. Bernstein is way too stuffy.

"*B'seder* then, Raymond." Mira replied with a smile.

"Perfect!" He replied with a laugh that caused his whole body to jiggle. "I can see that we're going to get along just fine. An awkward pause ensued until he spoke again. "Well, I'll let you get settled in. Here's your identification card, which will have to be validated by the local authorites, your temporary, three-months driver's permit, the keys to your car, which is parked in the garage behind our building, and," he pulled out a typed sheet of paper, "your itinerary for the next week, complete with places you'll go, and some important people you'll meet. For the next few days though, feel free to get aquainted with the city and our people. Drive around the area. Visit Jerusalem, Haifa, the Galillee?" He let his suggestions hang in the air for a moment, while his round face, with its black gotee and moustache, broke out into a warm smile. "I know it's like stepping into a whirlwind, but you'll catch on fast."

"Thank you, sir. I'm eager to get started."

"That's the spirit. Well, if you need me, my office is always open and... welcome aboard!" They shook hands once again, and then she was finally on her own.

***

The cloud cover that had stolen the sunlight for most of the day now gave way to bright sunshine in the waning afternoon hours. Major Azerah, Natan, and Benni huddled together outside the columned opening of the Garden Tomb. "Here's our plan as I see it," Major Azerah offered. "When the call comes in from command, we'll take our prisoners and make our way down the wadi to the ruins of Qasr Al-Bint. The only remaining wall of the ruins will give us adequate cover. Caleb and Levi will remain at their posts, and provide us with surveillance and protection in case there is an attack."

"What do you make of the disappearance of Bin Saladen's men, major?" Benni asked, concern showing on his face.

"General Haver at Central Command and I agree that they were most likely abducted by the Jordanians. That, plus the fact that the normal workforce in the museum and the restaurants, as well as any tourists, have not appeared today, shows me that Jordan is playing a heavy hand, and will probably rush in and attack sometime tonight. My prayer is that we are gone by then."

"What about our prisoners, sir? What's to be done with them?" Asked Natan.

"We will keep them hostage until the moment we board the helicopter. Then we will let them loose. The Jordanians will deal with them after that." He paused and looked at both men. "Any other questions? No? B'seder. Natan, check on our guests and make sure they haven't squirmed away.

* * *

"Layish, Kastel here, over." Came a clear voice over the sat phone.

"Go ahead Kastel, you are five by five, over." Major Azerah answered.

"We are inbound and will arrive your site in twenty minutes, over."

When Benni overheard this, his heart rate increased several beats.

"Roger that Kastel, we will be waiting at the Qasr Al-Bint ruins. You're to land between the ruins and the wadi. Acknowlege, over."

"Roger Layish. We will land between Qasr Al-Bint and the wadi, over and out.

"Nu, Benni," Azerah smiled broadly, "the bus will be here shortly, let's collect our prisoners and proceed to the bus stop."

"From your mouth to my heart, major. May the Eternal One deliver us to safety."

* * *

"General Husseini, we've intercepted several satellite transmissions going to and from Petra." The excited intelligence officer reported, saluting his commander with the back of his right hand in the old English style.

The general returned his salute. "At ease, major," he replied calmly, and leaned back in his chair.

"We have also picked up broken radar signals of air traffic moving generally in the direction of Petra, and believe them to be possible Israeli assets."

"This is the Israeli rescue in progress. Order our helicopters to be ready to move out in five minutes." He commanded, stood up and strapped on his holstered sidearm.

"Yes general." The major replied, and walked out of the tent.

General Husseini picked up his own satellite phone, and dialed the private number to the King of Jordan. "Your majesty, all is in place, and the trap has been sprung." He said reverently.

"Excellent general, you may proceed with your plan. Keep me informed of all developments."

"As you wish, my king."

* * *

The small group walked out of the Garden Tomb, then along the wadi, just as the sun was setting above the cliff tops to the west. Caleb and Yochanan were both pulled from their observation posts, and, while Yochanan joined the men in the Garden Tomb, Caleb took up a position at Qasr Al-Bint, and watched for any signs of movement.

The rest of the group walked down to the valley floor, turned right, and in a few minutes walked into the ruins of the long abandoned temple. One wall stood on the eastern side, and it was here that they seated their three prisoners, now with mouths taped shut, and tied their legs once again.

"You hear that major?" Natan asked. "By my life it's the sound of helicopters."

"It's sharp ears you have, seargent." Azerah replied, looking off to the west. "Levi light off the smoke signal."

Levi ran out some distance between the wadi and the temple, and pulled the pin from the canister, and set it in the sand. Immediately, a large plume of red smoke erupted and swirled up into the sky.

"I see them! There!" Shouted Natan.

Climbing over a ridge to the west came two helicopters. In the lead was an Israeli AH-64-D Apache Longbow attack helicopter, protecting a much larger CH-53W Yas'ur 2000 helicopter transport. The Apache peeled of to the left, and landed further back to the south, while the Yas'ur found the signal, and quickly landed on the sand, some fifty yards away.

"Levi, collect the prisoners, and bring them with us." Major Azerah commanded, while the men moved toward the helicopter.

"Major! Caleb yelled, running up from his position. "Jordanian helicopters coming down from the north!"

Major Azerah turned to see ten Jordanian helicopter gunships, leading out a large Chinook type transport. "By my life they've found us! Quickly, get inside the chopper!" He directed at a run, just as the leading edge of the Jordanian attack helicopters overflew the site. When Benni and the prisoners were safe inside the Yas'ur, Major Azerah posted his men with their sniper rifles on either side of the helicopter. "Don't shoot until we know what their intentions are." He ordered, as he unholstered his sidearm.

"What do we do major? Yelled the pilot. "Those wasps up there are carrying air-to-ground stingers."

"We will wait and see, *en brerra*, he replied.

The Jordanian transport landed some forty yards away, turned off its engines and quickly emptied two squads of armed soldiers with rifles and mortars. The soldiers immediately spread out in a curved line facing the Israelis. A few moments later General Husseini stepped out slowly, flanked by two armed guards, and sat down in an awaiting chair. An aide hurriedly produced a megaphone and the general's sat-phone, and then disappeared into the belly of the helicopter. The general raised the phone, and speed-dialed a number on the phone. "Your majesty, we have them in our power."

* * *

Reb Berkowitz paced wearily back and forth in his room. His intercessory prayer, which had started in the morning, continued through the waning afternoon hours. "Be faithful and help our Benni, dear Lord; You who uphold all things through your word and power. In some grave danger he is, nu? Be with him heavenly Father, in his hour of need."

* * *

General Husseini casually picked up the megaphone, and pointed it towards the now encircled Israelis. "Throw down your weapons!" He demanded, speaking in fluent Hebrew. "You are now the prisoners of his imperial majesty, King Hussein Ammani."

"We have no choice, men," Major Azerah conceded, and threw his pistol into the sand in front of him.

His men reluctantly complied, and along with the flight crew, threw down their weapons as well.

"Excellent. Now come forward and stand in a straight line in front of me."

The group, including the prisoners, came forward and spread out some ten feet in front of the Jordanian helicopter. Immediately several soldiers, at a nod from their commander, ran up to the Israelis and patted them down, making sure that there were no concealed weapons. They came to the prisoners, untied their hands, and brought them before the general.

Bin Saladen and his men immediately kneeled down, and bowed low to the ground. "May the face of Allah smile on all your days, O regal prince of Jordan," bin Saladen intoned without looking up. "You have delivered us from the snare of the viper and we are in your eternal debt. Let our vengence mingle with yours in the blood of our common adversary, even as Allah wills."

General Husseini disregarded bin Saladen's prayer, lit up an English cigarette, and blew smoke down on the three prostrate men. "Get up, sons of *jinn*, you devils, and stand away from me." He motioned for the guards to take hold of them. "You are also my prisoners. Pray that your esteemed father's ransom will be sweet enough to deliver you from the wrath of the king."

The sun was now fully set, as shadows from the western cliffs lengthened into the dusk of night. The Israelis were allowed to sit in the sand, while the general continued smoking in his chair, apparently waiting for some order, or directive. Finally Major Azerah stood up to speak. "Sir, what are your intentions?" He asked in fluent Arabic, producing a slight smile on the face of the general.

"You'll receive an answer in due course. You are an Israeli officer?"

"Major Moise Azerah, at your service."

"Yes, out of necessity, no?" He quipped. "I'm curious major, with a professional curiosity, why it was that you allowed yourself to be trapped in Petra?"

"Quite simple, really. We were trapped by your pincered troop movement, and by coming here we had at least the possibility of a quick rescue." He explained.

"Excellent, major. If I had been in your position, I would have done as much. Were it not for the brief communication with your rescue helicopters, you might have escaped."

Major Azerah sat down again. As darkness enveloped the site, portable lighting units were set up around the perimeter, while several Jordanian soldiers passed out water bottles to the prisoners.

"What could be the holdup?" The major wondered, as the chill of night descended on the valley floor. *"Surely they are not willing to release us... or are they?"*

General Husseini was sitting motionless in his chair when his sat phone rang "Yes your highness. I understand. Upon my honor it will be done immediately." He replied, and ended the call. "Major Azerah!"

"Yes." Azerah replied, somewhat startled; knowing instinctively that a decision had been made.

"You will accompany me inside the helicopter. Tell your pilots that they are to warm up their engines." The general commanded.

The major relayed the orders, and then followed the general into the Jordanian helicopter.

"My king has decreed that it is the will of Allah, the merciful, that you and your men are to be set free." The general declared without emotion. This produced both shock and relief to Major Azerah. "You can understand that this must be done secretly for the sake of my men, and the three prisoners. We will all leave together, and then my gunships will escort your helicopters to the Israeli border. Are there any questions?"

"And the *quid pro quo* will be?" The major asked warily.

General Husseini managed a thin smile. "That is a discussion for the politicians; I am but a humble servant." He held out his hand to shake hands, a move that surprised the major once again.

Major Azerah took the general's hand, and then snapped to attention, and saluted him. "Salaam Aleikum, general."

"Shalom, major. May Allah return you safely to your people." Husseini replied, bowed low, and touched his forehead, lips and heart with his right hand in the traditional Arabic salute.

They walked out into the cold night air, the general shouting orders for his men to prepare for departure, while Major Azerah gathered his men together, and ordered them into the Yas'ur.

The guards positioned in the front of the Jordanian helicopter, led Yosip Bin Saladen and his two men to the back of the airship.

Yosip kept looking at the Israelis preparing to leave, and realized that his mission to capture the escaped pilot now lay among the ruins of Petra. *"This is not possible! This cannot be the will of Allah!"* He said to himself in anger. The anger turned to rage when he saw Benni approaching the door of the aircraft. *"Aaiee! Allahu Akbar!"* Yosip screemed, deftly pulled a pistol from the surprised guard in front of him, and fired several shots in rapid succession in the direction of the Israeli helicopter door; hitting Benni and one of the aircrew members. The guard behind him, after recovering from his initial shock, hit bin Saladen in the back of the head with his rifle butt, and knocked him to the sand, unconscious.

Pandemonium broke out, as several of the Jordanian soldiers, thinking they had been fired upon, started shooting wildly in the direction of the Israeli's.

"Hold you fire!" the general ordered through his megaphone, and immediately silenced the gunfire. He then turned to the Israeli helicopters. "Proceed with your takeoff!" he shouted, then quickly radioed his gunships, and directed them to escort the Israeli helicopters with all haste.

The rotors of the Apache and Yas'ur spun up to full speed, and, after joining with the Jordanian aircraft, sped off for the west.

Had the Israeli's crossed the border more to the north, they would have seen thirty, former Jordanian prisoners, crossing the Allenby Bridge into Jordan, and freedom.

* * *

Inside the Yas'ur helicopter Major Azerah was confronted with a medical emergency. "Where is your medical kit?" He yelled at the co-pilot above the noise of the engines.

"Under the seat in that bay." The co-pilot replied, and pointed to a section in the middle of the helicopter. The major quickly lifted the seat and pulled out a large duffle bag full of supplies. He handed a compress bag and some bandages to Natan, who had cut away the left trouser leg of the air-crewman, which revealed a bleeding hole in the side of his thigh. He covered the wound with the compress bag, and wrapped it with gauze bandaging.

Benni's wound was more severe. The bullet had penetrated his back, just under the right collarbone, and lodged in his chest. He was unconscious, and rapidly losing blood. Major Azerah tore away his shirt, applied a compress to stop the bleeding, and with Caleb's aid, wrapped the gauze tightly around his chest. He then gently laid Benni's head down on the small stretcher pillow, and bowed his head for a short prayer, tears welling up in his eyes. *"No time for tears."* He admonished himself. *"En brerra."*

He crept up to the opening between the pilot and co-pilot. "We have to make for Tel Nof." He shouted. "The airbase has an advanced surgical team there."

"Ruth," the pilot replied.

"They're peeling off!" The co-pilot announced, as the Jordanian gunships veered right and left to head back to their base. "We're now over Israel. Hundred percent!" He shouted, smiling.

"It'll be ten minutes to Tel Nof, major." The pilot said.

Major Azerah clapped him on the shoulder. "Make it a very short ten. A man's life depends on it."

He sat down next to Benni, propped his head with his hand, and fell fast asleep.

CHAPTER 22

Jack Quinn literally bounced with renewed energy and joy into his office at the United Nations. He took out of his briefcase; a new, four-by-eight picture of Marcia and him, taken on their honeymoon at the Cold Springs Resort in Northern Idaho, and lovingly placed it on his desk.

Their honeymoon had only lasted three days, but they had filled up their time with boating on pristine Priest Lake, hiking in the rugged Selkirk mountain range, and taking casual walks and talks along the sandy lake front.

"The best part is that instead of going home to an empty house, I now have Marcia waiting for me with arms open wide." Jack spoke softly, while unpacking a few incidentals, and placing them strategically on the desktop.

He pulled up the messages on his vis-a-phone, and scrolled down the list, complete with pictures of the callers, and stopped at the hypnotic image of Ilya Stanas, and hit the play button.

"Mr. Quinn, congratulations on your recent marriage! I hope that you had a wonderful honeymoon. The Selkirks of Nothern Idaho, how I envy you! Please find time to meet with me as soon as you get back. It is a matter of some urgency. Until then."

"How did he know about our honeymoon in North Idaho? We didn't tell anyone where we would be." Jack wondered.

He turned his attention to the other calls. "See me when you get back." Said, the ever-scowling, Ambassador Stanton.

He scanned a few others of minor importance, and then found a message by Jim Hughes. "Jack, glad you're back, we need to talk. Call me right away." Jack was concerned that his friend's face and voice seemed strained.

He leaned back in his chair, and prioritized his calls. *"Stanas will have to be first. No choice there."* He thought to himself. *"I'll call Jim next, maybe go to lunch together, and then meet with the Ambassador."* He scrolled to the Stanas message once again, and placed a call to his office.

"Secretary General's office," said the soft, efficient voice of his secretary.

"This is Deputy United States Ambassador, Jack Quinn, and--"

"Yes, Mr. Quinn, his excellency has been expecting your call. Would ten thirty this morning work for you?" She asked.

"Ah, yes, that'll be fine, thank you." He hung up and saw that another call had just come in.

"Jack, darling, I just called to say that I love you. Have a fine day, dear." Marcia's beautiful face and birdlike voice greeted him on the screen. He gently caressed her face with his hand, and sighed contentedly.

* * *

Carla paced back and forth at the taxi stand feeling like she'd forgotten something. "The apartment's clean; the cats are with my aunt. I've got my tickets..." She reached ininto her large, sequined, mauve colored purse, and pulled out the tickets for her flight from New York's JFK Airport, to Israel. "There's something missing..." she insisted.

"The keys! She blurted out while diving into her purse once again. Her apartment keys were to be dropped off at the property management company. "No, I've got those too." She realized. "What could it be?"

The yellow taxicab pulled up with a screech, and the Punjabi driver, wearing a tan turban, moustache and beard, got out, and placed her two suitcases in the trunk of the car. She noted, with irritation, that he was only wearing flip-flop sandals. He got back into the car, and waited for her to get in the back seat.

Carla hesitated. *"What is it?!?"* She screamed to herself.

"Passport! That's it! My passport--where is it?" She clawed through her purse once again, but didn't find it.

"We go, yes? The driver asked with an oversized smile.

"Umm, Uno momento. No--you're not Spanish. Ah, one minute please." She replied, gesticulating wildly with her arms in the direction of the building. "I must...I'll just—momento!"

She left him there uncomprehending, and made a mad dash for the elevator. At the door to her apartment she fumbled with the key, finally opened the door, and raced inside. Stopping in the middle of the kitchen, she turned in several directions, not knowing where to look first.

"Think Carla, think!"

She placed her hands on her hips, thoroughly exasperated, and there, sliding her right hand into her pocket, found the missing passport.

"Oh Carla, you knucklehead." She complained, and quickly locked up the apartment once again, took the elevator, and jumped into the back seat of the waiting cab.

"We go, yes? Asked the toothy cabbie.

"Oui, merci. I mean yes, thank you." She sat back, and took a deep breath. *What a way to start my journey. I'm coming Mira. I'm coming baby!"*

* * *

Jack took the private elevator to the penthouse office of the Secretary General, and stepped out into a large, sparsely furnished waiting room, which was overseen by two very attractive assistants.

"You're to go right in, Mr. Quinn." One of them said with a winsome smile, pointing to the door on her left.

He took a deep breath, opened the door, and walked into a large room that had floor to ceiling windows covering the entire left and back walls, which displayed a gorgeous view of the East River, and the Borough of Brooklyn beyond. In front of the wall-to-ceiling bookcases on the back wall, were two leather lounge chairs separated by a coffee table, containing a service tray of coffee and pastries. On his right, was a wall-to-wall media center, where several large monitors displayed news and events from all over the world.

"Most impressive don't you agree?" Stanas inquired, with a trace of Eastern European accent. He rose from his large mahogany desk, and walked over to the blinking screens. "From this vantage point, I can reach almost any part of the globe, and communicate quickly with any of my associates. If a trouble spot develops, I can follow events in real time, and if need be, order an, ah, appropriate response."

"Are there other systems like this one?" Jack asked, entranced by the awesome display of technology before him.

"This is one of a kind, my dear Quinn." He replied smoothly. He extended his right arm, and pointed Jack to a seat in front of his desk. "I hold all the rights to this, so it cannot be duplicated by any other nation or federation of nations." He sat down, paused for a minute, and leaned back in his chair. "However, an even more advanced system is being designed, which will incorporate several interesting innovations."

"Such as?" Jack asked, trying to dispel the feeling that he was being drawn into a web of some sort. Stanas had an aura about him that almost demanded subservience: one that he was finding difficult to resist.

"Tut, tut, my friend. That's for another time." He chuckled lightly. "For now it is enough, no?" He leaned over his desk, a look of malevolent pleasure on his face.

"Now, as for the reason I called you here. I know why you were sent to the United Nations my dear Mr. Quinn." He paused to see what Jack's reaction would be.

Jack sat stone-faced, but inside alarm bells were going off.

"Your little gang of conspirators has been rounded up and are, shall we say, living for my pleasure." He spoke casually, eyeing Jack like a cat eyes a mouse he'd been toying with. "Did you really think you could succeed with this fantasy?"

Jack collected himself and summoned his courage to answer. "It was worth a shot. An underground resistance was better than submitting to tyrannical hegemony."

"Ha ha! Excellent, my dear Mr. Quinn. Did I not compliment you at our first meeting, and call you a true patriot? You still resist even when your plot has failed. You and your comrades are a rare breed, much like those men that began your country, yes? I admire that in you. I truly do."

He got up and walked over to the coffee table, poured himself a cup of black coffee and sat down. "Would you care to join me?"

Jack walked to the chair, but refused to eat or drink. He was too wary for that, and sat down. *"Why is he keeping me dangling like this? Send in the goons, and take me away!"*

Stanas eyed him over the brim of his coffee cup, and guessed what he was thinking. "Then why am I telling you all this, eh? The truth is, my friend, that I like you. I liked you from the moment I met you. You have courage: the courage of your convictions. That is a rare quality, and one that I find useful. You see, I will be leaving for Europe soon, to become the head of the European Union. It is Bulgaria's turn to chair that seat, and they've graciously selected me to be the leader for the two-year term."

Jack was taken aback by this new revelation, seeing in it a glimmer of hope as well. "Then what about your position at the United Nations?"

"Oh, I will still retain my office as Secretary General, and preside over the business of the Security Council and the General Assembly." He smiled broadly. "That's where you come into my plans, my dear Jack Quinn. You will serve me here as assistant director of my transition team. Your country is to merge seamlessly with the states of Canada and Mexico into the new North American Union. It will be your task, under my appointed director, to ensure that the union will be achieved as smoothly as possible." He leaned back in his chair; tented his fingers in front of him, and smiled.

"And if I choose not to join in your audacious plan?"

Stanas leaned over the coffee table, took a croissant, gave it a vicious bite, and swallowed it whole. "Let us just say that I would no longer require the services of your former associates."

Jack was trapped. This man, both gentle and brutal at the same time, held all the cards. He had no choice but to work for him, but only until he could somehow break free and rescue his friends. "Who is the director then?" He asked without emotion.

"An excellent question, my dear friend." He walked back to his desk and pushed a button on his vis-a-phone. "Send him in, please."

The door opened, and in walked Jim Hughes.

CHAPTER 23

It was already hot and humid, in the early morning hours, when Carla exited her jumbo jet at Israel's Ben Gurion International Airport. After a rigorous screening by Israeli security, Carla came down the ramp, and found Mira waiting for her, waving her hands and jumping up and down.

"Mira! Mira!" Carla shouted, waving her hand. She ran up to her and hugged her close, rocking back and forth excitedly.

"You're finally here." Mira gushed. "It seems like forever since I saw you last."

"Well, babe. You're stuck with me now." She quipped, as both women walked hand in hand to the baggage area.

"Carla, it's so exciting. There's so much to do and so much to see." Mira said.

"Oh, I can't wait." Carla yawned, trying to catch up with Mira's enthusiasm. "I can't believe it's only eight o'clock and I'm tired like this. I sure hope they have some strong coffee here."

"You're going to have some jetlag but I'll fix you up. They've got this Turkish coffee that's guaranteed to knock your socks off." Mira placed the suitcases on the cart and lead the way to the waiting car.

"Wow, nice wheels." Carla remarked after the bags were stowed in the front trunk.

"One of the company perks, of course." Mira grinned and climbed into the driver's seat of the sleek, silver, French Citroen. "It's a newer version of the older hybrid, but it works out well especially in the rural areas."

They drove out on the causeway, and joined the freeway heading north to Tel Aviv; Mira chatting away, and pointing out things of interest, while Carla bravely kept from falling asleep. Ariving at the apartment, they brought up the suitcases, put them into Carla's room, then zipped off to the office, where Carla met some of the staff. and was greeted by Mr. Bernstein. In minutes they were out the door and, after a quick stop for the promised Turkish coffee, headed eastbound for the city of Jerusalem.

"Yikes! You were right. This coffee is pretty strong stuff." Carla exclaimed after her first sip of the black brew. Why are the grounds floating on top?"

Mira laughed. "That's the way the locals make it. I don't much like it myself. *B'seder,* they have other kinds of coffee, and…"

"B' what?" Carla asked.

"*B'seder.*" Mira replied, laughing. "It means of course, or okay in Hebrew. I've already had my first Hebrew class, you're enrolled with me as well, and I'm trying to use different phrases when I can."

"Oh, okay, er, b'cider then, ha, ha. Like this Turkish coffee, it'll take some getting used to."

They drove out of Tel Aviv across the coastal plain and onto Route 1, heading east to Jerusalem. "On the left, Carla, is Latrun, the former British fortress that defied Israel during Israel's War of Independence, blocking any supplies from reaching Jerusalem. You know what the Israelis did? Built another road! They called it the 'Burma Road,' and it bypassed this fortress, and allowed food, water, and medical supplies, into the beleaguered city. Latrun was finally taken in 1967 during the Six Days War and is now a war memorial. Isn't that fascinating, Carla? Carla?"

She looked over and saw that Carla was spralled out in her seat, with mouth agape, and fast asleep.

Mira drove through the hill country west of Jerusalem, humming a Hebrew song she had learned, while Carla slept beside her. Coming to the outskirts of the New City of Jerusalem, she pulled over, took out her map, and traced the route she would take.

"Carla." She called, and shook her gently. "Car-la!"

"Skhaark! Yes, snookums. Momma's coming." She replied, still enmeshed in sleep.

"Carla!" Mira yelled laughing and shook her harder.

"Huh? Oh…Mira…Hi!" She yawned and stretched.

"I'm sorry, but we're almost there, and I need a copilot." She handed Carla the map.

Carla turned the map around and upside down. "Er, um, me and maps don't really get along too well."

Mira righted the map and pointed to the lines marked in neon green. "It's simple. Just follow the course, and let me know when a turn is coming up."

"Oh, okay, I can do that." She replied. "But…where are we now?"

Mira threw her head back and laughed. "I can see that we're in trouble." She pointed to the place on the map where highway 404 meets route 1. "From here we go south and get off on Sderot Shazar. That will take us to the Israeli Interior Ministry's office on Kaplan Street, there."

"Got it. 404 to Sadrot Shabam, then Kaplan. Piece of cake." She exclaimed slapping the map.

They got on the 404 and headed south when Carla called out, "There's that Shabam Street!" just as they drove past the exit.

"Carla!" Mira shook her head laughing, and took the next exit. "Okay, where to now?"

"What's the name of this street?" Carla asked pointing at the street sign.

"This is Sderot Yitshak Rabin.' Mira replied, while pulling up to a stoplight. "We can take this to Yoel Zusman which will turn into Kaplan, here."

"That'll work. Hey, this's not so bad. At least we're still in Jerusalem… aren't we?" They both laughed.

Several minutes later they they came to Kaplan Street, and found the building for the Ministry of the Interior. Mira looked at the time on her satphone, and saw that they were ten minutes early for their two o'clock appointment. "You've got your documents and passport, Carla?

"You bet. Got 'em right here in my purse." She replied confidently, then rummaged through the purse to make sure, and was relieved to find that they were there.

They walked to the main desk, where they were told to take a seat, and five minutes later were lead through a maze of cubicles to the small nondescript office of Mr. David Shuchman.

"Miz Rozen, I believe." He said in a heavily accented English, while shaking Mira's hand. "And you are?" He asked gently, turning to Carla.

"Carla Nordquist, your honor, er, sir. My mother is Jewish. "She was nervous as she shook his hand.

"Very happy to make your acquaintance." He said, motioning them to two chairs in front of his desk, while he sat down in his faux-leather, black chair. "I usually allow my staff to deal in these matters, but in your case I make exception, yes. You have credentials to show then?" He asked, putting on his small wire-rimmed glasses that sat on a prominent nose. Shuchman was in his mid fifties, slight of build, with salt and pepper, short-cropped hair.

Mira handed him the company paperwork, and both passports and birth certificates. The minister perused them with knitted brow, signed the documents and stamped the passports. He handed Carla back her birth certificate with a smile but held onto Mira's. "You were born, Miriam Cohen, at Kibbutz Maoz, close to Mount Hermon, I see."

"Yes, minister. I recently learned of my true identity from my adoptive father. My brother Benni and I--"

"Binyamin Cohen, an Israeli pilot, I understand." He interjected.

"Yes, he's the one I called you about. The last word I received was that he was still missing in action. When I was a child we were both separated from our parents during a terrorist attack on our kibbutz, and then separated from each other. He managed to stay in Israel, and the Rosens adopted me. You see, that is the main reason for my taking this job with Global Satellite Network. I want to find my brother, and my roots in Israel."

"The roots may take some time to grow, but I have some news about your brother." He handed her the birth certificate, and located another paper placed strategically on his desk. "Your brother has been rescued but--"

"He has? When? Where?" Mira asked excitedly.

The minister gave her a fatherly look of concern. "Miz Rosen, Binyamin was shot in an escape, and is in critical condition in hospital at Tel Nof airbase. That is all the information I could gather, I'm afraid." He sat back heavily in his chair, while a pall of silence descended on the room.

"News such as this affects all of us, my dear." He stated solemnly after a few moments. "It has been said that every family in Israel has suffered the loss of a family member at one time or another. I pray that the Eternal One will heal your brother, and allow you to truly find him."

* * *

He looked off to the north as he walked toward the fighter jet sitting on the tarmac. The hot Khamsin wind, that had been blowing in from the east, was now replaced by fierce northerly gusts, that threatened to topple him over. Huge black thunderheads were piling up into the sky, laced with intermittent lightning, heralding a massive building storm. "I have to get into the air before the storm breaks."

He scrambled into his cockpit. The wind blowing over his opened canopy seemed to be forming words. "Ninth…ninth…ninth of Av!"

Benni woke with a start and immediately felt a painful tug from the bandages on his chest. *"Only a dream. By my life, only a dream!"* He said to himself, gritting his teeth against the persistent pangs of pain. After a few moments he looked up, and saw that he was tethered to several IV's and some sort of a tube that disappeared just above his abdomen. He was alone in a long, powder blue, walled room that contained an empty bed, and ended at a large window, where early morning sunshine was now pouring in.

"What happened? How did I get here?" He wondered and tried to recall the events in Petra. Just then a young nurse, perhaps in her early twenties, Benni guessed, dressed in a matching two-piece, powder blue uniform and a clipboard tucked under her arm, came up beside him.

"Shalom, commander. It's good to see that you're awake." She offered cheerfully, while jotting down notes, and eyeing the monitor above his head.

"En brerra," he said lightly. "How am I doing? I don't remember much of what happened." He tried to sit up a little, but found that the pain allowed for little movement, and settled back in a prone position.

"You'll be in some discomfort for awhile, but you are healing well. The drain tube and two of the IV's will be taken out today, since there is no sign of infection, and that should allow you more movement. Soon you'll be sitting up eating normally, yes?" She smiled brightly. "For now you must rest." She pumped some medication into one of the IV's. "This should help." She turned on her heels and left the room. No sooner had she gone when Benni drifted off into a deep sleep.

* * *

Reb Berkowitz awoke from the best sleep he had had in days. He had prayed fiercely for Benni, feeling the pull and tug of spiritual warfare over his life, until the burden lifted, and he knew that all was well with his grandson. "It is time to give thanks to the Almighty One, who keeps watch over His people." He said and dropped to his knees beside his bed.

After several minutes of silent praise and worship, he rose stiffly and prepared for the new day. "First with a journey into your Word I should think, and then the time will be for my yeshiva class at Congregation Beth Israel."

He opened his well-worn bible to 1st Corinthians, the 15th chapter, and began reading. *"Ah... the gospel so brilliantly yet simply shown."*

Just then a light knock came at the door. He opened it and in hustled Marta, Avram's wife, with a small tray of hot tea, homemade bread, and cheese. "I brought you this because I know you haven't been eating. You're wasting away before my eyes, what with all the time you are spending in prayer, I am that concerned for you." She gently scolded.

"Oy, my dear Marta. You shouldn't bother so with me. Enough you have to care for that giant of a husband, and your beautiful children." He replied, taking the tray from her, and looked forward to breaking his fast. "May the Eternal One bless you."

"It's my joy, abba. And who will take care of you if I don't? *L'chaim!* Yes? To your life, so that maybe later you will share 'the Life' with our little ones, nu?"

"Yes, yes, already I'm eating, you see? And yes, later I will teach at the yeshiva." He took another bite of cheese and then a sip of his favorite black tea. "Thank you, Marta."

"Seeing you eat is my thanks." She paused at the door. "Tonight I'll expect you for dinner, yes?" She gave him a warm smile and closed the door.

"Blessed are you, Creator of the universe, for providing me with such dear ones. May your blessing rest on them, and on this house. Omain."

* * *

Jim Hughes walked into Jack's office and closed the door behind him. Jack offered no greeting, still fuming over the revelation that he would now be working under Jim, at the behest of Ilya Stanas, in the very conspiracy they both pledged to fight. He watched suspiciously as Hughes sat down.

"Ironic isn't it?" Jim began, with a sheepish grin, while sitting down. "We were the idealistic crusaders riding to the rescue of our country, like so many Don Quixote's chasing windmills."

"Jim, I trusted you; the others trusted you. We put our lives in your hands. For what?" Jack asked in anger.

"Not so fast, friend." He warned holding up the index finger of his left hand. "I've already crossed the Rubicon and back again for you and the others."

"What do you mean?"

"Why do you think Stanas is leaving you to breathe, Jack? It's the same situation I faced at the White House. I wanted to resign, but was told that my resignation wouldn't be accepted. I told Stanas to take a hike, and he said no way, and—oh by the way—I have your wife, kids and grandkids, Jack and his wife, the others in your clandestine group, and—you ready for this—even our dear Dr. Clarke, in my crosshairs. So, you'd better play ball, or it's game over, buddy." He paused to let his anger subside. "So what's your story?"

Jack slumped in his chair, and let out a big sigh. "Same script, but with a few exceptions." He leaned over his desk and held out his right hand. "I apologize Jim. I thought--"

Jim shook his hand. "You thought that I was a player for Stanas. That about right?"

"Yeah. The way he set it up…It was almost like a spell or something. I don't know, it was crazy that's all."

"Look, Jack. He does that to people. He's done it to me before; the man has this thing about him."

"So what do we do now, Jim?"

"Well, you're gonna' love this, we're to fly to Washington in a couple of days and meet with our new boss, the chairman of the North American Union steering committee."

"Who would that be?"

"None other than Zoltan Bielchek."

* * *

A thousand butterflies fluttered in her stomach as Mira drove up to the heavily guarded gate at Tel Nof airbase. After an early morning meeting with her boss, and quick instructions to Carla, Mira excused herself, and drove the forty-five minutes or so to the base. She smiled nervously as she presented her pass and identification card to a stern faced, female guard, who was dressed in green fatigues and sky-blue beret. The guard said something to her in Hebrew and gestured with her hands.

"I'm sorry," Mira replied in English, while shaking her head from left to right, and gesturing with her hands, "I don't understand."

The guard repeated the same instructions, but more slowly this time.

"I, I still don't understand." Mira said helplessly.

The guard then walked past the gate, motioning for Mira to follow her, and then pointed to a small, tan colored quonset hut on the left. Mira parked her car, and walked into the air-conditioned office. A petit, dark-skinned female receptionist walked up to her. How may I help you? She asked in Hebrew.

"Um, I don't speak Hebrew." Mira waved her pass in front of her. "Is there someone here who speaks English?"

"*B'seder.*" all right. "Sit an moment, yes?" She replied with a heavy accent, took her documents, and walked into an adjoining office.

"*There's that word 'b'seder' again. It's like aspirin in language form.*" She chuckled to herself.

The receptionist came back to the counter, and motioned for Mira to follow her. Mira entered the small, wood paneled room, and stood behind a neatly organized, metal desk. Behind it, sat a squat built, muscular officer in tan uniform, with short-cropped, salt and pepper hair.

"Miz, eh, Rozen, yes? Please to sit down." He said in polite but forced English, while looking at her pass. "You are to visiting Binyamin Cohen, yes?" He looked up, and handed back her papers and ID card.

"Yes, that's right, sir." She was nervous, but hoped it didn't show.

"You are brother? I am sorry. He is brother?"

"Yes. You see we were separated when I was a child, I was adopted and lived in America, but--"

"Ah yes, Americansky. I have, er, family, yes, in Novy Yorku." His face opened into a wide grin as he said this.

"That's wonderful." She smiled, hoping this interview would end quickly.

"So, you say Benni is cuzin to you, eh? He leaned on the desk, tenting his fingers in front of him.

"No, brother. I recently found out that he's my brother. I moved to Israel so that I could see him again. That's why I'm here--To see him." She was becoming a bit irritated now.

"Yes, yes, I see ze papers." He leaned back in his chair, and much to Mira's chagrin, lit a cigarette, offered her one, which she declined, and took two thoughtful drags. "He iz hero, your brother, no? He has, how you say it? *Ometz, courage* in the French."

"Courage." Mira replied flatly.

"Oy, same as French then. Yes courage. I like this word courage." He noted, while looking to the side, and took another long, thoughtful drag.

"May I go now?" Mira asked impatiently. "To see my brother?"

Just then the receptionist rapped lightly on the door, walked past the desk, handed the officer a piece of paper, and whispered something in Hebrew in his ear. She then turned to Mira, smiled, and silently walked out the door.

"Yes, Mira Rozen, you may go now. He opened up a drawer, pulled out a base map, circled the gate, the office building, then the base hospital, and drew a line weaving through several buildings linking the two. He gave the map to Mira. "You are here and brother iz here, yes? Follow line to hospital." He stood up and shook Mira's hand. "*Shalom*, Miz Rozen, and, *Kol Ha'Kavod*, all honor, to your brother."

"*Shalom* sir, and thank you for your help." She walked out the door, past the smiling receptionist, and into the heat of the midday sun.

Mira followed the map, found the base hospital, parked her car, and walked through the pneumatic doors to the main counter. An orderly pointed her to the ICU section of the hospital where she was told to take a seat. The butterflies now fluttered wildly in her stomach at the prospect of finally meeting her brother.

"Will he even remember me? What if it's too soon to see him? He's been wounded for heaven's sake. Not the best time for a family reunion!"

Just then a slighty built doctor walked up to her. "Shalom, Miss Rosen." He offered, greeting her with a Brooklyn-American accent. "I'm doctor Frantz. Benni has been placed in my care."

Mira shook hands with him and both sat down. The doctor had calm, sincere eyes behind his silver, wire-rimmed glasses. "As you may know, Benni was shot during a narrow escape from Jordan. The bullet went into his back and lodged very close to his heart. The operation was completely successful, our chief surgeon here is top-flight, if you'll pardon the pun, and we expect a full recovery."

Mira, who had been holding her breath through the brief explanation, finally let out a whoosh of air. "So, he's going to be fine then?"

"Yes, he should be up and running in a few days." He said smiling.

"Doctor, I haven't seen my brother since we were kids. Obviously I'm anxious to see him. Do you think it might be too soon though? Should I wait a bit?"

"Actually, I think it will do him good. His wife, you know, is still in a coma in Tel Aviv?"

"No I didn't know that." She said in surprise. "I guess I hadn't thought about other family."

"We haven't told him about that yet, so please don't say anything. We're waiting until sufficient healing has occurred. That's why it would be good for him to see you. A reunion may be just what the doctor ordered, eh?" He smiled again and patted her arm. "There's another person in there with him right now. As soon as he's gone, I'll send a nurse over to walk you in. *Shalom.*"

* * *

"So then, Moise, you're leaving tomorrow." Benni acknowledged with sadness. His bed was reclining in a sitting position, the spider web of tubes and IV's all gone. He was eating real food again, and was scheduled to leave intensive care later that afternoon.

"I'm afraid so." The major replied, while leaning his arms on his knees and absentmindedly twirling his red beret. He was dressed in a clean and pressed, tan jump suit, with high top, black-laced boots. "Duty calls. *En brera,* eh? Although it would be nice to be a prince like you, being waited on hand and foot." He teased, and patted Benni on the knee. "And with a harem to respond to your every wish!" He smiled, as a pretty, dark haired nurse entered the room, bringing in some fresh water for Benni. She blushed shyly at Major Azerah's comment, and quickened her pace out of the room. "Oy, I've been out of country too long. Now that's worth fighting for."

"Believe me all this is overrated. I can't wait to get out of this bed, and back on the flight line." Benni stretched himself. "Will you be going back, you know, there again?

"No. That mission, because of you sitting here alive and breathing, has been accomplished. My next stop is for some training in the north, and then on to another assignment. Where that will be is anybody's guess." He looked at his watch. "Which reminds me, my plane leaves in about an hour." He stood and got ready to leave.

Benni was choked with emotion, as tears filled his eyes. "I don't know how to thank--"

"I know my friend." Moise broke in, and took Benni's proferred hand and shook it. "We are comrades in arms, and have shared great adventures together. Perhaps one day..." Azerah couldn't finish the sentence, as emotion gripped him as well. He reached over and hugged him, and then stood upright at attention and saluted him. "May the God of Israel guide you in the days to come." He prayed, and then turned on his heels and left.

Moise walked through the metal, Intensive Care Unit door, into the narrow hall bustling with busy staff, and nearly ran over Mira. Major Azerah grabbed both of Mira's arms to keep her from toppling over, and came face to face with her. He was speechless.

"Oh, excuse me, sir. I was just getting up to visit my brother and..." She began to explain, and blushed because of his fixed gaze.

"No. Is my fault, yes? You are well, okay?" He asked in halting English, and stepped back to a proper distance from her.

Mira fought to control her emotions. This was a handsome, muscular officer, a little taller than her, with gentle, yet strong, peircing eyes, and he had unnerved her. "Yes, um, I'll be fine, thank you for your concern." She said in rapid-fire succession, finally taking in and releasing a deep breath.

The major also needed to summon up control, after being struck by Mira's soft, warm eyes, and the statuesque beauty of this evidently American woman. "You have brother here?" He asked, wanting to make conversation, and keep her a bit longer.

She swallowed, and took another cleansing breath before answering. "Yes, his name is Benni, um, Binyamin Cohen."

Moise crossed his arms across his chest. "I know this Benni, yes? We have, uh, mission together, you see?" He smiled broadly, wishing to continue, maybe to sit down for a coffee with her, but knew he had to leave.

An uncomfortable moment or two passed. "I must to go. I have to make plane flight." He said with reluctance in his voice.

"Oh yes. Well, it was nice meeting you." She said pertly, and extended her right hand. "I'll say hi to Benni for you, ah..."

"Major Moise Azerah into your service." He replied, shook her hand, and bowed low at the same time. "Your name is please?"

"I'm Mira, Mira Rosen--well—Cohen. Actually, I was adopted...but that's a long story." She was nervous, and chided herself for her lack of control, and for acting like a schoolgirl on prom night.

"Then Shalom, Miss Mira. Until we meet again." His warm smile brought goose bumps to Mira's arms. After fastening his beret to his head, he slowly walked away towards the main entrance.

* * *

Carla sat riveted to her computer screen and had barely touched her onion bagel with chive cream cheese. She had found a wonderful Jewish deli on her way to work that morning, which comforted her, and helped displace her homesickness. She hated not having Mira around her, even if it was for just a few hours in the morning. She had given her clear instructions on how to ferret out news stories of interest on the Israeli web, and she was homing in on the government sites, determined to find something of interest before Mira returned.

Raymond Bernstein casually walked through the beehive of activity in the office, and came up to Carla's desk. "Well, Ms., ah, Nordquist, you seem to be settling in here nicely?" He smiled broadly and sat down on one edge of her desk.

"Uh huh." Carla replied, barely looked up, and went back to her hypnotic posture behind the computer screen.

"I, um, told Mira, how, uh, happy I was for her to have such a competent assistant." He said self-consciously. He was not used to getting less than undivided attention from his staff. "And the fact that you both worked together, and are close friends, well..." He continued, making a gesture with his hands to try to draw her attention.

"Yeah, we go way back." Carla allowed, took a quick sip of coffee, found that it was cold, and went back to her work. After a few moments she turned to face her boss. "I'm sorry, Mr. Bernstein."

"Ah, Raymond, please."

"Thank you Raymond. Is there something I can help you with? Because I'm looking for an eye-popping story here for Mira, and I'd like to do that before she gets back." She replied curtly, with a thin smile.

"Oh, oh, of course, Carla. By all means continue." He answered, stood up, and adjusted his tie. "Nice to see such dedication, heh, heh. Carry on then." He turned and walked back to his office.

"Talk, talk, talk." Carla whispered, and went back to her monitor. "It's a wonder anything gets done around here."

She scanned a news page for Hebrew University's Archaeology Department, and found an announcement regarding a press conference to be held in two days time, about the possible find of recent aritifacts of religious significance.

"Good start." She said to herself. *"I'll place that at the top of the list. Israelis, and the world, love stories about archaeology."*

* * *

"This way please." The nurse said to Mira in fluent English, opened the door to the Intensive Care Unit and followed her in.

Mira froze in place.

"Is there anything wrong?" She asked with concern.

"Just a minute please. This is the first time I've seen my brother in years, and I'm a bit nervous."

"I understand." She replied, and put a reassuring hand on Mira's arm. "Would you like to sit down for a moment?

"No thank you, I'll be fine." The butterflies in her stomach now turned into angry bees.

The nurse led her into the hospital room, and there, laying flat on the bed with his eyes closed, *(was he sleeping?)*, was her brother. Mira's eyes filled with tears, as she sat down beside the bed and pulled out a handkerchief from her purse.

"I'll get you a glass of water." The nurse gently whispered, and quietly left the room.

Mira looked at her brother, and would not have known him, if she had met him on the street. She reached over and gently stroked his hair. "Still the touselled, curly mess."

"Monika, Monika--hamoodah!" Benni shouted, while rolling his head back and forth. He opened his eyes and looked at Mira. "Moni? Oy! Ah, *Shalom*." He looked at her with a quizzical look on his face.

"I'm sorry to have startled you." She said, hoping that he spoke English.

"You not Monika; er, English?" he replied, while slowly recalling a language he hadn't used for some time.

"American, actually." She braced herself, as a lump formed in her throat, and tears began to fill her eyes. "No, I'm not Monika, Benni. I'm your sister, Miriam." She gently touched his right hand as tears rolled down her cheeks.

Benni was stunned and uncomprehending. "Miriam? Miriam? My little--Miriam?" The scene of his running through a field, urging his sister to run, came vividly into his mind. "Miriam!" He shouted again, sat up, and held out his arms to her. She fell into them sobbing with joy. "I lost you Miriam." He cried between sobs, holding his face close to hers. "I am ranning back...not to find you...I run--The field burning...rifle shots--forgive me?" He pleaded with deep sobs, hoping for some relief from a burden that had haunted him for years.

"Shh, shh, my dear brother." Mira replied, took him in her arms and gently rocked him. "There's nothing to forgive. We were children, thrust out of the love and comfort of our parents, into the caldron of terrorist violence."

Benni held her at arms length, tears running down his cheeks. "You... different...beautiful."

She blushed and dropped her gaze to the floor, and then back to him again. "And look at you; all grown up with that curly mop of hair." She wiped the tears from her eyes, and mussed his hair playfully.

"Blessing is Eternal One, nu? You back at me!" He shouted, and spralled out on the bed with joy. The outburst quickly produced a concerned nurse, who then exited with a smile. Both looked at each other and laughed: a deep, heartfelt, intense, laugh.

They lovingly held hands, and spent the next hour or so catching up on each other's lives. The talk was both spirited and somber, and underscored by the poignant fact that there had been such a long time gap between them. They rejoiced to learn new things about each other, but were also saddened that they hadn't been there to share in the story. It was like the bare outline of a book without the details of the pages.

"This why here in hospital, nu?" He yawned, and felt a nap coming on. "Two things you do for me, motek?"

"Of course. Anything." She patted his hand, and got up to go.

"Find what is happened to my Monika. They give only the, how you say it, a 'run round' here. "Other is to call zaide--sorry, um, grandfather. He is to live Old City Yerushalayim, in room over Robinson's Arch by *Ha'Kotel*. Must warning you he haves strange beliefs."

"How so?" Mira enquired with concern, sitting down once again.

"Not to be sure. I do not to heem talk of it. Please to try stay away of religion."

She reached over and kissed him on the cheek. "All this and more I will do, and I'll hope to have some answers for you when I see you again."

"Thanks to you, motek. Soon we make escape and have many adventure, yes?" He gushed.

"As long as the adventures don't involve walking through a field." She joked, and they both laughed. "Get well first, okay. I don't want to lose what I've just found."

"*En brerra*. That is to mean, no choice."

"I like another one more." She said. It always brings peace to my soul: *Shalom!* Mira smiled lovingly, and walked slowly to the door.

"This another for you Miriam, *Lehitra'ot,* See you later." He said in a sleepy voice as she walked out. He then collapsed in his bed, and was asleep in an instant.

* * *

Reb Berkowitz walked slowly through the dark, narrow lanes of the Jewish Quarter to the Street of the Chain on his way to the Western Wall. He stopped to rest, leaning on his briar wood cane, took a deep breath, and sniffed the ancient air. *"Oy! Still I can smell the burning buildings, and the choking stench of rotting corpses from the siege of Jerusalem, during our War for Independence."* He remembered, choking back tears.

He walked into *Ha'Kotel* plaza, sat down on a folding chair, in the late morning shade, and closed his eyes. "Heavenly Father, God of the universe, Israel's Lord, I adore you." He began with a whisper, and continued for some time in an attitude of worship.

A mighty burden fell on him to pray for Israel, his country and people. The burden weighed heavily on him as he knelt on caloused knees. Then the Lord spoke to him:

"A mighty wind with fire and hail will descend upon my people." The Lord spoke in a still, small voice. *"Surely Dan will know it. Publish it in Judah. Shall Benjamin escape? A furious beast, thirsting for blood, will seek to devour the land, and inhabit my holy mountain. You are my watchman, Shlomo. Therefore, stand on the wall for your people Israel, my beloved. Watch for the lion's whelp and a cub, my messengers against the day of battle!"*

Large drops of sweat saturated the black felt fedora he wore, ran down his cheeks, and trickled onto his long white beard. The ache in his heart eased, and he lifted himself wearily into the chair. "I do not understand all of this, your word to me, yet, I am your servant, Lord. I will set up a watch for my people and your people. Deliver them, I pray, from this evil about to befall them. To this end I pray. Omain."

CHAPTER 24

The defense minister walked from the private elevator into General Borodin's command bunker, and stood at attention in front of the gray, oval conference desk located in the situation room beneath the Kremlin. Major Pavel Illych Petrovsky, and several cabinet members had arrived, but President Primakov was absent.

"You sent for me general?" Ivanov asked somewhat tentatively. He always felt like a schoolboy coming before the principal, whenever the leader of the Russian Republic summoned him.

"Yes Ivanoff. Sit down." He commanded, without looking up from the papers he was studying. "Pour yourself some coffee, and try to relax--that's an order."

"Yes, general." He replied submissively, but was still uncomfortable.

Borodin returned to the paperwork, took a drag from his cigarette, and followed that with a sip of coffee. "I'm studying your report, comrade. It appears that reasonable progress has been made in our clandestine stockpiling of weapons caches, and I find your calculations of troop strength in our allied nations acceptable. The Arabs seem to be cloaking their preparations well, so that to date, there has been no Israeli reaction." He took another sip of coffee and walked over to a map of the Middle East beside his desk. "Pavel, bring us up to date about our own preparations?"

The major shot up from his chair, walked over to the map stand, and picked up a telescoping pointer from the tray. Battle Group Six, located in the Crimea, is at full strength, and prepared to deploy into the Mediteranean for joint war game exercises with Turkey, Syria, and Libya. This will, of course, be a feint to draw Israeli attention away from the troop movements of our allies. Force One, consisting of Egypt, Libya, Sudan, Somalia, and Ethiopia are assembling in place, and will soon be ready to cross the Suez, to strike through the Sinai Peninsula, here." He pointed at the triangular tongue of land, framed on two sides by the Red Sea. "They will be the spearhead of the attack. Force Two will begin with Iran appearing to attack Iraq, whose forces will flee towards Syria. After Egypt's thrust from the south, the combined forces of Iran, Iraq, Syria, and Lebanon will then turn on Israel, sieze the occupied Golan Heights, and fall upon the Galillee region. This time they will drive their tanks and troops to the sea, and cut Israel in half."

"Da, da." The general said with a smile. "What of command and control, major? Are all our advisors in place?" Borodin asked, while lighting another cigarette.

"Yes, my general. All forces will be commanded by our own C-10 cadre of officers, and will have on-site control of all operations, with direct sattelite comm links."

"Ivanof!" Air Force General Sergie Chertov barked. He still chafed over Ivannof's impertinent questioning at their recent cabinet meeting. What is the disposition of our Il-476 long range transports?"

"Ten transports from the 51st Transport Wing at Ivanovo Air Base outside of Moscow, have been detached with special forces troops, to Incirlik Air Base in Turkey."

This brought a congested laugh from General Borodin. "Comrades, the former Americansky base in Turkey is now host to the strength of the Rodina." The seven men around the table laughed at the irony. "Continue Ivanof."

"Other transport wings, with several infantry and mechanized battalions, are deployed at Krasnodar and Mozdok airbases in the Caucasus Region, and are on yellow alert." He finished, looked at the general, who nodded his approval, and sat down.

"General Chertov, what of our new combat aircraft?" Borodin asked, while taking a long pull from his cigarette.

"This will indeed be a surprise for the Israelis." He smiled, while standing to attention. "We will have ten fighter and bomber wings deployed throughout our strike forces, with a reserve force of twenty wings each deployed at Krymskaya and Morozovsk airbases in the Caucasus. These will be our latest aircraft, the Sukhoi T-50 fighter and the Su-34 fighter-bomber. The Israelis have never seen these aircraft in action." He declared proudly. "This alone will be a shock to their system; one that they will not be able to recover from." He sat down amid nodding approval.

"Excellent general." Borodin said clapping. "These aircraft alone could bring the decisive blow to the Israeli gangsters, comrades." He smiled, and then turned to Major Petrovskiy who had been standing patiently by the map stand. "Pavel please continue."

"Thank you sir. Force One and Force Two will attack from the south and northeast," he pointing to the positions on the map, "effectively cutting Israel in two. These will be supported by an amphibious operation, Force Three, which will sail from Cyprus as soon as hostilities begin, and will land either in Haifa, in the north of Israel here, or Joppa in the south, depending on which of our land forces has made the quickest progress. Our own Russian forces will be held in reserve and may be deployed for mop-up operations thereafter. Computer estimates, comrades, is that the entire war will last two to three days."

"Thank you major." The general stood facing the men at the table. "Are there any questions?'

"Sir, what influence, if any, will the Americansky have on our operations?" Major General of the Army, Igor Kaminsky asked.

"None whatsoever comrade. They are mired in the cesspool of their failed capitalistic greed. United Nations troops will soon overtake their government. Martial law has already been imposed in many places, and many of the states are rebelling against the national authority. They are an eagle without claws, and will not be able to mount a challenge to us. Besides, we have a bit of surprise for them, before we begin, courtesy of our Iranian comrades." Borodin answered cryptically.

"Then what of Stanas and the European Union?" Chertov asked.

"Stanas has lately been installed as the new European president. He and the Union are in disarray due to worldwide collapse of the dollar, and the muddle of the market basket currency scheme. Our operation will tweek Stanas' nose, and he will have to pull his troops from Jerusalem. I don't see anything but a possible verbal challenge coming from that quarter." He replied chuckling, taking a thoughtful drag from his cigarette. "Besides, the European Union, for the most part, hates Israel as much as we do. They may even give us their tacit approval."

A round of laughter went around the table.

"If there are no further questions?" He asked, snuffing out the stub of his cigarette, while looking from man to man. No one replied.

"The operation will be code-named, 'Sudden Lightning.' You will submit your final operational plans in three days. *Spasiba*, thank you, comrades. You are dismissed."

CHAPTER 25

She drove into a parking spot on Ben Yehuda Street across the street from a small non-descript office building that was to serve as the Jerusalem bureau for the Global Satellite Network. The office was above a two-car garage, and Mira was pleased to see that the workmen were busy putting the finishing touches together.

"Carla, it's eight o'clock, and we've got to be at the press conference in an hour." Mira said, gently shaking her friend, who had been sleeping, mouth agape, in the seat beside her.'

"Wha--huh?" she snorted, stretched, then pulled the seat up to a sitting position. "Oh, okay. Friday, right? That must mean we're in Jerusalem."

"Find Sha'ul, warm up the van, and I'll get us some coffee and bagels."

"You got it babe." Carla responded, and stepped out into the already hot, early morning sunshine. She was growing to love Israel, and found that her ever-present sinus problems had shriveled up to nothing in the dry climate. Just as she crossed the street, one of the garage doors opened, and the GSN blue and white uplink van coughed to life, rolled backwards into the street, and parked by the nearby curb. Sha'ul, the GSN cameraman, engineer, and jack-of-all-trades, rolled down the window and greeted Carla with a wide grin. "*Boker tov*, good morning, Carla from Amerika." The thirty-eight year old, dark complected sabra, with short, brown, curly hair, said cheerfully. "We are already to go, yes?"

"Booker tow to you too, Saul." She replied, calling him by the English version of his name, and trying to match his accent. "The boss has gone out for coffee, and will be back in a minute."

"No, no, Miss Carla from Amerika. You say 'boh-ker,' not 'boo-ker,' see? You try."

"B-Bow-ker. Right, I've got it, thanks." She said, a bit annoyed, and still groggy. "It'll be a wonder if I'll ever learn this language of yours."

Sha'ul lighted happily from the van. "Is okay, nu? You will learn some day." He chuckled and patted her on the back.

Just then Mira rode up, and passed out the black coffee and fresh, hot bagels.

"Wow! It doesn't get better than this." Carla gushed. "Thank you dear."

"Yes, thanks to you, and now we go, yes?"

"Right. We'll follow you." Mira answered.

Sha'ul hopped in the van and Carla took her seat in the car. The two vehicles drove a few blocks until they came to the Jaffa Gate, on the western side of the Old City, went through the Armenian Quarter, came to the Jewish Quarter, and arrived at the Western Wall.

* * *

"I tell you Shlomo, if what I heard is true, this will be a complete balagan, a disaster!" asserted a sweating Chaim Podhoretz. He took out a large, white, handkerchief and wiped his flushed face. "A rest I need, it's that winded I am."

They stopped for a few minutes, both leaning on their canes, only a few blocks from the news conference at *Ha'Kotel*.

"My dear Chaim, if you should the prophet Daniel read, and then the Revelation of Yeshua Ha'Mashiach, as given to Yochanan, you would understand that--."

"Shlomo, please! This is not the time or place for this discussion?" He mopped his brow, and both men started walking again. "The Sanhedrin has pleaded with the Chief Rabbi to halt the news conference, until further study can be made, but, oy! *HaRosh Mistovev*! How the head is spinning!

"Chaim, Chaim. Have faith in the Eternal One, blessed be His name. There is nothing done that cannot be used for His purpose. True?"

"*B'seder. B'seder.* Of course you're right. *Baruch Ha'Shem.*"

They turned the corner to the left, saw the great retaining wall of The Temple before them, and found that an excited crowd, filling the entire plaza, had already gathered.

Lead by Rabbi Podhoretz, both men plowed through the throng, until they came to the front, fifteen feet from the limestone wall, where chairs were provided for them. Sitting on the end of the second row of seats, Rabbi Berkowitz noticed that on his left a news crew was filming the proceedings.

"Sha'ul take a few cuts of the people in the plaza for background." Miriam directed.

"As you wish. I climb ladder there and shoot."

"Shhh! Easy with that word, babe," Carla cautioned. "You're likely to get us arrested."

"Oh, yes, I see." He said smiling, and climbed up a wide, eight-foot ladder with a small platform on the top.

At precisely nine o'clockm a barrel chested rabbi, dressed all in black, with a long gray and black beard, made his way to a bank of microphones, and prepared to speak. To his left was an ordinary rectangular table, dressed with a white and blue stiped tablecloth. Sitting serenely behind it, was the shrunken figure of the eighty-two year old patriarch and Chief Rabbi, Yitzak Shimson, with a single microphone in front of him. His white forlocks dangled beneath the Borsolino black felt hat he wore, to ward off the sunshine.

"*Shalom uv'racha le Yisrael!* Peace and blessing to Israel, and to all who are gathered here. In a moment the Chief Rabbi of Israel will give a short statement but will not be available for questions. Following him, Conrad Tershoal, distinguished director of The Ministry of Antiquities, will make a follow-up statement and answer a few questions. And now the Chief Rabbi, Yitzak Shimson."

"*Shalom haverim*! Peace to you my friends! I am here to announce a momentous discovery for the children of Israel; indeed for the whole world." Rabbi Shimson began in a raspy voice. "A short while ago a team of archaeologists headed by the chairman of The Ministry of Antiquities, Doctor Conrad Tershoal, believe they have found what may prove to be the most significant archaeological find of our time. He started sobbing and brought out a white handkerchief to wipe away the tears, while the crowd in the plaza buzzed with excitement. The Chief Rabbi regained his composure, and raised his hands, calling for silence. "Our friends and enemies alike must know that things are now falling into place as we await *Ha'Mashiach*, who will then build his temple. Shalom."

With that the old Rabbi followed by two of his assistants left the plaza as Doctor Conrad Tershoal, dressed in a double-breasted khaki shirt and khaki pants, stepped up to the bank of microphones amid a cascade of animated conversation. He paused for a few moments until quiet resumed.

"First a brief statement. I will take a few questions but it should be known to all that I will not make known any clues as to the whereabouts of this significant site. Suffice it to say that the facts of the matter are in the possession of those who need to know. I would also like to acknowlege the contributions of my colleagues on this project, my dear friend Dr. Yigael Alloni, and his assistant, Zev ben Suchar. Gentlemen would you please stand and be recognized."

Both men stood in front of their seats on the front row, and were greeted by a warm round of applause. "It was these two, really, who have been leading our efforts, and without them I would not be standing here before you." He took out his pipe from his pocket, lit it, and took a couple of puffs.

"I'll take a few questions now." He pointed to a man he knew in the second row.

"Max Spiegel, Reuters World News. "Can you tell us what led you to begin your search for the artifacts?"

"Actually if was Dr. Alloni and Zev Ben Suchar who began the search. I was brought on the scene only after there were significant developments. They began searching in an area that was considered quite ordinary, but near to another promising site. At a whim, during a break, Zev dug up a shovel full of dirt which lead us to the conclusion that we are about to uncover a major historical and archaeological find."

"Yes," He pointed to a woman a few rows back, who was then handed a remote microphone.

"*Mazeltov!* Congratulations, Doctor Tershoal. Sheena Rivlin, Ha'Aretz. Can you give us a description of the possible items you hope to find?"

"The best description I could give you would be found in the *Tanakh*, the Bible. In Exodus 25, you'll find instructions given to Moses for the building of the Ark, the Table of Shewbread, the Altar of Incense and the Candlestick. What you have there, accurately describes what we hope to find." This produced more murmuring in the plaza.

He looked to his right and picked someone he didn't know. "Yes, you my dear."

"Thank you. Miriam Rosen, Global Satellite News."

"I understand that you're new here Miss Rosen." He said to her in English.

"Yes sir, GSN recently opened a bureau in Jerusalem.

"*Mazeltov!* I wish you good success." Tershoal said smiling. "And your question?"

"Could you tell us how far beneath The Temple Mount you were when you found this site?"

"We were—oh--that was very good, Miss Rosen." He paused to recover his composure. "I will neither confirm or deny that we were ever under The Temple Mount." He said curtly and went on to another questioner.

Mira now knew that the search was occurring under The Temple Mount. She was thrilled to note that her probing question drew admiring glances and nods from several of the other media men and women.

"What just happened?" Carla asked seeing the reaction to Mira's question. "Did I miss something?"

"I just left a calling card for the director of the Ministry of Antiquities. He'll certainly remember me the next time we meet." Mira said smiling.

"Huh?" Carla looked at her confused. "I don't get it."

"You will dear. I'll explain it to you later." Mira patted her on the back, while looking at her notes.

During the first few questions Rabbi Berkowitz had been in prayer. It was interrupted when Mira began to speak. The Lord spoke to him in the midst of her questioning: *"Shlomo, this is one of those I spoke to you about."* He looked over at the business-like woman to his right and determined that he would meet her when the news conference ended.

"Okay Sha'ul, Carla, that's a wrap." Mira declared, after they had filmed an editorial piece in front of the Western Wall. She picked up her notes, placed them in her brown leather briefcase, while the others carted off, and stowed the equipment in the van. She looked up to see two elderly Rabbi's with long white beards, dressed from head to toe in black, standing before her.

The one with the perspiring, flushed face, spoke to her in heavily accented English. "Miz, eh, ah, Rozen, yes?

"That's right." Mira smiled, looking at each face. "May I help you?"

"My name iz Chaim Podhoretz. This, mine friend iz Rabbi Shlomo Berkowitz. He comes to ask you some things, yes?"

"Um, okay. Would you like to take a seat?" She asked, while motioning them over to row of seats to her left.

"Yes, thanks be to the Eternal One, nu?" The rabbi replied, while pulling his beard, and sat down beside Reb Berkowitz, who wore a quizzical look on his face. "Eh, Miz Rozen. My friend Shlomo has queztions for you, yes?"

Mira nodded in reply, as Reb Berkowitz began speaking to Chaim in Hebrew.

"Eh, d' Rabbi asks of you, do you know heem? Have you, how you say, be with heem, maybe?"

She looked Reb Berkowitz in the eye, and sat back. "No, I don't believe so. Should I know him?"

He gave her answer to his friend who then asked another question. "He sayz you must to know each and de other. Can you tell how you come to Izrael?" Chaim asked, as both men looked at Mira intently.

"Well, this is a bit strange. I don't think I would forget a face like his." She replied. "If you must know, I recently learned that I was adopted at an early age from Israel, after both my parents were killed in a terrorist attack, north of here."

Upon hearing the translation, Rabbi Berkowitz sat bolt upright, and fired a quick question to his startled friend in Hebrew.

"Eh, he azks, what were they name, the parents?"

"The last name was Cohen." Mira responded, now startled by the old rabbi's reaction.

Shlomo's eyes widened and his already white face turned whiter still when he understood what she had just revealed.

Chaim wiped the sweat off his face with his white handkerchief, and nodded several times to something his friend was heatedly telling him. "The good rabbi azks, do you have family other that you know?"

Mira was distressed to see the old man beside her so agitated, and reached her hand out to touch his arm and comfort him. "Um, yes. That's one of the reasons I took this job in Israel. I have a brother named Benjamin, Binyamin in Hebrew, who's a pilot in the Israeli airforce. I visited him recently and--"

Tears welled up in Shlomo's eyes, as he cried out: *"Adonai Tzid'kenu! Adonai Tzid'kenu!* The Lord is our righteousness!"

"Mira, stunned, looked from Rabbi Berkowitz to Rabbi Podhoretz.

Both men talked back and forth to each other excitedly, until Chaim, swobbing down his face again in the heat of the early morning sun, finally spoke. "Miriam, daughter of Izrael, Shlomo Berkowitz is your *zaide,* your grandfather!"

CHAPTER 26

The first formal meeting of the new North American Union Interim Governing Council, or NUIGC, took place at The Plaza Hotel across the street from Central Park in downtown Manhattan. The ornate Global Room of the Plaza played host to over two hundred delegates from Canada, Mexico, and the United States, who had come to New York to vote on a new constitution for the nascent North American Union, modeled after The Charter of the United Nations. On the dais were the ambassador's general from each country, Zoltan Bielchek, Chairman pro tem of the Council of the United States, his counterparts in Canada and Mexico, several staff members, including Jim Hughes and Jack Quinn, and the keynote speaker for the night, Special Envoy for Secretary General Ilya Stanas, Mr. Benjamin Stuart.

After a brief introduction by Bielchek, Stuart got up to speak. He was a tall man in his early seventy's, with a thick mane of white, curly hair, and piercing black, almost hollow eyes. He bounded up to the podium with youthful energy, hugged the black-robed Bielchek, and enthusiastically snapped off the mike with his left hand.

"ONE WORLD NOW! ONE WORLD NOW!" He shouted, and raised the microphone to the ceiling. A few in the audience joined in.

"Come on, you can do better than that. ONE WORLD NOW!"

"One World Now!" One WORLD Now! ONE WORLD NOW!" The crowd stood up and shouted until the chant grew to a crescendo.

Jack Quinn looked over at Jim sitting beside him, who was looking down into his coffee cup, and wore a troubled expression on his face.

Stuart allowed the crowd to go on for a few moments, until the chanting ended in a loud round of clapping. "Please take your seats." He paused, and took a sip of water. "I want to welcome you to the dawning of a new day. I have in my hands an envelope that contains the results of your vote for, or against, a new constitution for a new entity called The North American Union." Several whistles and claps came sporadically from the room. "This is an exciting moment isn't it?" He smiled, while tearing the envelope open, like a Hollywood Oscar presenter. "I'm pleased to report," he began, "that the vote to adopt a new constitution for the North American Union is unanimous: two hundred to nil!"

Thunderous applause greeted him from the floor, as thousands of suspended balloons, mixed with a blizzard of multi-colored confetti, cascaded down from the ceiling, accompanied with shouts of, "ONE WORLD NOW! ONE WORLD NOW!"

Stuart stood basking in the celebration for a few minutes, and then held his hands up to still the crowd. "As wonderful as this is, we have a lot of work ahead of us. The nations of the US, Canada, and Mexico are divided today." Several boos came from the floor. "The small minded, the bigoted, the Christian fundamentalists, the right-wing, terror seekers, are doing their best to undermine our just cause." More boos and shouts of "No! No! No!" filled the hall. "All over the world the rotting corpses of intolerance and indifference are giving way to a new order—a benign and prosperous system of government—one that will be free of bloodshed and fear—one that will enoble humanity and provide for its deepest needs and desires. A NEW WORLD ORDER!"

Shouts of, "ONE WORLD NOW! ONE WORLD NOW! ONE WORLD NOW!" rang out from the standing, jumping, and dancing crowd.

"Makes me want to vomit." Jack said under his breath.

Jim was quiet, and glanced over at Bielchek, who gave him a knowing look.

Stuart relished the heady emotion that filled the room. "Will you join me in this critical hour? Will you stand against any who seek to countervail our holy alliance? Will you--?"

"We will stand with you!" Several shouted. "ONE WORLD NOW! Others declared. Still others started singing a song, *We are the World*, and then the whole room joined in.

Everyone on the dais stood up and began singing along, and clapping.

Jack, reluctant to participate, nonetheless felt compelled to stand, and join in as well.

Stuart let the singing continue for several minutes, before concluding his remarks. "Let me say in closing that you have the strength and will within you to bring about this new world order. But you lack the power." He leaned over the podium. "How do I get that power, you ask? You need to be initiated into *The Plan*. With the help of our benevolent 'ascended masters,' whom I serve, you will reach your full potential, and each of you will become the god you were meant to be."

Cheering and clapping erupted once more from the room.

"As soon as we're done here, you're all invited to join me in that far room to my left where the initiations will take place." He pronounced with a broad smile that transformed into a wolf-like leer.

"You're dismissed." He hissed, and walked down the stairs to join the crowd streaming toward the initiation room.

"That was really frightening." Jack observed, as both he and Jim left the hall, caught an elevator, and walked through the revolving glass doors and out into the street.

"Don't let it get to you." Jim replied, while hailing a taxicab, which quickly came to a screeching halt beside the curb. "Just stay the course, Jack. Our friends' lives depend on it."

"Aren't you coming?" Jack asked.

"There's something I've got to do upstairs, Jim replied. "You take care." He answered sadly, and watched as the cab sped away. He then took the elevator to the Global Room, walked over to the room to his left, and several minutes later became initiated into *The Plan*.

* * *

Ilya Stanas sat motionless behind the mahogany desk in his United Nations penthouse office, when the intercom woke him from a trance. "Sir, Ali Abdullah Alawi the Palestinian Prime Minister is here to see you." The secretary intoned.

"Er, yes, very well, send him in." He stood up, adjusted his tie, and buttoned his suit jacket.

"Salaam Alaikum, mister Prime Minister." He acknowledged, while bowing, and directed him to a leather chair in front of his desk.

"Alaikum Salaam, your Excellency," replied the short, balding Palestinian leader, and returned the bow. He wore an expensive Armani two-piece black suit that fit snugly to his heavy-set frame. His left hand revealed a large diamond encrusted gold ring, and a gold Rolex watch wrapped around his wrist. Alawi was accustomed to luxury.

"I know that you are a busy man, so I'll come right to the point, Stanas began. My sources tell me that you are going to stage an intifada against Israel in a few days, is that correct?

The prime minister lifted his black eyebrows in surprise. *"No one was to know about this. No one!"* He thought to himself. "Eh, merely a rumor your Excellency. The decision has not been made at this time."

"Very good. You will to see to it that no action of any sort is taken at this time. I've already contacted the leaders of Lebanon, Syria, Jordan and Egypt and they have agreed to do the same." Stanas commanded, and then sat back in his chair.

"This is not possible!" Alawi exploded. "My nation is poor and starving, and a prisoner of the Zionist entity. We will never be satisfied until they are driven into the sea. Has not the Prophet Mohammed said, peace be upon him--"

"I understand Ali." Stanas interrupted, a sly look spreading across his face, "I am one with the plight of your people. All your wars and strikes have amounted to nothing, true?"

The prime minister sat smoldering in his chair, a charred look of resignation on his face. "The jihad must continue, even though it has failed to date."

"And it will my friend, it will. But we must take a different approach now. We will put our enemy to sleep, and make him believe that we are his friends. When he closes his eyes..." he slammed his right hand on the desktop, startling his guest, "then we will crush him!" Stanas smiled wickedly, and sat back in his chair once again. "You will be rewarded for your patience. Humanitarian aid for your people would need to be increased, and, of course, a sizeable contribution would be made to your personal fortune."

The prime minister sat back with a glazed look on his face. "What would you have me to do, Excellency?" He asked, his thin moustache twitching involuntarily.

"I'm glad you asked, my friend. You and I must follow *The Plan*."

CHAPTER 27

This time Mira was quickly waved through the Tel Nof airbase gate. Sitting somewhat uncomfortably beside her, unaccustomed to riding in modern conveyances, was her dear grandfather, Shlomo Berkowitz. She reached out and touched his hand. "*B'seder zaide?* It's okay, grandfather?"

"*B'ezrat Hashem, tateleh.* With God's help, little darling." He replied with a smile, while patting her hand.

Miriam guided her grandfather through the busy hospital. They walked up to the help desk, enquired about Benni, and found that he was no longer in ICU, but in a room in the main part of the hospital. Upon entering the room they found Benni pacing back and forth beside his bed, seemingly fully recovered from his wound.

"Zaide! You found him, Miriam! " He shouted with joy, and ran up to hug them both.

"It's more like he found me." She quipped, and gave her grandfather a warm hug.

"One part of de mission is finished, yes? One hundred percent! What of Monika?"

"Binyamin sit down already. You're not that well yet, nu? Shlomo began, speaking in Hebrew. "I will tell you of Monika, but you must be brave." He sat back, and then laughed at what he had just said. "Hah! I'm telling you to be brave, and through fire and water you have just returned from."

Benni translated to Mira, and they both laughed.

"You were not aware of this, but Monika was pregnant at the time you left on your mission." He began, with a serious face. "A few days after you were shot down, I got an urgent call from her, asking me to come and help her. By the time I arrived, she had already miscarried, and because of complications, later lapsed into a coma."

A pained expression clouded Benni's face. "It was my fault then, for leaving her, when I could have been here for her. The crash upset her and--"

"Not so my son. She came out of the coma at one point, and I was able to briefly talk with her. Both of us felt that you would come back safely. She sincerely believed that."

Benni looked down disconsolately, as tears welled up in his eyes. "Thank you, zaide. So now?"

"She is in hospital, in Tel Aviv, and is still in the coma."

"Then I must leave here at once and go to her." Benni resolved, stood up, and began pacing again.

"Binyamin sit." Shlomo demanded. "You are to get well. This is why the doctor decided not to tell you earlier."

Mira walked over and sat next to her brother on the bed. "Benni. I live in Tel Aviv. I will visit the hospital and leave word that if anything changes in Monika's condition, they be should contact you immediately."

"*Todah*. Thank you, Miriam. This takes great weight from me." Benni replied, and lay down on his bed.

"Do you want to rest Benni? We can come back another time?" She asked.

"No please, a bit tired I am from stress about Monika. Please, now I need ask my grandfather." Benni said and switched from English to Hebrew.

"Zaide, I've been having these *meshuga*, crazy, dreams lately." He began, which caused Shlomo to become alert.

"I explain to grandfather strange dreams I have lately." He explained to Mira. This prompted her to remember her own dreams.

He returned to his zaide. "The dreams all have one thing in common. They involve scenes from battles or warfare, and even a nuclear exchange of some sort. Then there's a warning: 'Tisha b'Av.' I know that it relates somehow to our month of Av, but, well, what do think it means?" Benni asked.

"Tisha b'Av?" Shlomo replied with alarm. He scratched his head around the edge of the black kipa he wore, and then pulled on his beard.

Mira saw his reaction, and became concerned. "What did you ask him?"

"I spoke dreams I am having are with warfare, and end with, warning: 'Ninth of Av.'

Miriam turned white, and almost passed out.

Benni saw her reaction, and put his hand on her shoulder. "Miriam what's wrong?

"Benni, I've been having the same kind of dreams for some time now, and they all end with that same cryptic phrase, 'Ninth of Av.'"

They both looked at each other in stunned silence for a moment, and then both turned their gaze to their grandfather.

"Nu?" He replied with a smile.

Benni translated what his sister had just told him. After several thoughtful minutes he finally responded. "The dreams are one and speak of a calamity that will soon befall our people. You have been chosen by God, as I have foreseen by His grace, to prepare our nation for what is soon to come to pass."

Upon translation his grandchildren both gasped.

"This is incredible. How can this be?" Benni asked.

"The Almighty, blessed be the Name, like Esther and Mordecai of old, has called you for such a time as this.

"But zaide you're the zealous one, why didn't He show you these things?" Benni pleaded, uncomfortable with being confronted with something religious in his life. He thought quickly back to the boxes of bibles he had found in Petra. *What do they mean?*

"Binyamin, the Lord chooses whom He chooses, His will to perform. You are both His vessels, and I must explain to you the deep meaning of these dreams. Please translate for your sister."

Tisha b'Av has a profound place in the history of our people. At the beginning of the Exodus, while in the wilderness, Moses sent out spies to search out the land of Canaan. Most of the spies believed that the land was too strong, and that Israel could not prevail. That night, *Tisha b'Av*, the people cried to go back to Egypt. The Almighty One became angry at their lack of faith, and because of this, the whole generation died in the wilderness, and only Joshua, Caleb, and their children entered the Promised Land.

Then the First Temple, built by David's son, my namesake Shlomo, was destroyed by the Babylonians on *Tisha b'Av*, and, amazingly, so was the Second Temple, by the Romans.

In 133 A.D., the Jews rebelled against the Romans. They believed that their leader Shimon bar Kochba was to be their Mashiach. Their hopes were dashed at the battle of Betar, on *Tisha b'Av*.

There are a few others." The rabbi said pulling at his beard once again. "In 1290 A.D., Britain expelled the Jews from their land. In the same year that Columbus sailed for America, 1492, King Ferdinand and Queen Isabella of Spain also expelled the Jews. The date in both cases was *Tisha b'Av*."

Benni and Miriam were shocked to silence for several minutes, while all that their grandfather shared sunk in.

"The Eternal One has shown you both that something of grave consequence is shortly to come to pass on *Tisha b'Av*, the 9th of Av."

CHAPTER 28

The hastily arranged press conference announcing a message of worldwide import was arranged, significantly, in front of the *Let Us Beat Swords into Plowshares* statue in the garden area of the United Nations compound. The statue, showing the muscular figure of a man wielding a hammer against a sword, was donated to the United Nations by the Soviet Union in 1959.

A minute before 9:00 a.m., on a bright and sunny morning, Ilya Stanas, accompanied by four men, stepped up to a bank of microphones. In front of him were newsmen and women, ambassadors, and dignitaries from all over the world.

"I will make a brief statement, but will not take any questions at this time." Stanas began. "Standing behind me are Israeli ambassador, Mordechai Brinn, Arab League chaiman, Fara al-Malaki, Palestinian Prime Minister, Ali Abdullah Alawi, and UN Special Counsel for Religious Affairs, Sir Benjamin Stuart. We are gathered here, in front of this glorious symbol of peace, to declare that the blueprint for a sustainable and true peace between Israel and its Arab neighbors has been accepted by all parties." Excited discussion went up from the assembled crowd. "I will be flying to Jerusalem this afternoon as a representative of the United Nations, and as the President of the European Union, to negotiate and finalize the details of the plan."

The noise level increased dramatically, and several calls went out from the press to answer a few questions.

"I'm sorry, but that is all we have to say at this time. I'm sure we'll see many of you in Jerusalem. Thank you very much." Stanas smiled broadly, and marched off with the others into the Secretariat Building.

* * *

That same afternoon, General Borodin, President Primakov, several members of the cabinet, and a few trusted aides watched Stanas' news conference in the grand meeting room of the Kremlin. It produced an immediate concern and a round of argument around the table.

General Borodin patiently took a sip of coffee, and lit a cigarette until the room quieted down, and all heads turned towards him.

Finally, Air Force chief Sergei Chertov crashed through the silence with his booming voice. "Has not this move by the peasant Stanas imperiled our plans to invade Israel?

Borodin looked at him with indifference, and took another drag from his cigarette.

When an answer wasn't immediately given, the Defense Minister discreetly chimed in. "I should think that a general re-appraisal would be in order, general? What if our coalition has had second thoughts? After all the Arab League--"

"Nyet!" General Borodin yelled, and slammed his left hand down on the mahogany conference table. "Our plans have been finalized, and we will proceed with our attack strategy."

Silence greeted him from the stunned faces.

"I will alert our diplomatic staff in our allied countries to determine what damage this new development may have caused, and then we will apply whatever pressure necessary to keep our children in the fold. Is that clear?" He took a long drag from his cigarette, and flicked the ashes into the tray beside him. "Besides comrades, do you not realize how this move by Stanas has played right into our hands?" He looked from one blank face to another. "We will not need the diversion we had devised to draw away Israel's attention from our movements. Stanas has given us his own diversion. They will become so occupied with their peace negotiations, which, like all the others before this one, will drone on forever, that we will be able to attack in force, and still take them by surprise."

* * *

He took the elevator to the penthouse suite of the Secretary General of the United Nations, went past the reception desk, and straight into the plush office. Ilya Stanas was standing by his desk, busy loading various papers into folders, and the folders into a large black briefcase.

"Jack Quinn!" Stanas gushed, with a sly smile. "Thank you for coming at such short notice. As you can see preparations are underway for our departure to Jerusalem."

"*Our* departure, sir?" He replied.

"Yes, my dear friend, you and your wife, of course, are to accompany me and my entourage to Jerusalem. Tickets and accommodations have all been arranged."

Jack was stunned, but soon recovered. He cared nothing for his new position, and had, in fact, been making careful plans to eventually sabotage certain elements of the proposed North American Union. "But my work with the transition team? Jim and I?

Stanas kept packing, and answered without looking up. "Zoltan has assured me that Jim has, ah, taken on a new vision for his work, so-to-speak, and will be able to get along very well without you. Whereas, I shall need your counsel, and you will coordinate certain aspects of my itinerary." He looked up and smiled, while gauging Jack's reaction. "You will serve me as you once served President Williams, yes?"

Jack's mind searched for some way out, but quickly realized that he was trapped. For the sake of his compatriots, he could not refuse.

"I will tie up some loose ends here, and join you in Jerusalem, sir."

"Splendid! I will look forward to seeing you at our staff meeting there, and also, to meeting the lovely and gracious Mrs. Quinn as well."

* * *

Mira and Carla were cheerfully chatting, as they walked into the Global Satellite Network office in Tel Aviv the next morning.

"Did you hear Stanas' speech yesterday?" Their animated boss, Raymond Bernstein, asked as they came through the door. Both looked at each other, and shook their heads. "Here, come into my office, and I'll replay it for you." He quickly lead them into the large room, sat them in front of his desk, and swiveled the over-sized monitor to face them. The video clip came on, and showed Stanas speaking once again to the large crowd in the United Nations garden. While they watched, Bernstein nervously paced back and forth beside his desk until the end of the speech. "Well what do you think?"

"I'd say we'd better hustle up to Jerusalem; the sooner the better." Mira answered.

"I'm with you Mira. We'll camp out if necessary." Carla added.

"That's the spirit. I knew I could count on you girls." Bernstein acknowledged, sat down behind his desk, and handed Mira a manilla envelope. You've been booked for unlimited stay at the King David Hotel. There's a purchase card in there to take care of any expenses you might have, and an itinerary of the hastily planned meetings. Those may change quickly, so you'll have to stay on top of it." He smiled and leaned back in his chair. "This could be the dawning of a new day for Israel."

Both women were caught up in his reverie.

"So, what are we waiting for, already?" He chuckled, while taking his normal position behind the desk. "Go have fun! Let me know if you need anything. Shalom."

The women left the office and hurried to their car. After a quick stop at their favorite deli, for hot coffee and sandwiches, they hustled out of Tel Aviv, towards the baked hill country of Jerusalem.

* * *

The day that Benni had waited for had finally arrived. Over the objections of his doctor, who would have preferred that he waited a few more days, he was being discharged from the hospital. He was just packing the few items he possessed, when Major Moise Azerah, who was on leave, popped through the door. "Your chariot awaits, master." He quipped.

"Moise!" Benni cried, and ran up to hug his friend. "It's good to see you. How was your training?"

"Boring, but thankfully brief and to the point. Looks like I'll be staying close to home for awhile, so, unfortunately, you'll be seeing more of me." He replied cheerfully. "Um, I'm also you valet, sir, so if you'll allow me?" He picked up the duffel bag, and both men walked out of the room. "So where to now?"

"How long are you available?" Benni asked.

"You've got me as your slave for the whole day, my friend. It's the least I can do for allowing you to get shot." He joked, and slapped Benni playfully on the back.

Benni stopped for a second and winced in pain.

"Oy, you're still injured." Azerah noted, dropped the bag, and held out his arms, ready to catch his friend.

"Shh!" Benni said looking around. "It's nothing. I just need a little time to heal, but not here."

"I hear you. Never did like these places myself."

They walked up to the service desk, where Benni signed himself out of the hospital, and then got into the major's car. "Where do you want to go? Breakfast, a movie, a sight-seeing trip to Petra perhaps?" Moise quipped. They both laughed.

"If you don't mind, I'll go to my base apartment, pick up my car, and we can drive seperately to Tel Aviv. I'll park by my sister's place, and then we can go on to the hospital."

"*B'seder*, but only if you'll take me to the commissary, so I can grab a quick bite for the road. I'm starving."

"There you go, just like in Jordan, always thinking with your stomach, eh?" They laughed again, as Moise pulled up to Benni's apartment.

"I'll wait until you're ready to go." Azerah offered, knowing instinctively that it might be difficult for Benni to be back in his apartment for the first time since his mission.

"Be right back." He replied, then turned, and noted his late model BMW 749i sitting forlornly by the curb. "Come to think of it I'll probably need a jump start. Do you have any cables?"

"Got some in the boot."

Benni walked to his apartment, and paused at the door. "*The last time I was here I held Monika in my arms.*" He thought to himself, unlocked the door, was greeted with a dusty smell, and almost everything the same as when he had left it. He walked to their bedroom, opened the door a crack, and smiled when he saw that the bed was still unmade. "Not like you at all *motek*." He observed. He found the car keys on the counter in the kitchen, and, after a thoughtful look around the apartment, locked up, and rejoined his friend.

Moise attached the cables to his car battery, and after a few sputtering tries, the engine hummed to life once again. Both men drove their cars out of the base, and headed north for the half-hour trip to Tel Aviv, when suddenly, Benni's satphone rang.

"Hey! What about some food?" Moise demanded.

"Is eating all that you think about?" Benni joked. "Listen, there's a great café in Tel Aviv we can hit, after we park my car."

"You're on!"

The drive through the sun-drenched, browning landscape was uneventful, but Benni rejoiced in the freedom of the open road, and the sights and smells of his homeland.

He parked his car in front of Mira's flat, and jumped into Moise's rented hybrid.

"Hey is this your sister home? You know I literally bumped into her in the hospital hallway the last time I saw you. "I thought we really hit it off together."

"No, she called me earlier. She's on an assignment in Jerusalem, and didn't know when she'll be back." He gave his friend a defensive look. "Now don't get any ideas about her. I just got reacquainted with her, and would like to get to know her more before she gets involved with anyone else."

"Oy, *b'seder*, I just want to marry her, that's all." He joked, and both men laughed. "But that can wait until you feed me."

"We'll take care of that right now: drive on major." Benni said, and directed him to the Café Americain on Dizengoff Street.

Benni, nervously awaiting his visit with Monika, could only manage a cup of Turkish coffee, while the major feasted on a large plateful of cheese blintzes, topped with currant marmalade, and a demi-tasse of espresso coffee.

"Moise, I don't know how it's going to go in the hospital with Moni. Perhaps it would be better if you just dropped me off." He suggested.

"I understand Benni. Whatever you think is best. I don't mind hanging around, if that would help." He offered, while taking a final sip of coffee.

"*Todah*. Thanks. It would be good to have someone close by."

* * *

Mira checked herself and Carla into the King David Hotel, and took the elevator to their third floor room. "Wow, this elevator and the hotel are ancient." Carla noted.

"I love the old-world atmosphere in this place; it's kind of romantic." Mira replied as the doors opened. They walked down the hall, almost to the end, and found their room. "There's a lot of history here, Carla. Did you know that the hotel, in fact the wing we're in, was bombed by Israeli radicals before the War of Independence?" She noted, and inserted the card key into the door receptacle.

"Bombed? You mean like dynamite bombed?" Carla's eyes went wide with fear.

Mira laughed. "That was a long time ago, silly. We're a lot safer here than with the gangs and terrorists in New York."

They unpacked their suitcases into a pair of dressers across from the two twin beds, and surveyed the room. Warm beiges and browns dominated the modern oriental arrangement of walls, drapes, carpeting, and furniture.

"Hey, we've got a balcony." Mira cried out with delight. They walked out onto a stone-walled patio, and sat down on two white, wrought iron chairs, divided by the same style round table.

"Woo--hot!" Carla exclaimed, and sat up and then down, until she could sit still.

On the table was a crystal bowl filled with a fragrant spray of fresh cut summer flowers. Mira stood up, sighed happily, and walked to one corner of the patio, and then the other, where large, potted yellow and pink roses stood, and gently caressed a few of the delicate blossoms. "I could learn to like it here, Carla." She allowed, while leaning on the sand colored, stone and mortar wall, which overlooked the Tyropoean Valley, and the Old City of Jerusalem beyond.

Carla joined her on the wall. "Yeah, a bit snooty for my taste, but you've got a gorgeous view here." She observed. "We'd better get out of this hot sun though, before we get sun stroke." She cautioned, and hustled into the room just as the phone rang.

Moments later she walked back out to where Mira was standing. "That was Sha'ul. He said the news conference scheduled for today was postponed, and will be held at eleven tomorrow."

"That's great. It'll give me a chance to visit with our friend the Interior Minister. Before that, though, how about some lunch?"

"You're on babe. Let's see if they've got a McDonalds or something around here."

"Carla! You can't be serious. No way. We'll drive to the Damascus Gate and walk down to the Souk. They've got fresh flat bread, couscous, fava beans, skewered lamb…"

"Well, if you say so. But later we've got to find a Big Mac. I'm craving junk food right now."

Mira chuckled. "No wonder Sha'ul calls you, 'Miss Carla from America.' We'll get you some fries and a coke as well."

"Now you're talking." Carla replied.

* * *

Benni and Moise walked solemnly into the Sourasky Medical Center. They took the elevator to the third floor, and proceeded to the nurse's station, where they asked to see Dr. Ezra Patek. A few minutes later, the doctor came bustling through one of the swinging doors, and approached the men.

"Mr. Cohen?" He asked, looking from man to man.

"I'm Binyamin Cohen, doctor."

"Doctor Patek." Come let us sit for a moment." He ushered the two men to a small, unoccupied waiting area.

"Your wife, Mr. Cohen--"

"Please call me Benni."

"Very well, Benni. Your wife is still in a coma due to complications resulting from a miscarriage some time ago. Of this I'm sure you're aware. She is in good health otherwise, and shows no degenerative signs."

"How long, I mean, is there anything that can be done?" Benni asked with concern.

"All that can be done has been done. The rest is in the hands of the Eternal One. She could awake in a minute, or, some time from now. We simply do not know."

"Can I go in to see her doctor?"

"By all means. Your coming might even be of some therapeutic value." He stood up. "Come, I'll take you to her, but then I must quickly leave."

Benni turned to his friend. "Moise I'll be back soon."

"I'll be here." He replied.

They walked down the hall to her room. The doctor gave Benni a warm, paternal look, patted him on the shoulder, and hustled down the hall.

Benni walked quietly through the door, and found Monika lying on a single bed on the left side of the room. Above her, a dim light shined on her face, while a heart monitor kept its silent watch. He saw that she was calm and peaceful, with angelic beauty he thought, and appeared as if she might be just taking a nap.

He sat on the edge of the bed, and stroked her face gently with his hand. "Moni, it's Benni." He whispered tenderly. "I've come back to you." He combed through her hair with his fingers, and gently kissed her forhead. "I'm home now *motek*." He said as tears welled in his eyes.

There was no response.

The only sound he heard was the soft repetition of her beathing. He held her hand, as tears streamed down his cheeks, then kissed her lips. "I'll be here for you, Moni. I'll be back later." He paused to look at her once more, tears refilling his eyes, and then silently left the room.

He walked up to Moise, and nodded for them to go, and said nothing until they got in the car. "Just take me home, Moise. I need to be alone."

Moise drove him to Mira's flat, and without another word said between them, dropped him off.

* * *

Mira let Carla off at the hotel, and proceeded to her late afternoon appointment with the Israeli Interior Minister, David Shuchman. She walked into the office, then up to the reception desk, and was immediately ushered into the minister's office.

"Thank you for seeing me at such short notice, minister," she began, while taking a seat in front of Shuchman's desk. "I don't know many people in government yet, and you were so kind to Carla and me at our first meeting, that I decided to come to you."

"I'm happy that you did, my dear. Rest assured that my door is always open. You said on the phone that the matter you wish to discuss is of some urgency?"

"That's true." She found it hard to come to the point. "What I'm about to tell you will sound a bit strange, but please hear me out."

"Please, continue." He replied, and leaned back in his chair.

"It started for me several months ago." Mira began, and retold several of the dreams she had been having. "When I met the second time with my brother, he told my grandfather and me, that he had been having similar dreams as well. The common thread, in both our dreams, was a coming storm, or battle of some sort, followed by the cryptic pronouncement, 'Ninth of Av.' My grandfather, who is a rabbi from the Old City of Jerusalem, informed us that, historically, the Ninth of Av had been associated with several devastating events regarding the nation of Israel. Were you aware of that?"

The minister took out a notepad and began jotting something down. "No, my dear. I must say that this is all new to me. You say this all revolves around the ninth day of the Jewish month of Av?"

"Yes. That is the one constant in our dreams." Mira replied.

He paused, and looked at his notes. "Pardon me if I seem a bit skeptical, my dear. We are a practical people, and have all but lost contact with our God, or anything supernatural for that matter." He sat back and looked up at the ceiling. "So you believe that these dreams you've been having are some sort of warning from God, I take it, that Israel is about to face another trial of some sort. Is that about right?"

Mira felt her cheeks turn red. "Well, yes. We hadn't really thought about the source of the dreams, but I suppose they must be from God. I mean, who else would have have planted them there. We surely didn't ask for them, and to be honest, speaking for myself, I would rather not have had these dreams at all. But here they are, and all I can do is try to warn you, and the people of Israel, that something devastating may be about to happen."

The Interior Minister leaned forward on his desk, and gave her a fatherly look of concern. "But my dear, which Ninth of Av will it be? The current one, which will arrive in a matter of days? The one next year, the one after that?"

Mira looked down and felt silly. "We don't know, sir."

"I see." He jotted down another note, and put down his pen. "I will, of course, pass on your concern to the defense minister, this is a routine precaution, but I wouldn't worry about it my dear. You see, the Secretary General of the United Nations is here, and from all that I've heard, there is a real chance for peace from the negotiations under way." He looked at Mira and saw that she was saddened by the way their discussion had ended. "Let me give you, off the record of course, a bit of information I just received."

Mira perked up and returned to her role as a reporter. "Do you mean that this information came from 'a highly placed source in Israeli government?"

Shuchman smiled. "And nothing more. We have received word from our contacts inside the Mossad, that Ilya Stannas' mother was Jewish. This is a closely guarded secret, but it is also the probable impetus that seems to be motivating him, viz-a-viz, Israel. So you see my dear, I believe that your premonitions may be somewhat premature."

* * *

Benni sat in the gloom of his despair over Monika for several hours until he had had enough. "Nothing's getting better by my sitting around like this. If I leave right now I can still make my meeting with Ehud. It's time to move."

He got up from the couch, grabbed the keys to his car, and headed back to Tel Nof airbase. Half an hour later he was saluted through the gate, and parked his car in front of the base headquarters.

"Shalom Hanna. Is the boss in?" He asked the secretary in a nonchalant voice.

"*Kol ha'Kavod!* All honor. It's really you! She gushed, and stood up to give Benni a vigorous hug. "Alive from the dead, eh? But of course, you're as late as ever."

"What can I say, some things never change."

"Sit, sit, already. He's been waiting for you, so I'll tell him you're here." She disappeared behind the base commander's door.

A few minutes later, Ehud ben Ami bounded through the door and clasped Benni's hand in both of his. "My boy! By my life it's wonderful to see you. Come in. Come in. Hanna some refreshments, please."

"Right away, sir."

They both took their respective seats in the rectangular, wood paneled office, which was adorned with pictures of different types of aircraft, and the pilots who flew them.

"It's good to see you out of hospital, and so soon. I'm sure that it was more your desire than the doctor's, eh? Are you fully recovered?"

"A few aches and pains, but nothing I can't handle."

"You're not reporting in for duty then? You still have ninety days of leave ahead of you."

"No, not yet. I need some time to heal, and stay close to Monika."

"Yes, I'm sorry about Monika, Benni. Has anything changed?

"I visited her several hours ago," he replied, a lump forming in his throat, "but there's been no change."

"We'll continue to pray for her, Benni." Ben Ami said solemnly. "So, what can I do for you my son?"

"Brace yourself, commander. What I'm about to tell you will sound a bit strange, even *meshugah*, crazy, maybe, but please hear me out."

A serious look replaced the warm, paternal face of his commanding officer. "Go on."

Benni took a deep breath and began. "Several times in the past few months I've had dreams of impending disaster for our country, each ending with the cryptic phrase, *Tisha b'Av*, ninth of Av."

"*Tisha b'Av*? As in the ninth month of Av in our Hebrew calendar.

"Exactly, sir. I didn't make the connection until a few days ago. You see, I was recently reunited with my sister, Miriam, and was amazed to find that she had been having similar dreams, each of which also ended the same way."

"Extraordinary!"

"Yes sir, I believe it is. My *zaide* was with us when all this unraveled, and gave us a short history of the significance of that particular day in the life of Israel. Have you heard any of this?"

"I remember well the history courses I took in college, and the bitter significance of that day." He responded dryly. "So it is your contention that something of notorious significance is about to befall Eretz Israel."

"I'm not sure sir. All I know is that this is more than mere coincidence. Added to this is the fact that my *zaide*, who you'll remember is a devout rabbi, several days before we got together, had a vision. In that vision he was told to expect two people, who would have a message of importance for the nation of Israel.

A stunned silence descended on the room, until the commander spoke once more. "By your life Benni, your story is intriguing. On the one hand, there appears to be a warning from heaven of a disaster about to befall our land. I know such things are real. On the other hand the Secretary General of the United Nations is here to negotiate a treaty that may finally bring peace in our lifetime."

"Perhaps this warning we've received is for some time in the future?"

"That is a possiblility. Nevertheless, as you know, I have always been a stickler for being prepared. This years' ninth of Av is only two days from now, and it would be prudent for the Zahal to be on alert against any threat. *En brerra*."

The general began writing on a legal pad. "I'll pass a note on to Yossi Peleg at Central Command, saying that, due to new threat intelligence we've received, it is my recommendation that we go on full alert, the day before, during, and after the ninth of Av. You might have to back me up, if he calls me to task on this."

"By all means, sir."

"Good. Thank you my boy. Stay in touch, and, uh, be ready to come back on board if the need arises."

He stood to attention. "At your command, sir."

Just then Benni's satphone rang. "Major Cohen, Dr. Patek here."

"Yes, doctor."

"We've had some new developments with Monika. How soon can you get here?"

Benni held his breath; then asked, "Is everything all right?"

"She's fine, but we think that she might be waking."

He sat down, closed his eyes, and said a quick prayer, while the commander came beside him and put his arm on his shoulder.

"I'll be there as quick as I can, doctor."

CHAPTER 29

General Borodin sat behind his massive desk,

and flicked the ashes from another cigarette onto the floor. His coffee cup remained full; he had had too much coffee already, and had a painful acid stomach ache to remind him.

A knock came at the door and in came his aide Major Petrovsky with a sheaf of papers in his hand. He walked in front of the general's desk and stood at attention.

"Da, da. What have you got for me major?" The general asked without looking up.

"I have the update you requested on 'Operation Sudden Lightening.'" He held out his hand with the papers.

"At ease malor. Just give me the ghist of it."

"As you wish, sir. "There have been several defections from our alliance, notably Saudi Arabia, the Emirates, and Jordan.

Borodin turned his chair to the wall behind him, and studied the large map of the Middle East. "Da, they are not important. What of the others, and what position has the Arab League taken?"

"The others remain firm in their resolve, and the Arab League, while playing along with Stanas' peace plan, for the time being, is firmly in favor of war.

"That is as it should be. Never forget Pavel Illych, that they are a duplicious people. Fence stradlers. They play both sides, until the strongest side emerges, then claim to have been with them all along." He stood and studied the map.

"If I may ask, sir, what are your intentions?"

The general sat down at his desk, tented his fingers in front of him, and stared straight ahead. "When Stanas announces his peace agreement, we will attack!

* * *

Rabbi Berkowitz found his friend and fellow rabbi, Chaim Podhoretz sitting in his favorite spot in front of *Ha'Kotel*, the Western Wall. "My dear Chaim, so good that you should meet with me, and at such short notice."

"Well Shlomo, you said it was a matter of some urgency, and although you've been banished by the Sanhedrin, your friendship is still important to me."

He sat down in a chair beside him. "Good, good. I knew I could count on you. Now listen to me. Several nights ago, the Lord spoke to me while I was praying. He told me that there was a grave danger facing Israel."

"Nu, has there ever been a time when that wasn't true?" Chaim interjected.

"Yes, yes, of course true. But the Lord spoke of an invasion coming that could destroy Israel."

"Invasion!"

"Exactly. He also said that I should look for two, who would confirm what I was being shown."

"And?"

Just the other day Miriam and I visited with Benni in the hospital."

"How is Benni doing then?"

"Chaim, please. He's fine. The point I'm making, one that I should like to stick to, so that I don't get all muddled, is that while there, I found during our conversation that Benni and Miriam both had had a series of cataclysmic dreams that all ended with the words,'*Tisha b'Av*'"

"*Tisha b'Av*?" He shouted in surprise. "A day renowned for judgement and distress for Israel!

"Yes, my friend."

"So then, you believe that the Eternal One, blessed be the Name, is warning us that a time of trial is soon to come upon our country?" Chaim responded.

"It would appear that the war predicted in the book of Ezekiel in chapters 38 and 39 are upon us."

"You mean the war of Gog and Magog? The confederacy of Russia and the Islamic nations is included in this warning. Should not that be confined to the time of the end?

"I'm afraid, dear brother that we are on the verge of the 'last days,' so long ago predicted by our prophets."

Podhoretz was visibly shaken. "Why haven't you brought this to the attention of the Sanhedrin?" He asked bluntly.

"I tried, but they wouldn't give me a hearing. That is why I asked you to come. Perhaps you could get a better ear."

Chaim sat upright, his hands folded over his ivory-topped cane, and mulled over what he had just heard. "I will try Shlomo. That is all I can do. I will request a meeting with the Chief Rabbi and a few others, and see if they will listen."

"Thank you, that's all I ask." The Reb replied. He looked over at his friend, and patted him on the back. A strange emotion came over him. "You have always been dear to me, Chaim. Even though we haven't seen eye to eye on many things, I want you should know that I could not have asked for a better friend than you."

"Oy, Shlomo. Now look what you've done." He brought out his white handkerchief from his coat sleeve, and wiped tears from his eyes.

"I know dear friend. Some things are better said sooner than later."

* * *

Benni entered the hospital ward, and found Dr. Patek looking at a clipboard in front of the nurse's station. He looked up and smiled. "My, you must have sprouted wings."

Benni grinned. "How is she doctor?"

He motioned for Benni to follow him. "Her movement has stopped for now, but it is a good sign. I've seen cases like this before, and almost every waking event was preceeded by movement of some kind."

They paused at the door to Monika's room. "You may go in, but don't expect anything dramatic to happen. It may still be days before she moves again. I'll be close by if you need me."

Benni paused, and said a quick prayer before entering the room. Everything was the same as when he had left that morning. Monika lay still, her breathing barely lifting the covers over her chest.

He sat beside her on the bed, and gently caressed her cheek with the backside of his hand, and then quickly pulled it back, when she responded and began moaning.

She was trying to say something. Benni put his ear to her mouth and faintly heard words that brought tears to his eyes. "Benni, Benni."

"I'm here motek. It's Benni."

"Benni my love. Benni…"

"Shh, shh! I'm here Moni." He laid his head on her shoulder and started to cry.

"Benni, it's you. My Zahal flyboy! You're home! She stroked his hair, and kissed his forehead.

Stunned by what she had just said, he sat upright, and saw that Monika's eyes were opened.

"Moni! He cried, and buried his head into her shoulder once again, amid a flood of tears.

"It's alright motek. You're here." She replied in a faint voice, while stroking his hair. "I knew you would come back to me. They said you were lost, but I knew in my heart that you would come home to me.

He sat up and wiped away his tears. "How, how are you. I mean, how do you feel?"

"I'm fine," she yawned. "Just a bit tired; like I've had too much sleep."

He laughed through more tears, and took her hand in both of his, alarmed that it was so limp, and she so fragile. "Please stay awake and I'll be right back. I've got to find Dr. Patek."

"Alright my love. I'll just close my eyes and rest for a minute then."

Benni dashed out the door, and ran to the nurse's station. "Where's Dr. Patek? I need him right away!"

The nurse was alarmed, but immediately paged him.

A few moments later, Dr. Patek came running down the hall. "Benni, how's Monika?"

"She woke up doctor! She knew who I was, and we talked. But she's so frail. I'm concerned for her."

They both walked rapidly down the hallway. "That's to be expected. Her body needs time to respond to wakefulness."

Benni led the way into the room and sat on the bed. "Moni," he said gently, while touching her shoulder. "I've brought the doctor."

Monika slowly turned to face them both. "Shalom, doctor. That sleep therapy you prescribed really worked." She joked, bringing light laughter from both men.

""We're thrilled that you've enjoyed a nice rest. Now you will soon be ready to resume your normal daily activities." He put on his stethescope and listened to her heart and breathing. "Everything appears to be fine. I"ll have the nurse come by in a few minutes for a thorough examination, and then perhaps something to eat, nu?"

"Thank you doctor." Benni said, as Dr. Patek left the room.

"How long have I been here, motek, do you know? It seems like just yesterday that I had the--oh Benni!" Her eyes widened as she reached up to hold his face in her hands. "I, I had a miscarriage and--"

He leaned over and hugged her close. "Yes, I know my love. I'm just happy that you are well, and that Elohim has spared you.

A thought occurred to her, and her face brightened once again. "Motek there's something else I want to share with you."

Just then the nurse came in for the tests. "Well, Mrs. Cohen, it's a *mitzvah*, a blessing, to see that you are up and about again. This won't take long, sir, and the doctor has asked that you meet with him."

He kissed his wife on the forehead, and found Dr. Patek waiting in the hall.

"Benni, even though Monika's come around, we'll want to keep her here for observation. We need to make sure that this is not an episode, but that she's truly wakeful.

"Of course, doctor, whatever you think is best."

"As strange as it might seem, she'll still need to sleep, and then begin to return to a normal wake/sleep pattern. I shouldn't stay with her too long tonight, as much as I know you would both like it to be otherwise. We will observe her through the night, and make a further determination in the morning."

"Sounds good, doctor. I'll be here bright and early."

Dr. Patek smiled and patted him on the back. "Don't make it too early. I won't be in until nine."

After the nurse finished her examination, Benni went back into the room to say goodnight, and thought Monika had fallen asleep. Her eyes opened again when he sat down on the bed.

He took her hand in his. "Moni, the doc thinks it best that I leave and let you rest, so I'm going to say goodnight."

A look of concern crossed her face. "Motek, there's just one thing I've got to tell you. Something wonderful has happened to me."

"He patted her hand. "I know, I know, dear one, I feel the same. I thought I had lost you and now--"

"No, it's not that, *hamoodah*. You see, I awoke once before, and *zaide* was there."

Benni's face clouded over. "He didn't try to lay his religious trip on you, did he?"

"It wasn't like that at all. He comforted me, and opened up the word of God, and--"

"I knew it! I've told him before to keep his beliefs to himself."

"Benni that's not fair." Monika blurted out as tears filled her eyes.

He saw that he would have to be more sensitive, reached down, and gently held both her arms. "Moni, I'm sorry, please don't get upset. I'm thankful that *zaide* was there for you. Could we discuss this tomorrow? Please?" He gently kissed her.

"Alright. If you promise?"

"I do." He sat up, and held both of her hands. "Now will you do something for me?"

"Of course, motek, anything."

"*B'seder*. Rest now. Dr. Patek says that you need to develop normal sleep patterns once again."

She pouted playfully. "Well, if you insist. I am sleepy though, so it shouldn't be a problem."

He reached down and kissed her once again. "I love you. I'll be back first thing in the morning."

Benni helped pull the blanket over her shoulder and tucked her in.

"Motek? I want you to know that I have always loved you, and always will." She said sincerely

Tears came to his eyes. "I know Moni. Goodnight." He kissed her, and walked out the door.

Monika prayed that Benni would come to know Yeshua as his Lord and Savior, and that God would give her the right words to say when he came in the morning.

She then keyed the intercom to the nurse's station, and requested some paper and a pen. "I'll write down what I want to say. That way I can rest tonight in your arms, Lord."

CHAPTER 30

Mira woke out of a dead sleep at one o'clock in the morning, while Carla snored away on the bed beside her. *"Grandfather! I've got to see grandfather."* She said to herself, got up, threw on some clothes, and drove into the Old City of Jerusalem. She found the Jewish Quarter, and came to the house belonging to Avram Shmuel.

She paused at the door and stepped back a pace. *This is ridiculous. They're going to think that I'm crazy or something."* Yet a compelling urgency gripped her, and she pressed on to see her grandfather.

She knocked several times, but no one answered. After a few more knocks that she hoped would not wake the neighbors, Mira tried the door and found that it was open. Her heart beating wildly, she walked into the darkened house, and found her way to her grandfather's room. She knocked gently, and, after getting no response, opened the door and walked in.

"*Zaide, Zaide,*" she whispered with her heart in her throat.

No one answered.

Mira turned the light on and looked over at the empty bed. "*Zaide!*" she screamed. There was nothing there but his nightgown neatly folded on the bed.

Mira, terrified, flipped on the lights in the main part of the house, ran to wake the others, but found that the same had happened in each room of the house.

Her *zaide*, the Shmuel's, and their children had all disappeared!

* * *

The satphone rang several times before Benni, who had been in the deepest part of his sleep, answered it. "Shalom." He answered, while rubbing his eyes. He glanced at the clock on the nightstand, and saw that it was only 3:12 in the morning.

"Benni, Dr. Patek. You must come to the hospital at once!" He shouted, and hung up the phone.

Alarmed, Benni jumped out of bed, threw his clothes on, and sprinted out the door, only to find that he had forgotten his keys. Cursing under his breath, he ran into the house, retrieved the keys, and sped off through the sleepy Tel Aviv streets, until he found the hospital parking lot.

The hospital was in turmoil when he arrived there. Nurses, doctors, and patients were scurrying around the floors. Some were weeping, others calling out for loved ones, and still others walking around, trance-like, in a daze.

The scene only heightened Benni's concern, and he wondered if there might have been a terrorist incident of some kind.

He found Dr. Patek sitting behind the nurse's station, his head buried in folded arms on top of the desk.

"Dr. Patek, I'm here." Benni announced with a strident voice.

He looked up, as tears welled in his eyes. "Monika's gone Benni. Disappeared!"

"What! How?"

The doctor got up from his chair, and walked quickly to Monika's room, motioning for Benni to follow him. Both men entered the room at the same time, and found her bed empty. Benni pulled the covers back, only to find Monika's folded hospital nightgown, and her pillow indented, where her head had lain.

He recoiled from the sight, and looked at Dr. Patek.

"The same scene has been repeated in several rooms throughout the hospital," he said vacantly.

Both men stood still, not knowing what to do next, until Benni, filled with grief, ran out of the room, through the front entrance, and into the black maw of night.

* * *

It was five in the morning when one of Ilya Stanas' aides knocked loudly on the door of his suite, instantly waking him up.

"Come!" He shouted in anger.

"Your Excellency, I beg your pardon," his ashen-faced aide began, "but there's a serious situation developing."

Stanas flung himself out of bed, put on his red, silk bathrobe, and walked to his desk. "Go on."

"We have been getting numerous reports that scores of people, that is to say, men, women, and children, have been disappearing all over the globe. More in some countries, and less in others."

The Secretary General was unmoved, and powered up his computer. He accessed his encrypted database, and found it crammed full of incoming messages.

"Sir, what are we going to do?" The aide blurted out in fear.

Stanas looked at him with eyes filled with loathing. "Stop whimpering like a child. Send for Jack Quinn, and then order me breakfast.

"Yes, your Excellency." He replied in a humble voice, and left the room.

Alone once again, Stanas went into a trance, blanking his mind from any thought or image. Soon a voice spoke to him. "You are not to concern yourself with this happening. It is part of *The Plan*. You will be given further instructions.

"Yes, my master. I live to serve you."

Another knock at the door brought Stanas back to reality.

"Come!"

"You sent for me?

"Yes Jack, you and your wife are well?" An agitated Stanas asked.

"As far as I know—oh, you're concerned about the disappearances." He had never seen Stanas ruffled before. "What do you make of them?

"I've been in touch with my, er, advisors, and will have more to say about that later. Right now, I need you to contact the Palestinian and Israeli prime ministers, and the chairman of the Arab League. They must be at my news conference--do you understand?" Stanas screamed, which caused the hair on Jack's neck to stand up. At the same time he felt the presence of something dark and malevolent.

"I'll get right on it." He replied, glad to leave the room.

* * *

All over the world people simply vanished! In the United State husbands woke up to find that their wives, who had been sleeping beside them, were gone. Other wives lost husbands. Older children were bereft of their parents. In Australia, office workers became missing. Several villiages in eastern India were completely empty. All the children and Christian workers in an orphanage in Kenya disappeared. Many government workers including the President of Korea were gone. From every country, rich and poor, young and old, blue collar and white collar, members of every level of society simply vanished!

Chaos ensued in many places. A jumbo jet crashed, killing all on board, because the pilot and co-pilot, despite strict regulations in place by the airline industry to prevent this from happening, were both Christians. Other planes and jets fell out of the sky. Cars suddenly veered off roads, some causing accidents in the process. Farmers vanished from their farms, business owners from their businesses, clerks from their jobs, while panic filled the places they left behind.

Those awake and those who later awoke to the unfolding drama clamored for an answer. The world looked on with fear and trepidation.

* * *

Mira ran out of the Shmuel home in terror, and drove back to the hotel. She had phoned Benni several times without success, and had left several messages. (Is he missing as well?) She then called long distance to see if her father had disappeared, and was relieved when he answered the phone.

Sleep was out of the question; her grandfather's empty bed and the empty house haunted her. She was grateful when the dawn appeared, and inwardly hoped that she was only dreaming.

She got up to take a shower when her sat-phone rang.

"Mira? Bernstein. Have you seen what's going on?"

"Well, yes and no. That is, something's going on here that I don't understand, but--"

"That's an understatement. Listen, turn your television on and get caught up. The whole planet's in an uproar. People are missing everywhere. Get your team together, and get over to Stanas' hotel. There's going to be a major news conference sometime this morning. You couldn't be in a better place to cover this story. Keep me posted. Shalom."

"Shalom." Mira ended the call, and felt a deep fear welling up inside of her. "It's true then. *Zaida* and the others are gone, and we are still here."

She voiced on the television, and watched as news of the mysterious disappearances poured in from all over the globe.

Mira thought of her brother, as her eyes filled with tears. *"What on earth is going on?"*

"H-hey Mira. You mind turning that thing down a bit." Carla asked, while pulling a pillow over her head.

"Carla, you've got to get up. We're...they..." She lost control and started sobbing.

Hearing her cry, Carla sprang out of bed, and put her arm around her. "What's wrong dear? Is everything okay?"

Mira struggled for control. "Grandfather's gone. People all over the world have vanished into thin air. Benni..." She couldn't finish and cried harder.

Carla held her close and handed her a box of tissue, as both watched images and reports of the disappearances.

"Unbelievable!" Carla shouted; stunned.

After watching for several minutes, they suddenly heard sirens sounding throughout the city. They ran out onto the balcony, and there, moving slowly in the sky above them, in the brightening early morning sky, were six large shiny disks.

"What kind of aircraft are these? Mira wondered with fear.

"Those aren't aircraft dear." Carla stated without emotion. "They're spaceships. I've seen others like them before. I'll bet that whatever's causing those people to disappear has something to do with what's up there in the sky there. I've waited years for them to make themselves known to us, and now here they are. It's about time!"

Then Mira became business-like once again. "Carla, call Sha'ul. Tell him to meet us at Stanas' hotel as soon as possible. I'm going to jump in the shower. Oh, and tell him to get some shots of the aircraft, or spaceships, whatever they are.

"Will do." Carla said in a distracted voice, still looking up. "I knew you'd come one day."

* * *

Ilya Stanas also heard the alarms and was looking out of his penthouse window at the strange discs in the sky, when a knock sounded at his door.

"Come!"

Benjamin Stuart, impeccably dressed as usual in a shimmering black silk suit, silenty strode into the room. "Your Excellency, you called for me." He said bowing.

"Have you seen what's in the sky? What have our masters told you about them?"

"I am as surprised as you are. They must have something to do with the exodus we've just witnessed."

"Ah, yes." Stanas said with a sarcastic smile. "Truly an exodus of biblical proportions, eh?" Both men laughed.

"Let us wait on our masters then." Stuart intoned, while Stanas pulled the window drapes closed. Stuart shut off the lights, and both men sat in the middle of the floor with legs crossed and arms raised in a lotus position. After a few moments Stuart went into a trance and started to speak in an unearthly voice:

"The enemy has again acted foolishly, and removed from us the obstacles to The Plan. The apparitions you see in the sky are designed by your masters to show the world that all resistance has been eliminated, and that those who have been obstinate in their rebellion have been safely taken away by their supposed, alien brothers. We will say that the rebels will be held for indoctrination, and reeducation, and will one day be returned to earth, when they have embraced The Plan."

"We hear and obey." They replied together. Both men stood up, faced each other, and began jumping up and down and laughing with a strange, cackling laughter.

CHAPTER 31

A huge crowd had gathered in front of the Hotel Semiramis in the New City of Jerusalem, eagerly anticipating the news conference to follow. A bank of microphones, representing the world's major news organizations, was set up on the front sidewalk.

"Let's go down to one end of the street, Sha'ul, and do a preliminary take before the news conference gets started. I want to get the mass of people in as a backdrop." Mira directed. "Carla, get a definite start time for Stanas' speech, and see if you can get one of his people to give us his itinerary for the next few days."

"Gotcha."

Sha'ul panned the crowd with his camera, and shot some footage that would later be embedded into the news conference replay. He then brought the camera to ground level and zoomed in on Mira. She touched up her makeup and hair, and then counted down: "3, 2, 1. I'm standing in the midst of a sea of concerned onlookers, all who are hoping to receive answers to the perplexing developments of the past several hours. Added to the dilemna of people vanishing all over the globe, we now have witnessed the appearance of strange objects lingering in the morning sky above Jerusalem. Are these aircraft alien spaceships? Are they somehow linked with the mysterious disappearances? The world watches breathlessly, and hopes for answers. This is Mira Rosen reporting from Jerusalem for GSN news."

She held her pose for a moment and then said, "okay cut. That's a wrap, Sha'ul. You took some shots of the space, um, the flying objects, right?"

"Yes, Miss Mira. I took many from many angles. But what are they? Do you know?"

"No, I don't, but according to this press release, we're soon to find out. Let's get set up for the main event."

Sha'ul set up the camera in his reserved spot, some fifteen feet back and left of the podium. A hush came over the multitude, as the dignitaries, including the Israeli Prime Minister, some of his cabinet ministers, religious leaders from all the major faiths, the Palestinian Prime Minister, and members of the Arab League delegation, filed into their seats behind the bank of microphones.

At precisely 11:00 AM, Ilya Stanas, dressed smartly in a tailored dark gray suit and red silk tie, walked out of the revoving doors of the hotel, accompanied by Benjamin Stuart and several of his aides, and approached the podium.

"Mister Prime Minister, distinguished guests, citizens of the world," he began, smiling earnestly. "We have come upon momentous times. As you know, last night, multitudes of people from all over the world suddenly disappeared from the face of the earth. Today we have the appearance of alien spacecraft."

The crowd, including the dignitaries behind him, erupted into boisterous conversation.

Stanas paused until the chatter subsided. "You heard me correctly. You see above us, a contingent of a huge force of our alien brethren, who have been orbiting our planet, ready to intervene at a moments notice. Do not be alarmed! They are here for our protection and have been watching over us for centuries.

While hundreds of cameras flashed, animated discussion continued.

After a few moments, Stanas, with a knowing smile, held up his hands, and pleaded for quiet. "Through the science of channeling, we have been in direct contact with these, our masters. I would like to ask my protégé, Dr. Benjamin Stuart to come forward and communicate to you a message coming directly from the commander of the alien host."

Stuart embraced the Secretary General, and then walked up to the podium. His black silk suit, shimmering in the sunlight, produced an electric, ethereal glow. "Mr. President, honored guests, and people of the *new world order!*" He shouted, throwing his right fist into the air.

The multitude of people responded with loud clapping and cheers, with a few shouting, "one world now!"

Benjamin Stuart, a leering smile on his face, waited patiently for the cheers to subside. "We are privileged to witness the most tremendous event in the history of mankind. The coming together of two worlds: our planet earth, and a culture far in advance of our own. While the SETI project has for years unsuccessfully tried to make contact with extraterrestrials, it is your privilege to be the first generation to make true contact with these gods of the universe." He stated, and, with both arms extended, immediately went into a trance.

The disembodied voice that spoke through him was authoritative and terrifying:

"Greetings and peace to the people of earth. At this momentous time in your evolutionary struggle we have decided to establish communication with you. You have been watched in regards to your development with growing concern for millennia, and we now find it necessary to intervene in your affairs. To this end we have extracted a cancerous tumor from your midst, one that has long restricted your progress towards personal godhood. The vanishings you have seen and heard about have been caused by us, and have occurred so that you may continue to evolve on the path of peace and prosperity, prescribed for you from the time of the beginning, when members of our order planted the first seeds of life on your planet.

Let this be a warning to you! We cannot, and will not, tolerate obstructionist, fundamentalist religious viewpoints, or any religionists who maintain that there is only one-way to god. All roads and beliefs lead to god. You only need to discover the fact that each of you is a god!

Those we have removed will be held by us, reeducated, and will one day be returned to earth, to become productive members of your new world order.

A glorious new day is before you. We will be eagerly watching your progress."

As soon as the message was given, the six spacecraft sped off as one over the Old City. Passing over the Temple Mount, they picked up speed and quickly disappeared over the Mount of Olives and the Judaen Hills.

The hush that had settled over the crowd erupted into a cacophony of voices, cries and discussion. Some were moved to tears of joy, others were frightened and in a panic. Still others stood in awe of what they had just seen and heard. The dignitaries seated behind Stanas were no less affected, and talked passionately one to another.

Carla held on tightly to Mira, who was lost in her own thoughts. "I knew it. I knew it all along." Carla said relaxing her grip. "People wouldn't believe me, but I knew that those aliens had been visiting and experimenting with us all along."

"Grandfather, my dear, sweet grandfather. I was just getting to know him, Carla." Mira responded in a far away voice."

* * *

Jack and Marcia Quinn, standing behind the row of seated dignitaries, were dumbstruck.

"Oh look Jack, There's Mira and her crew filming the event." She said, while waving her hand, trying unsuccessfully to get her attention in the sea of people.

She turned to her husband again. "Darling, what an honor it is for us to be here. To think that generations have desired to witness what we have just seen. I believed all along that there was some truth to all these ET sightings. I don't think I've ever told you this, but I've seen them myself."

Jack remained quiet for a few moments before replying. The revelation that there were actual alien entities, warred with his carefully held preconceptions that no such beings could possibly be real. The desire for tobacco and a stiff drink became almost overpowering.

"Then there's the Secretary General, basking in the afterglow of this historic moment." Jack thought to himself. "The man I have been fighting is actually a superhero! Who else could have pulled this off? Maybe I've got him all wrong..."

"Jack dear, are you alright." Marcia asked with concern, while pulling gently on his arm.

"I'm, uh, fine. Just a bit overwhelmed by all of this."

"I know what you mean." She replied. "It's all happening so fast. How can a body keep up with it?

Jack pulled his wife close in his arms, and looked towards the podium where Stanas was about to speak once more. "One thing is sure. In this new world we're in, we'll have to be brave."

* * *

Ilya Stanas allowed the discussion to continue for a few minutes, and then brought everyone to attention. "'Let not your heart be troubled,' Jesus once said. He, along with Moses, Buddha, Confuscious, Mohammed and others were the forerunners, some of the sixty-six masters; the adepts of the New Age. Through their combined wisdom, they have bequeathed to us the foundation upon which we will build a shining new city on a hill. A city built with unity, strength, and above all peace."

The mesmerized crowd, who had been milling about in turmoil over the strange happenings, found their unity by focusing on the Secretary General, and stood as one man applauding, and showering him with shouts of Shalom! Salaam! Stanas!

Mira and Carla were both overcome with emotion, and joined in as well.

Stanas acknowledged the acclaim with feined humility, while inwardly he lusted for more.

"To this end I have a truly epochal announcement to make. As if we needed more, eh?" He grinned as a wave of laughter echoed down the street. "The Prime Ministers of Israel and Palestine and the Chairman of the Arab League will please join me at this time."

He looked behind him and extended his right arm in welcome. The men came up and stood beside Stanas, bewildered by what exactly this announcement might be, and how it involved them. He shook hands with each of them, and as he did so, looked hypnotically into each man's eyes.

"Since the unfortunate war of Israel's independence in 1948, really the history goes back even further to Abraham, Ishmael and Isaac, men have sought to find a solution to peace between Israel and his Arab brothers. Many nations have offered various proposals and sent countless delegations to solve this enigmatic puzzle. Much blood has been shed, and countless lives lost in an elusive quest for peace. It is my honor and priviledge to announce to you today that the three parties standing before you, the State of Israel, the State of Palestine, and the member nations of the Arab League, have all agreed to a seven-year unconditional peace treaty!"

Wild clapping, and shouts and cries of, "Peace! Peace!" rang through the crowd. Some began to dance, others held up their hands making the peace sign, while still others closed their tear-filled eyes and were quietly praying.

Benjamin Stuart made his way to the podium, and unfolded a leather bound book that contained the articles of the peace treaty. Ilya Stanas stood to one side, an expectant look on his face, while each man signed all three copies. Stanas added his own signiture to the documents, and all four men shook hands with each other, while the throng of people cheered wildly.

The three men were bewildered by what had just taken place as each made their way back to their chairs. Later, each leader would not be able to recall that the signing had actually taken place.

Stanas, a ravening, wolf-like look on his face, took the binders, held them over his head, and shouted, "there is now peace in our time!"

* * *

General Borodin was furious at what he had just seen on television in his office at the Kremlin. "Petrovsky!" He shouted through the intercom to his stunned aide.

"Yes, general."

"Arrange for a full cabinet meeting at once!"

"At your command, sir."

* * *

Benni watched the live news coverage with its ongoing commentary, and replayed it several times on his sister's television, with grave interest. There was just too much information to absorb all at once. Monika and others were gone; abducted by aliens? He had never believed in their existence before, and found the possibility impossible to grasp. Now, the much longed for peace treaty with Palestine and the Arab nations? It was just too much, too fast.

He replayed the news conference once again, paced back and forth, and was riveted to the screen when the announcement of the peace treaty came on again. He hadn't noticed this before, but for a brief moment the camera had panned the crowd, and there was Mira standing beside a man holding a shoulder camera.

"I've got to see Mira, and *zaide*," he decided, and quickly threw on a change of clothes and bolted for his car. It would be close to midnight before he would get to Jerusalem.

* * *

Borodin was seething with rage, as he called the special cabinet meeting to order. The dark gloom of night seen through the conference room windows matched the mood in the room. "You have all seen the theater taking place in Jerusalem this morning." Several nods went around the large rectangular table.

"What do you make of it?"

General Chernov stood up. "I believe I can speak for all of us here, comrade. What we saw today amounted to nothing more than a cheap trick, meant to fool the world into thinking Stanas has the answer to these strange vanishings. We have had our share of people missing in the Rodina as well, but aliens taking away Christians? Nyet! The Russian Orthodox Church is still here today. The pope in Rome has appeared with his cardinals at the Vatican. This is nothing more than a magician's slieght of hand.

Our scientists have told us that there have recently been strange occurrences regarding the earth's magnetic field. Whales have foundered on beaches; schools of fish have washed up on shore, and flocks of birds have collided and killed each other. These strange anomalies might yet explain the strange happenings we have just witnessed. There is a practical explanation for these people disappearing. We just haven't found it yet."

"Thank you, general. These are my sentiments exactly. Now what of the treaty?"

"That presents an altogether different problem." The defense minister offered. "I have met briefly with our military chiefs of staff, and it is our consensus that we should wait and see how this treaty plays out with our Arab allies. It's bound to have a deleterious effect, and--"

"Nyet!" The general interrupted. "We cannot wait for our simpering allies!" Borodin shouted. We must act now before they have had a chance to dissemble again. Once the forces of war are in motion, and positive results are achieved, they will run ahead of us, hungry for the spoils of war."

He looked from man to man, and was pleased to see a grim determination on each face.

"I am hereby ordering the full mobilization of our Russian and Allied forces. Inform our agents in all countries to commence 'Operation Sudden Lightning!'"

CHAPTER 32

Rabbi Chaim Podhoretz sat alone in the back of the synagogue, and wept quietly for his friend Shlomo Berkowitz. He had watched the news conference on telelvision but came away unimpressed. *"Only time will tell the truth of these events,"* he had thought to himself. Taking his white handkerchief from the sleave of his black coat, he blew his nose, and placed it back.

"Nu, Shlomo, my dear friend, you have fled from us, and we haven't said Kiddush for you. Where will your soul find its rest?"

He bowed his head in sorrow, and began weeping again. "The whole Shmuel family gone as well. Others, who claim Yeshua as Mashiach also gone. To where, Adonai, to where? Are they in your presence now, or damned to Sheol, the home of the unrighteous dead?" He produced the hanky once again, dabbed his eyes, and mopped his brow.

"I will miss you my friend. Though I never seriously listened to your talks about *Yeshua Ha'Mashiach,* by my life, I swear upon the sacred scrolls, that I will look into those things you've said, until I find the truth about *Yeshua.*"

* * *

Benni parked his car and dashed up the stairs, not bothering with the elevator, to Mira's room, and knocked.

Carla wasn't expecting anyone, and became immediately frightened. She gathered her courage and opened the door a crack. "Who's there?"

"Shalom. Eh, you must be Carla, yes? I am Benni, Miriam's brother."

Carla was relieved and opened the door. "Oh, hi. But Mira's not here. She said she needed to take a walk by herself. To be honest with you I'm a bit concerned. She told me that she was going to the Wailing Wall."

"Oy, very good. Thanks to you. I will find her to bring home."

With that he ran to his car once again, glanced at his watch, and saw that it was just before midnight. He weaved through the dark and narrow streets of the Old City, found a place to park nearby, and walked the rest of the way until he found the plaza of *Ha'Kotel*. The wall itself was bathed in light, which turned the huge limestone blocks into a soothing tan hue, while a large crowd of people thronged the plaza. Benni looked in every direction until he found Miriam sitting by herself in the roped off women's section. He picked up a folding chair and placed it beside hers.

Mira looked over at him and sprang into his arms. "Oh Benni, you're here!" She cried, hugging him close. "I called; left messages…thought you had been taken away like *zaide*."

"*Zaide's* gone?" Benni exclaimed. "First Moni and now him too?"

Mira began weeping. "Not Monika? Oh Benni, I'm so sorry. This is horrible." She buried her face in his shoulder and sobbed. Benni put his arm around her, as tears formed in his eyes.

They sat together, mourning their loss, when Benni saw a large crowd of people milling in front of the wall on the men's side of the plaza. Suddenly, the throng quickly backed away to some twenty feet from the wall, revealing two curiously dressed, very old looking men. Both were of medium build and had long beards. The taller of the two had on a white robe, and held a long wooden walking stick in his hand. The other was bald and wore a coarse brown garment. Benni saw that the tall one was saying something to the startled crowd while the other lifted a long *shofar* to his lips and prepared to sound.

Benni got up to find out what was being said, when his satphone rang. "Binyamin Cohen?

"Yes, this is Benni Cohen."

"Sir, this is Major Lukas, duty officer at Tel Nof airbase. You've been requested to report for duty immediately. This is a red alert. I repeat this is a red alert!"

"Can you tell me what's going on major?"

"There's been nothing official yet, but the rumor has it that Israel is under attack."

"Very well, I'm on my way." He turned to give Mira the news, when both heard sirens begin to wail all over the city. At the same time the sound of the shofar echoed throughout the plaza.

Brother and sister looked at each other in fear.

"Mira, what day is this?" He asked cradling her in his arms.

'It's August the 10th, why?'

"No, no. I mean what day is it on the Jewish calendar."

Mira thought for a moment, as her eyes widened...

"Today is the Ninth of Av!"

Printed in the United States
By Bookmasters

Printed in the United States
By Bookmasters